The Keepers of Horns & Wings

The Keepers of Horns & Wings

A. GRAY

Contents

Chapter One

Think About Her

Elle

It was an odd feeling when the days and nights blurred together. Each evening seemed like my last, while the days stretched on forever. My days had become a series of robotic motions, a hollow mimicry of a life devoid of purpose or passion.

Cream lace curtains billowed in the breeze, their gossamer edges caressing my cheek. I smacked the fabric away, halfheartedly. Nothing was worthwhile out the open window, not even the soft breeze or the sparkle of fireflies. With my face pressed into the crook of my elbow and my long, golden hair twisted around me, I stared into space, my mind on nothing and everything.

"Come on, Ellise… What are you doing to yourself?" I breathed, my eyes burning. I glanced at the clock on the wall. It was nearing 9 P.M. "At least find a better place to crash than your desk."

Neck throbbing, I gradually stood and clutched the back of the office chair. I needed to stop feeling sorry for myself. My parents were dead, and there wasn't a single thing I could do about it. But the weight of despair continued to drag me down. It coated my skin like thick grease. I couldn't push past the grief, and maybe a part of me didn't want to. Perhaps the fact that the numbness shielded me from confronting the truth was why everything felt so hard. My parents were never coming back. I was alone, and exhaustion was a bottomless pit that promised sweet nothing.

A small, morbid part of me wished I'd been with them. I could almost see myself in the back seat of the car as they swerved to avoid whatever was in the road, careening off the edge of it and crashing into the rocky mountainside. Those same pine-cloaked slopes had greeted me when the taxi brought me home from the airport. Whenever I ventured outside, the towering, familiar outline of the endless trees loomed over me, a constant reminder of all I'd lost. What was in the middle of the road that made my father swerve so drastically, demolishing his car and ending their lives in the span of a heartbeat?

They left me alone. I have no one.

I missed my father with an ache that settled into my bones. There wasn't a day that went by that I didn't long for the infectious cadence of his laughter, the way he'd tilt his head like a puzzled Labrador when something confused him, and even his mud-caked shoes that inevitably ended up under the coffee table. My sweet, easily bewildered father.

Walking over to my bed with tears streaming down my face, I tried to bury my emotions in the darkest recesses of my soul, hoping they'd never again see the light of day. If I thought about how much I missed my father, I would think about how much I missed *her*.

My limbs grew heavier. The rush of sorrow I knew was coming, because it always came, was followed by a low sob quivering through tear-soaked lips. I missed my mother peeking through my cracked door before bed to ensure I was safe. I'd trade the breath in my lungs to go back to watching her dance around the kitchen to a song we both knew while we sang at the top of our lungs, my father laughing at us from the living room. The void she'd left behind was cavernous. I missed her so, so much.

They'd been taken from me, ripped from my life like a page from a book the author didn't like. I ran the fleshy part of the inside of my bottom lip through my teeth repeatedly until the bitterness of blood filled my mouth. *I can't do this. I don't want to do this.* Pulling back the blanket, I folded myself under it, tugged a pillow to my chest, and curled my knees around it. Sleep might let me hide from my emotions, if only for a little while, but those feelings would still be there, waiting for me when the sun glared through the curtains in the morning.

The symphony of songbirds outside the window pulled me from a deep sleep. Spring was rolling into summer, the air losing its chill, turning frosty mornings into lazy, warm afternoons. The night air had been warm enough that I'd left the window open. I pulled back the blanket and walked over, closing the window with a soft thud. Rubbing at my sore neck, I looked down at the messy pile of paperwork on my desk that needed attention.

Among the documents were bills I barely knew how to pay with my newly inherited money, which I barely knew how to access. I was drowning in a sea of papers that demanded my signature. Buried at the bottom of the nightmare stack were ominous letters from the college I'd been attending. I didn't bother reading them; they were all the same. If I missed another week of school, I shouldn't bother coming back. The word *withdrawn* was stamped across the back of the envelope of the very last letter they'd sent.

"Pfft," I muttered to nobody, "if only they knew how withdrawn I truly am."

I had the slight urge to tackle the growing pile of responsibilities, and for once, I considered grasping at the desire instead of ignoring it entirely. Deep inside of me, there was a need for reprieve from the repetitive, mind-sucking depression that clung to me like an insolent leech, even if that meant paperwork.

Staring at the stack, I made the decision before I could change my mind. I went through the motions of showering, brushed my unkempt hair, dressed in an ivory sweater, pushed my legs into dark jeans, and put on my sandals. I moved the paperwork into a stack on the dining room table and hesitated. The burden of feeling overwhelmed crept up my spine, making me shiver as the fine hairs across the back of my neck stood on end. It was as if someone was watching me fumble, judging me. *Where do I start? There are so many papers. It's all too much.*

Blinking back the incessant numbness, I thumbed the edges of the papers at the top of the stack, puffing a stubborn strand of hair from the front of my face. It settled languidly back in its preferred spot, over the corner of my eye.

I needed to see the property that my mom left to me— the property I never knew existed, the one with her name on the deed.

Shining black ink scrawled across the signature line. Bought, paid for, and now mine. Maybe curiosity would pull me out of the endless funk life had handed me. If I were going to give in to what a functional life demanded of me, I'd have to do it before I lost momentum and let the abyss always waiting for me take over.

I needed my phone to get to the property, but finding it would be a nightmare. It was buried somewhere among the piles of old take-out containers, paper plates, pizza boxes, and wadded-up tissues that littered every flat surface. Not that it mattered; the phone was probably dead anyway, and it wasn't like anyone important called me. The most important people couldn't. They would never call me again. Despite it all, I needed to find the dang thing, so I dug and dug until I saw the rectangular shape of my purple phone case. I barely registered that it still had battery power before shoving it into my pocket.

Picking up the keys from the slate-gray island, I walked out to the garage and climbed into my mother's Jeep. I set the papers on the passenger seat and jammed the keys into the ignition. With a slow twist of my wrist, the car came to life, and my insides spun with a wave of nausea. It hit me so hard that I pushed my palms into my stomach and put my clammy forehead on the steering wheel. *I can do this.* I wouldn't let myself waste away in the house I'd grown up in just because I was alone. I didn't need to move on, but I did need to move forward.

Entering the address into the GPS, I pulled out of the slanted driveway. The drive didn't seem too long, perhaps because I knew the twisty side roads around the base of the mountains well. Yet, the pull-off was unfamiliar to me. The Jeep bumped up the muddy, potholed lane until it had to stop at a gate that spanned the width of the long, hazardous driveway. The gate was enclosed on either side with crumbling wire fencing. A large *No Trespassing* sign took up the space on the right, and a big lock hung from a chain on the other end.

Maybe this was why my mother insisted on getting an off-road vehicle instead of a more practical car like my sedan. I'd thought it was overkill for the roads of our sleepy town, but a Jeep could handle getting to wherever this was. I killed the engine, pocketed the keys, and exited the car. The scene before me was unexpected and seemed at odds with everything I knew about my mother. A long, winding gravel lane had seen better days behind the rusted gate. Dense trees lined both sides of it, their branches reaching toward each other like contorted fingers.

My mother adored our tiny town and never expressed interest in living far from it. She'd taught math at the town's small school of around three hundred students, where all the grade levels were consolidated into one building. She'd built a life in Belview. So, what business did she have with this secret parcel of land in the middle of nowhere?

My skin crawled as I climbed over the dilapidated fence. The eerie solitude of the woods made me feel like I'd stumbled onto a movie set. But there wasn't a tornado on the horizon, no magical wardrobe waiting to be discovered, and certainly no wand tucked into my back pocket.

"You're fine," I muttered, trying to quell the unease.

I started down the overgrown lane, each step crunching loudly on the gravel beneath my feet. The feel of the ground under me, the whisper of wind through leaves, and even the weight of my body in motion struck me as absurdly novel after being cloistered in the house for so long. *My house now,* I corrected myself, my fingers instinctively curling at my sides.

There had to be some way of opening the gate, so I could've driven further in. Recalling a set of keys my parents' lawyer had given me, I groaned. I could see them in my mind, a big red panda keychain with seven silver keys. If I had brought them, I wouldn't have had to walk.

For about half a mile, there was nothing but the dirt lane, the various trees, and the vegetation that lined it. The scent of fresh grass grew stronger the further I went. Nature bloomed tall and proud, as vegetation tended to do without human intervention. Bright yellow dandelions, lavender, loosestrife, and purple nightshade twirled along the edges of the forest as if tempting me further down the lane. Butterflies gracefully flew among the flowers springing from the grass. They were so mesmerizing that I didn't notice the meadow until I was in it.

Who is it? A masculine voice whispered. I froze, toes jamming against the front of my shoes. The words were barely there—a thread of sound woven into the forest's tapestry. Leaves rustled, branches creaked, and the question lingered in that near-silent symphony.

"Hello?"

The entire meadow fell into an abrupt stillness. If I called out, I was sure my voice would echo through the dense forest and the rugged slopes of the mountains around me. The stillness felt surreal, as if time itself paused. Adrenaline pulsed through my veins. I tilted my head to catch any faint sound that might break the eerie quiet. *Weird…*

Is it her? A dainty, feminine voice answered.

My head snapped in the direction of the voice. Twenty or so feet away, through tall grass, were the ears and glimmering forelocks of several horses.

Horses? I blinked.

I loved horses. At one point, I was obsessed with them and even took riding lessons throughout my childhood. I'd spent those years begging my parents for a horse of my own, only to be met with the impracticalities of their cost on an engineer's and teacher's salaries. Horses were too expensive. When I realized I'd never own one, I'd lost interest. Yet here on the land my mother owned and left for me stood a small herd of horses.

It took me a moment to remember I'd heard someone call out… surely it wasn't the horses. Perched on my toes, I attempted to look over the tall grass to see if I could spot who it might be. The sets of silvery white, black, and tan-tipped ears remained rapt in my direction.

The only logical explanation for all of this was that my parents were renting the field to someone who owned the horses. Or perhaps the horses had managed to make it onto Mom's land of their own accord; horses were escape artists, after all. *My land,* I reminded myself, my fingers jerking. They certainly couldn't have belonged to my parents, who complained about the cost of breeches and riding boots.

"Hello?" I called again.

A sudden chill tightened around my chest, and the feeling of a revelation followed by a deep sadness swept through me. The feelings weren't even mine. *What the heck…* It was as if someone were projecting their grief onto me, and the last thing I needed was more emotions to wallow in. The meadow's silence grew dense, almost palpable, as if the very atmosphere conspired to drown me in this inexplicable mourning. Even the sharp cries of the flock of starlings circling overhead and the high-pitched scrape of grasshopper wings had disappeared.

She was gone. My mother was gone. Hopelessly, I tried to fight the despair that choked me. The despair that was somehow not mine but was everything that I had become. Fighting it was pointless, and I coughed to relieve the aching pressure, covering my mouth with a fist. I didn't possess the ability to keep the wretched feelings at bay because they were being cast into me from someone else. I was a shallow pool, and the emotions swimming around me were a depthless agony.

Desperate to outrun the thoughts and far too familiar emotions, I spun away from the meadow and fled. Tripping out of my sandals, I ran down the gravel drive as fast as my legs could carry me over the jagged ground. I jumped over the fence and threw myself back into the Jeep. The overwhelming anguish followed me like a black cloud, even when I turned off the property and sped down the road toward the safety of my home.

Chapter Two

Her Secrets

Elle

The house was too quiet. I needed noise. I turned on the television, and the sound of a game show filled the room. The sound was necessary, but not even the spinning clicks of the wheel as the contestants spun it drew my attention away from my racing thoughts. I started to pace. The old oak floorboards creaked under me when I repeatedly passed in front of the couch.

There were horses on land my mom never informed me of, voices I couldn't explain, and emotions that weren't entirely mine but were left lingering in the meadow. None of it made any sense. Sure, I didn't always follow my mother around, but this secret was far too big for someone like her to hide. Had my father known about the meadow? Had anyone besides our attorney known it existed? What would I do with a herd of horses when I couldn't even care for myself?

Head pounding against the barrage of questions that pelted through it, I sat heavily on the black suede couch, sending it sliding a few inches into the table beside me. A glass of juice sitting on it toppled over, its contents cascading in a gleaming arc before splashing onto the intricate heirloom rug below. I scrambled to my feet, grabbing a towel from the kitchen before dropping to my knees to dab at the growing stain.

The dark liquid crept across the rug quickly, and the towel wasn't soaking it up fast enough. Desperately, I grabbed a corner of the rug to check if the juice had seeped through, lifting it just enough to notice a floorboard that didn't fit correctly. My panic over the spill faded when I ran my fingers over the board's edges. They gapped at the smooth surface of the floor as if it had been placed there intentionally. *Had Mom used the rug to hide something?*

Kneeling forward and bracing against the wet rug, I pried the board loose. It popped up easily enough that I lost my balance, landing squarely on my butt, the corner of the damp rug hitting my leg with a loud smack. *Perfect.* Moving back to my knees, I pulled the rug back further. A narrow wooden box was tucked into the space with a small lock dangling from it. I dug the box from the floorboards, fingernails catching the thin trim. Lifting the tiny silver lock, I studied it before setting it down to grab the keys the lawyer had given me from the table.

Fumbling through them, I found the only key that looked like it might fit. The key opened the lock with a tiny click. For a second, the world around me grew fuzzy. Apparently, my parents were living a secret life because I'd lived in this two-story house since my mom brought me home from the hospital, and I never, not once, stumbled upon this hiding spot. Yet, there was a meadow, a key, and inevitably more secrets hiding inside the box I was holding.

Lifting the lid, I found a journal inside. Its pages were weathered, and when I inhaled deeply, it smelled of vanilla. The cover was made of a scaled material, much like a black snake, if the snake happened to be very large. I opened the cover and read the inscription on the inside: BOOK XII. If this were Book Twelve, where were the others?

I flipped the journal open, and a page fell out. Unfolding it, I started to read…

My name is Melody Portier. It is August 6th, 1999, a quiet, sunny day. I have been initiated as the Keeper of my herd for a month. My job is to protect Nimue, Dolfan, and the others from the Dothians, the Keepers of the Dragons. My mother is gone. She sat me down before she died and told me about the Unicorns in the meadow. I didn't believe her, but on the day of her funeral, I drove out and walked into the mountains. My mom was telling the truth. I knew there was something spectacular about them the second I saw them.

Being their Keeper is not just about watching over them. It's about understanding the ancient bond we share. The responsibility is overwhelming, but my connection with these magnificent creatures is beyond anything I've ever known. Their fate rests heavily on my shoulders, and I am determined to honor it, no matter the cost.

Unicorns? Dragons? The words were clearly my mother's handwriting, but the fairytale I was reading was entirely unlike my mother. Mom was exceedingly practical and honest, lacking the imagination to make up bedtime stories, let alone stories about Unicorns. Her creativity ended with failed hobbies and attempts at new recipes in the kitchen that generally fell flat when she improperly seasoned them or cooked them for too long.

Unicorns… I scoffed, slowly shaking my head.

The horses in the meadow did not have horns, but Unicorns most assuredly did. I looked down at the journal in blatant confusion, flipped to a page, and kept reading.

September 19th, 2002 – It has been a while since I've gotten to know Dolfan and Nimue. Dolfan, the herd leader, has a blindingly white coat. His mane and tail are so long that they nearly drag the ground. He is old and wise, older and wiser than anything I've ever known.

Nimue is his constant companion. She has a coat that reminds me of a deer. She has been with Dolfan for many years. Nimue is the mother of Itha and Ayda. Itha is like a wild rose, with a coat, mane, and tail the color of a brand-new penny. Itha is mischievous and spirited. Ayda is her opposite. She is stubborn and firm. She is a faded version of Itha's coloring, with white hairs throughout her coat.

Dolfan's brother, Aire, is nearly white. He is standoffish and doesn't trust me, but I admire him for his regal beauty. Last is Elska. Elska was born before my mother took over. None of them is as perfectly beautiful and lovely as she.

For the next few hours, I sat on the floor in disbelief as I read and reread the words my mom had written on those first few pages of the journal. I traced the flat ink on the paper with my finger until it felt raw. Despite my desperate desire for answers, something inside me prevented me from reading further. I was stuck on her words.

Unicorns don't exist…

Everything felt unfathomable, like an unending illusion I couldn't grasp or comprehend. Curling into a ball, I sobbed softly until I eventually drifted off to sleep on the couch, the book lying nearby. In my dreams, I saw my mother and a majestic snow-gray creature that, despite its appearance, was not a horse at all.

Chapter Three

My Discovery

Falling awake is not nearly as satisfying as falling asleep. My left side was already throbbing before I hit the floor. I stumbled to my feet, the unnatural half-sitting position I'd slept in causing my joints to crack. Rubbing my side, I looked toward the stairs out of habit. My bed was calling to me, a potential sanctuary from the disorienting reality that grew heavy as I made sense of the previous day.

Pushing my hair back, I picked up the journal that sat open on the coffee table. Its cover bore the telltale signs of frequent use—edges softened, spine creased, a patina of handling that showed hours spent with pen pushed into paper. My fingers traced the marks, and a knot formed in my stomach. I know I needed to drive out to the meadow, confirm it was all nonsense, and dismiss the words on the pages as my mother's hidden imagination.

Before I could change my mind, I dressed quickly and climbed into the Jeep, taking the keys to unlock the gate and driving further down the lane. Sometimes, especially before my parents passed away, I could think intelligently enough to make rational choices, like remembering the set of keys. Sometimes…

Opening the gate and pulling onto the potholed lane, I drove until the Jeep's tires crunched to a halt at the meadow's edge. My feet touched the ground, and the air shifted, uncertainty rooting me in place. They stood—waiting, expectant, their gazes fixed upon me with an intensity that stole my breath. *Me.* These creatures looked to *me* like I held the key to their salvation. Each step forward was an effort, my trembling legs threatening to betray me—seven of them. The number registered dimly in my mind, a discrepancy from the number in the journal. Two stood closest to where I'd stopped, one as white as pure snow and the other the color of sun-kissed sand.

Dolfan.

Nimue.

Behind them stood a young black colt, its coat gleaming like polished obsidian in the sunlight. I was drawn to him, and as he stepped forward, I tentatively reached out, my fingers shaking. The colt's large, curious eyes locked onto mine, and the world seemed to hold its breath momentarily. The connection was instant and undeniable, a whisper of something almost otherworldly.

He walked to me, placing his muzzle against my palm, and I gently caressed his velvet nose. A calm settled over me. It was a momentary reprieve from the wildfire that was becoming my emotions. Then, with a breath that felt like my first in years, I drew back his long, silky forelock from his forehead. Time seemed to slow, my heart hammering loudly against my ribs like it could fill the silence of the meadow. The small, twisted stump of a ragged, black horn lay where the flat expanse of his forehead should have been. It looked like someone had sawed it off. I gasped, the sight of the horn shattering the last remnants of my disbelief.

For a fleeting second, I was a child again, lost in the pages of a storybook where such mythical creatures roamed free. But the touch of the rough edges of the hacked-off horn under my fingers, the undeniable reality of its texture, anchored me firmly in the present. My hands shook, not from the chill of the spring air but from the overwhelming realization of what stood before me.

"It's real," I whispered, the words a lifeline as my mind raced to catch up with what my heart was already accepting.

The world as I knew it had just expanded beyond the confines of reason and into realms I could only dare to dream. The unicorn watched me, its gaze deep, almost understanding, like it could see the turmoil that raged inside. In that gaze, I found an echo of the loneliness and longing that lingered from the moment I'd been told my parents had died, and a whisper of something else… hope.

With the horn still beneath my fingertips, I allowed myself to truly see the creature before me. I dropped my hand, the raven-colored hair falling back into place across the creature's forehead, and took a step back. My arms hung uselessly at my sides as I looked into the creature's eyes.

"You're real," I admitted, not just to him but to myself.

The acknowledgement was like a key turning in a lock. There was a world where such beauty could exist, the kind of beauty every child wished for but never thought they'd see. Yet here it stood, right before me. The last of my skepticism cracked, allowing the light of pure fascination to seep through.

She knows, a feminine voice spoke.

Hello Keeper, a younger male voice chimed. *My name is Flint.*

"Hello," I whispered.

Their voices were the same from the day before. These creatures before me could communicate, and I could understand them. My breath caught in my throat. I was losing my sanity. It was the only plausible explanation. Perhaps I finally plunged into madness, imagining scenarios where horses talked and grew horns like Unicorns. Flint nuzzled my arm gently in understanding. A single breath and a profound sense of tranquility enveloped me.

They allowed me to stand there and process my back-and-forth thoughts while they regarded me. I could sense everything they felt, their emotions swirling around me like a dust storm, coating my skin and digging into my lungs. It didn't take me long to realize they were projecting their sentiments onto me as if our feelings belonged to each other. When I'd hurriedly left the meadow the day before, it was their sadness that flooded through me as they came to terms with the fact that my mother had truly passed away. Only my mother. They didn't know my father when he was alive. I could feel that, too.

Her death is a travesty.

Whispers hung in the air, soft conversations that revealed Dolfan denied my mother's passing despite sensing it. Their curiosity came in gentle ripples of unspoken questions. The youngest, eyes soft and warm, radiated inquisitiveness. More direct than the others, he searched for my intentions, and I felt the burden of his wordless inquiry seep into my consciousness. This unspoken exchange was a delicate dance of mutual fascination. The elders gazed at me, their solemn expressions suggesting an awareness I didn't fully understand.

What is going to happen to us?

"It's okay," I told them, but I wasn't sure why I said it.

How could I promise them everything would be fine if I didn't know what I was doing? Despite my uncertainty, I was determined to do my best to keep them safe from whatever threats they might face, even though I had no idea how to protect them from Dragons. I was still holding onto the hope that Dragons weren't real, but if Unicorns are real, why not Dragons? Just thinking about it left me feeling vulnerable and small.

They are real.

I closed my eyes and did my best to push aside everything welling up. I was both lost and found. Lost because my mother had not prepared me for her version of life. Found because I wasn't alone anymore. The Unicorns weren't my parents, but they represented a part of my mother. They offered something tangible amidst the void of emptiness. For the first time since my parents' death, there was purpose.

The murmurs around me quieted as I approached their leader. Dolfan studied me calmly, dipping his head in my direction. Patiently, he allowed me to inspect him. Running my hand over his pure white coat, he took a deep breath under my fingers. Dolfan's gentle caramel-brown eyes remained fixed on his herd while they grazed quietly, absorbing the presence of their new Keeper.

Nimue stood as close to Dolfan as she could, her nose at his hip, napping quietly while I circled her slowly, committing every detail to memory. She was slender yet soft, her dainty head and arched neck giving her an air of superiority. Her mane was wavy and silky, her forelock dropping off her nose like a curtain.

Standing a few feet away was Flint, his curiosity keeping him close. I could tell I would like him; he looked intelligent, absorbing my actions and emotions keenly. He was black as a shadow from the tip of his nose to the end of his tail. The colt was perhaps the equivalent of a two-year-old horse, though I knew nothing about Unicorn maturity.

I am much older than a two-year-old horse, he quipped, his voice resonating more profoundly than the others, a fact that did not escape me.

I smiled at him, gently rubbing his face before moving away. Itha and Ayda, I presumed by the descriptions my mother had given in her journal, stood together, nuzzling each other while casting unsure glances my way. When I approached, Ayda's rusty-colored coat trembled under my touch, though she allowed me close. Itha, on the other hand, leaned into my caress. Ayda nudged Itha with pinned ears, warning her to be careful, I suppose.

Elska hid behind the rest of the herd, her head low. She was my mom's favorite, and it was easy to see why—she was beautiful. Her mane was so long it touched the ground, her tiny ears drooped to the side, and her face was delicately dished like the Arabian horse I once rode in lessons. Her legs were slender, with tufts of hair around her fetlocks. Elska looked as close to a classic depiction of a Unicorn as one could get. I put a hand on her neck and scratched under her silky, flowing mane, sharing briefly in her grief. My mother wrote that she was special, that their souls sang for each other. I couldn't help but wonder about the bond they shared. It must have been deep with how much sorrow the little mare carried, filling the space between us.

Aire, the last member of the herd, was perhaps the most handsome of them all, with his regal build, long silver-colored mane, and steady sky-blue eyes. He kept his distance, tossing his head when I tried to come closer. I stopped a few feet away, lowering the hand I intended to use to pet him. I understood; he didn't know me. My mother wrote that he was standoffish, a trait he hadn't lost. Something set him apart, though I couldn't pinpoint what it was.

I could have spent all night in the meadow, enjoying the breeze and the company of the beautiful beasts that surrounded me. They did their best not to burden me with their thoughts, and I tried to return that favor, aware my emotions were already overwhelming. Sitting on the meadow's edge, I continued reading through more of my mom's journal, hoping it might guide me on how to honor my promise to keep them safe. I skimmed through the pages, looking for one that might offer guidance.

Dragons, I swallowed.

I looked up at the Unicorns grazing in the field around me. They resembled horses in many ways, yet there were differences. They seemed so otherworldly in how they moved, graceful and ethereal. Quietly, they grazed the long strands of forage covering the meadow from tree line to tree line. When I flipped to the journal's last page, another folded paper was stuck against the cover, and an odd pensiveness washed over me. She'd kept her first entry tucked in the front and her last in the back. I opened the page knowing these were my mother's final words. The last she'd ever write.

April 7th, 2011 – It has been a long time since I met the Unicorns, though only a few weeks have passed since I discovered the older journals. They are so fragile, I must handle them with utmost care. I've been painstakingly transcribing them. If you're reading this, the transcribed journals are where my mother rests.

And if you're reading this, it means I am gone, and there's much you need to know. The journal you hold now will always be the most recent, but there are details I dare not include in it, for fear they might fall into the wrong hands and jeopardize the very creatures I've sworn to protect. Soon, you will face critical decisions. I trust you'll choose wisely. This may be one of the last remaining Unicorn herds, and their existence is pivotal to the balance of the Keepers. Should they disappear, so too will those who have safeguarded them since their creation. Answers that you need to ensure their safety lie within these journals. Seek them out.

Chapter Four

Then I Saw Him

Elle

The following day was painfully chilly. My father had never taught me how to use the ancient thermostat, and I still hadn't quite figured it out on my own. Messing with it either left me unbearably hot or without heat at all. Layering a long cream sweater over leggings, I grabbed the papers and headed for Belview Brews, the coffee shop near the middle of town, to sort out which bills needed to be paid and when. The task seemed mundane yet daunting, but most importantly, it offered me a semblance of normalcy. Or it should have. After the tumultuous days I'd endured, it was like I was stuck in the eye of a cyclone with no way out.

I opened the café door, and the wind kicked it shut behind me. Pressing my hands to my chest, I tried to ignore the eyes that snapped in my direction. It had been a while since I last visited, perhaps well before I'd left for college. The friendly barista who always knew my order was still working there, and I recognized the cozy nooks throughout the room. However, they'd done a lot of redecorating, giving it a quaint, cottagecore vibe unlike the hippy theme it once held. The walls were painted a soft sage green, the hardwood floors stained dark brown, and brown loveseats with matching cushions were scattered around scalloped white wooden coffee tables. The upgrades were geared toward tourists, not the local townies.

Several townies were sprinkled among unfamiliar faces. I recognized a few of them and exchanged brief acknowledgments. Most seemed engrossed in their phones, books, laptops, or conversations. It struck me how familiar I was with so many of them, yet I was still overcome with feeling alone in a crowded room. The loneliness made my heart sink.

I glanced over the menu, which had changed, along with the sparkling espresso machines lined up on the counter. Ordering an iced mocha and a blueberry muffin, I grabbed my tray and weaved through the tables, seeking refuge in a far corner. A lone brown couch offered the semblance of privacy I needed. Perfect. With a steadying deep breath, I spread the papers across the coffee table. I was determined to tackle them in this public place to hold myself accountable. Pen in hand, I diligently drew lines across a piece of blank printer paper, scribbling some numbers next to them.

Sliding the first bill from its envelope, I opened it and jotted down the amount owed. Slowly, the air filled with a static charge, freezing my pen mid-air. A sharp breath caught in my throat, and adrenaline surged through me, setting my heart pounding like a caged bird. It felt as if someone's eyes were boring into me. Glancing around, I looked from face to face, but nobody paid me any particular attention. Puzzled, I scanned the room again, scrutinizing every shadow and corner. Nothing seemed out of place until a flicker of movement caught my eye. A person in a high-backed chair facing away from me shifted, revealing a sliver of a man's profile.

I leaned forward to see more of him. He was hunched over an art pad, studiously avoiding eye contact with anyone who looked in his direction, and several people were, in fact, looking his way. Black jeans, a deep crimson shirt, and a mossy green bomber jacket. His hair was dark brown, and even though I couldn't see his eyes clearly, I envisioned them as blue. He had a strong jawline and thick lashes; from my line of vision, his nose had a curious arch to it.

One glance his way, and my heart somersaulted, even though he didn't spare me a single look. The hand hovering over my notepad trembled. *Great… Now, all of my focus is gone. Seriously, what is wrong with me?* This stranger was having a bizarre effect on my nervous system. My leg bounced in agitation, and I again tried to focus on my paperwork.

"You okay?" he said, staring at me now. His voice was velvet night.

My head snapped up. He twisted in his seat, leaning toward me, his arm stretched languidly along the armrest. Like a deer caught in headlights, I blinked twice, forgetting myself. Then I noticed his eyes. My imagination hadn't done them justice. His eyes weren't just one shade but a mesmerizing spectrum of shades reminiscent of something cold and vast. *Chilling…* Nearly white at the center, deepening to a celestial blue, and finally fading to a midnight black around the edges. It was like staring into a moonlit winter sky, with shadows of trees dancing across a blanket of snow. I could swear I was falling, tumbling endlessly into their captivating hues. My breath hitched. Like a record scratch in my mind, consciousness rushed back. My knee stilled abruptly, and I smacked my heel against the white vinyl floor with a sharp click.

"Good?" I replied, mentally smacking myself for the girlish, high tone I couldn't suppress.

The corner of his lips lifted in a slow smirk, those eyes traveling over me like I was something he was trying to figure out. My cheeks burned under his scrutiny, the heat spreading to my ears. Those eyes were bedroom eyes. They spoke of secrets whispered in the dark, of tangled sheets and mornings that bled into afternoons. This guy was trouble with a capital T. I nervously pressed my tongue to the roof of my mouth.

"Cat got your tongue?" he drawled, his smile widening as if he could see right through me.

I shook my head quickly.

"Feels like the whole world does," I mumbled.

He tilted his head, a glint crossing his narrowed eyes as if he were trying to assign emotions to my expressions. Heat flooded my face again, and I looked down momentarily, tucking my chin away from his relentless gaze. When I looked up again, our eyes met for a fleeting moment, a spark passing between us. It was almost as if I found something I'd been desperately seeking yet instinctively knew I should evade. He was a siren's call personified – alluring yet dangerous, a temptation that promised both fulfillment and ruin.

"The entire world," he responded, coming out as a statement rather than a question.

With a soft, sad smile, I nodded and asked, "What's your name?"

"Kairo," he told me. "What's yours?"

"Elle. What are you drawing?"

He glanced down at the art pad on his lap, his brow furrowing for a moment like he'd forgotten its existence. The cover was soft brown leather, weathered and worn. Some pages peeked out with aged, sepia-toned edges contrasting the crisp, clean ones beneath. It was almost magical, as if the pad could add pages as needed, defying what little I knew about bookbinding. With a sharp snap that startled me, he shut it and then held it out to me.

"Want to see?" he asked.

Curiosity gnawed at the part of me that screamed to play it cool, to decline and stick with my bills. Before I could talk myself out of it, I reached forward and accepted the art pad. The moment my fingers brushed the worn leather, a jolt shot up my arm, raising goosebumps and stealing my breath for a beat.

I flipped the pad open to the first two pages. Detailed charcoal sketches filled the spread, depicting towering trees like ancient sequoias on one side, their branches framing a path that snaked through them, leading toward a majestic mountain range. It was as if Kai had captured a seamless narrative across the two pages. The detail was so incredible, so vivid, even in grayscale. I could almost feel the cool, damp earth beneath my feet and the scent of the crisp mountain air as I imagined myself walking the path.

Turning the page, the mood of the sketches shifted dramatically. In it, a fire blazed in the center of a cavernous void, its flickering flames illuminating intricate cave paintings that depicted an epic battle. Soldiers, clad in armor, clashed with monstrous beasts and rearing horses. The soldiers' mounts wore frightened expressions, with wide eyes and gaping mouths. Each line captured the intensity and drama of a battle fought long ago. *He is good... very good.*

Enthralled by the meticulous detail that breathed life into his art, I flipped the page again. My eyes widened in horror, and my heart plummeted to my stomach. The page held a monstrous winged beast, its talons clutching a struggling horse. The creature's ferocious expression, captured with chilling details, tightened my chest.

A strange familiarity tugged at me. The sketched scales were oddly similar to the ones adorning the mysterious journal hidden in my room. Studying the page again, the art's enchantment suddenly shattered when I truly took in the creature's prey. It wasn't a horse. It was a Unicorn, lying limp in the Dragon's razor-sharp talons, its horn snapped off. Its once lively eyes were now empty, devoid of any spark. This wasn't just art. No, this was a looking glass reflecting a nightmare. A cold dread settled in my stomach, leaving a bitter taste in my mouth.

"Look at the next one," he said, his voice incredibly low.

I could sense he'd found something in my reaction to his sketches. Peeking through the curtain of hair falling across my face, I studied his calm expression and figured my assumption was correct. My reaction alone seemed to answer a question he hadn't even asked. Swallowing the lump in my throat, I flipped to the next page. And there I was. At least, the woman in the white dress looked a lot like me, standing in what looked like a sun-drenched meadow. A magnificent black Unicorn stood beside me, its head dipping toward my hand. It was a scene straight out of a dream, a memory I didn't yet possess.

The sketch was like an awakening, and as I studied its details, the thoughts I'd been keeping at bay slammed into me. *Dragons are real.* It was a terrifying confirmation; all etched across the page in charcoal. Panic bubbled up, constricting my throat. I dropped the sketchbook as if on fire, scrambling to gather the scattered papers with hands that trembled like leaves in a strong wind.

No. I took in a shallow breath of uncertainty as my eyes met his.

"It's nice to meet you," Kairo said to me. "Unicorn Keeper."

I didn't pause when I left, not even to collect my coffee and muffin, see if he would follow, or tell any of the townspeople goodbye.

Chapter Five

I Felt So Alone

Bursting through the front door, I slammed it shut and locked the deadbolt with a click. For the second time in as many days, I cowered in my own home, and the sense of déjà vu was nauseating. Leaning heavily against the cool wood, my legs gave out under me, and I slid down until I sat against the door. My chest heaved and I gulped for air, each breath a ragged gasp that tore at my throat. Sweat beaded on my forehead, trickling down my temples despite the chill that gripped me.

If I was right – and every throbbing nerve, every racing thought, screamed that I was – I'd just encountered a Dragon Keeper. I'd refused to believe that Dragons existed in the meadow, but the denial was stronger inside my home, and I wanted to shout and yell at the top of my lungs. *'They aren't real!'* Yet the evidence was undeniable. The sketch flashed before my eyes, its lines etched in my memory like a hot-iron brand: a Dragon, majestic and terrible, feasting on the broken body of a Unicorn.

What did he want from me? My fingers curled into tight fists, nails biting into my palms. Was it even me he was after? Or my herd? An unnerving realization crept over me. I was responsible for what could be the last of their kind. The thought left me reeling with its implications as fear, cold and sharp as an icicle, lanced through me. I had to act, but what could I do?

Every fiber of my being screamed at me to stay home, where I felt safe, but I knew I couldn't stay. I needed to leave and check on the herd. Yet, if he truly was a Dragon Keeper, and every horrifying image in that sketchbook seemed to confirm that fear, leading him straight to them would be a death sentence for us all. *I can't leave. It's too dangerous.*

Hugging my knees, I fought the overwhelming urge to collapse under the pressure of this twisted existence I'd found myself in. I needed information or a clue—anything—to tell me what to do next. Raking my fingers through my hair, I willed my racing thoughts to slow and forced myself to take several measured breaths to calm my fraying nerves. My legs wobbled as I stood, walked to my bedroom, and sat on my bed. Grabbing the journal, I flipped through the pages frantically until the word "Dothian" jumped out at me.

MARCH 19th, 2008- The day my mother died, she summoned me to her bedside and told me about a curse she termed the Curse of the Keepers. The curse of the Unicorn Keepers, known as Allorians, and the Dothians, or Dragon

Keepers. According to her, the Allorians and Dothians were locked in a bitter conflict over two centuries ago.

In her final moments, she directed me to a specific journal that would unveil the origins of the enmity between the Allorians and Dothians.

The following day, I uncovered the journal secreted away in a chest in the attic. Within its pages, I learned of a tragedy: the Dragons had fallen ill, and the sole remedy was Unicorn blood.

In response, the Dothians started hunting the Unicorns, desperate to save their charges. Meanwhile, the Allorians, aware of their adversaries' plight, devised cunning strategies to outwit and deceive the Dothians. Their tactics often led to the demise of the Dragons caught in the crossfire.

The conflict escalated so direly that Albadine, known as the Keeper of All, intervened by casting a curse upon the Dothians and the Allorians. This curse extended to their charges, Dragons and Unicorns alike.

According to the journals, the initial aspect of the curse dictated that Dragons and Unicorns could no longer reproduce freely. This decree led to a significant decline in their populations. Each loss of life was mourned deeply, while every birth was celebrated with profound joy.

The second aspect of the curse demanded that Keepers face a choice. Each Keeper must vow their undying loyalty and faithful protection to their Unicorns or Dragons. Due to this, Allorians could maintain their immortality only by staying with their Unicorns and avoiding intimacy. Dothians could remain immortal only if they avoided falling in love while living with their Dragons. This dichotomy presented all Keepers with a stark decision: to live eternally as a Keeper or to pursue a relationship and risk passing their fates to future generations.

At that time, I had already begun seeing someone. He was practically a nobody in the grand scheme of things after my world shifted, but I found myself drawn to him. He offered a sense of normalcy I desperately needed. He held me when I was upset, thinking it was because of my mother's passing. In truth, my distress stemmed from the impossible task she entrusted to me. She'd thrust me into this unfamiliar world with scant information, and I struggled to grasp why.

He didn't ask questions when I disappeared for hours, claiming I needed fresh air. He didn't call me crazy for sitting in my bedroom all night surrounded by old journals.

Instead, he made me laugh. He wiped away my tears and promised to always be there for me. So, when I had to make the choice, I chose him. I chose him, knowing I was passing my duties as a Keeper onto my child and that I would die to ensure that happened.

My mouth went as dry as sandpaper. *Immortality?* The word echoed in my skull, bouncing off the walls of my mind. *Impossible.* The information from the journal had a surreal edge to it. Perhaps it was because this enemy had materialized out of thin air just days ago. Goosebumps rose on my arms, and I rubbed them roughly, leaving angry pink marks on my skin. I needed to focus, to find myself in the here and now before this situation spiraled out of control.

I clenched the journal shut, the worn leather cool against my fingers. My mind was a battlefield. This was becoming less about coping with losing my parents and more about figuring out how to survive all of this on my own. A fierce part of me wanted to be brave, to face whatever this new existence held. But another, quieter part whispered that I should escape, run as far away from the Dragon Keeper and his dark truth as possible.

He needed the blood of my Unicorns? Literal blood?

My teeth scraped against my bottom lip, and I rubbed my palms nervously against the rough fabric of my pants.

Protect them. Keep him from finding them. These thoughts pulsed through my mind, synchronizing with every beat of my heart. What began as a conscious decision quickly became instinctual. I took a deep breath, forcing myself to focus. My mom's entries stated that the key to unraveling this mystery lay in the first set of journals. I ran my finger down the page before me, scanning my mother's familiar handwriting, and reread the words 'the journals rested with my grandmother'.

Closing my eyes, I let my mind drift back to when I'd visited my grandmother's grave. The memory was hazy, obscured by time and childhood inattention, but I clung to every detail I could muster. The scent of wildflowers, the whisper of wind through tall grass, the solemn weight of the moment—I grasped these fragments, willing them to coalesce into a clear picture.

The bumpy, narrow road leading there was strangely familiar, tickling the edges of my awareness. A weeping willow, its branches like a cascade of green silk in the wind, stood on a rise overlooking a small family cemetery. My mom's hand tightened around mine as she led me through a rusted, broken gate. The grass inside was a fresh green carpet, meticulously trimmed. In my mind's eye, I saw aged stone crosses and mossy headstones arranged in neat rows within a small, wooden-fenced plot.

Then, with a jolt, my eyes flew open. My brows furrowed in concentration. I'd been there. The willow tree. That meadow, the one where the Unicorns live, I'd visited there as a child.

The following day, I sat at the kitchen table, laptop humming against the white wood. My mother's journal lay beside it, but I couldn't bring myself to read it. The discovery of her secrets now fell to me, and reading her words left me torn between anger at her secrets and my love for her. Needing a break from the emotional onslaught, I shoved the journal aside and turned to the internet. However, the information I found offered few concrete answers, which frustrated me. Where were the clear instructions, the step-by-step guide on how to deal with a freaking Dragon Keeper?

I scoured the web. Every search engine declared fire-breathing Dragons a myth, and Unicorns? They were hairy rhinos in outdated textbooks. Forums, social media, and even fringe conspiracy chat groups were all dead ends. The information online was either laughably fake or so heavily edited that it was useless.

Finding someone who understood and knew what I was dealing with was a fool's errand. The Keepers, whoever they were, had done a damned good job of keeping their secrets. Dragons, though? Keeping those under wraps seemed like a logistical nightmare. Unless, of course, they weren't precisely the mountain-sized beasts I envisioned. Maybe they weren't as large as I'd imagined? Though Kairo hadn't portrayed them as smaller in his artwork. No, in his sketches, they were a lot larger than the Unicorns.

Slamming my laptop shut, I chewed on my lip until it was sore. The sour taste of failure was a poor substitute for a real plan. I wanted to check on the Unicorns. I couldn't stand the thought of them being exposed. But leading the Dragon Keeper straight to their field was dangerous. I'd serve them on a silver platter to the predators lured here… *By what? How did he know where to find me?* My grip on my pen tightened in frustration, and I twisted my fingers around it until my knuckles turned white.

I would have to find another way. I reached for my phone and scrolled through my contact list. It was filled with names of so-called friends, most of whom were at college or scattered across the country. I hadn't talked to any of them except Chase in months. Chase was sometimes a staple—a quiet text after a hard day, a meme sent late at night, a check-in that never demanded a response. He understood my need for space since the day my parents died. Despite my pushing him away, he never let me go. Without a second thought, my thumb tapped the call button.

"Elle," Chase answered. "You called for once."

"I did," I breathed. "I need a favor."

Before he could reply, I went right into what I needed from him. Drive down to Ellory Lane, turn down a driveway to the middle of nowhere, find the meadow, and look to see if there are horses in a field. If Chase thought my request was odd, he didn't let on. He listened to me, asked me to clarify that he wouldn't get shot for trespassing, and then said, "Okay." Simply, "Okay". As if he didn't have anything better to do.

The click of the call ending was barely audible over the rush of blood pounding in my temples. Had I just thrown Chase into some unseen danger? Unable to stay still, I bounced from window to window, only pausing to peek between the curtains. Between looking, my fingers flew across my phone screen, searching for any scrap of information I may not have found. It was still a rabbit hole of useless information. After an hour of restless pacing and mind-numbing online research, I collapsed onto the couch and reached for my mom's worn diary.

MAY 16th, 2004– It's the middle of May, and I find myself halfway through the old journals. This spring rushed in so fast. It feels like we were just gathered around the Thanksgiving table a few weeks ago. Now, as I gaze out the window, watching lilies bloom in the flower bed, I'm struck by the passing of time.

In the third journal, I stumbled upon something intriguing, something so significant I felt compelled to note it here. The Unicorn horns are what shield them from the Dothians. There's a protective quality in these horns, a safeguard against discovery. But in this modern era, the risk has become too great. They had to be removed.

My great-grandmother was the one who discovered the secret. She found she could carefully saw off the horns, collecting them each year when they grew back enough to peek through their forelocks. It became a semi-annual ritual. When my mother acquired the land they now roam, she took it a step further. She buried the horns deeper and deeper around the meadow, experimenting to see if their magic could act as a protective ward against intruders.

The Unicorns have remained hidden from prying eyes all this time. I imagine it as a protective bubble surrounding them, blending with anything inside of it and its surroundings. However, if the Dothians managed to breach the bubble, they would no longer be concealed from their sight. My mother did the same to the house, burying dozens of horns among the flowerbeds that I'm looking at now to protect our home from those who are searching for us.

I re-read the last paragraph and relaxed into the chair. It was comforting to know the Dothians might only locate the Unicorns if someone managed to cross their barrier. Yet, it was hard to imagine how the horns could provide this level of protection. Confused, I leaned my head against the couch cushion and closed my eyes.

Chapter Six

I Would Find Her

I was twirling down a damp, endless, dark well filled with mist, creepy voices, and unfurling night. Just as I was about to discover where the voices came from, a sharp knock ripped me from the nightmare. Blood roared in my ears, and I startled awake, fumbling for the worn journal beside me. I stuffed it under the couch cushion and got to my feet. My sleep-rumpled T-shirt twisted around my torso. Smoothing it down, I crept to the window and peeked out. Even though it was dark outside, I could make out Chase's form on the porch. It wasn't Kairo. *Why would Kairo knock? Why was I expecting him?*

"Elle," Chase breathed when I opened the door for him.

He beamed at me, and I ran my eyes over him, relieved to see he was unharmed. His hair, a sun-kissed brown, was neatly trimmed in his usual crew cut. There was warmth in his root beer brown eyes. He had a straight nose, eyes that weren't too big or small, and features that were neither sharp nor soft. There wasn't anything remarkable about him. Not to me anyway. To me, he was just Chase, the same guy I'd known since the first grade.

"Chase," I replied, quickly checking behind him for Kairo before letting him in.

"I tried to call you," he told me as he walked past.

"You did?" I blinked, pulling my phone out of my pocket to check it.

I frowned at the four missed calls. *The herd! Were they okay?*

I scrutinized Chase's face. He didn't seem to come bearing bad news, but a preoccupied furrow to his brow developed when he wandered into the living room. Casting a worried glance around the messy space, disapproval hung on his face, unspoken but clear.

"Are they okay?"

"The horses," he replied, "are fine."

I let out a long breath of relief and followed Chase's gaze, finally registering the state of my living room. Shame burned in my cheeks. How long had it been since I'd even noticed the mess, let alone cleaned it up? The laundry room door was obscured by a pile of clothes that threatened to topple over. Dishes on the coffee table were abandoned, and trash littered every flat surface. It was all a testament to my months-long neglect. I grimaced. I couldn't even tell what was clean and what wasn't anymore.

"I thought my brothers were bad."

"I kind of," I replied, trailing off as I folded my arms under my chest.

"Grab a trash bag."

I did and passed it to him. He started gingerly picking through the clutter on the coffee table, filling it with my forgotten trash, stuffing in the crumpled receipts, half-eaten bags of chips, and an ancient, dog-eared paperback until it stretched thin. Following Chase's lead, I started with the kitchen. For a while, the only sounds were the soft clink of dishes and the rhythmic whoosh of the washing machine. Without a word, we fell into the rhythm of our tasks. It wasn't exactly bonding over conversation, but focusing on cleaning was strangely comforting. And when we stopped, an awkward silence settled.

Chase perched on the edge of the couch, his hands clasped in his lap, and his gaze darted around the room. I sank into my dad's worn recliner, the leather cool against my flushed skin. Our eyes met for a fleeting moment before I glanced away, unable to absorb the emotions brewing beneath his gaze. It was a look I knew all too well, a mixture of concern and something more, a wordless longing trapped just below the surface. But the truth was, Chase was like a cousin. There was no romantic spark for me, and there never would be, no matter how much he wished otherwise.

"What was your mom doing with a herd of horses?"

He placed his hands on his knees and leaned forward, as if trying to close the gap between us.

I took a deep breath. "I wish I knew," I lied. "I didn't even know they existed until a couple of days ago. I drove out to the property, not sure what to expect. Horses definitely didn't cross my mind. Remember when my mom gave me a hard time about riding lessons?" Pausing briefly, I didn't wait for his answer, since it was a rhetorical question. "She always told me they were too expensive, so finding a whole herd out there was…" I trailed off.

"Maybe she meant them as a gift to you?"

I forced a smile, the truth burning on my tongue. Little did he know how right he was about my mom's bizarre, out-of-this-world gift that I never asked for.

I shrugged, forcing another lie. "Maybe she was saving them for my graduation present?"

Chase chuckled. It was a warm sound that did little to ease the knot of stress tightening in my stomach. Mom couldn't keep a secret if her life depended on it. She'd always managed to blurt out what birthday presents were or ruin holiday surprises. Her inability to hide things turned me into an expert at faking shock and delight, mostly to spare Dad's feelings, though I suspect he knew all along.

"Elle, if you need anything, all you have to do is let me know. You can't just disappear and do… whatever this is." He motioned around the house at the rest of the mess that still needed to be cleaned.

"I know," I mumbled. "It's just… everything changed so fast."

Chase squeezed my shoulder. "There's no way to sugarcoat it. This sucks. I can't even begin to imagine what you're going through." He paused and studied me, as if choosing his words carefully. "But listen, your parents wouldn't want you to shut yourself away. At some point, you'll need to find a way out of this funk and start living again before life passes you by."

His words hit a raw nerve. He was right. I knew he was right. I'd told myself the same thing a thousand times already. The responsibility of the Unicorns meant there was something to live for. But the despair wouldn't ease up. It was the same bottomless pit of grief that still clung to me, leaving me exhausted. Its heavy pull whispered promises of a blanket, a pillow, and the oblivion of sleep.

"I don't even know where to start," I confessed, tears pricking at my eyes.

Chase didn't hesitate. He walked over and kneeled beside me, offering a silent invitation with a wave of his fingers. When I leaned into him, he pulled me close, his hand gently stroking my hair. His touch was so tender that I had to fight back a sob.

"You'll figure it out," he murmured into my ear. "I'll help if you want me to."

But I didn't really know if I wanted him to.

Kairo

Why did she make me so angry? My gaze lingered on the empty path the Allorian had gone down. Running out after her, I'd watched her turn a corner where she'd vanished into thin air, leaving me with a bitter cocktail of irritation and grudging respect. It wasn't that I doubted her ability; the Allorians' talent for slipping through Dothian fingers made them resourceful, a quality I found both impressive and infuriating.

Had she given me a nickname to use instead of her full name? The letter L or Elle possibly… What sort of name was that? Was it shortened from Eleanor or Ellen? It was annoying… but quaint, as quaint as the charm of Elle's small town that grated on me. I muttered a curse under my breath. My thoughts returned to the fact that everyone else in the town likely knew the Allorian's whereabouts while I was unable to track her down. It wouldn't last long, and I wouldn't continue to be outsmarted. I'd find her because I had to.

Cobblestone sidewalks flanked picturesque houses like a scene straight off a postcard. I hadn't been in a town like this for more than a few hours, yet I'd been stuck in this modern sprawl for several damned days. The houses were crammed together in a fashion that was very different from the open spaces I was used to. Wide roads buzzed with various vehicles, and the towering utility poles bristled with wires, giving the whole place an industrial vibe that made my skin crawl.

I yearned for the desolate beauty of my valley, the comforting emptiness that was more like home than this suffocating town ever could be. The constant hum of traffic, the garbled chatter from televisions through windows, and the ever-present tang of overflowing trash cans were all harsh reminders that I was very much in a modern-day town, not some romanticized picture.

I was fine in Dothan Valley. But when I'd felt the familiar tug of Sula-umbra, I had no choice but to uproot my life and fly my Dragons far from their home, guided by a beacon I hadn't felt in almost thirty years. The Sula-umbra, or the enlightening of a new Keeper, marked the passing of the previous one, and with Keepers' numbers dwindling, these beacons grew rarer. This particular one had yanked me from the solitude of my own devices and deposited me right here, on the corner of the road, nestled amidst this idyllic yet irritating town where I'd run into her.

My meeting with the Allorian had been as unintentional as my openness. I hadn't expected to bump into her so quickly, let alone find her so… unprepared. She reminded me of a fawn in a field of lions—doe-eyed and innocent, trying to go unnoticed as she navigated through sharp teeth and slanted eyes. Every one of her movements was tentative, and each glance held a flicker of uncertainty she couldn't fully mask.

Her naiveté was jarring. Clearly, she was clueless about who she truly was or about the world she'd been thrust into. But that wasn't the most unsettling part. No, the truly bizarre thing was the unwelcome thrum of protectiveness lingering in my ironclad will. It was an absurd notion, like those lions she was navigating, feeling paternal toward that fawn. Yet there it was, a stubborn ember refusing to be extinguished by logic.

The very idea of wanting to shield her from harm went against everything I knew, everything I was. A frown creased my brow as I wrestled with this unwanted impulse. There was something about her beyond the honey-gold hair cascading down her shoulders and those gold-flecked eyes that widened when she saw my sketches. A raw vulnerability drew me in, and I couldn't pinpoint why. It was a disconcerting development; one I needed to nip in the bud before it blossomed into something more troublesome.

I hadn't seen an Allorian since I was a kid. Back then, Dothians and Allorians coexisted in harmony, and deaths among our Dragons and Unicorns were rare. Until the Dragons were poisoned, and the cure was discovered, it was the blood of Unicorns. When my parents heard an Allorian had poisoned them, rumors of deliberate sabotage spread like wildfire. As our Dragons began to sicken, the Allorians refused to surrender any of the Unicorns to save them, despite their abundance at the time and the rumor that multiple were needed for the cure to work. It didn't take long for the Allorians' betrayal to fester, morphing into a gaping chasm of distrust between the Keepers.

For years, the abrupt disappearance of the Unicorns and their Keepers caused a fissure among my people. One day, they were there, grazing peacefully in the meadows; the next, they were gone. Our once-healthy Dragons grew sicker, their powerful bodies wracked with the sickness from the curse. Panic bloomed in the village, becoming a suffocating pall that choked out all reason.

The Dragon burial grounds overflowed with the remains of once magnificent creatures. Some Dothians found Unicorns in time to save their Dragons, but for others, the hunt continued. It was a desperate chase echoing through the decades as our Dragons withered away with each passing day. Artok would not meet the same fate. Determined to save him at any cost, I was left with no choice but to brave every obstacle the Allorians constructed around their Unicorns.

Leaning against the cold metal of a lamppost, the chill seeped through my jacket. The sight of jagged mountain peaks clawing at the sky stirred a pang of unwelcome nostalgia. Sure, the houses here were a far cry from the sturdy log dwellings I called home, but the rolling hills, the burbling creek, the vibrant tapestry of green—it was very similar to the valley of my childhood.

The Allorians seemed drawn to these familiar landscapes–a detail that wasn't lost on me. Maybe they wanted to come home? The idea caused a small rip in the fabric of suspicion my parents had woven so tightly around my heart. They'd spent years drilling warnings into me about the cunning and cruelty of the Allorians. But seeing the raw fear and surprise flicker in Elle's eyes when she realized who I was… for a fleeting moment, doubt dared to sprout. Was she merely protecting her charges, like I was?

Glowering at the empty street, I realized standing around wouldn't get me anywhere. I ran a hand through my hair and conceded defeat. Elle wasn't coming back tonight. *Fine.* I'd find her another day. But at the moment, my Dragons needed me. With a final disgruntled sigh, I turned and retraced my steps, the echo of my boots the only sound breaking the natural stillness of the approaching night. I didn't bother to search the streets for her as I returned to my Dragons.

I scoured the town's outskirts the following day, walking the same path where the Allorian woman had vanished. Each house lining the street could potentially be hers, yet their windows offered no clues. There wasn't a flicker of candlelight, nor a lingering scent of herbs hinting at arcane practices. The houses revealed nothing.

Allorians typically resided near their herds, but for reasons unknown to me, this one seemed to prefer the compact, crowded space of town. Perhaps she believed staying under the radar, blending in with the human populace, offered a sliver of safety. If someone stumbled upon her, they might not locate the Unicorns she protected because she wasn't with them. Not that her reasoning mattered. Such concerns paled in comparison to the problems I faced.

Kicking a rock across the blacktop of an empty parking lot, I swallowed. My Dragon, Artok, had been waging a losing war against his illness for far too long. That past year, the sickness had worsened. Every labored breath, every flicker of weakness, reflected my inability to care for him. Having explored every other avenue and exhausted every Dothian remedy, I couldn't stand by and watch Artok die. What I needed was Unicorn blood.

The eldest of the three Dragons entrusted to my care, Artok, had been a legend in our valley for as long as I could remember. My father's stories made sure of that. He would often regale anyone who would listen with tales of his enormous onyx Dragon with clever golden eyes.

He was so unlike Dalya, who was resentful and calculated. The ivory-colored Vermidias Dragon clung to her bitterness, despite my persistent attempts to build a relationship. She'd tolerated me before my father's death but resented me from the moment I took over his position, having shared an unbreakable connection with him. Try as I might, I could never understand why Dalya chose me. Over the years, I often thought she'd be better suited for Koa, my twin sister. They shared similar personalities and a general disdain for… well, pretty much everything. But Dalya had a particular aversion to Koa's brand of prissy know-it-all-ness. When she'd made her preference abundantly clear, I accepted her without hesitation.

The fact that our father had left all three of his Dragons to me had instantly ignited an anger in Koa. Artok was invaluable, Tattu was practical, but Dalya… She represented the future of our kind. When Koa had received Chuff, the only Dragon our mother had raised, the disappointment curdled into bitter animosity. I still recall her storming out, vowing revenge, and severing all ties with everyone in our valley. Chuff possessed a powerful heart and an unbelievable tolerance for her volatile temper. Yet, he would never be enough to fill the void left by the future she'd thought she'd deserved in the hatchlings that Dalya could produce.

At the end of the parking lot, butterflies milled around a blooming garden. I scanned the windows of the apartments lining the flowers, then paused at the end of a short lane. Small children played at a nearby playground with their parents in tow. Watching them, a pang of something akin to longing hit me, a reminder of the missing parts of my own life. With both my parents and my only sibling gone, there were moments when I'd felt adrift. I'd been the one to distance myself from Koa's drama, intentionally avoiding her chaos to preserve my sanity and ensure the safety of my Dragons.

It had been years since I'd seen her. The last I'd heard, her rage had boiled over, and threats were thrown around. Some of which included stealing Artok and Dalya. The very idea was outrageous. Stealing a Dragon was unheard of in the Keeper world, as bonds tended to be for life. The only legitimate ways to acquire another Keeper's Dragon were through a Dothian ritual that reassigned the bond, the passing of one through lineage, or the murder of a blood relative. However, killing another Keeper came with a blight that clung to the killer's soul. Thinking about the stories around flickering campfires of Keepers driven mad by the tortured spirits of those they'd slain, I grimaced.

A desperate part of me wondered if things might have been different with Koa. If we'd gotten along, I could have found solace knowing she'd take care of my Dragons because if I died, my unclaimed Dragons might waste away. Not that I had to worry about dying. Dothians didn't die of old age or illness–unless, of course, they fell in love, which, because of the curse, was a death sentence of its own. Beyond falling in love, if death did visit a Dothian, it was typically at the hands of another Keeper.

Looking down the street, I narrowed my eyes. I wasn't making any progress finding signs of the Allorian, and darkness was setting in. Parents began to bribe their children in the playground, and more lights brightened the apartment windows. My day of looking had come to a close. Reluctantly, I turned back to my Dragons.

50

Chapter Seven

I Will Protect Them

Elle

The turmoil over my forced seclusion led to an inescapable conclusion: I needed to return to the meadow. I'd spent the previous evening scrubbing and cleaning the house to distract myself, but it didn't work. I tried not to think about the Unicorns being alone, which only made me think about them more. Chase's welfare check wasn't enough. I needed to see them for myself. My confidence in leaving the house was bolstered by the knowledge that they had the ward around them. But navigating from the house to the meadow? That was a whole different challenge because the ward wasn't an invisible force that followed me… Not that I was aware.

Raiding Mom's closet, I yanked dresses off hangers and flung them aside. Floral monstrosities, long floor-length plain skirts, pantsuits… *Pantsuits?* She'd never worn most of this. A dark blue sundress was tucked in a drawer under her blouses—simple and hopefully inconspicuous. I threw it on, followed by a wide-brimmed sun hat and black sunglasses. Twisting my hair into a high bun, I tucked it under the safety of the hat's brim. My honey-colored hair sometimes stood out among the brunettes, redheads, and dyed varieties of the locals.

Grabbing my keys, I opened the garage door and looked at the two vehicles inside. Maybe Kairo didn't know about either? I'd walked to the coffee shop when we ran into each other, so he likely hadn't seen me driving. Although if he was watching me, he probably saw me driving my mom's more reliable Jeep versus my older black sedan. Cautiously settling on the smaller car, I didn't even stop to consider how it would fare on the rocky gravel lane that led into the meadow.

I pulled out of the driveway, eyes darting between the rearview mirror, side mirrors, and every window. What exactly was I looking for? There wasn't a shred of evidence of real, fire-breathing Dragons, so spotting one soaring through the sky was unlikely. Yet, here I was, scanning the clouds for leathery wings or puffs of smoke. Kairo, however, was a different story. He could be anywhere, unless he possessed some magical invisibility shield of his own. Was that a possibility? Maybe he *had* been watching me all along? The idea made me shiver, cold chills covering my skin.

The ping of gravel against my car's side jolted me back to the moment. I crept down the narrow road, forcing my attention back to driving and scanning the two-lane street. Thankfully, it was empty save for a few wind-blown branches and my little black sedan. The location of the meadow, I realized, had been chosen deliberately. Dense trees arched overhead, offering zero visibility from the sky.

Despite the meadow's seclusion, I debated driving past the driveway entirely, just in case. But slowing down now would look suspicious, wouldn't it? Sighing, I pulled in, dirt and rocks crunching beneath my tires and my brakes squealing in protest. Everything looked the same, except for the fresh truck tire tracks that marred the dirt path, ending abruptly at the gate. Chase's truck. He must have walked all the way into the meadow.

Chase was definitely too good a friend for this. Helping each other out here and there was how our relationship worked, but he didn't sign up for this whole mess. Sending him here could have been dangerous, and that was something I had only briefly considered. If I added the complication of dealing with his unmistakable feelings for me… feelings I would continue to politely ignore until he chose to make a big, awkward deal about them, I shook my head, pushing away the guilt that threatened to surface.

The creak of rusty hinges pierced the stillness when I swung open the old gate, got back in my car, and eased onto the rutted path. The vehicle groaned in protest, its undercarriage scraping against the uneven ground thanks to the potholes. I crept forward at a snail's pace, barely touching five miles per hour, my knuckles white as I repeatedly curled my fingers around the steering wheel.

The lane cleared ahead, and the Unicorns stood under the trees, their forms glowing against the dark foliage surrounding them. They emerged from the shadows, like apparitions materializing in the soft light. The tall grass barely stirred at their passing. The grinding of my tires seemed almost sacrilegious in the hushed clearing. Dolfan strode forward to meet me as I rolled to a stop and parked the car. His eyes were tight, the skin around them crinkled.

Dragons are here? Dolfan inquired, his tone flat.

"How did you know?" I asked.

In the years we have lived here, we have rarely had a human stumble upon us. Our horns are kept short, not only for the ward. If a human ever did stumble through, they would assume we are just horses and leave of their own accord. No human has ever intentionally sought us out. Either you were hurt, or Dothians were surely somewhere nearby. Seeing that you are standing before us, I assume there are Dragons near?

I slowly nodded, confirming his suspicions.

"I met a Dragon Keeper," I told him. "His name is Kairo. Do you know him?"

The herd stood frozen, their massive bodies taut. Their stasis was deafening. Vast, liquid eyes stared at me, pupils blown wide like those of deer caught in the headlights of an oncoming train. Their expressions were so eerily unlike horses that it made me fidget. I'd already made a mess of being a Keeper. Was I really cut out for this role? And if I wasn't cut out for it, what then? Where did that leave us?

Dolfan was the first to break the spell. He nudged his head against my car door with a snort, prompting me to step out. I turned the car off, got out, and readied myself for their scrutiny, not liking the ache of foreboding that settled in my heart.

No, Dolfan answered, and it took me a second to recall my question.

Frowning, I pulled the stuffy hat off my head. "How do I protect you?"

Beyond the ward, our safety has been our Keeper's concern for generations. I do not know how to help you.

My fingers bit into the straw hat. "I know about the wards. Have they ever been broken?"

They haven't been breached since they were created. They will hold.

As long as Kairo stayed outside the ward's perimeter, they were safe from him, from anyone like him. But how long could I keep him away? Avoiding the meadow seemed the only option, but that meant sacrificing my time getting to know my herd. It was an impossible choice. I could either be with them and risk their safety or stay away and miss the only part of my life that was becoming valuable to me.

My stomach wouldn't stop churning. Sensing my distress, Flint appeared beside Dolfan and nudged my arm with his velvety muzzle. I reached out, burying my hand in the smooth expanse of his dark neck when he leaned his massive form against me. He exhaled a long, slow breath that vibrated through me, a silent attempt to steady my emotions. Reluctantly, I pulled my hand away from his side and let it drop to clear my head from his influence.

Flint is foolish and young. We have been left in the hands of an inexperienced Keeper whom Dothians have already discovered. He needs to understand the danger, and his ignorance is a problem, Dolfan stated with a sideways glance at his son. Flint tossed his head at him but didn't disagree. I got the sense that doing so would be an act of youthful foolishness and prove his father correct.

Dolfan held me in his stern gaze, his silent concern manifesting as a heavy, physical burden, pressing down on me like a damp blanket. He twitched his magnificent ears back and forth, listening to everything around him and silently relaying the frantic questions to which I couldn't find answers. How could I keep them safe from a threat I barely understood?

"I want to understand," I whispered. "I'm sorry."

Dolfan's nostrils flared as he released a puff of hot air and turned to nuzzle Nimue's flank. Something was off about her, a soft glow coming from her middle. It was a visible representation of new life and added responsibility, shimmering beneath her coat and filtered through the dappled sunlight. She was pregnant. I let out a surprised breath and leaned against the side of my car. There was another life on the way I'd need to keep safe, and I wasn't sure how to feel about that. All I could do was offer myself to them in earnest.

"I'll find a way to keep all of you safe," I vowed.

Nimue remained quiet, dipping her head into Dolfan's side in withdrawal—a silent retreat from her Keeper. I didn't want to disappoint them. If they didn't believe in me, then who would? Since the accident, self-doubt had become a constant companion, but Nimue's reaction was somehow worse. Knowing the only one who believed in me was Flint saddened me deeply. I bit my lip hard to stave off the tears that threatened to brim over.

Flint's warm breath tickled my hand, and he nudged it with his nose again. I ran a finger down his smooth cheek and then across the expanse of his muzzle. Even if he couldn't grasp the situation, his unwavering presence was like a spark in the growing darkness. It fueled a renewed determination within me. There was no turning back. Giving up wasn't an option. It meant failing the herd, myself, and the memory of my mother. But most importantly, it meant failing the magnificent creature who was becoming my friend.

With a heavy breath, I walked away from him, heading up the path toward the weeping willow on the other side of the meadow. After some effort, I located my grandmother's old headstone and cleared away the dirt around the grave. There wasn't a birth year, only the year of her death and her name beneath it. There were no signs of the journals anywhere near her burial spot. It was clear that the only way I was going to find the journals was to get supplies and dig.

A question drifted across my thoughts as I took in the neglected cemetery. Why had my mother chosen cremation when she could have been buried with her family? I recalled that she'd wanted her ashes scattered beneath an ancient willow tree above her mother. However, I hadn't received them yet because I had purchased a specialized urn that hadn't been delivered. Without the ashes, the thought hadn't crossed my mind. Then, it hit me. In her final act, my mother ensured I would find the creatures surrounding me.

I studied the old weeping willow, its branches draped like a curtain in the still air. It wasn't just any willow; it was the one I used to sketch and paint endlessly when I was younger. The very tree I remembered but could barely recall. The long, graceful limbs were dotted with buds, and wisps of moss hung like delicate lace curtains between the boughs.

It's a beautiful spot for a cemetery, I thought.

Out of the corner of my eye, I saw one of the unicorns approaching. Elska.

Do you have a plan? She asked.

Did I? I didn't. I couldn't lie to her. So, I shook my head and ducked my chin. I knew I needed to come up with something, but there wasn't anything to go on yet.

"I will come up with one," I promised, more to myself than to Elska.

Elska was silent for a moment, considering.

Our Keepers have a choice. For some reason, they always choose not to stay with their herd. They choose someone, and when they do, we repeat this cycle. A new Keeper comes. We are at risk. The Keeper meets someone, and we are left here, lingering. Will it ever change?

Her question made me feel empty, blank. I wasn't going to make promises I couldn't keep because, truthfully, I didn't know what my future held.

"I don't know."

Elska's head dipped, her forelock dropping over her eyes. She let out a breath.

I see, she responded before slowly turning back to the herd.

I watched her go, my insides hollowing out, scooped clean with each graceful step she took. So many before me seemed to turn down the option of immortality for family and love. Here I stood, living proof of that cycle. Evidence that each Allorian in my lineage, destined to become a Keeper, chose marriage, children, and a finite existence. It was like a betrayal, a flaw woven into something bigger than I could imagine. Perhaps love, in all its messy glory, was our downfall.

Could I choose the Unicorns' happiness over my own? I looked over them and could see both paths, duty keeping me from ever finding love or choosing that love over the preservation of their Keeper. I wasn't sure which path was the right one, and my steps became heavy as I left the meadow, contemplating my choices.

Back in my car, I quietly closed the door. The sun finally set over the mountains. The days were stretching longer, the evenings shrinking. A strange sadness settled over me as I watched the sunlight linger, a silent lament for the quiet darkness that used to usher me to sleep. It felt like the world itself was conspiring against me, the lengthening days stealing the opportunity for me to disappear in sheets and pillows.

Chapter Eight

Fate Brings Us Together

Kairo

This wasn't how this was supposed to go, I thought while I sat on the mountain's precipice, watching the sunrise paint the horizon with fiery oranges and pinks. Below, the valley exploded with spring. Vibrant green shoots and colorful bulbs pushed through dirt, and the first blossoms unfurled their delicate petals. It was a beautiful day, but its beauty was wasted on me, soured by my inability to find the Allorian. I whittled the edge of the spear I was making, cursing lightly at myself for letting her slip away.

A flicker of movement caught my eye amidst the fluffy white clouds—a ripple that grew larger until it revealed a magnificent Dragon shedding its camouflage. Tattu landed gracefully at the cave entrance. His sleek, green, and black wings folded against his back. There was a playful glint in his large, almond-shaped eyes. Despite the obvious mischief, I knew he was here to share something important by the catty way he postured before me.

Chuff near, Tattu told me with a rumble, the low sound echoing inside the cave.

My hands froze, and the Dragons within the expanse behind me stirred, sensing a shift in my emotions. I forced a deep breath. Artok, especially, wouldn't respond well to my rising anxiety. He'd take any threat seriously, even if it meant facing off against my sister's healthier, younger Dragon. Dragons were duty-bound. When the bond was great, a Dragon would do anything for its Keeper, including die. I wouldn't let Artok risk it.

How did she find us?

Didn't find you, Tattu yawned. *Found Allorian.*

I squeezed my eyes shut, my lip curling. Of course. The Allorian's Sula-umbra. The fleeting window triggered by the curse, when a new Unicorn Keeper came into their power, was the only time Dragons could mate. Some Keepers would answer the call, but others, with healthy Dragons like Tattu, wouldn't risk exposing them to the modern world for a shot at Unicorn blood. The remainders were so scattered that the journey wouldn't be worth the immense energy drain on their Dragons for the benefit of blood or breeding.

Some would come, though. Some would seek to capture Elle and the Unicorns for their own purposes. Some sought the blood of the Unicorns for its healing properties, while others coveted both Keepers and the Unicorns themselves for their own gains. Whatever those gains might be. My sister was likely in the latter category. From what others had told me, she made no secret of her contempt for Allorians. To her, they were beneath her, serving only one purpose, making their lives as unimportant as the Dragon's meals scattered around the base of the mountain.

I tried to convince myself that Elle's safety wasn't a priority. Tried to tell myself my sole focus should be securing the Unicorns. This single-minded objective, I told myself, was the key to keeping my emotions in check. Yet, a nagging worry for Elle burrowed into my thoughts regardless, refusing to be dislodged. My Dragons and their well-being *should* be my sole concern. But the more I tried to push this unfamiliar concern away, the more persistent it became. It was an unwelcome complication. I should not be concerned with the well-being of the Allorian…and yet, I was.

Behind Tattu, I saw Artok's eyes glowing like golden embers in the darkness at the back of the cave. The Dragon looked tired and weak. I knew I had to find Elle before my sister did. Yet, being away from Artok for long periods left him vulnerable to what someone might do if he were discovered.

See if you can find Koa, I instructed Tattu.

Figuring out how Elle was masking her location became even more urgent. Without help, it could take days or weeks, but the only Dothians who might selflessly assist me were miles away. Running a hand through my hair, I surveyed the sprawling mountains below me. Tattu was already airborne on the mission I'd just given him. Artok, weakened from the journey here, wouldn't manage another long flight. And Dalya wouldn't willingly make the trip without complaint unless something was in it for her. That was a recipe for disaster. I was stuck.

I once stupidly wished my life were more exciting, and now I'm kicking myself for it. The unexpected chaos made me long for the days of reading books by the river's edge while the Dragons lazed in the sun.

Elle

Half an hour later, I started to pull into the hardware store lot, only to find it sealed off with a maze of bright yellow caution tape strung between orange cones. The "Open" sign hanging lopsidedly in the window seemed almost mocking. It hadn't occurred to me until that moment to drive to the bigger city miles away, even though Kairo would be less likely to find me there. This store's convenience led me straight into a potential dead end. Stuck in my car, frustration built like freshly lit coal. Why didn't my dad have a spade shovel?

Looking down at the gas gauge, it warned me that a trip to the city would require gas, adding considerable time to the already rushed timeline I'd given myself. Between driving there, finding a store with shovels, and returning, I'd lose hours I felt I couldn't spare. Staying local seemed wiser, though finding parking nearby proved to be difficult. There were so many people shopping that I had to park a block away. Taking the keys out of the ignition, paranoia crept in. It felt like someone was watching me. I scanned the area, eyes darting from car to car, searching for any sign that someone stood out in the crowd. Nobody was paying me the slightest bit of attention. Shaking it off, I rushed to the hardware store only to face a hand-scrawled sign on the door.

"Be back in fifteen minutes. Great," I muttered under my breath.

I looked back at the Jeep. I regretted bringing it, but it would fit a shovel, and my sedan wouldn't. It was a struggle to keep my suspicions at bay. I knew someone was searching for me, and my exposed position made me an easy target. With a sigh, I decided sitting in the car wasn't an option. My only other choice was to keep moving and find somewhere to go. I knew this town better than most. If someone were after me, they would have more luck snatching me from a stationary vehicle than in the town center, where shoppers were milling around.

Besides, it was a beautiful morning, and I was drawn to the quaint courtyard. I stuck my hands in my pockets and started toward the gazebo that took up the center. Roses were budding in the bushes, and mourning doves perched on the low branches of the giant oak tree in front of the small convenience store. I told myself I was safe here. Nobody would find me among the townsfolk I'd grown up with. I flipped my sunglasses down just in case.

Kairo

I stood outside a diner the morning after Tattu departed on his search for my sister. Ordinarily, pride would have kept me far from such establishments. I preferred self-sufficiency– foraging, hunting, and living off the land without relying on society. Yet today, something had shifted. The usual desire to hunt was nonexistent, and the thought of skinning an animal and cooking it over a fire held no appeal. Instead, I caved to the diner's promise of quick, ready-made food.

The outing served to satisfy both my craving for coffee and my hope to catch a glimpse of the Allorian. Perhaps she would gather a hint of bravery and venture out before my sister could smoke her out of hiding? I caught my reflection staring back at me in the tall glass door when I entered the building. It was the same scowl and steely glint in my eyes. Koa's appearance, Artok's illness, and the repercussions of being away from home wore me down.

Dolly's Diner was mostly deserted, surprising given the number of people walking the streets. Brown tables and chairs, worn but comfortable-looking, lined the beige-painted walls that contrasted with the white and black checkered tiles covering the floor. Along the kitchen, a stainless-steel counter gleamed under the fluorescent lights, punctuated by weathered white stools. Despite its lackluster interior, the air was filled with the delightful aroma of freshly brewed coffee and syrup.

The middle-aged waitress with curly dark hair who seated me, her face etched with lines from years of serving, patiently waited for my order. Thankful for her patience, I gave her an easy smile as she placed a steaming mug of coffee before me. Returning my attention to the town square, I caught a flash of blonde hair from the corner of my eye.

It was her, the Allorian. She appeared out of nowhere, a fleeting figure pausing by the diner to glance across the street. Adrenaline surged through me, and it wasn't from the sip of coffee I'd taken. My excitement at seeing her was quickly stilled by the knowledge that if I let my emotions spiral, the Dragons would sense it. This intense and unexpected anticipation might translate as distress to them, drawing them straight to my location. That wouldn't be helpful at all.

I doubted the Allorian would stay if Dragons came crashing into the town's small courtyard.

The diner window framed her pretty little face. Elle, the Allorian. I needed her like lungs needed air, and she didn't even realize it. She frowned at her phone before pausing by the window. My knuckles rapped against the glass, an impulsive gesture. Logic screamed at me to snatch her, ending this frantic hide-and-seek before she vanished again. But a strange curiosity bloomed in my chest. Would she come to me of her own accord?

Chapter Nine

Like Ice And Water

Elle

The crosswalk sign blinked a warning hand when I crossed the main road. I paused once I was on the other side to check the time on my phone. There were still ten minutes to kill before I could head back, assuming the person who had put up the 'be back in 15 minutes' sign had left just before I arrived. Glancing back toward the hardware store for clarification, I heard a rapping noise on the diner's window beside me. I spun toward the rap and froze under the gaze of a man with arctic blue eyes. His sharp features were partially obscured in the dim light, but there was no mistaking who it was.

It was him, the Dragon Keeper. I'd run into him… again. Which somehow didn't surprise me one bit, but also shocked me to my core.

Watching Kairo study me, I met his intense gaze as steadily as possible. He scrutinized me, his gaze making me feel unexpectedly warm. I was rooted to the spot, unable to move. Then, with a casual flick of two fingers, he beckoned me inside. My mind screamed a warning, yet my traitorous legs twitched with the urge to obey.

Shifting from one foot to another, my heart hammered against my chest. I wanted to bolt, but laced with the fear lay a spark of defiance. Who was I kidding? Running wouldn't solve anything. I had a feeling he'd just keep finding me, and I couldn't hide forever. This might be my chance to see what I was truly facing. Besides, Dolly's Diner wasn't exactly the most inconspicuous place for a kidnapping. He couldn't be foolish enough to think he could disappear with me unnoticed.

I straightened. If I asked the right questions, he might give me information. At this point, any information would be useful because I knew very little. If I could get details, I could possibly show the herd that I was someone they could rely on. That I was someone who would do whatever was necessary to keep them safe, including meeting with him. I needed something to take back to them. *Something, anything.* Taking a deep breath, I pulled my shoulders back and headed for the front entrance. Was I making the biggest mistake of my life? Probably, but it was time to play this game.

The surprise that I'd obeyed his request was written all over his face, and frankly, it mirrored my own. Taking a hesitant step in his direction, I let my gaze travel over the sharp lines of his dark jacket and snug black pants. There was an undeniable charisma swirling around him, a force that drew me in even as I fought it. He seemed like a figure carved from myth, as if he were capable of haunting nightmares or stirring dreams. One brow was raised, his chin was ducked, and his plump bottom lip drooped inquisitively. His face was beautiful, and it would be easy to hate myself for being drawn to him. He was a confusing mix of fascination and unease.

I lowered myself into the chair across from him and waited for a sign of what he might do, studying my cuticles against the light blue linoleum table. Would he speak first? Or was I, the idiot who'd just walked into a potential Dothian trap, expected to break the silence? I was nearly afraid that speaking might attract unwanted attention. We would sound like idiots discussing mythical creatures known only to the two of us. Yet, worse than appearing ridiculous to the public was the possibility of sounding foolish to him. I wasn't sure why his opinion mattered, and I realized that caring about it was something I was going to have to work on.

"You are awfully brave," he said finally.

My eyes snapped up and met his. "Or foolish."

He chuckled deeply, sardonically.

"I'm not going to bite you."

"I guess I'm not afraid of you biting me," I admitted, my cheeks heating.

The waitress materialized beside me with a notepad clutched in her hand.

"Can I get you anything, Elle?" she asked warmly.

"Just water for now, please," I muttered, my voice barely above a whisper. It was a noncommittal choice, a clear message that I could leave at any second. My stomach, however, disagreed with a loud, traitorous growl.

The waitress winked conspiratorially. "Sounds like you need a proper meal, dear. You know we have the best pancakes in town."

I flashed her a weak smile. "Maybe later."

Silence descended when she sauntered away, thick and heavy as fog. My empty stomach rumbled again, a poignant reminder of my unintended hunger strike. Last night's dinner had been sacrificed to the search for information about the other journals until near dawn, and breakfast? A casualty of oversleeping. I was weary and tired. The tension of being so close to Kairo was a live wire lashing against my last remaining nerve. I contemplated making a break for it. Sensing my unease, Kairo leaned forward. His eyes met mine with an intensity that messed with my head.

"You aren't afraid of me?" he asked, his tone serious.

"I don't know whether or not to be afraid of you," I lied smoothly. "I just know that you want something that I've been tasked with keeping away from you. So, you can see why sitting here in the diner I've visited since I was a baby is a little awkward."

He glanced around as if he had just noticed where he was and then returned his attention to me. I couldn't help but fidget under the weight of his stare, but I also couldn't bring myself to look at him directly.

"I didn't expect you just to walk by. I've been looking for you, and suddenly, there you were."

His face grew calm, almost unreadable, and he adjusted himself in his chair, pushing backward to give me space. The odd energy between us lingered until the waitress appeared, and the clink of dishes briefly broke the silence, a respite from our quiet exchange. She set his plate down and placed my glass of water beside it. The interruption allowed us both a moment to collect our thoughts until the waitress ambled off to take other orders. The weight of his stare returned, and a knot of apprehension tightened in my gut.

My eyes flicked across his features, and I felt a blush creep up my cheeks. My earlier anger at myself for finding him undeniably handsome seemed misplaced. It would be so much easier to channel my frustration toward him, to truly despise him, if he weren't so ridiculously attractive. But here I was, struggling to stop myself from drooling. He was absolutely off-limits, yet I couldn't help but find him desirable. I'd have to convince myself to stop salivating over him at some point.

His brow furrowed, a silent conflict playing out behind his eyes, as if he were debating another bite or breaking the relentless silence between us. I took a sip of water, buying him a moment to eat. He poked at his food with a detachment that surprised me. That was not exactly the behavior of someone about to pounce. In fact, he seemed content to let the awkward silence hang, allowing us to size each other up. The tension was getting the better of me. Uncertain about what was safe to ask, I waited until he paused between bites before carefully choosing my words.

"You've been looking for them?"

He nodded. "How much do you know?"

I raised a brow and looked out the window.

"Clearly not enough. But enough to know that if you have a sick...." I paused, looking around to make sure nobody was listening. Leaning forward, I rested my elbows on the table, gesturing with my hands as I spoke. "If you had a sick dog, you might need... medication to help them. Medication that I have."

The corner of Kairo's lips twitched.

Kairo

Trying to adjust my expression from curiosity to boredom, I sat back in my chair and adopted the demeanor of someone who might pose a threat if necessary. Under different circumstances and in another place, her naivety and innocence might have been amusing. However, our current situation marked the difference between life and death. All I needed from her was one thing, just one thing. I hoped to persuade her without resorting to force. She needed to believe I would do whatever it took to get what was required. I glanced over her shoulder briefly, checking the room, before speaking.

"Here is the thing. I know you have the medication I need, and I do need it. My dog," I said, my lip twitching slightly, "is very sick. I don't know how much medication you have, but it seems like you have enough to sustain a lot of dogs. So, if you were to give me just one dose, you'd never have to set eyes on me again, and you'd still have plenty left to keep you occupied. Keeping them safe is going to be a chore in itself. The last thing you need is me, or someone like me, lurking around, waiting for you to turn the wrong corner when they feel they've run out of options. Especially when someone knows your pretty face as well as I do now."

My words came pointedly. Being honest was worth a shot, I told myself. Elle wanted to hear what I had to offer. Yet, as I spoke, she didn't cower as I expected. Instead, she stared at her cup, spinning it on the table with her fingers, tracing a pattern in the condensation with her thumb. Elle seemed to be contemplating what I'd said. I had anticipated shock or fear from her, yet she remained silent. So, I continued.

"I'm not the only one who felt the Sula-umbra. The others won't ask; they will just take. They will take your medicine and you with it. They might keep you alive, but you'll wish they hadn't."

She looked confused when I spoke of other Keepers taking her, the corners of her lips twisting downward, indicating she likely didn't understand her value. This girl was clueless. Didn't she see the bullseye painted on her back? The burden of being a walking pawn, a bargaining chip in a dangerous game she wasn't even aware of. I gave her a moment to think, but when she didn't respond again, I looked down and studied her through the shadowy filter of my lashes.

"They'll exploit you, Elle. They'll take whatever knowledge you have and twist it for their own gain. And trust me, you don't want to see what they're capable of. If you give me what I'm seeking, I won't tell them who you are or where they can start searching." I leaned forward, my gaze holding hers. "That is my offer."

I held up one finger, punctuating my demand. Slowly, she transformed from fawn to lioness. Anger darkened her eyes, her brows forming a thunderous V above them. Her lips pressed into a thin line, her jaw clenched tight. The raw protectiveness blazing in her gaze surprised me, yet, strangely, it was a compelling sight. For a fleeting moment, something primal roared to life within me. My damn thighs twitched involuntarily as she leveled me with her gold-flecked eyes.

"Let me clarify something for you," she said firmly. "I will never willingly hand one of them over to you or anyone else. Over. My. Dead. Body."

Fury surged through me, hot and volatile. She'd left me with no choice. Slamming my palms on the table, I started to rise, ready to snatch her in the middle of the greasy diner. One of my Dragons awaited me, and getting her on its back before another Dothian noticed her was the only way out of this mess. Come hell or high water, I would get what I needed.

But Elle was faster. She flicked her thumb upward before I could reach my feet, sending the glass of ice water tumbling. A wave of icy liquid cascaded onto my lap. I lunged back, cursing under my breath. Her chair clattered over as she dashed out of the diner. Cursing, I thrust a twenty onto the tabletop and, without waiting for change, I flung myself toward the door. Every eye in the diner was drawn to me, and a moment of stunned silence followed as I left. I sprinted after her, catching only a fleeting glimpse of her figure before she disappeared around a corner.

She knew this town better than I did, all the back alleys and shortcuts. By the time I reached the corner, she'd vanished, and the street was empty. Again. Scanning both directions, a humorless chuckle escaped my lips, thwarted by a cup of ice water. Maybe she was better suited for this life than I had given her credit for.

Checking every sidewalk and road near the diner, I made my way out of town. Tattu was asleep at the edge of the tree line, and for a moment I was surprised, because Dalya had been the one to bring me to town. Approaching the Dragon, my frustration simmered beneath the surface. I had hoped Tattu would have come back from his search with some clue about Koa's whereabouts, but the Dragon's presence suggested otherwise. He slept too much, but never when he wanted to gloat over gossip or information. Watching the faint rise and fall of his chest, that subtle movement stood out as the only sign of life in the otherwise still forest clearing.

Yet, even in slumber, Tattu maintained his camouflage. Until I was close enough, his form had melted into the backdrop of trees, grass, and stone, blending better than a chameleon with its surroundings. Anyone foolish enough to wander near would feel the prickle of unseen danger and steer clear. It was one of the few magical remnants Dragons retained after the curse.

I walked closer, and a flicker of movement stirred as one silver eye blinked open, the iris narrowing when he recognized me. A low rumble emanated from his throat, a question hanging heavy in the air.

"Looks like Koa managed to slip away again."

Tattu blinked and stretched. *Find her*? he yawned.

"I did," I replied aloud. "She got away. She's going to be trouble."

The Dragon smirked, lifting the corners of his scaled lips.

Like trouble, he drawled lazily.

I shook my head at Tattu's comment and climbed onto his back, using his front leg as a mounting block. Running my hands down his scales, I took a moment to consider everything that had happened. Maybe this was a fool's errand. Soon enough, the Dothians, who were further away, would arrive, and I would be up against potential enemies with a sick Dragon, one who barely cared for me, and one of the smallest Dragons that existed.

Even Chuff had a size and strength advantage over my current situation. However, I certainly had the upper hand as far as my sister was concerned. Chuff's deep-rooted loyalty to our family meant I was untouchable, no matter how much she might want to prove otherwise. I wasn't sure I could one-up her when it came to Elle, though. The look on her face had given me pause. She could appear innocent one moment and then conjure fire in her eyes the next. I hated to admit it to myself, but for a brief second, I couldn't think of anything more attractive than the look on her face when she transformed from a confused fawn to a lioness protecting her cubs. What kind of trickery was she using on me?

Tattu took to the sky, and I spent the flight considering what I should do. For Artok, I had to keep trying, I told myself as I returned to my Dragons.

Chapter Ten

When My Soul Fractured

Elle

When I was six years old, all I'd wanted for my birthday was a kitten, even though I knew the cruel fates had bestowed my father with a severe allergy to cats. So, Mom told me no over pancakes in a tiny diner in the middle of our tiny town. In my youthful mind, an allergy was not a good enough reason not to get a cute cream-colored kitten. Not when I really wanted it. So, when Mom said no, I stood in the middle of the diner and took off. I was going to run away and get that kitten on my own.

As awareness dawned that my parents were looking for me, I became frightened that I would face punishment for disappearing. So, I chose to hide and ran around to the side of the diner. I found a spot so well-hidden it took nearly two hours for anyone to find me. Beside the building, in the narrow alley that ran alongside it, there was a fenced-in area where Dolly's Diner kept their dumpster. The tall, weathered wood fence stood about three feet from a set of rickety stairs that led up to the kitchen.

Underneath those stairs was a small square cut into the concrete. I squeezed into the gap and held my breath whenever I heard footsteps or voices nearby. Back then, this square had seemed roomy enough to stay in until my parents could deliver the cream-colored kitten I never received. Instead, I'd been found by one of the diner's staff and handed back to my very distraught parents. Now, I barely fit as I tucked my knees to my chest and wiped the tears from my face. The gravel and dirt I was sitting on dug into my butt, making the tiny space almost unbearable.

I leaned my cheek on my legs and bit into my palm. I didn't like being completely clueless. It hurt me so severely that I had to fight back the inward sobs that wracked through my lungs. For some reason, I had been under the delusion that if worst came to worst—if I failed at my mission—I could leave all the surreal things happening around me behind. In the back of my mind, a small part of me had thought I could make this someone else's problem. But something Kairo said made me realize I wouldn't get out of this even if I wanted to.

I could never be a bystander in this mess. Kairo had made it clear—I was part of the package, like it or not. Forget the naive hope that the Dothians would deem my Unicorns more important and leave me behind. No, I was just as valuable, a bargaining chip someone could use if needed. With a choked cry, I retreated further into the wall, desperately seeking refuge from the harsh reality that the Unicorns were, undeniably, my fate. Though I already knew that they were, the fact that there was no getting out of this made me, for a moment, feel like I was drowning.

My skin grew clammy, and my chest squeezed, a familiar ache returning that pulled me right back to that six-year-old girl wailing beside a dumpster. Right now, I was the girl who truly believed nobody understood her. Right now, I am as alone as I could ever be. But I wasn't that six-year-old, and this was a million times more significant than a kitten. Left clinging to the only things that mattered—my Unicorns. I decided I would stand by them. I had to stop thinking I could escape this and face the fact that I shouldn't want to get out of it, no matter how terrifying it all seemed.

The past few days left me feeling like I was in a pressure cooker, seconds from bursting. Maybe it was the constant tension or the terrifying realization that I was at a total loss on how to keep the Unicorns safe. I forced myself to breathe slowly and deeply, inhaling through my nose and exhaling through my mouth. With each breath, my frenzied thoughts settled slightly. Finally, I relaxed my legs, unknotted myself, and rubbed a hand over my face. It was time to face whatever came next, one unsteady step at a time.

Needing some sort of resolution, I considered every viable option. From what I understood, Kairo wasn't the worst Keeper out there. Others would hurt me or use me without a second thought. They all wanted my Unicorns, but at least he wouldn't stoop to ruining me to get them unless I made things difficult for him. Though I wasn't sure that wasn't an empty threat. Something made me think he was merely posturing to get me to give him what he wanted.

Posturing or not, the worst part about our conversation was that he knew. He knew I had a herd of them, not just one or two. And like a fool, I hadn't denied it. I sat there at a loss for words, all self-pity and too little fight. But that was over. I wouldn't give up a single one of them, and I was less bumbly with each passing day. He clearly wanted to help his Dragon just as much as I needed to protect my herd. And if we wanted the same thing…

After running into Kairo twice, it was beginning to appear less coincidental and more like an unnatural habit for two supposed enemies. He could just be very good at tracking me down, but I'd gotten the feeling he hadn't expected to bump into me either time. One thing was for sure: if these unexpected encounters with him continued, I'd be left with the impression that what little control I had over my life was slipping away. I had no choice. My next step would be to deal with him because he obviously wasn't going anywhere until he got what he wanted. The next time we meet, it will be on my terms.

My thoughts hummed. Something nagged at the back of my brain, but my head still ached. What I needed was a solution to both problems. If I could find a way to keep my Unicorns safe and help Kairo heal his Dragon, it would be one less issue to deal with. Emerging from the concrete hole, I uncurled myself, stood up, shook my limbs, and walked toward the hardware store. I had to find the journals and contemplate a solution. Then, I needed to persuade Kairo to follow my plan. But first, I needed a shovel.

Dolfan watched over his herd while they rested. With a swish of his ears, he regarded me languidly when I approached. Needing the calmness I knew he would provide, I went straight to Flint, stretched out on his side. The black colt exhaled slowly as I lowered myself to sit against his chest. He tipped his nose toward me, his breath skimming my bare legs. I pulled my mother's journal out of a canvas sack.

The clouds rolled in slowly, casting shadows over the setting sun and deepening the dusk settling over the meadow. I fumbled in my bag, finding the small flashlight. Clicking it on, I shone it onto the page I'd bookmarked before leaving my house.

April 14th, 2008—Ellise will be six years old in a few days. I fear for her future as I watch her play beneath the willow tree. Ellise is a brave young girl who takes on the world with unyielding fervor.

I hope when you see this, Ellise, you'll know how important you are. One day, you'll realize I missed my chance to make a difference for my herd, so I had you. I had hoped that one day you could fulfill the destiny that might have been mine to bear, and I would have been honored to bear it.

The day you were born, I could have sworn I saw the shadow of a Dragon flying across the hospital's windows. I held you close that entire night, fearing the worst. Looking back, it was an omen. You were meant for things far greater than I could have imagined for myself. I see it in your eyes as you pick the dandelions from the field and rub them against your chin. There is no fear, only a great determination to take on whatever challenges lie in your wake.

Ellise, I am giving you the most incredible gift when I pass on. I know you will mourn my passing, but know that when you are done crying, you must find the other journals. You must persevere. There is little time left. You are one of the last Allorians who can do what must be done. I love you with all of my heart, and I know you can do this.

Blinking back the sting of tears caused by my mom's words, I realized Flint had nudged his head into my lap. His big, brown eyes were half-closed, watching me with a soft, concerned gaze. I gently ran my fingers through his forelock, feeling the smooth curve of his growing horn against my palm. A solitary tear escaped, tracing a warm path down my cheek, but I quickly brushed it away.

My mother was right. The weak, solemn girl I'd become was unlike the person I was before my parents' death. I was more fire and bite than I was letting myself believe. I could do this. I would stop standing in my own way and figure this out. I tucked the journal back into the canvas bag. Lying across Flint's neck, I ran my fingers over his silky coat and stared into the distance. It was time to implement my plan.

Chapter Eleven

I Decided To Save Her

Kairo

The mountain air bit at my face when I emerged from the pass, muscles coiled with anticipation. We'd found Chuff, which meant we'd found my sister. Years had passed since I'd last seen her, but I knew she was still bitter. I knew there was a chance that she'd do anything to stop the progress I was making with the Allorian if she knew the things that I did. My doubts about Koa's intentions weren't unfounded. Her philosophy on the Keeper-Dragon relationship was diametrically opposed to mine, and I was about to confront her… about the Allorian.

To her, everything and everyone served a purpose that should benefit her somehow–even Dragons, even her only sibling. To me, Dragons were more than loyal followers or weapons.

Keeping them safe was an unwavering responsibility, a bond we'd forged in trust and respect. I didn't exploit my Dragons like she did. They were my partners. And because of that, at least a couple of them would fight tooth and nail to protect me, but it wouldn't be out of obligation.

In a way, I pitied Chuff. He was a big, stupid brute of a Dragon who didn't deserve to be treated the way my sister treated him. I'd heard a rumor that she used him for pit fighting. These fights often left Dragons battered and broken, some with permanent injuries. Before the curse, pit fights had been bloody, but with the rarity of Dragons, few risked their lives so carelessly. Still, it astounded me that some Keepers would demand their Dragons participate in such a cruel spectacle. Even from a distance, as I crested the ridge, I could see the jagged scars that marred Chuff's once pristine wings. Pit fighting wasn't a test of strength. It was a travesty disguised as tradition.

I was surprised that the Dragon's cloaking was lifted. Chuff's dark scales glistened in the bright spring sun. He had a large male elk tucked between his front legs, which he chewed on gamely. My scent finally alerted him to my presence, and he turned his head in my direction, flaring his nostrils. His pupils dilated as he halted his chewing. Studying me, he sniffed the air lazily before disregarding me in favor of his meal.

Here I was, holed up high in a cave with my Dragons, insisting they maintain their cloaking to avoid detection, while Koa left Chuff exposed in the middle of a mountain range. Her lack of care was concerning, as if prying eyes were a mere inconvenience to her. Even with a female intent on finding a mate, I still demanded they remain as hidden as possible. Koa's cavalier attitude threatened not just Chuff but also the very foundation of our way of life if someone found him.

"What do you want?" I heard from behind me.

Spinning around, I narrowed my eyes at the female version of myself. Koa had always been as silent as a cat and as pissy as a cornered badger.

"It's nice to see you too," I replied. "What are you doing here, Koa?"

"I would like to think you are smarter than that, brother," she sighed, pushing her black hair over her shoulder and tugging the sleeves of her shirt down over her wrists.

"Chuff isn't ill, and you've torched nearly every alliance that could make harboring a Unicorn or its Keeper profitable."

I schooled my features into a mask of neutrality, hoping she'd fixate on my discovery of her whereabouts rather than probe into my knowledge of the Allorian. Even more crucially, I hoped Koa wouldn't suspect I knew about an entire herd. Elle's expression when I'd mentioned that she had more than one confirmed my suspicion. She had an entire herd, not just a solitary Unicorn. A Keeper with a single charge would defend it to the death, but one responsible for many might reluctantly sacrifice one to ensure the survival of the rest. This information could prove invaluable to my sister.

Koa laughed, her husky tone sounding false and haughty.

"You think you know everything. I can build a bridge just as fast as I can destroy one. The Keeper is mine. I don't care about the Unicorns."

"Why would you need a Keeper?"

"Wouldn't you like to know?" She raised a bored eyebrow.

"Artok is dying," I said, intentionally confirming whatever suspicions she may have had.

Koa's face flushed scarlet, and her eyes flashed angrily as she sucked in a sharp breath between her teeth. I'd expected…sentimentality? Or perhaps a flicker of grief for the old Dragon who'd been there our entire lives? Instead, she looked like a cornered viper, venom pulsing beneath the surface. My hackles rose. I straightened, fingers curling into fists, ready for whatever poison she might spew at me.

My lips twitched as a low, menacing growl reverberated from the tree line behind me. In response to the growl, a soft snort drifted from the clearing as Chuff's massive head rose, his senses attuning to the sudden shift in the air. Dalya's timing was impeccable. With Artok still battling his illness, I couldn't risk a confrontation with my sister. So, I had to bring a lure to occupy her Dragon. Despite my plan, I couldn't risk Dalya emerging from the woods. Her presence carried a multitude of risks—not least of which was the allure she'd present to a virile male Dragon. I turned my gaze deliberately toward Chuff with a subtle tip of my chin.

"Your Dragon is restless," I purred to my sister. "You might not want to let him go exploring."

Koa looked over my shoulder to see that Chuff had abandoned his meal in favor of the sound coming from somewhere behind us. Realization dawned on her face. I'd brought my only female Dragon as bait.

"Get out of here!" She balled her fists, panic setting her expression ablaze.

When I didn't move, she huffed and rushed to her Chuff, easily stepping up his leg and swinging onto his back. I could barely make out the scowl she aimed at me as the Dragon cast his cloaking and then took to the sky.

Watching her fly away, I emerged from the tree line, and Dalya's form came into view. Our bond thrummed with desperate need and anticipation. Amplified by my sister's presence, our shared energy threatened to shatter Dalya's fragile remaining self-control. I approached cautiously, placing a steadying hand on her warm, scaled nose. A part of me yearned to hear her thoughts, but I knew better. She'd never talked to me due to the torture she'd experienced as a yearling. Dalya had only ever entrusted her words to my father—her savior.

Our relationship, though strained, still held the unbreakable thread of Keeper and Dragon. So, despite our history, I murmured soothing words to her, and each whispered comfort calmed her turbulent emotions. Slowly, reluctantly, she settled, her gaze drifting skyward as she took on a faraway look. Yet, beneath this hard-won serenity, I could sense her urges churning—the instinct to pursue Koa and Chuff warring with her need to stay with her Keeper. It took every ounce of my influence to keep her grounded.

If Dalya reached Chuff and they mated, a bond could form between them—one that might lead Chuff to abandon my sister's Keep for his new mate, or vice versa. It was a risk my sister wouldn't tolerate. Despite the tempting prospect of a strong male offering protection and contributing to the Dragon population, I was reluctant to entertain it. Koa's attention was a problem that I wouldn't wish on anyone.

With a resigned sigh, I climbed onto Dalya's back, her ivory scales flattening beneath me. She cast one last longing look at the horizon where Chuff had vanished before spreading her magnificent wings. The delicate balance between Dalya's needs, our safety, and the fate of Dragonkind hung in the air around us, as tangible as the wind beneath her wings.

The tremor from Dalya's landing vibrated through the cavern when her back legs found the ledge. Artok was at the edge of the cave, looking out into the sky. Dismounting, I strode toward him, scanning the wide, expansive mountain range for the source of his attention. Artok's exhales were raspy, and each of his lengthy inhales was a weary huff.

"Get some rest."

Too much rest, Artok responded, his voice half as deep as normal.

"I'm trying."

Artok gave me a look that said he knew I was. He would never second-guess his Keeper.

"I don't know what to do."

Do what's right.

I ran my hand across the back of my neck, wishing it were that simple. I wanted to save my Dragon, but I didn't want to dig up the dangerous dark part of me that would do anything to make that happen. The path kept leading straight back to Elle, and her safety was a line I wasn't sure I wanted to cross. I rolled my jaw. Elle. Why did her well-being hold such weight? The answer seemed annoyingly elusive.

I trudged toward the makeshift bed of elk and moose hides. Artok's once proud head drooped, reflecting the growing desolation in my chest. Sleep would be a battlefield tonight.

Chapter Twelve

I Decided To Save Myself

Elle

Since my run-in with Kairo, I'd accomplished three things. First, I was sure I'd come up with something that might help both of us. I smiled down at the jug tucked safely in my bag and imagined the look on Kairo's face when I showed it to him. My second accomplishment was figuring out how to reach him. I squeezed the pouch in my hand, feeling a bit more confident. While the first two things were necessary, the last was a true victory—I'd found the journals.

The previous day, I'd started to dig a hole above my grandmother's grave while Flint watched me curiously. I'd managed to create a two-foot-deep by three-foot-wide dirt cavity before taking a break. Sitting in the grass with sweat running down my back, I'd drunk a bottle of water and reconsidered my life decisions. People on television made digging graves to dispose of bodies or digging up graves with bodies already in them seem effortless. This hadn't been easy. This had been a poor choice indeed, and at the rate I'd been going, it would have taken me a month to dig deep enough to see if the journals were in my grandmother's coffin.

Sensing Elska before seeing her, I glanced behind me, and it was like she'd materialized. Her dark lashes had briefly lowered before her eyes locked onto my face. I'd held her gaze as if hypnotized, hearing her every breath. An icy sensation crept up my limbs, and then I suddenly experienced Elska's movements as though I were inhabiting two bodies simultaneously.

I saw myself standing where she was, arms hanging limp at my sides, my expression a blank canvas. When I blinked, I saw what Elska saw. When her eyes roamed, so did mine; our gazes perfectly synchronized. We'd focused on the tombstone and the ornate arrow that pointed skyward, its intricate design etched into the weathered stone. As if pulled by invisible strings, Elska and I had tilted our heads back in unison, our eyes trailing up into the sprawling canopy of the ancient willow tree.

For what felt like an eternity, I stood transfixed. Its graceful, draping limbs swaying gently, adorned with leaves in a palette of colors I'd never before witnessed. Shades of greens and yellows that I assumed only the Unicorns could see. The breeze animated the tree, its motion almost playful.

I blinked again, and my perspective shifted. I found myself abruptly back on the ground, lungs heaving like I'd been running for miles. Disoriented, I'd turned to Elska for answers. But there she'd been, grazing peacefully, the picture of equine nonchalance. It was as though our shared vision had never occurred.

Freaking mind games, I'd thought to myself as I stood up and walked to the other side of the tombstone.

Carved into the back of the white stone, an ornate arrow pointed up into the tree, and where it pointed, I could see a notch a few feet above my reach. Something was peeking out from it. Walking over to the tree, I stretched onto my toes to reach the notch, but found that I was too short. I didn't need a shovel. I needed a ladder. Huffing, I looked around and realized there was nothing I could use to reach it. Then my eyes settled on the Unicorns.

One second, I'd been digging a hole, and the next, I attempted to line Flint up as close to the tree as possible. I had yet to learn if I was even supposed to get on the Unicorns to begin with. The journals never explicitly mentioned using them as climbing equipment. What I did know was that Flint would give me plenty of height to look into the notch, and he was by far my favorite. He seemed willing enough when I'd put my hand on his nose to get him to take a step back, resisting the temptation to cluck at him.

Come on, big guy, just a little closer.

Stop talking to me like I'm a horse, Flint had replied.

I playfully stuck my tongue out at him and nudged him into position. His curious gaze had met mine, and then he'd let out a slow, amused snort as if he understood the game we'd been playing. Kneeling, he gracefully lowered himself so that it was easier for me to climb onto his back. I chuckled, marveling at his cooperation and wondering if he was secretly enjoying our little adventure as much as I was. As I'd settled into place, I patted his sleek neck.

I didn't realize how much I'd missed the feeling of being on the back of an animal like that. It wasn't just the sensation of riding but the connection, the subtle thrill of Flint's muscles and movement beneath me. The wind whipped through my hair, and I felt a sense of unbridled freedom. I'd surrendered to it for a stolen moment, letting my fingers comb through Flint's thick, luxurious mane.

Balancing precariously on Flint's broad back, I didn't have to stretch to reach into the tree's gnarled notch. My fingers brushed against a heavy canvas material, and a wave of relief washed over me when I extracted a heavy bag. Inside, several plastic sacks unmistakably held the journals. I had been elated for a brief moment, but the initial thrill evaporated when I examined the contents more closely.

The plastic sacks had deteriorated. I'd gingerly brushed my thumb across the covers and pages, and my heart had sunk. The once-crisp paper had transformed into a soggy, warped mess. Time and moisture had taken their toll, leaving the journals weathered and fragile. What should have been a moment of triumph now felt hollow. As I cradled the canvas sack, I couldn't help but wonder how many of their secrets had been lost to the ravages of nature.

Pulling one out, the musty scent of aged paper hit me, and I carefully flipped through it. Maybe, just maybe, the damage wasn't extensive. To my relief, the topmost pages, while damp at the edges, seemed salvageable. The writing was nearly legible, but all the pages needed to be dried. Mom had worked so hard to translate the originals, but they'd almost melted in the rain because the sack meant to keep them dry hadn't done its job.

Slowly and gently, I set the bag on the ground, wrapped my arms around Flint's neck, and scratched his chest.

"Thank you."

You're welcome.

He'd tilted his nose back toward me as I dismounted, and I missed the sensation of being on him the second my feet touched the ground. It felt like I was meant to be on him. I would definitely have to explore if riding was a possibility later. But at that moment, I'd packed the journals into the Jeep and had driven back to my house with them. The trip home had been quiet, with my attention divided between driving and reflection. If Kairo or another Dothian had found me while the journals were so visible, there was no telling what could happen. I'd looked down at them in the passenger seat, wondering just how dangerous the information in them could be if they did end up in the wrong hands.

The sack of journals seemed far heavier when I'd carried them from the garage to the house. Once inside, I'd placed them across the living room floor in the order they were numbered and fanned out the pages so they could dry. Some of them had gotten wet multiple times and would require a lot of work before I could make sense of them. These, I knew, would be a battle to salvage. Yet, some were in pretty good condition, and I could probably read them right away. I'd still need to dry them out to keep the paper from sagging apart in my fingers.

I wanted to read the journals in order, and it just so happened that the most damaged journal was journal number one. It had the stubborn ghosts of water rings clinging to the parchment, and I'd traced the damp circles. The site of the damage made me sad.

Counting them, I'd realized that there wasn't a number six, and a pang of irritation had shot through me. I'd come so far, unearthed them, only for one to be missing? Anxious to dry out the remaining journals, I'd shoved my frustration aside and rummaged through the downstairs closet to find a fan. And as delicately as possible, I placed items on the top of the pages and then set the fan on low to let the pages air out. While I was flipping through the driest one, something caught my eye. A small note was scribbled on the edge of the cover of journal number three, with a sketch of a tiny Dragon above it.

The best way to attract a Dragon is to find a clearing, start a fire, and lure them with treasure.

A genuine, unadulterated smile had stretched across my face for the first time in an eternity. I had something that could be considered treasure, and thanks to Flint, I had something that might solve my Kairo problem. Things were looking up. The next time I saw Kairo, he wouldn't know what hit him. I could almost see his face, all clueless and confused. It was going to be amazing. The hunt was on, and this time, I wouldn't be the oblivious one.

As the next day's temperatures rose to almost unbearable levels, I stood at the edge of the clearing and pulled out the satchel of old coins my father had once collected. Starting a fire the easiest way possible—with a fire log, a lighter, and many dry branches—I watched the flames grow. I didn't know how big it needed to be, but setting the forest on fire didn't seem like a great idea, so I contained it with whatever rocks I could heft into a small circle. With a silent prayer and a lump forming in my throat, I tossed the coins one by one into the flickering heart of the fire. The sound of metal clinking against stone was the only response.

I searched the sky, my skin growing hot from the flames. I'd run through the one scenario that could cause my plan to fail. If another Dothian found me before Kairo did, there'd likely be nothing I could do to stop them from taking me and using me as Kairo described, especially with the evidence of who and what I was tucked in my rucksack. My smile faltered, emotions flip-flopping. I retreated from the fire's burning embers and watched from the solace of the shadows of the trees. While I walked, a shiver traced its way down my spine, a prickle that felt suspiciously like eyes on my back, but there was nobody there. Despite my paranoia, I didn't waver from my objective.

He will come to me. This plan will work.

Chapter Thirteen

My Stupid Move

Kairo

The sky hung low, a tapestry of gray and white stretching as far as the eye could see. As I strolled out to the edge of the cave, Tattu's restless ripple caught my attention. The Dragon kept taking to the sky, circling, then coming back. His wings beat in wide arches as he surveyed the immediate area, his eyes tracing the treetops in slow sweeps. Initially, I thought Tattu had spotted Chuff, but he didn't seem defensive; the armored scales lining his back lay flat. If he felt threatened, they would be lifted for protection. Reaching out through our shared mental bond, I silently called to him, and he landed beside me, shaking his scales with a series of rustles. He eagerly eyed the edge of the mountain range.

"What's gotten into you?"

Treasure, Tattu answered.

A frown creased my forehead. Someone was trying to lure Dragons. It was most likely a trap, and only Dothians knew how to attract Dragons. But why would a Dothian want to trap a Dragon? I couldn't think of one single good reason.

Sensing the disturbance, Dalya poked her head out of the cave entrance, her attention flickering between Tattu, still fidgeting, and me. This wasn't going to end well. With their insatiable curiosity and ingrained love for shiny things, Dragons couldn't resist the lure of treasure for long. Tattu shifted his weight onto his powerful hind legs, wings twitching with the urge to take flight.

Oh no you don't, I commanded.

Treasure... He rumbled in response, the air practically vibrating with his anticipation.

I'm very aware. It's a trap.

Tattu's golden eyes narrowed, the glint of defiance momentarily replaced by a flicker of understanding. He lowered his head with a reluctant sigh, his powerful body radiating a tense stillness. We couldn't ignore the threat, but sending Tattu in blindly was a recipe for disaster. Looking over the horizon, I searched for clues pointing to the source of what was beckoning him.

I rubbed the back of my neck. My conscience wouldn't allow me to remain behind while Tattu searched for answers without me. Walking into the cave, I pat Dalya on her nose to calm her. Artok briefly opened one eye to take in what was happening before curling his nose to his side and falling back asleep. The old Dragon was often exhausted, and though I was sure he felt the lure, he was too sick to care. Grabbing my jacket, I reluctantly climbed onto the back of a jittering Tattu as we prepared to face whatever trap someone might have set for us.

A few moments later, Tattu landed on an old softball field. His hurried landing sent a tremor through the ground, and with a dismount less agile than heroic, I stumbled onto the soft grass.

Seriously? I admonished, but my Dragon wasn't the least bit interested in manners.

He bounded toward the fire, a low rumble emitting from his chest. Before I could even think of stopping him, he was snuffling at the crackling embers, his long, nimble tongue plucking through the ashes. It was a comical and unnerving sight—a Dragon, even though a small one, delicately fishing out… tiny gold coins?

I looked around warily, glancing over the lush green grass that stood tall and still against the wind. Searching the tree line, I spotted a flash of golden hair peeking from behind a thick trunk, confirming my suspicions. The hair didn't belong to a Dothian. I froze.

Most certainly a trap, I thought, rolling my eyes.

Elle's gaze was glued to the massive ripple playing in the fire. From her confusion-laced posture, I knew she couldn't see Tattu, but she surely knew he was there. She looked thoroughly flummoxed— her lips parted, her eyes wide, and her stance tense. My invisible Dragon must have been a strange kind of mesmerizing to her, the way the embers writhed and shimmered with an unnatural light. Though Tattu remained cloaked by magic, his presence was undeniable—a subtle shift in the air, a vibration that ran through the ground beneath our feet.

My attention was drawn back to Elle, standing a few feet from me, a silent gasp escaping her as a particularly large ember pulsed and winked out entirely. I took a moment to study her. Dressed in a light blue T-shirt and practical denim pants, with a worn leather satchel slung over her shoulder, she exuded an air of casual determination as she strode in my direction.

"Kairo," she breathed. "I wasn't sure if it would work."

The utter nonchalance of her greeting, as if I were a long-lost friend encountered at a market rather than a Dothian summoned by his Dragon's need to find treasure, sent a jolt of disconcertment through me. She had an abundant amount of audacity for assuming I'd come running. Her casualness was a deliberate transgression of the boundaries set by our ancestors.

"Then why did you do it?" I asked, my tone demanding.

"I needed to talk to you," she replied, her eyes still on the mess that was once a fire.

"About what?"

Elle blinked, a flicker of surprise crossing her features before she turned her full attention to me. She focused on me so intently that her eyes nearly crossed, and I could see determination on her face that bordered on recklessness. Her unwavering attention was unsettling, as if I were the sole point of reference in a world suddenly blurred around the edges. Drawn by unexplainable magnetism, my gaze landed on the dip in the middle of her bottom lip.

"I have something for you."

I wasn't sure what it was, the tone of her voice or her proud stance that made me angry, but a shadow formed under my lashes, and my eyes flashed to hers. She was foolish, a danger to herself. Luring Dragons and their Keepers straight to her, while she stood alone in the middle of the field like naive bait. What was she thinking?

"You stupid, stupid girl," I growled and stalked forward.

Grabbing her arms, I pulled her toward my chest. My sight dimmed the moment our skin met, and a keen ache coursed through my hands. My breath hit the air in cold wisps, and my vision faded until I could only focus on the illusion surrounding me. I wasn't in the old baseball field any longer. No, I was home… The field of golden wheat that lined the valley swayed like ocean waves under a clear, cerulean sky. The familiar scent of sunbaked earth filled my senses, but that wasn't the only thing I smelled. Vanilla drifted through the air, pulling my attention to the person beside me. It was her. Elle. We stood on the bank of a familiar river; the silhouettes of ancient mountains etched against the horizon. My house was nestled among the towering redwoods I'd scaled countless times as a child.

Then, another cold, wispy breath passed, and she was in my arms while I wrapped a blanket around her shoulders. We sat in the tall grass, my hand pressed to her swollen belly, while two vibrant wood ducks soared overhead, their wings catching the sunlight. I leaned down, a phantom warmth blooming in my chest, gently kissed her forehead, and pointed at the birds. That kiss, that soft, innocent brush with my lips, was all the comfort I'd ever needed.

Just as it materialized, the vision shattered, leaving behind the ghost of what could be. The moment was so real I could sense Elle's hair on my lips, the breeze on my skin, and hear the calls of bullfrogs lining the banks near the tall cattails. For a stolen moment, trapped in that idyllic illusion, I felt a strange sense of peace.

Snapped back to reality by a whimper, a sound laced with confusion and pain, I reacted instinctively. My grip on her arms slackened, and my hands flew up, palms facing outward, forming a subconscious barrier between us. My skin burned, my face flaming with the onslaught of emotions stirred by the visions. Blinking rapidly, I tried to clear the lingering remnants. She remained rooted to the spot, arms held out as if I were still holding them, her gaze fixed on me.

Thinking she caused it, I wanted to demand answers from her, but the illusion wasn't because of Elle. This… this was me. And I knew this because if she'd experienced the same vision, her face wouldn't be a mask of… uncertainty? There was no sign of the mirrored shock I'd expected. She didn't look satisfied or triumphant either; instead, a wrinkle creased the bridge of her nose, and a frown etched between her brows. Perturbed—that was the word. Perturbed, as if I'd just tracked mud over a freshly cleaned rug, but she wasn't one to punish. The incongruity that she hadn't experienced what I had shook me all the way down to the depths of my soul, leaving me feeling exposed and bared before her. What just happened?

"What did you say?" I asked, my voice hitching as I recovered.

"I told you I have something for you, then you called me a stupid girl."

I had called her a stupid girl… I shook my head at her in disbelief. Caught up in illusions of my home and wood ducks, I was momentarily disassociated from reality. I pinched the bridge of my nose and squeezed my eyes shut, battling the sudden urge to hold her, promise her everything, and tuck the stubborn strand of hair falling over her eyebrow behind her ear. What in the seven hells is wrong with me?

"It was a stupid move to set that lure," I told her. "There are other Dragons in the area. If we were close enough to have felt the lure, they likely felt it too."

I watched her closely, waiting for the hint of fear that should accompany my warning. She didn't flinch, and no flicker of surprise crossed her features. It was almost as if she'd expected the chance of others finding her.

"I was hoping you'd feel it first," she admitted. "That you'd be closer."

Looking across the sky, I searched for any telltale shimmering that might indicate another Dragon closing in. Relief washed over me when I glanced over to see that Tattu had doused the embers entirely. No fire, no lure. Even if something was nearby, the trail had gone cold. Hopefully, other Dothians would be left circling, wondering where the source of the treasure had come from. The silence stretched, and I finally broke it when she did not explain further.

"Well, here I am," I exhaled. "What do you have for me?"

"I'll show you, but first, we have to work out a deal—something binding."

I raised a brow at the request. Did she think Dothians made pinky promises?

"What do you have in mind?"

"I have something you need," she answered, looking over where she supposed the very invisible Dragon remained. "I need something as well." She paused, searching my face in an apparent attempt to gauge my reaction.

"What do you need?" I prompted, my throat tightening.

"I need protection."

My brow furrowed even further. *Protection?*

"What could you possibly give me that would make me want to offer you protection?"

A sly smile played on her lips, and she reached into her satchel. A simple jug peeked out, but the silver liquid swirling within sent a jolt through me. Instinct took over, and my hand darted forward to snatch the container. She yanked it back with surprising speed, dropping it back into the bag before stepping away from me.

"What are your terms?" I huffed… *a trap indeed.*

Chapter Fourteen

Surprise Me

Elle

Watching Kairo wearily, I took a step back to put distance between us. The shock of his appearance was still flooding my nerves, tingling through my fingers. The ground had tremored from a massive weight landing on it, then the air had rippled, and Kairo solidified before me as if conjured from nothing. I'd considered the fact that I might die, having to quickly come to terms with the fact that I knew nothing about what Kairo could do to me.

Reminding myself that I had the upper hand, I straightened my shoulders. If I flinched away from him, it would only give him the illusion that I was afraid. Perhaps I was afraid… Or full of apprehension and still reeling from the shock that ran through me at the change in his attitude only seconds before. Kairo tucked his hands behind his back, his eyes darkened by his lowered lashes when he narrowed them. Chewing on my lip, I rocked back on my heels.

"I need protection," I repeated. "Not for a few weeks or until my current threats move on, but for a year... A full year to learn, train, and become whatever I'm apparently meant..." Noticing his scrutiny, I faltered mid-sentence.

Every word that came out of my mouth was shadowed by thoughts of why he'd looked distant for several heartbeats, then blinked his thick lashes at me as if seeing me for the first time. Or why he'd gone from touching me one second to dropping my arms with a flick of his wrists as if I burned him the next. After he'd snapped out of his strange trance, he didn't seem fully engaged in the conversation until I pulled the jug from my bag, and the abrupt shift had puzzled me.

To top it off, my circumstances had evolved beyond fighting for survival; they now involved the tangled mess of destiny that thrust me into Kairo's path. A year. That was the gamble. A year to prove my worth, to become more than just the girl who'd summoned a Dothian with a desperate plea.

Kairo's chest widened, and it dawned on me that my requests may have become too desperate and rushed. His expression was both confused and amused, the latter evident in the slight upturn of his lips. Determined to appear composed, I rooted myself to the spot, curling my toes inside my shoes as if they could anchor me in place.

Despite the medley of emotions playing across his features, there was an undercurrent of desperation in his eyes. It was subtle but unmistakable—as if he might snatch my bag and bolt given half a chance. Instinctively, I tugged it closer, still wary he might try to rid himself of me and my apparent madness. The way he was looking at me, it was clear he thought I'd lost my marbles to some degree.

"If you protect me for a year, I'll give you the blood."

"I don't think there is enough in that jug to cure my smallest Dragon, let alone the one who is sick," he replied, his eyes flicking to where I assumed his Dragon was.

There are Dragons of different sizes? All of my Unicorns were about the same size. I followed Kairo's line of sight toward the fire where the coins had been. Though I couldn't see him, I imagined the Dragon was still there. It'd been big enough to make a massive mess of the branches and ash in the middle of the now-destroyed fire ring. I was so shocked I couldn't see it; I almost hadn't come out from behind the trees. I shuddered. If this was his smallest Dragon, I didn't want to get near his biggest, even if it was somehow invisible. Protection from creatures like that is precisely why I needed him on my side.

"Who said the blood has to come from the same Unicorn? And who said it has to be all at once? If I give you a jug now and another in a couple of weeks, we can see if it might, at least, improve your Dragon's… circumstances." My forehead creased. "If that doesn't work, I can bring it to you sooner. Of course, you know better than I do. I've just begun to read the journals. I'm sure you've had access to all of this information for… what, decades?"

Instead of confidence, he looked perplexed with his eyebrows bunched and his lips parted as if he wasn't sure about what I'd said. His expression confused me. He obviously possessed a deep understanding of his world. So why did he look as if there was a sudden lack of knowledge about something as fundamental as treating a sick Dragon?

"To be completely honest," he admitted, "I've never had the opportunity to use Unicorn blood, and my parents never described how it works, probably because they were unfamiliar with it as well."

My blood ran cold. "Your parents were alive before the curse?"

"Yes. I was the last of the generation of Keepers who lived when the curse was set. My parents were alive and well until they died within a year of each other."

"Because they chose love over being immortal?" I blinked.

He inclined his head in silent confirmation. Raising a brow, his gaze fell to my mouth. I wished he would stop looking at me like that. The intensity of his attention was both confusing and strangely intoxicating. I wasn't supposed to be attracted to someone who'd threatened me. This was supposed to be a business proposal and nothing more.

"Did you learn about Keepers, the curse, and immortality in your journals?"

"It was one of the first things I learned," I admitted.

His features pinched as he considered me. I let him have his moment of silence while I gave him a once-over. Fatigue etched lines on his face, the exhaustion evident in the dark circles beneath his eyes. The different shades of blue held a depth that seemed to pierce right through me. Even as tired as Kairo looked, he exuded a raw power that left me weak-kneed and strangely breathless.

Tall, lean, and broad-shouldered, he filled out his dark gray shirt. His hair hung loosely to the middle of his ears, split near the middle, and mostly straight except for the ends that curved slightly toward the nape of his neck. I'd been mistaken, thinking it was just brown.

In the sunlight, his hair was nearly black, giving off a deep cinnamon glow when light caught it.

The corner of his lip twisted into a crooked smirk. "Are you checking me out?"

I rolled my eyes at him. The question clashed with his earlier skittishness. He'd recoiled from our touch not five minutes ago, flinching like I'd shocked him the same way a static-charged shopping cart jolted me sometimes.

"I was waiting for you to stop looking like you were going to have an aneurysm."

His face contorted as if he were biting back a retort.

"If neither of us is careful, we'll spend the next few hours bickering over trivial things and lose focus on what's important."

"I agree. Besides, we've stood out in the open for too long," Kairo told me. "I have a lot to consider, and I'm not sure I can give you a year."

Looking down at my shoes, I ran my lip through my teeth again. I needed a year, wanting the security that time could give me. Sometimes, time seemed to stand still; at other times, it rushed by so fast I found myself sitting on the same date a year later, asking where the days went. If time chose to move quickly, a year didn't seem long enough to learn what I needed. Yet, I was desperate, and at this point, I would take whatever he could give me.

"Just enough time for me to figure out this mess," I ventured, the urgency in my voice betraying my growing fear. "However long that takes."

His earlier amusement returned, dancing across his features hesitantly. "What if 'however long' takes longer than a year?"

"Then consider this a commitment, not a deadline," I pressed. "I'll help you heal your Dragon, but you must guarantee my safety until I can handle myself—until you or the danger disappears… Up to a year, if needed."

His lips quirked into a reluctant smile. "Elle…"

I fought the urge to pace, forcing myself to appear confident. Here I was, offering a potentially life-saving elixir, and Kairo was deflecting. Perhaps I'd been naive. Maybe the Unicorn blood wasn't as valuable as I'd thought, or perhaps he was wary of making a deal with a complete stranger, especially one who, according to the journals, was supposed to be his fated enemy.

"How long do you need to think about it?" I asked.

"Can I have a day?"

"Yeah, Kairo," I sighed. "You can have a day. Can you meet me back here tomorrow at the same time?"

"Sure," he replied, ducking his head a little.

He glanced down at my bag, and his gaze lingered for just a moment too long. He desperately needed what I was offering, and I couldn't bear the thought of him returning to wherever he was staying empty-handed. Besides, maybe a clear head might help him see things better? Without thinking, I reached into my bag, the sunlight catching the silvery liquid inside the jug.

Holding it out, I surprised myself with my words. "Consider this a token of good faith. I don't want your Dragon to suffer because of me."

The look of shock he gave me was followed by the slow exhale and relaxed shoulders of someone releasing something they'd carried for far too long. Taking the jug, he was careful not to touch me. A strange fluttering filled my chest, but I quickly stomped on the feeling. This wasn't some fairy tale romance. This was a deal, a necessity. No matter how attractive I found him, he was just a means to an end.

"I'll be here," he promised.

"Same," I replied.

Chapter Fifteen

Things Change

Kairo

Tattu cleared the tree line of the field, and the hair on my neck stood on end. I couldn't shake the suspicion that someone was watching us, but the expanse of the sky above was a canvas of clear, unblemished blue, as empty as the ground below. Regardless, I clung to the jug like the lifeline it represented.

Sensing my urgency, Tattu had never flown faster, and it took mere minutes to make the trip back to Artok. The wind tore at my face when Tattu swooped toward our cave's entrance. I let the windswept droplets of moisture fall from my eyes without wiping them away. Every whoosh of air around me matched the thudding of my pulse. Tattu folded his wings close to his body, readying himself for his approach. Stupidly, I leapt off the Tattu's back before he landed, sending a sharp jolt of pain through my legs.

Scrambling toward Artok, I was certain the dragon had to drink the blood for it to work, though a knot of unease twisted in my chest that this might not be the most efficient method. I tilted the jug into his cavernous maw; my fingers trembled against the plastic bottom. I urged every last precious drop onto his massive tongue. He lapped up the liquid, a grateful rumble emanating from deep within his chest. Before my eyes, his form seemed to inflate, his ribs softening. The Unicorn blood was working.

While these subtle changes happened, my thoughts were drawn back to Elle's offer. It was made on a promise as flimsy as smoke. There was no way that I could offer her a year. At some point, I wanted to return home. Perhaps, sensing my reluctance to agree to her deal, her intent had been clear when she'd offered it; that jug wasn't supposed to leave with me unless I committed. The way she'd looked at me, she'd been determined to convince me to provide protection. She must have seen the anguish on my face when I told her I needed time to think, and she had unexpectedly given me the jug out of pure kindness.

I wasn't even sure how much the jug would help. Beyond rumors that it required an entire Unicorn's worth of blood, there was nothing on how much or how little a Dragon needed to get better or how long it would take to make a difference. Because there was no frame of reference for the supposed miracle cure, I sat beside my sleeping friend and waited. His deep, rattling breaths went on for what seemed like forever. I watched his every movement until fatigue overcame worry, allowing me to fall asleep beside him.

The piercing cry of a hawk shattered the cavern's silence, jolting me awake. My body was stiff and achy from the hard cave floor. As sore as I was, hours must have passed. Artok stood by the entrance, head held high, gazing at the cloudy sky. A half-devoured moose lay at his feet. Relief washed over me in waves. The journey from Dothan Valley had zapped Artok's strength; it'd been hard for him to eat. To see him eating, even partially, was a minor miracle.

Rising cautiously, I approached him. "Look at you," I whispered.

He wasn't fully recovered, but he was no longer on death's doorstep. Moonlight glinted off his scales, catching a spark from his narrowed eyes. They seemed to bore into me, searching for something in my soul, something new. Swallowing back shame, I knew what he was looking for, and I lowered my head, a futile attempt to conceal emotions he was already aware of.

You went to her. I saw you.

Heat flooded my face as his words sank in. The edge in his voice made it clear he knew exactly why I was avoiding eye contact. The Dragon let out a hot breath, and I had no choice but to meet his steady gaze. Artok sent me an image of Elle and me along the river that ran through our valley. The image told me our bond was strong enough that he must have seen the vision that coursed through me when I'd touched her. The cool evening air filled my lungs when I sucked in a sharp breath. The pressure of his stare intensified, urging me to speak.

"What does it mean?"

It means change, Artok answered quietly.

"What if I don't want to change?"

Sometimes, change is not a choice.

My eyes burned. Elle was an enigma, a stranger thrust into my desperate situation. Had she tricked me? Was the jug some elaborate trap, a way to manipulate me into her clutches? The thought hadn't crossed my mind before because I'd been blinded by the desperate need to save Artok. Before I could question a dozen different theories further, logic forced its way in. She'd offered the jug freely, without holding it hostage over our intended agreement. Still, I'd been so mindlessly hopeless that I hadn't even considered that what she'd given me could have been poisoned. It obviously wasn't, judging by the way Artok had recovered.

Would Elle know how to poison Dragons? She'd seemed so lost, adrift in a world she didn't understand. It had to be because she was new and hadn't learned the Allorian ways. Or maybe… perhaps this was all a carefully crafted illusion, a desperate attempt to manipulate me to get to my Dragons. Even if she seemed terrified of them? Even if this supposed deal cost her something as precious as her herd's safety?

My ears started to ring, my mind racing with potential scenarios. The fragile trust I was beginning to build with her teetered on the balance of my decision. Do I stay and help her? Or take what she'd given me as enough to head back home?

"What do I do?" I asked, my voice barely louder than the wind whipping into the crevices behind me.

Sometimes, we give in, and sometimes, destiny finds us regardless.

To give in to whatever that premonition was… Lying on the blankets with her in the field at home, I'd felt so strongly about my affection for her. In that vision, she'd been mine. We'd belonged together, and that feeling had felt so right it terrified me. The notion of doing anything to be with Elle wasn't just a fleeting sentiment. It was imperative, a force compelling enough to make me consider the unthinkable. Would I forsake my duties as a Dragon Keeper if that's what it took to be by her side?

My responsibility to my Dragons was everything to me, and the allure of an unknown future with Elle seemed pitted against my loyalty to them. Choosing Elle meant sacrificing my life, eventually leaving my Dragons without a Keeper, and potentially placing them in my sister's hands.

Not to mention that the thought of wanting Elle was terrifying. My chest twisted harshly against the reality of considering what the future would look like with her. I wouldn't do it. I couldn't let my feelings jeopardize the safety of my Dragons. I was going to tell her no. Yet, when I looked at Artok, I still saw weariness about him. He looked exhausted, wearing his illness in his dull scales and tucked-in waist. I would need more Unicorn blood, and I doubted Elle would continue to provide it in good faith.

I moved to sit on the mountain's ledge and gazed at the clouds rolling across the horizon, contemplating my options. Time was ticking, and I needed to give Elle an answer I wasn't sure I could deliver. She would expect me to come and agree to her deal, and logically, it would be wise for me to do so. I could stay in this mountain a little longer while Artok recovered. The Dragon needed the rest. A trip home would be hard on him, if not fatal, unless he were mostly healed.

There had to be another way. I could bury it all, pretend the vision never happened. I could focus on protecting Elle long enough to get Artok the blood he needed. Then, I would distance myself and keep things strictly to the agreement. However, I knew that if I stayed, I wouldn't hesitate to protect her regardless of the deal. It was a fierce, unexpected proclamation that rocked me to my core.

I tucked my face into my palms. Even if I stayed, there was no guarantee Elle would ever return my feelings. Maybe she just saw me as a temporary solution, a source of stability in this strange new world. Sure, I'd seen a flicker of something in her eyes, but was it desire for me, or a reaction to her circumstances? The terrifying truth was I could stay, pine after her, and have her never feel the same way. Was that worse than staying and forcing myself to keep my distance because of the Dragons? Perhaps I didn't even have to worry. I was sure she didn't feel like her heart was walking a thin line between circumspection and devotion like mine was.

Looking over the peaks, I noticed silver streaks dancing among the clouds in the distance. Dalya and Tattu were celebrating Artok's recovery. I realized that my emotions did not need to become theirs, and if I didn't contain them, I would cast all of my fears, desires, and discernment onto my Dragons. Letting myself relax, I decided to meet her in the meadow to give her my decision, but for now, I needed to let my Dragons' enjoyment become my own.

Chapter Sixteen

Then I Was Taken

Elle

The clock read eight, though I'd been awake since dawn. Six hours remained until Kairo and I were supposed to meet, and my patience wore thin. Would I look desperate if I arrived an hour or two early? Honestly, I wasn't sure if it was desperation or just a ridiculous hope that he'd arrive as soon as I did. A part of me didn't understand why he was making me wait. We both knew he needed to take this deal unless he planned to get blood elsewhere.

My stomach grumbled, and I couldn't tell if I was hungry or nervous. I swung open the refrigerator door and went over my food options before realizing it was basically empty. There was nothing but condiments, rancid takeout hosting a thin layer of mold, and milk that had outlived its expiration date… by three weeks. I rolled my eyes. Since when had I become so distracted that I couldn't even make time to want to eat? And when did staring longingly at a half-full jar of jelly become a valid breakfast option?

Tapping my fingers against the handle, I contemplated going back to bed instead of shopping, but my stomach rumbled again, deciding for me. With a heavy sigh, I grabbed my car keys from the kitchen island and headed to the garage. Waffles that popped out of a toaster, chocolate syrup, and a hot mug of coffee sounded incredibly good because, if I was honest, sleeping and waiting for Kairo's answer wasn't all that appealing. Determined to do something other than sulk, I pulled out of the garage and turned my car toward the center of town.

I stopped at a red light and tapped my fingers on the steering wheel. What could Kairo be thinking? Could I change his mind if he chooses not to help me? Uncertain of his age, I imagined changing his mind would be challenging. I shook my head. With immortality on his side, changing his decision would likely be as easy as convincing a mountain to move.

Lost in thought, I nearly missed the store's entrance. I jerked the wheel at the last second to pull into the lot, the wheels squealing against the asphalt. Bypassing the first available space, I maneuvered into a spot where I could pull through rather than reverse in case someone tried to trap me. The irony wasn't lost on me—my hometown, of all places, wasn't safe, and I couldn't help but feel a surge of resentment. This was yet another reminder of how woefully unprepared my mother had left me for all of this.

The pain of her absence was constant, compounded by the anger of being left in the dark about my heritage and my new responsibilities. Sometimes I found myself forgiving her, considering that perhaps she wanted a normal life for me. But then reality hit, dragging me back to the challenges that felt insurmountable without her guidance, leaving me with an anger I wasn't sure how to deal with.

Walking into the grocery store, it hummed with an unsettling normalcy. Shoppers strolled the aisles, blissfully oblivious to my inner turmoil, likely pondering mundane questions like what to make for dinner. It was all so ordinary. I gripped the cart tighter, the cool metal reminding me of how abnormal my life has become. My worries inflated, and for a fleeting moment, I wanted to announce to everyone the sheer absurdity of my situation. But the image of wide-eyed shoppers and a bewildered cashier staring at me like I'd lost my mind quickly squashed that impulse.

Oddly enough, the only person I could talk to about my situation was supposed to be this evil presence that kept me awake at night. But last night, I found myself awake for an entirely different reason. Stupidly, I wanted to see him. Not only to hear his decision, but because I craved someone who wouldn't look at me like they needed to grab a straitjacket and the keys to a padded cell if I discussed my life right now. Kairo could easily fill the void where a friend should be, and I wasn't sure how to feel about that.

I threw a bag of chips onto the pile of food I was accumulating in my cart and shuffled my way to the checkout. There I was, getting groceries, but my mind was still very much waiting in that field for Kairo's decision. It was like playing pretend. Maybe I could get there three hours early to wait for him? I could unpack my groceries, make waffles, and sit in a folding chair with a tumbler full of hot coffee and a book.

After paying for my groceries, I exited through the sliding doors. They opened with a slow hiss. The wind picked up, blowing cold against the back of my neck. I paused to figure out what was causing my sudden sense of unease. Looking around, I didn't see anything unusual. There were about two dozen cars in the lot, and only one or two people were around. I caught the gaze of a girl walking by; she smiled and nodded at me, and I nodded back slowly. The girl was beautiful—unreal-looking—as if she could stop people in their tracks with just a glance.

She reminded me of someone, but I couldn't pinpoint who. A hazy memory danced at the edge of my mind with her in it. It teased me, just out of reach of deciphering what it was. Blinking to clear my thoughts, I turned back to my cart, reaching for a bag. Suddenly, goosebumps rippled across the back of my arms, raising the fine hairs and sending a shiver down my spine. The adrenaline rush was so similar to how I felt when I'd met Kairo that I nearly searched for him.

I attempted to catch a glimpse behind me without being obvious about it. As I tilted my head, a whisper ghosted across my ear, so soft I thought I'd imagined it. The soothing aroma of lavender overlaid with the sweet smell of chemicals hit me all at once, and a wave of dizziness dragged me down, leaving me feeling disoriented and strange.

"Sleep," the girl whispered.

I couldn't quite grasp what was happening. Why was she telling me to sleep? It made no sense, not even as my limbs became lead weights and my thoughts muddled. I tried to grip the grocery bag I was lifting from the cart, but my fingers wouldn't cooperate. It slipped from my grasp, hitting the ground with a dull thud. I watched in odd detachment as cans and produce rolled across the asphalt.

The overwhelming urge to lie down flushed through every nerve and muscle. I fought against it, but my eyelids drooped traitorously. The world tilted and swayed. Vaguely, I registered the sensation of being moved. My body sagged against someone before cold leather pressed against my skin. Was I in the back seat of my car? How did I get here? I fought to cry out, but the encroaching darkness swallowed me, and I couldn't summon the strength. My last thought was of Kairo before everything went black…

It took an eternity to pry my eyes open because my body was protesting the idea of waking. When I finally did, my vision was blurry. I blinked several times, struggling to bring the small room into focus. A fire crackled in a wood-burning stove, casting flickering shadows across the small space. An old wooden chair sat opposite me; its weathered back created a frame around the flames. Taking in the ancient, tattered, colorless rug that covered the entire floor, I tried to place where I was.

I was definitely on a cot of some kind; the unforgiving canvas wrapped around the frame that was biting harshly into my hip. Attempting to adjust myself, I bit back a groan. I couldn't move my arms, and even turning my head felt impossible. The girl from the parking lot was cooking something on the stove. She looked at home and hummed a familiar tune, though I couldn't place it.

"Oh, you are up," the girl spoke, smiling at me as she made her way over with what looked to be two bowls of steaming soup. "Just in time."

Taking her in, I tried to remember as much as I could. Her pitch-black hair cascaded to her waist in sleek, glossy waves. She was all elongated limbs and taut, sinewy muscle. Her skin-tight black leather pants tapered down to knee-high boots. A crisp white tank top clung to her slender torso, and she wore a studded black belt that cinched her narrow waist. A tattoo of something ornate twined its way around her arm, ending just below her shoulder. I couldn't make out the details through the haze—perhaps leafy vines or a series of flowers and butterflies. She looked young, but the way she held herself, graceful and upright, made her appear older than the years her features suggested.

She set the bowls down on a table near the edge of my cot and pulled a chair over. Fanning the hot soup with her hand, she smiled at me politely. My jaw slackened, and my brows drew together, shock rippling through me and wiping away any trace of confusion. Had I seriously just been kidnapped? Was my captor serving me soup as if she knew me? Did I somehow know her? She seemed oddly familiar. I tried to sit up, every motion so laborious through the fog that it took all the concentration I could muster.

"You," she said, "are probably wondering who I am."

Was she insane? Of course I wondered who she was and where she'd taken me. She stepped closer, her expression soft, making her appear inviting, but there was a hint of something else. Her eyes flickered, and I saw a wicked glint that lay just behind the friendly mask she attempted to portray. She was dangerous. I opened my mouth to demand where she'd taken me, but my stomach cramped. Swallowing back the bile rising in my throat, the room spun around me.

"My name is Koa," the girl told me. "I'm a Keeper, just like you."

I tried to comprehend what she was saying; truly, I did. Who was this girl? What did she want? Did Keeper mean she was an Allorian? Like me? I wasn't alone. But then, why had I been kidnapped? Why was the room spinning? Why did my stomach feel like I'd been punched in the gut? The realization that I might not be alone in this new life should have been comforting, but it only added to the growing knot of apprehension forming within me.

"Do you need help eating your soup?" the girl asked, the corner of her lip twisting upward as she grabbed the spoon from the bowl nearest me.

I lifted my hand to refuse, but she was insistent. She pushed the food toward me, and even with my mouth partly closed, she poured some of the soup in. The rest dribbled down my chin and onto my shirt. After repeating the process six more times, I collapsed onto the cot with a thud, the effects of the drugs taking control. My vision faded again, and I began to slip away, powerless to resist the encroaching darkness.

"If you are tired, feel free to go back to sleep. We can talk tomorrow. We have all the time in the world."

Chapter Seventeen

My Decision Was Made

Kairo

Tattu swooped into the field ten minutes after Elle and I were scheduled to meet. I landed softly on the ground, shaking my head at the Dragon that bounded toward the fire pit to check for any overlooked treasures from the previous day. Searching the tree line, a weird sensation crept over me. I wasn't sure how I knew something was wrong, but I did. An icy dread blasted through me like a barrage of raw, desperate vulnerability. I scanned the trees again but didn't see anyone. Elle isn't here.

Sprinting to my Dragon, I hurled myself onto Tattu's back. As he took to the sky, the Dragon shifted away from the fire, dirt, and leaves exploding from under him. The ash accumulated on his nostrils from the smoldering fire flicked back at me when the wind kicked up around us. I wiped the grit off my face and eyes, cursing under my breath.

Searching below us, I guided him to a small clearing amidst the rugged terrain near the quaint mountain town where Elle resided. We landed as close to the rows of postcard-style houses as we could. When Tattu's talons grazed the earth, I slid off his back. Landing in a crouch while sweeping the area for any signs of her. The streets held the same scenery as the day before with a smattering of cars, a black cat striding down the sidewalk, and a couple strolling, paying no mind to the goings-on around them… No signs of Elle.

Crossing the street briskly, I examined each car and peered through every window—the thought of Elle arriving in the meadow while I searched for her barely registered. Something was off. I knew deep down she was gone. I knew that something had happened to her. The spot deep inside of me that was reserved for her was somehow emptier, which terrified me. It frightened me so much that I didn't feel when something shifted as I stepped over a large crack in the sidewalk.

A roll of tension crossed my chest and shoulders, and my pace faltered as a stiff breeze stirred, kicking up the dirt around me. For a second, I considered turning around and heading in the other direction, the need clinging to me. *Turn around,* my thoughts screamed. I didn't listen. No, I wouldn't listen. Passing a yellow two-story house surrounded by a beautiful green lawn, I walked toward the neighboring house tucked behind it. It sat unassumingly with its overgrown grass and lace-curtained windows, but something about it made me bristle. I couldn't shake the feeling that the house was inexplicably connected to Elle.

I paused in front of it just as a boy walked up the three steps to the porch. He approached the house, opened the screened door, knocked, glanced down at his phone, and repeated the process several times. Running his hand through his hair, he peeked into the window beside the front door. I tried to hide my interest but couldn't help slowing my steps, taking in every detail regardless of what the boy might think. Wondering if he was connected to Elle's disappearance, I watched to see if this stranger might unknowingly provide me with a clue.

Maybe his distress was related to Elle? Would she associate with someone so utterly unremarkable? He was unsatisfyingly human, with no distinctive traits. I was convinced my assessment was correct; she wouldn't be involved with someone so boy-next-door.

The boy put his cell phone to his ear, with his head turned away. I barely caught the tone of his voice, but from what I did catch, it was unmistakably laced with concern. My focus wavered, and a strange panic began to fester again. The possibility that this seemingly insignificant human might actually be linked to Elle sent a jolt of unease through me, alerting me to complications I hadn't considered. She'd been raised here, among them. Of course, she'd have human friends… possibly even a human boyfriend. The thought made me want to gag.

"Elle?" the guy called out loudly, after placing his phone back in his pocket. "It's Chase…" He knocked on the door a few more times.

I whipped around so fast my heel caught the edge of the sidewalk, nearly causing me to trip—something that hadn't happened in ages. Straightening the cuffs of my shirt, I approached the house as the shock of hearing her name reverberated through me. Elle wasn't in the field. She wasn't home. I was right. Something was wrong. The fact that this guy, who clearly knew her, was worried about her not answering the door or her phone only amplified my concern.

"Is she not home?" I asked when I was near enough. "I've been looking for her."

The boy startled and turned to face me, appraising me boldly from head to toe. I allowed it, raising a brow at his audacity.

"Who are you?" the boy asked, his tone tinged with jealousy.

The corner of my lips turned upward, and Elle's disappearance was momentarily forgotten. This boy thought I was competition. I took a step forward, intentionally invading his space. But my transgressions were short-lived when I reminded myself that while I was sure this boy was no comparison, my concerns lay elsewhere, far beyond his opinion of me.

"A friend," I told him, trying to appear non-threatening. "We met at the coffee shop a few days ago, and I came over to make sure she was okay. It seems like she is going through a lot."

The boy studied me, his face cycling through various emotions. First came a flash of false bravado, quickly replaced by intimidation. Finally, his features settled on something that resembled reluctance, confirming my initial assessment. No comparison.

"She's not home," he told me firmly, his tone a poor attempt at masking his unease.

With his words, the boy stiffened. His stony expression suggested Elle was not at liberty to interact with someone like me, and the notion piqued my interest. Did Elle have any say in this matter?

"Do you know where she is?" I kept my voice deliberately neutral, though curiosity stirred beneath the surface.

"Out," The boy's clipped response came with a slight shift in his stance, positioning himself in the archway at the top of her stairs so that he was blocking her doorway completely.

"Out where?" I peered past him at the windows.

"She's just out," the boy's jaw tightened. "Even if she were here, she wouldn't want visitors."

Noting how his fingers curled into fists, his protective stance only heightened my interest. What exactly was Elle to him that he felt entitled to guard her door with such conviction? The boy appeared to consider their relationship significant, which would have been amusing if it weren't for the fact that Elle was missing.

"And you often speak for her?" I let a hint of my amusement color my words, and his shoulders tensed.

"That's not your concern," his chin lifted defiantly.

"Everything about Elle is my concern." The words slipped out before I could catch them, sharper than intended. Almost unnecessarily so.

The boy's eyes narrowed. "Is that so?"

As intrigued as I was by the boy's attitude, it wore on my patience. Still, I wasn't sure who he thought he was or what role he filled for her. What I was sure of was that my confusion as to his place in Elle's life only made me want to understand her more. Was she merely an object of contention, or did she hold power or choice in this boy's assumed relationship with her?

Briefly, I considered her not merely as a Keeper or a means to an end in my situation but as a person with her own will and desires. The reflection brought complexity to my feelings, blending respect with my growing fascination with her. When I caught the boy staring, I merely smirked, but the smirk was a mask, a facade hiding my growing respect and genuine interest in understanding Elle's true role in our intertwined fates. A mask that was also hiding my seemingly depthless worry.

"Let's try this again," I said, forcing a smile that didn't reach my eyes. "When will she return?"

The boy's face reddened. "She'll return when she returns."

"You seem quite invested in protecting her." I observed. "Does Elle know you're turning away her visitors?"

"I said she wouldn't want visitors," he countered.

"And yet here you are, speaking for her as if you have the right." My words carried a subtle challenge, and his shoulders tensed. "Tell me, does she appreciate being treated like someone who can't make her own choices?"

The boy lifted his upper lip. "You can be as persistent as you want, but that isn't going to make her appear. I don't know who you are, but today doesn't seem like a good day to show up at her doorstep." *Or any day, for that matter, if it's you,* his expression implied by his cold once over.

"Persistent?" I couldn't help but smirk. "I've only just arrived. You've been here longer than I have. Though I'm beginning to wonder what she'd think about this particular welcome." My words seemed to pull him out of his posturing.

"If you see her before I do, tell her Kairo stopped by," I said finally. "I'm sure she'll be… amused by your dedication to her safety."

"I don't need your permission to protect her," he shot back, but uncertainty had crept into his voice.

"No," I agreed, "but you might need hers," I added, before spinning in the other direction and walking back toward the edge of town. Behind me, I could feel the boy's gaze burning into my back, his suspicion tangible.

Elle wasn't there, and posturing with the boy was a waste of time. I needed to find her, and I needed to find her soon. I only momentarily cataloged the fact that I'd found where she lived. I'd broken the ward she'd put in place to keep me out. The moment I walked back over the crack in the sidewalk, trepidation swept over me. The only thing that had kept me from rushing off was my concern for Elle's well-being.

Adrenaline spurred me into a jog when I was nearing where I'd left Tattu. I spotted the old factory at the edge of town, its better days long behind it. Crumbling brick walls and missing windows, some haphazardly boarded up, told me it hadn't functioned in decades. Local youth left their mark with obscure graffiti decorating the deteriorating exterior. My Dragon was stretched out along the building, his head resting on a mound of dirt and his legs tucked tightly against him.

"Tattu, Get up."

Tattu peeked at me lazily, his lips curling into a wicked grin. He yawned greatly and settled his chin back on the dirt mound.

I sleep.

"You always sleep," I replied, unable to contain my exasperation. "Now you wake. The Allorian is missing."

That woke him up. It seemed he'd taken a liking to her because she'd gifted him treasure. He raised himself carefully, sitting almost like a dog. Eyeing the woods around him, he turned to me and came to the same conclusion. We had to find…

Chuff?

"Chuff," I agreed. The implications of my sister's involvement angered me because I had no doubt she was somehow involved.

I leaned close to Tattu's side as he circled the mountain lazily, nearly suspended in the cool, swift spring air. For two long days, we'd searched tirelessly, hope dwindling with each fruitless pass over mountains and valleys surrounding them. Searching through the trees and clearings below, my eyes narrowed. Suddenly, Tattu hesitated, his wings catching an updraft as a slow plume of white smoke rose in the distance.

Spotting Chuff's tail dipping into the tall evergreens, I exhaled. His cloaking was dropped, revealing his massive form. My sister was, once again, blatantly disregarding her Dragon's safety by not demanding he remain under the camouflage that kept them hidden. For once, I was grateful for her stupidity. Her careless actions had inadvertently led us to her, and she probably didn't even realize it. Or she didn't care.

See him? Tattu inquired.

"I do," I called over the whipping wind.

I craned my neck, searching the sky behind me to ensure Dalya was still following somewhere close behind. Her sleek form cut through the clouds, and the sight of her so close was reassuring. She'd stayed with me when I'd asked her to, without knowing the plan. A great lump rose in my throat, and my heart pounded so fiercely I feared it might burst from my chest. Dalya's presence was to ensure I could go through with my plan without a fight, but her presence also reminded me of what was at stake to retrieve Elle.

I shouldn't want to save her. Yet, the thought of Elle in danger sent a surge of dread through me, an unfamiliar sensation threatening to unravel my sanity. It was a wild, unreal thing, this fierce protectiveness that took root in my soul. I knew my sister all too well–Koa's moral compass had always been as fickle as the wind. If someone dangled the right price tag before her, she wouldn't hesitate. She'd hand Elle over in a quickened heartbeat, unmoved by the consequences.

Tattu landed downwind from Chuff's location, and I dismounted onto my toes, my boots barely making a sound on the soft forest floor. Silently, I navigated the woods. I used the trunks of the tall aspen trees to maintain my cover, the moss and the dew making their roots slick. Hiking over them, I circled the meadow to approach from the west of the smoke plume. I moved swiftly, cautiously, each step placed on the soft ground with intent. Pausing only briefly to reorient myself, the noises of the birds and wind masked what little sound I created.

The trees began to thin, and I halted with one hand against an old, tall stump. Near a clearing, I caught sight of a dilapidated hunter's shanty. Its metal roof sagged pathetically over a tiny wooden porch, and the whole structure looked so fragile that Tattu could've reduced it to splinters with minimal effort. I spotted Koa's dark hair through the grimy windows when I approached, and bile rose in my throat. I'd have to consider my every move if Elle were in the cabin. Rushing in blindly could jeopardize her safety, and I couldn't afford any mistakes with my sister involved.

I shook out my limbs, letting the tension roll through my shoulders before settling into a familiar cold detachment. Like armor, I masked my features piece by piece. The skin on my face tightened, and my lips curled into a scowl.

Drawing myself up to my full height, I crossed the cabin's threshold. The warm air of a fire hit me, the heat drastically different from the chill of the wind blowing through the mountain pass. The door creaked in protest as the wind pushed it, but it remained where I wanted it, open to the sounds coming from the surrounding woods. I nearly let my facade slip when I took in the scene inside the cabin. My sister turned to me, her expression morphing from shock to anger in the blink of an eye.

"Brother," she stated, her tone emotionless.

"Koa," I replied, matching her expression.

My gaze landed on Elle, and my hands tightened into fists. Every fiber of my being screamed to rush over, scoop her into my arms, and flee this wretched place. She lay motionless on an old cot in the corner, looking more like a corpse than a living being. When I caught her chest's subtle rise and fall, my knees threatened to buckle with relief, but it was short-lived. I locked onto the constellation of bruises marring her face, their angry colors contrasting with her sickly pallor.

"What, exactly, are you planning on doing with her?"

Koa's upper lip rose. "My plans are none of your business."

"It is my business. I found her before you."

Koa's laugh echoed in the small space. "Finders, Keepers," she said with a sneer. "Possession and all that."

"Be reasonable, Koa. You don't need her. Let me take her so I can get Artok the help he needs."

Koa's face hardened, reminding me of a little child who might have had her favorite toy taken away—spoiled, indignant, rotten.

"When will you learn, little brother? I do not care about Artok. I haven't cared about him since he was handed to you. I don't care about you either. The only person that I care about in this damned world is me."

"You don't mean that," I said, searching her face for a glimpse of humanity.

Koa's laugh was bitter. "Oh, but I do. You've always been so naive, so eager to see the good in everyone. It's pathetic."

"And you've always been selfish," I spat back. "But this? This is a new low, even for you."

Her eyes flashed dangerously. "You have no idea what I'm capable of. What I do with her is none of your business, and what happens with Artok is none of mine," she sucked in a breath, "And I'm not going to let you take her."

"I'm not going to give you a choice."

Koa sneered, waving a hand in Elle's direction. "You'd really fight me over her?"

"To save Artok?" *To save her.* "Yes, I would."

What appeared to be hurt and apprehension flashed across my sister's features for a second. She quickly masked it, glancing at Elle and then back at me through slitted eyes. Koa's hand moved to her back, as if she were going to draw a weapon. "Don't make me hurt you, brother."

I stood my ground. "I'm not the one making choices here, Koa. You are."

"If I'm the one making choices, then I'm choosing for you to leave," she seethed. "I don't want you here."

"I'm not leaving without her," I said, my resolve hardening. "And deep down, you know this isn't right."

Koa's face contorted with rage. "It doesn't matter if I'm right or wrong. Being morally right is a luxury I can't afford. This," she motioned around the cabin, "is about survival."

"No," I countered, "this is about having some sort of power. And it's corrupting you."

Her laugh was hollow. "Power is the only thing that matters in this world. You'll learn that soon enough."

I shook my head, sadness creeping into my voice. "What happened to you, Koa? We used to protect each other when we were younger."

"We grew up," she snarled. "Now, for the last time, leave. Or I'll make you leave."

Her words sent a flash of red-hot anger through me. A screech sounded from the woods, and my sister's brows drew together in confusion. Marveling at Dalya's impeccable timing, I caught Elle stirring out of the corner of my eye. Subtly, I extended my hand by my leg, holding down one finger, praying Elle would catch the signal to stay put. *Don't draw attention to yourself,* I silently willed her. The air vibrated with the calls and rumbles of Dragons, filling the cabin with their chorus. My cue had arrived, and the pieces of my plan were falling into place.

"Who…what was that?"

"That, my lovely sister, is the one thing you didn't plan for."

"Kairo, what do you mean?" she asked, her voice shrill.

"You forgot something," I pointed out.

I practically sauntered over to Elle and took her into my arms. She fell asleep again, her body limp against mine. Her head drooped over my arm, golden hair cascading like a waterfall. Adjusting her position, I cradled her against my chest. She fit perfectly in my arms.

"You forgot that Chuff cannot resist Dalya."

Koa's expression froze, her mouth slackened, and betrayal flashed across her features. The screeching intensified, and the wind swept into the tiny cabin, catching Koa's hair. She lurched out of the cabin, racing toward her Dragon. Looking down at Elle, I ran a finger over the bruises lining her cheeks, and her eyes twitched under her eyelids. My sister had been keeping her drugged. I could smell the sweet, plum-like scent of datura in the air, a plant I was well versed in, as it was found in the valley where I'd grown up. It was a drug she'd have to sleep off, but one that shouldn't cause her any harm.

Holding her tightly, I made my way out of the shack and searched the sky. Dalya and Chuff circled each other, their cloaked forms casting ripples that turned the clouds into a mesmerizing swirl of blue and white. I could imagine them without their cloaking, the giant male testing Dalya with arrogance while she artfully danced out of his reach. Their harsh cries vibrated through the trees. I hesitated on the cabin steps, aware that anyone within a hundred miles could hear them. Yet, I reasoned, they might be more concerned with my sister's anguished cries, which, most likely, could also be heard from a great distance.

Maybe my sister would get lucky, and Dalya would deny Chuff's attempts at mating. Maybe Chuff and Dalya wouldn't develop a bond even if they did manage to mate. But, judging by her shrill cries bouncing off the mountainsides, Koa didn't want to take the chance of either happening.

I knew there was a slim possibility Dalya might not return to me. Such was the rightful choice of a Dragon who took on a mating bond, if one occurred. The pairing would choose which Keeper to align with; generally, it was the males. Dalya was free to make whatever decision she wanted because even though she saw me as inferior to my father, I had faith in her. Our bond, over time, had been built on mutual respect and understanding, not force or dominance. I trusted she would return, that the tentative connection we'd forged over years of companionship would prevail, and she wouldn't choose to stay with Koa and Chuff.

Needing to get Elle away from my deluded sister before she managed to retrieve Chuff, I headed into the woods. Elle's head drooped over my arm again, and I shifted her. She seemed light and fragile in my arms. When her shirt slipped off her shoulder, revealing her thinning collarbone, I saw she wasn't eating enough. I pulled it back over her shoulder, and something settled deep, something I could no longer ignore; I must help her.

This had been my fault. I'd taunted my sister, making her want to find Elle even more. Instead of scaring her off, I'd presented her with a challenge—one she wasn't prepared for, but one that had caused Elle to get hurt. The bruises on her face were already darkening against her soft, cream skin. I ran a finger over them again and sucked in a breath.

Gently, I placed Elle on Tattu's back, sitting her up before I swung up behind her. She leaned heavily into me, and I wrapped an arm around her waist. The mix of emotions trembling through me was incomprehensible. Anger so vivid it was absolute. Fear so great it was polarizing. Relief so vast it could fill the gaps in the mountains we would soon fly through.

Tattu was quietly studying the sky, his mischievous nature held back by unwarranted jealousy. We both knew he wasn't a match for Dalya. He was too small, too unlike her. Patting Tattu on the side to get his attention, I tightened my grip around Elle. Tattu gave the sky one last longing look before silently taking off in the opposite direction.

Chapter Eighteen

When I Awoke

Elle

The haunting sound of the wind woke me, its howls echoing like a mournful prayer flowing through a tunnel. I drew short, quick breaths, each exhale a cloud of mist in the frigid darkness in the crisp, biting air. Running my fingers over the coarse fur beneath me, I gathered my bearings, turning toward the dim light filtering into the cave. Someone was silhouetted against the starry night sky, a solemn figure sitting silently in the vast darkness.

I clenched my fingers into fists around the thick blankets. *Kairo.* The soft glow of moonlight illuminated his features, giving him a godlike appearance. Studying his profile, I felt both relieved and uncertain. Uncertain because the look on his face gave nothing away, and relieved because it was him.

"I'm sorry," he said, breaking the silence.

His voice sent goosebumps down my arms.

"Sorry for what?" I whispered.

Without answering, Kairo turned toward me. He absently toyed with the dirt by his side, drawing figures into it with one long finger. The waning light highlighted his troubled expression. It was the same look he'd worn the evening before, standing in the cabin doorway as I attempted to lift myself off the cot. I'd strained so hard to hear snippets of the conversation between Kairo and the girl who took me, but only one word stood out—*brother*.

His eyes darted back and forth, as if his mind was racing, or as if trying to find the right words to explain whatever he thought he needed to. He picked at the dirt beneath his fingernail before glancing up and meeting my gaze.

His finger stilled. "I know you have questions," he said softly, his voice so low I barely heard him. "About what you might have heard. About…her." He paused, swallowing hard.

Kairo looked out into the darkness beyond our small circle of moonlight. The night was alive with subtle sounds—the rustle of trees far below, the distant call of an owl—but his breathing spoke to me above the other noises. The quiet hitch, the long inhales, and the delicate flare of his nostrils in the soft light betrayed what he struggled to conceal. His fingers twitched almost imperceptibly as if reaching for words he couldn't bring himself to say. He was nervous.

"But I want you to understand," he continued, turning back to me, "whatever you think you know, whatever you've pieced together—there is more to it."

Suddenly, I was holding my breath, my heart pounding against my ribcage. What could he possibly mean? What truths was he hiding? Despite the apprehension caused by my circumstances, I found myself leaning in, waiting for more.

"I'm sorry for what my sister did," he said, confirming their relationship.

His sister… The similarities… She'd looked so familiar. I blinked at him, not exactly sure what to say. It wasn't his fault his sister had kidnapped me… or was it? Then, it occurred to me that as much as I wanted to know about his sister, there were more important questions that I wanted answers to, or simply confirmation of the information I'd already stumbled upon.

"Why didn't she tell me? Why didn't my mother explain this all to me?"

He sighed, running a hand through his hair. "I'm not sure about all of this for you. The Allorians' side, I mean. But I don't think your mother had a chance to tell you that you are a Keeper. It is part of the curse for us, so it must be the same for you." Kairo hesitated. "In order for a Dragon or a Unicorn to reproduce, there are specific…" He paused again. "Things that need to happen. One of them is called the Sula-umbra. A new Keeper must become enlightened to their responsibilities around the death of the previous one. In most cases, the old Keeper knows they are dying and can explain everything to their successor. But in your case…"

"My mother died suddenly," I finished, sitting up straighter.

The car accident and the lack of warning.

A chill ran across my arms, not entirely due to the cool night air.

"Yes," he agreed, nodding solemnly. "I assumed your mother passed unexpectedly and didn't get a chance to tell you."

"Why do the Dragons and Unicorns need Solabra?"

"Sula-Umbra," Kairo corrected, saying it more slowly. His brow creased, forming deep grooves on his forehead. "I'm not sure. Someone cast a curse long ago, causing a ripple effect. The Sula-umbra was a part of that ripple. If there is reasoning beyond mating, I'm unaware of it."

I nodded slowly because that confirmed what I'd read. "So, this curse affects not just the creatures but Keepers, too?"

"Yes."

The silence that followed was thick with a tangle of vague realizations. I hugged my knees to my chest, trying to process everything I'd just learned.

"I know it's a lot to take in. I wish… I wish there were an easier way to explain all of this."

It was a lot to take in, but now I understood why my mother had kept this secret. It wasn't by choice—it was part of the curse mentioned in the journal, a curse I was only starting to comprehend. And if one could be cast, it could surely be broken. Despite Kairo's clarification, I still wanted and needed to know more. I looked up at him, studying his face. Despite the familial connection to my kidnapper, I found myself wanting to trust him. Trust that he was being truthful.

"So my mother, even if she'd wanted to, couldn't have prepared me for this until she was dying?"

Kairo nodded again. "Yes. The curse ensures that each new Keeper comes into their role with a clean slate. They aren't jaded by preconceptions or expectations. My guess is that it's a precaution but also a curse in its own right." He sighed, running a hand through his hair. "Being a Keeper means we are responsible for maintaining the balance between Dragons and Unicorns so that neither goes extinct. We are crucial to their survival and reproduction."

"What would happen if an Allorian were to tell the next in line the truth before their Sula-umbra?"

"It's… more complex than you might imagine," he began. "The curse has safeguards. If a Keeper were to attempt to reveal the truth prematurely, it could alter the Sula-umbra process. Typically, a Sula-umbra spans a few months. It's enough time for Allorians to fully come into their roles and Dothians to identify suitable pairings among their charges. But an altered Sula-umbra… that's something else entirely. It hasn't occurred in decades, perhaps even centuries. The consequences could be unpredictable."

"What kind of consequences?"

Kairo's fingers returned to absently tracing patterns in the dirt beside him, expression flat and distant. "There are rumors of Keepers whose Sula-umbras lasted a long time. Others tell of them being cut short. Since they only happen every few decades, each one is vital to the survival of our species, especially with the Dragons' illnesses and Dothians' necessity for Unicorn blood. The balance between Dragons and Unicorns is delicate. An altered Sula-umbra could tip that balance in ways we can't foresee. I think that is why most are so adamant about protecting the natural progression of a Keeper's journey. It's instinct for us to protect our Dragons at all costs, as I'm sure it is instinct for you as well."

I felt like I had consumed so much information that I was buried in a strange stillness.

"How am I supposed to handle all of this?"

Kairo's expression softened. "You're not alone in this. I can… I will help you if you let me."

It was almost exactly what Chase had said, but the difference was that I wanted Kairo's help. Chase wouldn't understand. He wasn't meant to be dragged into the life I'd been handed.

Searching Kairo's face for any sign of deception and finding none, I asked, "After what your sister did…"

"My sister and I don't always see eye to eye," Kairo said, his voice tight. "What she did was wrong, no matter her reasoning. I want to make it right."

Kairo moved across the cave. He found a closer spot and sat down again, leaning against the mossy side of the rock wall. Sick to my stomach with anxiety and confusion, I tried to place how I felt about him and was surprised that my fear of him was gone. It dawned on me that if he truly meant to harm me, we wouldn't be having this discussion about my deceased mother and ancient curses.

He, at the very least, wasn't about to let anyone toss my body into the woods or hurl me off the side of this mountain. Despite the circumstances, despite everything I'd been through, I realized I trusted him. It was a strange feeling, putting my faith in someone who, by all accounts, should be my enemy. But here we are, two unlikely allies in a cave, unraveling the mysteries of a world so foreign it barely existed to me. Barely existed, like the cave I was in. Glancing around, I took in the slick, moss-covered cave interior, the wide mouth, and the gaping moonlit sky. I was pretty sure that I was high up on a mountain.

"How did I get here? Where am I?" I asked.

"I needed to save you from my sister," Kairo answered, misunderstanding my questions.

Needed to?

"Koa?" I ventured, recalling the name I'd heard before.

"Yes," he said, letting out a weary breath. "She is a Dothian, like me."

My lips parted in surprise, and I shook my head. It didn't make sense. "She told me she was…"

"An Allorian?" Kairo cut in, his eyes sharp with understanding.

"No," I swallowed, feeling a bit foolish. "She just said she was a Keeper. I assumed the Allorian part." I exhaled. "That was stupid of me, especially considering she kidnapped me."

Kairo's voice lowered, his words colored with concern. "She drugged you. Koa is… She's been troubled since our parents died."

I fell silent, and Kairo did too, politely allowing me to piece together the trap his sister set. His sister was troubled. He needed to save me. What exactly did he mean by that? Was she dangerous? Unstable? I wanted to ask, but part of me feared the answer.

I sifted through my hazy memories and remembered waking up briefly while floating through the sky, my face banging heavily against something slick and emerald green. I'd been draped across… something, the ground terrifyingly far below. I'd tried to keep my eyes open, but the drugs must have pulled me under again. As the realization dawned on me, my stomach bottomed out. Had I been on a Dragon? The thought both terrified and fascinated me.

Kairo opened his mouth as if to say more, but before he could, a movement caught my eye. Near the far wall of the cave, something glittered in the moonlight. My hand found my chest as the form of a sleeping midnight-colored Dragon materialized far too close for comfort. I squinted, trying to make sure I was really seeing what I thought I was.

"He doesn't bite," Kairo muttered, echoing our conversation in the diner. "His name is Artok."

I continued to gawk. If Unicorns seemed unreal, seeing this Dragon sprawling across the cave wall was unimaginable. It was one thing to hear about seemingly fictitious creatures, but to see one in the flesh…

Sensing my gaze, the Dragon opened a lazy golden eye, studying me with an intelligence I'd never encountered. I was frozen in place, caught between awe and disbelief. This was the Dragon Kairo had been so desperate to save. And now here I was, sharing a cave with him.

I stood, my knees trembling, and walked toward the magnificent beast. He lifted his chin with a deep sigh that sent warm currents of air and flecks of dust swirling around me. Hesitantly, I touched the top of his gigantic nose, my hand looking impossibly small against its massiveness. The Dragon was a mountain of muscle and scale.

He watched me with old, wise eyes. Within them, flecks of amber and topaz swirled. The scales along his body ranged in size from fingernail to the palm of my hand, creating a breathtaking mosaic. Near his head, they were small and delicate, iridescent in the light, shifting from a deep dark gray to onyx. Further down his neck and body, the scales grew, taking on a burnished black hue that dulled as the spiked scales rose from his body. His expansive leathery wings were folded against his back, the tips meeting where his torso ended.

I ran my fingers over the planes of his face and marveled at the texture. The scales were smooth under my touch, warm and alive. The ridges above his eyes were adorned with elongated scales that added an air of regality to his majestic appearance. To my surprise, the Dragon tilted his head into my palm as if enjoying my touch. The movement caused ripples to flow across its muscular neck, the scales shifting and realigning. A low rumble emanated from deep within its chest, a sound I felt more than heard, resonating through my body like thunder rumbling through clouds.

Standing this close, I could see the subtle variations in its hide. Battle scars were etched into the scales, each mark adding to the Dragon's formidable presence. I stood there, my hand resting on him, feeling insignificant yet incredibly privileged. Here was a creature that had likely seen empires rise and fall, regarding me with curiosity and perhaps even a hint of approval.

I raised a brow and looked at Kairo, who kept watching me intently. The wonder must have been evident on my face, but concern quickly took its place when I remembered why we were here.

"What's wrong with him?"

Kairo's expression darkened. "He has been sick for a long time."

Recalling the entry in the journal about the sickness that spread among them, I nodded in understanding. I rubbed the spot where the scales ran together smoothly around Artok's muzzle, marveling at the contrast between his hard exterior and his surprising gentleness.

The warm, deep exhales felt amazing against my cold skin, like standing before a furnace.

I imagined what it must be like to be the Keeper of such giant, powerful beings. The responsibility must be immense, especially considering the danger if the public ever discovered them. So many people would want to harm them or use them as weapons. Suddenly, I was very grateful my charges were much smaller and could blend in almost effortlessly. Still, as I stroked Artok, I couldn't help but envy the bond Kairo must share with these incredible creatures.

Turning back to Kairo, I knew I had to do something. The Dragon was suffering, and I couldn't help but wonder how a curse could make him so ill, or if ending it would cure them, so Unicorn blood wasn't needed.

"How much more does he need?" I asked, breaking the silence that had settled over the cave. Kairo hesitated, and I could see the uncertainty in the narrowing of his eyes.

"I don't know," he replied.

I slowly nodded and pulled my hand away from Artok, immediately feeling the loss of his warmth. My lips parted, words hovering on the tip of my tongue. I moved back to where I'd been sitting before. The fur that lined the makeshift bed tickled against my exposed skin as I sat cross-legged among them, weighing my response.

"I can get you more."

"That would be helpful," he said, a troubled look crossing his features.

The implications of my proposal lingered between us, but I knew it was the right thing to do. Despite everything, I couldn't bear the thought of Artok suffering if I had the means to help. Though my offer of help was outside my proposed agreement, which meant that I was still without protection. The agreement we'd discussed earlier somehow seemed so far away, and after everything, I wasn't sure if I would ever feel safe on my own again. Oddly enough, the only secure place was here in this cave with Kairo and the Dragons.

"Maybe I should go. I need to check on my…" I didn't finish my sentence because bringing up the herd in the cave, so close to a Dragon, seemed unwise.

Kairo didn't argue my hesitation. Instead, his forehead creased and his shoulders tensed as if he didn't want me to go, but we both knew I was bound by instinct to return to my Unicorns. I needed to be sure they were okay, especially with Kairo's sister out there, angry and potentially willing to do anything to find me or them.

He held out his hand, and I walked to him, pausing momentarily before taking it. The instant we touched, my entire body reacted. The hair on my neck stood up, and my stomach filled with butterflies. I looked up at him and froze at the expression on his face. It was that same emotion that I couldn't place—an intense sort of concentration and indecision, as if he was finding it hard to figure something out and couldn't decide which direction to take. Something was holding him back from fully committing to whatever path he was considering. And that something, I was now sure, was me.

Kairo closed his eyes and let out a long breath, and the tension between us built, thick with conflicting desires. As we stood hand in hand, I became acutely aware of every point of contact. The warmth of Kairo's skin, the strength in his grip, the slight tremor I wasn't sure came from him or me. It was as if the world had narrowed to just this moment, just us, standing on the precipice of something monumental. Yet, the pull of my responsibilities to the Unicorns tugged at me, reminding me of the complications we both faced. And it must have been the same for him because he took a step back and motioned toward the cave's gaping entrance.

"Come on," Kairo said to me, and a smaller Dragon appeared out of nowhere.

I startled, my heart leaping into my throat. This Dragon was much livelier than Artok, swirling around like a flickering flame. Its wings stretched impressively across the cave entrance, and its long, serpentine body reminded me of illustrations I'd seen in ancient mythology books. The larger scales across its back were narrow, reminiscent of an iguana. There was mischief in its eyes as it ducked its head toward me knowingly.

"Tattu, meet the elusive Allorian," Kairo seemed to tease. "He can carry us back to the edge of your town."

Tattu…The name matched the Dragon perfectly. With a slow blink, his clever eyes shifted to me. Kairo helped me onto the flat scales between the Dragon's front legs. His hand on my back made my skin tingle. He signaled for me to move forward, allowing him to climb up behind me. As I unintentionally leaned against him, I could feel every muscle in his chest, and my body responded in ways I wasn't prepared for. I wasn't entirely surprised by my reaction. Kairo was, by far, the most beautiful man I'd ever been this close to.

Tattu prepared to take flight, and the thought of soaring through the night sky on the back of a Dragon was exhilarating and terrifying. It was something straight out of my wildest dreams. Yet here I was, letting the truth of their existence twist into reality like I had with the Unicorns. With Kairo's strong presence behind me, I took a deep breath and let myself feel the weightless ascension as we rose into the star-studded night.

152

Chapter Nineteen

I Agreed

Kairo

Being on the back of a Dragon with Elle passed out had been slightly uncomfortable. But now, with her awake, aware, and squirming in front of me, I grew uncomfortable in an entirely different way. My attempt to wait patiently for her to settle was a miserable failure. I gritted my teeth and scooted back a few inches, desperately needing space between us. If she kept moving, she'd soon understand precisely why. The predicament I'd put myself in was a complication I wasn't ready to deal with. I tried to focus on the wind whipping past us, the rhythmic beat of Tattu's wings, anything to distract me from the intoxicating presence of the woman in front of me.

As soon as Tattu took to the air, Elle scooted forward, much to my relief. She was a natural, adjusting her seat so the ridges of his scales moved with her, not against her. I'd seen many Keepers attempt their first ride, and few could stay as competently with their mount as she did. I wanted to hate her for how naturally it came to her, but instead, I found myself filled with a pure and damned desire I couldn't shake.

When we touched down in the glade by her residence, I steadied her dismount, gently clasping her hand when she lowered herself from Tattu's side to the earth below. We stood there briefly, amazement spreading across her face when Tattu seemed to disappear once we were more than ten feet away. Her stunned expression made my chest feel lighter. It was refreshing to see someone experience the magic of our world for the first time, and I found myself enjoying her wonder more than I probably should. I allowed myself to savor this moment, this connection, before the harsh reality of our situation came crashing back down on us.

"That's amazing," Elle said, her mouth open in wonder. "That's how you keep them a secret."

I nodded. She eyed where Tattu had disappeared, and I waited patiently for her to comprehend what I could barely explain myself. For the first time since meeting her, I fully appreciated how beautiful she was. Her hair cascaded down her back like golden silk, and her oval-shaped face bore high cheekbones framed perfectly by delicate waves. Subtly curved at the edges, her hooded eyes were a mesmerizing blend of honey gold and soft sage green. Her upper lip formed a pronounced Cupid's bow, two peaks rising from the center, contrasting with her full, pillowy bottom lip.

Turning away, a muscle in my jaw clenched, and I fought to control the surge of desire coursing through me. Elle looked over her shoulder at the road behind her, lips parting as if to say goodbye. Clearing my throat, I caught her wrist.

"Elle," I said softly.

"Yes?"

"I'll take the deal," I replied, the words tumbling out before I could second-guess myself.

She ran her lip through her teeth; I wished she wouldn't. How her teeth pulled at the soft flesh of her bottom lip sent a jolt of heat through me, creeping up my neck and warming my face. I ducked my chin, trying to hide the naked need I knew must be evident on my face. I'd just agreed to a deal I wasn't entirely sure about, but all I could think about was how her mouth would feel against mine, how my hand would fit in the curve of her lower back, how smooth her skin must be under the thin fabric covering her stomach. Letting out a breath, I forced myself to focus. This attraction was dangerous and potentially disastrous, but at that moment, it felt like the most natural thing in the world.

Elle jumped forward and wrapped her arms around me, her hands clasping at my back. The unexpected embrace hit me like a sucker punch. Every ounce of air left my lungs in a rush. Her fingers twisted under my flight jacket, and I swore I could feel the heat of her touch through my shirt. I stood there, arms hanging uselessly at my sides, torn between the urge to crush her against me and the need to maintain some semblance of control.

She didn't seem to care about my internal struggle, squeezing me tighter, our hearts pounding in sync. I didn't dare breathe, afraid that if I truly took in her scent—a mix of something sugary and uniquely her—I'd lose what little restraint I had left. The top of her head fit perfectly under my chin, and I fought the urge to bury my face in her hair. It took every ounce of willpower I possessed not to sweep her off her feet right then and there, consequences be damned. This woman was going to be the death of me.

"Thank you," she breathed.

Elle stepped back, her gratitude hanging between us. Realization crossed her face, no doubt reading the raw desire in my expression; she cleared her throat awkwardly. I let out another long, slow breath, rubbing my upper arm in a vain attempt to distract myself from the ache of wanting her. The distance she'd put between us was a canyon, and every instinct in my body screamed at me to close it. I wanted to yank her back into my arms, hold her for dear life, and beg the stars to let us stay that way forever. My fingers itched to explore every curve and plane of her body, to memorize her more thoroughly than anyone ever could or would. Clenching my jaw, I forced myself to respect the boundary she'd just established, no matter how much it pained me.

I cleared my throat. "I should be thanking you. You're saving Artok, which means more than you'll ever know."

Two pinkish spots formed on her cheeks, and she tucked her hands behind her back before asking, "How will we communicate?"

I raised a brow at her question. It hadn't even occurred to me that she might have expected modern methods of staying in touch. My world didn't work like hers. We had our own ways of communicating—slower, perhaps, but far more reliable than trying to find a decent cell signal in the middle of nowhere.

"I'll come to you tomorrow, explain how to reach me, and we will make the deal official."

Elle frowned, then nodded, turning away slowly. She gave me one last look before heading to her house. As she disappeared from view, my shoulders slumped, the tension draining from me like water from a sieve. I was glad to finally know where she lived—how many hours had I spent walking these roads, unknowingly diverted by the spell work protecting her house from me? I might still be searching if it hadn't been for that strange boy knocking on her door and calling out her name.

Knowing the general principles of their wards, this particular manifestation around her house had felt foreign. When the human had unknowingly pointed the way, and I'd stepped across what felt like nothing, the ward had simply given way. Almost too easily. It wasn't how an Allorian defense should yield. A cold shiver had crawled over me, a subtle fraying at the edges of my own certainty, almost like a Dragon's cloaking. But finding Elle was all that mattered then, and the weird anomaly faded at the terrifying thought of what could have happened if I hadn't found her.

When I was sure she wouldn't return, I returned to Tattu, my mind exhausted. I needed to recover Dalya and assess the damage done there. Yet, as my Dragon took to the sky, I couldn't shake the feeling I was leaving something vital behind. I scanned the streets below, catching a glimpse of Elle entering her house, the door swinging shut behind her. A long breath escaped me, the desire for her lingering.

Tattu dipped sharply beneath me, clearly unsettled by the cocktail of hormones I was exuding. The air around us felt thick with it, and my usually composed Dragon told me in no uncertain terms that I needed to get a grip.

Tattu landed at the cave, and I immediately reached out through my bond with Dalya, calling her back. My eyes swept the skies, searching for any sign of her return. Finally, I caught sight of a ripple and relaxed. Chuff wasn't with her. That was one less complication, and I was grateful for it. I didn't want to fight with Koa if she'd lost her Dragon. Caring for my own was challenging enough with the added task of keeping Elle safe.

Dalya landed on the ledge of our cave with a soft thud, shaking out her ivory scales and stretching her heavy body across the dusty ground. Despite her apparent fatigue, an unmistakable air of fulfillment surrounded her. The emotions she unintentionally projected answered my unspoken question—my sister hadn't prevented the Dragons from mating.

Artok will be thrilled, I thought sarcastically, though I wasn't sure he'd even care. He'd sired his share of hatchlings in the past, but this was Dalya's first opportunity. She might have missed her chance if she'd waited for Artok to recover.

Dragon mating wasn't like human coupling—it was often less complex and more deliberate. Usually, the Keepers picked the pairings, though sometimes the Dragons took over and chose independently. Most of the time, the pairing only mattered when it came to their offspring's future. Unless the Dragons were bonded, there were no outside pairings when they already had a bonded mate. Not every Dragon bonded, and it was a rare and beautiful thing when they did—something every Keeper was supposed to respect and protect. The offspring of these pairings often resulted in the best and strongest hatchlings. Chuff and Dalya were excellent matches in size and strength. If their coupling resulted in a clutch, I'd be elated, thrilled even. By the time they hatched, Artok would be well enough for me to enjoy the added responsibility.

Tattu snorted from somewhere in the cave, the sound dismissive and jealous. I chuckled to myself. Though his size and stealth had grown on me lately, I knew he and Dalya weren't compatible. Forcing them to mate would have been like breeding a ferret to a horse—the resulting offspring would be more curiosity than asset. The future of our kind depends on healthy, viable hatchlings from well-paired parents.

Pondering these things, my thoughts were drawn back to Elle. Even with the undeniable pull between us, our worlds were so different, and our breeding was as incompatible as my two Dragons. I was loyal to them, and wanting Elle wasn't part of the agreement. I couldn't afford to let my personal desires cloud my judgment. Our arrangement was all that could exist between us—anything more was forbidden and dangerous.

On the brink of another day, I'd changed my mind yet again.

Chapter Twenty

Are You Going To Let Me In

Elle

Maybe I was dreaming? Maybe that's the reason I felt like I was floating in an endless abyss. My limbs were so light that they didn't seem real. I'd been on the back of a Dragon, not once but twice. It couldn't be real. And Kairo. What was I going to do about Kairo? Why did he make me feel so... alive?

My steps slowed when I entered my house, and I abruptly stopped just inside the doorway—the Unicorns. I needed to check on them. No matter how exhausted I was or how much my body screamed for a hot shower and my bed, I needed to ensure they were okay. With a tired groan, I grabbed the keys off the entryway table and dragged myself to my mom's Jeep.

The drive to the meadow was a blur of yawns and hazy thoughts about Dragons and mysterious, irritatingly handsome Keepers. When I arrived, the sun was starting to rise. I did a quick headcount and made my way to Flint. For some reason, I couldn't bring myself to tell them about my little adventure. Maybe it was pride, or maybe I just didn't want them to think I was incompetent for being kidnapped. Flint sensed something was off, but had the good sense not to push. My relationship with the rest of the herd was still a bit like walking on eggshells, and I felt that if I told Flint anything, it would ripple through the herd quickly.

Clutching my dad's scrub brush, I held it out to Flint. It wasn't exactly a horse brush, but it was the closest thing I could find. Flint eyed it warily at first, but within minutes, he was leaning into it, his eyes half-closed in bliss as I ran it over his coat repeatedly. The others didn't take long to venture over, curious about this new grooming ritual.

Tension among the herd eased with each stroke of the brush. Even Dolfan took a turn, pressing his muscular chest against the bristles while I worked my way down his neck. The only one who didn't approach me was Aire. Leaving him to his own devices, I finished brushing Elska. They all seemed content to graze lazily amongst the clover and timothy grass. Glancing back only once, I stumbled to the Jeep. The drive home was hazy, and I nearly tripped up the steps to my front door.

I fumbled with my keys, the urge to check my phone strong enough that my fingers traced the edge of my pocket. A foggy memory of being in the backseat of my car floated through my mind—the same car I was sure was no longer in the grocery store parking lot. Shoving open the door, I put my hand on the frame. I didn't have a clue where my car was, which also meant no groceries. Fantastic.

Too tired to care about my missing phone or empty stomach, I glanced at the clock above the fireplace. It was six in the morning. I dragged myself to bed and collapsed fully clothed onto the sheets. I tried not to let my thoughts wander to Kairo, but it was a losing battle. He was there, mingled in my exhaustion, a lifeline when I'd desperately needed one. I boxed up the terrifying encounter with his sister, labeling it a problem for another day. Right now, I was too caught up in how Kairo's lip curled when he was deep in thought and those pale blue eyes that seemed to search my face for answers when I didn't speak.

I was lost as to what the rules were in this new universe I'd been thrust into, but a relationship with Kairo wasn't what would break this curse. Pulling off my shoes, I adjusted the blanket and closed my eyes. I definitely shouldn't be lying in bed contemplating everything on the edge of fatigue. Yet there he was in my mind, silhouetted against the night sky in the entrance to his cave, while I lay on what I was sure was an elk hide, watching him. That image was seared into my memory, impossible to shake.

There was a word for hero-worshiping, but as sleep claimed me, I couldn't help but wonder if there was a term for when the intended villain turns into the hero. My last conscious thought was of Kairo's face—concern and something deeper, something that made my heart race even as exhaustion pulled me under, written on it. The complexity of my feelings for him, the danger of our situation, and the utter strangeness of it all blurred together. But as I drifted off, one thing was clear: my life would never be the same again, and Kairo would be a big part of that change, for better or worse.

Someone knocking on the door woke me up. Cracking open a bleary eye, I glared at the clock on my bedside table—nine in the morning. I'd only gotten three hours of sleep. "Go away," I muttered, but I still threw my legs over the side of the bed. It must have gotten hot during the night because my shirt, socks, and pants were strewn across the floor. Feeling exposed, I grabbed the pink, fluffy bathrobe off the back of my bathroom door.

Chase had to be checking in on me or something. Since the last time we'd seen each other, we'd been texting a few times a day—just simple messages and mild conversations about the weather or whatever shows he was binging. With my phone MIA, he was probably worried I had finally snapped and ran off to be admitted somewhere.

Tucking the robe across my waist, I ran a hand through my tangled hair, which at this point resembled a bird's nest. I shuffled to the door and prepared myself to reassure Chase I was still among the living, just phoneless and in desperate need of coffee. But when I swung open the door, there stood Kairo. Not Chase. Kairo. Mr. Tall-Dark-and-Dragon rider himself looked like he'd just stepped off the cover of a magazine.

For a split second, we both froze. I was suddenly acutely aware I was wearing nothing but my undergarments, a very pink robe, and what felt like the world's worst case of bedhead. I blinked and unsuccessfully tried to flatten my hair. Kairo's lips parted in surprise, the corner of his mouth twitching into what might have been amusement if he wasn't trying so hard to look stoic. As his gaze swept over me, I had the sudden urge to check if I'd drooled on my chin or if my robe rebelled against staying properly closed. Because, of course, this is how the universe decided I should greet him—looking like I'd just lost a fight with my pillow and the concept of personal grooming.

"Elle," Kairo breathed, pushing a coffee and a brown bag toward me. Was he really standing on my porch at nine in the morning, bearing caffeinated beverages?

How on earth had he figured out where I lived? More importantly, how did he get through the ward? I blinked up at him, half convinced I was still dreaming. For a second, I was back at my desk, face smashed into my arm and curtains billowing in the breeze. Then I was standing before him, Kairo was indeed holding coffee, and I was still standing before him in my robe.

"How?" I managed to croak out, my voice rough from sleep and confusion.

Given the circumstances, it was the most eloquent response I could muster. What does one say when a Dothian shows up at your door with breakfast? *Thanks for the coffee. Where are your Dragons?*

"Oh," he responded, rocking back on his heels as he stood awkwardly in my doorway. "I went looking for you when you didn't show up to our meeting, and some guy knocked on your door and called your name. I put two and two together."

My mouth went dry. I was right; Kairo had broken the ward.

"Chase," I said, as if his name were a curse word.

"Yes. Are you going to let me in?"

I reluctantly stepped aside, allowing Kairo to gracefully stroll into my house. Closing the door behind him, I reflected on the absurdity of it all. Did he have to be invited inside? Like a Vampire? Is that why he'd asked to be let in? He walked into the living room, and I marveled at how much space he seemed to occupy, as if my house shrank around his presence. Looking over the contents of my living room, I was thankful for my recent cleaning spree. At least he wouldn't see what a mess I was—had been.

He didn't say anything as he perched on the edge of the couch, his gaze drawn to the journals spread across the coffee table under the whirring fan, their covers still damp. The solemn look that crossed his face made me wonder if I should collect them and put them away. He tapped his finger on his cup, his jaw rolling before he looked away. Clutching my coffee cup a little tighter, I suddenly became very aware I was standing in my living room, in my robe, with a man who commanded Dragons. All I could think was, *well, this will be an interesting morning.*

"Uh," I muttered, "sorry for the mess… thanks for the coffee." I peeked into the brown bag, and my stomach rumbled. "And the muffin."

"I thought you might need it," he replied. "I asked the barista if she knew you. She didn't, but one of the other employees did, and she also knew what you liked."

I took out the muffin and took a bite, freshly baked blueberries exploding on my tongue.

"Small towns," I said with a shrug.

"Small towns," he agreed.

Speaking of people who knew of me. "Would you happen to know where my car might be? Your sister sort of put me in the back seat of it."

"No," he said, leaning forward, "but if you tell me what it looks like, I can have Tattu find it."

I gave Kairo a brief description, hoping against hope my phone might still be in the car. With his coffee in one hand, he picked up one of the journals and absently flipped through it as I spoke. He didn't bother to look up from the journal, and my focus drifted to his hands, moving over the pages. Was this his way of trying to come up with a new topic of conversation, or was he avoiding a topic entirely?

"These were my mom's," I blurted out, gesturing to the journals with my half-finished muffin.

"Interesting," Kairo replied, withdrawing his hand from the pages.

"I haven't read them yet," I explained. "I only had access to one before, and the rest got wet."

He nodded, his expression impossible to read. Impossibly blank. I sat in my father's chair, cradling my coffee between my legs with both hands.

"What's the plan for today?"

Kairo's forehead creased, and he replied, "I need to take you somewhere. It'll take a while, and we'll have to take a Dragon. Tattu will be too slow with both of us, so we'll have to take Dalya."

Dalya? My curiosity piqued. Tattu seemed quite large to me—about the size of a school bus, though his tail made him almost twice as long, with his green, slender, lizard-like form and petite, dished head. If Tattu wasn't big enough to carry us both efficiently, Dalya must be massive.

"Take me where?"

Kairo

"I have to take you to the valley… where I live."

The idea worried me. It wasn't that I didn't want to take Elle. It was the risk involved. All the Allorians had dispersed many years ago. Anyone who happened upon us would know she didn't belong, and if I wasn't careful, I could be leading her straight into danger.

Elle was right—we needed a way to communicate and make her deal official. The only way to do that was to return home because the things I needed weren't available in Belview. I waited for her response, doing my best not to focus on the fact that she was barely clothed. When I stumbled upon her wearing a robe, it nearly brought me to my knees. Her bare legs, frizzy hair, and sleepy expression were enough to make me consider swearing off my oath to my Dragons entirely. She looked devastatingly beautiful.

Scolding myself, I attempted to redirect my attention back to our conversation, steering clear of my dangerously wandering thoughts. The last thing I needed was for Elle to catch me staring like some lovesick fool. My focus should be on keeping her safe and fulfilling our deal. But with her sitting there, looking both vulnerable and impossibly alluring, it was becoming increasingly difficult to remember why I'd sworn off romantic entanglements in the first place.

"Is it going to be dangerous?" she questioned, crossing one leg over the other, the robe dipping between her legs.

"Only if someone finds out you're an Allorian. We shouldn't run into anyone we don't need to. Most of the residents of the valley live on the opposite side of my house."

Elle seemed to think it over, her fingers tapping lightly on her coffee cup.

"Are you going to dump that on me like with the ice water in the diner?"

Shaking her head, she squinted her eyes at me. "Remind me why we have to go?"

"This is the only way to make the deal official where I'm from," I responded, resting my hands on my knees. "And it'll give you a way to communicate with me. I doubt there is cell service where I'm staying, and contracts from your world would be unenforceable in mine. We have our own methods."

She didn't falter, as if she was determined to do whatever she must to secure protection, and my offer to make it official was nothing more than a hurdle.

"How long are we going to be gone?"

"It shouldn't take more than two or three days."

She rubbed her thumb on the coffee cup and frowned, pausing for a moment before looking up, her expression resolute.

"Okay," she said quietly.

I stood before the word was entirely out of her mouth, wanting to leave before she could change her mind.

"Good," I stated. "Are you wearing that?"

Elle glanced down at herself, her cheeks flushing a pretty shade of pink. She disappeared, heading upstairs, and I silently berated myself, ducking my face into my hands and rubbing my eyes with my palms. I let out a low grumble of frustration. When I was away from her, logic came easily. But the second she was near, all I could think about was holding her in my arms, her touch pulling all the fragmented pieces of my soul together. It was maddening.

Hearing footsteps on the stairs, I took a deep breath and held it. When she came into view, she looked even more appealing in her skin-tight black leggings, knee-high tan riding boots, and a long, light blue T-shirt than she had in the robe. Her hair was pinned up with a blue clip, a few stray strands framing her face. A black satchel hung loosely over her back.

Damn it all, she was distracting. My mouth went dry, and I clenched my fists to avoid reaching out and tucking that stubborn strand of hair behind her ear. I cleared my throat, holding the door open for her before exhaling slowly. *Get it together*, I told myself. *You're a Dragon Keeper, not some lovesick fool.* But as Elle walked past me and out the door, the vanilla scent of something she'd showered with lingered in the air, and I knew I was fighting a losing battle.

Her trust in me was both remarkable and unsettling. For all she knew, I could be kidnapping her just like my sister had. But here she was, willingly following me to the clearing near her house without a hint of self-preservation. Something about it seemed perversely wrong.

Elle hesitated when we approached Dalya, likely sensing something off ahead. I reached out my hand, and she took it, her mouth pressed into a firm line as if she were pushing her doubts aside. The moment Dalya's cloaking dropped, Elle froze, her mouth gaping open. I couldn't blame her. Dalya was a sight to behold— pearl-white scales glistening in the sun, dorsal spikes lying flat against her back, and long horns curling slightly at the ends.

I took a step forward, tugging Elle's hand. Her fingers gripped mine, and my pulse kicked up a notch. Attuned to my emotions,

Dalya turned her head and let out a hot breath at my inability to keep a tighter lid on them as if I could help my reaction.

I'll do better, I told Dalya.

She shook her head, her scales rattling. Using Dalya's front leg like a ladder, I climbed onto her back and held out my hand to Elle. Grasping it, she pulled herself up to sit before me, her back pressed against my chest. The warmth of her body so close to mine was both exhilarating and maddening. This journey would be a test for every ounce of my self-control.

Without warning, Dalya launched into the sky. Elle tensed in front of me, trying to speak before the wind stole her words. She gave up, pressing her lips tightly shut. When I caged my arms around her, her shoulders stiffened, and her back went ramrod straight. Sensing her discomfort, I loosened my grip. Her fingers splayed across Dalya's flat scales, and it struck me again how new all of this still was for Elle. Dalya was three times Tattu's size, and I'd forgotten how intimidating that could be.

We flew for hours in silence, the landscape blurring beneath us. At one point, Elle tucked herself against me and dozed off, her trust in me and Dalya never more apparent than in her ability to sleep thousands of feet in the air. Tucking my arm around her, I found myself cramping up and shifting uncomfortably several times throughout the journey, unused to riding with another person relying on me to keep them on the back of my Dragon. When we neared our destination, she awoke, stretched, and relaxed her body into mine, riding with an ease that still surprised me. In the distance, I spotted familiar mountain peaks on the horizon. I pointed them out to Elle, signaling the end of our long journey.

"We are almost there," I whispered in her ear.

The old familiar rush of returning home warmed me, and I let out a breath of relief. My valley, protected by nothing but its sheer isolation from civilization, came into view. From above, it looked like nothing more than a long-forgotten ancient town. Its thatched roofs, bleached by the sun and blanketed in moss and time, blended seamlessly into the surrounding landscape. It would appear as little more than a curious relic to anyone flying overhead in a plane, but to me, it was home.

The Dragons mostly kept to the ravines and dense mountainsides surrounding the grassy valley for protection from the elements. The only ways in were to brave the harsh mountain pass on foot or to fly. During our descent, I pondered how Elle would react to the place that was both my sanctuary and my prison—a world so far removed from the one she knew.

Dalya touched down in the heart of our fields, her massive form disturbing the wheat that rippled like a golden sea around us. I surveyed the landscape, taking in the scattered dwellings dotting the valley floor. Some were modest log bungalows, while others were towering structures that seemed to defy gravity.

Tucked at the edge of the valley was my simple-looking log cabin built into the side of a mountain cliff. The outside of it was much simpler than the more ostentatious buildings, but it suited me. I helped Elle dismount and motioned her toward the front door.

"Let's go," I told her, glancing over my shoulder.

I released Dalya and instructed her to stay close. We walked along the edge of the fields, my hand on Elle's back. She took in what was before her the same way she studied me in the diner, with rapt curiosity.

"Why so much wheat?"

"Unicorns love it," I answered, recalling what I'd been told. She tilted her head, but she didn't question me further.

Over the noise of our feet crunching the tall grass, I heard something shift behind us. Pulling Elle behind me, I pivoted toward the sound, thinking it was someone who shouldn't be so close to my cabin. Instead, Nolan stood in the path, long-limbed and wide-mouthed. I relaxed, letting my hand drop from Elle's waist. My cousin's medium-length curly hair was somehow lighter, matching the color of the surrounding wheat fields. His sparkling green eyes held a mischievous glint as they made their slow perusal over us. I took in his familiar features—his elongated face, boxy cheeks, slightly arched nose, and playful, crooked grin that was spread across his face in response to my once-over.

"Nolan," I called, stepping forward and embracing him.

Pulling back, I felt a flush of relief that he was there. What we needed to do would be much easier with a third person. He always had a knack for showing up at the most interesting times. I glanced back at Elle, suddenly very aware of how this unexpected reunion might appear to her. By the tilt of her eyebrow, her thin lips, and the way that she crossed her arms over her chest, I could tell she was already skeptical. It was the first sign of self-preservation I'd seen out of her since the day she'd dumped ice water on my lap.

Chapter Twenty-One

The Way He Looked At Me

Elle

I shrank behind Kairo when he pivoted his back to me. My body was so sore from the long flight that my legs nearly gave out. Catching myself against Kairo's back, I clutched the fabric of his riding jacket, steadying myself, and eyed the stranger wearily.

Something had shifted during our long flight here. At one point, I'd leaned into Kairo and was met with a sense of safety I hadn't felt since my parents hugged me goodbye at college. It was a relief to let go of all my insecurities, even if only for a moment, while we were thousands of feet in the air on the back of a Dragon. I almost didn't release Kairo when I stepped forward to greet the man, fully intending to honor our agreement and let him assume his protective role. Reaching out, I tried to pull him back toward me, a light protest escaping my lips before I could stop it.

But as Kairo moved away, I was alone again. I stood on the path, knock-kneed and exposed. The sense of security I'd briefly enjoyed evaporated, leaving me acutely aware of my vulnerability in this strange place. Kairo embraced the other man, while I fought the urge to step closer, to reclaim the feeling of protection I'd so quickly grown accustomed to.

The blond man looked at me while hugging Kairo. *Nolan.* His gaze flicked to each of the bruises lining my cheek before he raised one eyebrow, his eyes roving up and down my body with all the subtlety of a neon sign. *Great*, I thought, *I've barely been here five minutes, and I'm already on the menu.* I was no stranger to lust. I'd seen how men looked at me and even caught Kairo giving me a few poorly hidden once-overs. But the way Nolan was looking at me? I felt like a mouse in the crosshairs of a feral cat.

"Nolan," Kairo repeated, seemingly oblivious to his cousin's slightly predatory gaze. "This is Elle."

Either Kairo was clueless, or Nolan's behavior wasn't out of the ordinary to him. I swallowed hard, mustering up a small smile so I didn't seem wholly freaked out by the heated look lingering in Nolan's eyes. Beyond the want dripping from him, there was also something else… Recognition? What made him so blatantly bold as to look at me as if he knew every secret I might be holding? He made my eyes twitch.

"Let's go in," Kairo stated, searching the wheat for disturbances.

His words filled me with relief. *Yes, let's.* We filed toward the doorway—Kairo first, me second, and Nolan behind me. I could practically feel his gaze burning holes in my back as I climbed the stairs. Shooting him a frown over my shoulder only resulted in him giving me a crooked, boyish smile. I narrowed my eyes at him. Just because Kairo trusted him didn't mean I would. His deep chuckle hit my ears, and it felt like a challenge.

My foot snagged on the high threshold, sending me lurching forward into what I'd expected to be a modest mountainside cabin. Warm fingers caught my waist, and I jerked away on instinct before catching Kairo's concerned expression. "Sorry," I mumbled, but the word died in my throat when I took in our surroundings.

The rustic cabin exterior had lied. We'd stepped into a cathedral of living stone, where rough-hewn walls stretched up into darkness. Firelight danced across the cave's natural curves, casting long shadows over hand-carved chairs and tables that formed gathering spaces. The scent of wood smoke mingled with something cooking—herbs and meat—drew my eye to an alcove where copper pots hung from iron hooks. A stone staircase spiraled up the cave wall, leading to a second level where ornate doors punctuated the rock face, their wooden surfaces etched with intricate patterns that seemed to shift in the flickering light.

Light spilled through jagged skylights, illuminating the cavern that could swallow my entire house whole. Natural stone pillars stretched from floor to ceiling like ancient sentinels, their surfaces worn smooth. Water sang against rock as it tumbled down the far wall, its silver ribbon catching the dimming light before vanishing through a moss-lined crevice.

My jaw went slack. Dragons could stretch their wings here—no awkward folding or squeezing required. Every surface was carefully crafted with the large beasts in mind—claw marks turned to artful grooves, rough edges smoothed to gentle curves.

"It's…" I said. "Incredible."

Kairo flashed a wide, toothy smile that caught me entirely off guard. I'd never seen him grin like that before—so unabashed and open. The dimples curving into his cheeks were downright lethal. I stared, mesmerized by how his entire face seemed to glow. It wasn't until Nolan cleared his throat behind us that I reluctantly tore my gaze away. Heat crept up my neck, and I realized I'd been caught gawking. Kairo's playful, crooked grin reappeared. *Boys*, I scoffed internally. *They never change.*

"Do you both live here?" I asked, desperate to change the subject.

"I do," Kairo replied. "My parents' estate is on the other side of town, but I rarely stay there. I prefer the seclusion here. Nolan is a nomad. He travels a lot, but when he isn't, he stays here."

"Sometimes I like the quiet," Nolan interjected.

"Did you build this?"

"Yes," Kairo admitted, a hint of pride in his voice. "Over the course of many years."

I swallowed hard. I'd avoided asking Kairo about his age, afraid knowing the truth would make him seem less human. But now, looking at the impressive home he'd built "over many years," I realized that the conversation was inevitable. My two decades on this earth suddenly felt like a blink compared to whatever time Kairo had witnessed. Before I could dwell on it further, Nolan's voice cut through my thoughts. He turned toward his cousin, one brow raised.

"Why'd you return early? I thought you weren't coming back until you found the…"

Nolan froze mid-sentence, and he let out a startled laugh before clapping Kairo on the shoulder.

"You found her," he laughed, his eyes darting between us. "And you led her here…" He paused, searching my face. "No, she came willingly. I honestly didn't think you could do it."

I was going to ask what he meant, but Kairo stiffened beside me, his posture shifting into something somehow regal—shoulders tense, back straight, head held high. He leaned away as if trying to put distance between us, and his sudden change in attitude made my stomach plummet to the soles of my feet. *What's he playing at?* I thought. One minute, we're sharing looks, and the next, he's acting like I'm radioactive. If this was some Dothian mood swing, I was going to need a manual.

"It's not like that," Kairo said firmly, his tone leaving no room for argument.

Nolan's gaze ping-ponged between us, his head tilting like a confused puppy. After a blink and shake of his head, he let out another laugh, taking Kairo's statement as an admission. Then his gaze bore into me with unsettling intensity, making my nose wrinkle as I fought the urge to squirm. Every thought played across his face—from the lift of his brow to the curl of his lip and that glint in his eyes… I could all too easily guess what those thoughts implied.

"Oh… you didn't," he scoffed.

"Nolan," Kairo said sternly, cutting him off. "I didn't. We are here for something serious. I need your help."

Nolan visibly calmed, looking almost relieved as he wiped his palms on his pants. His gaze briefly returned to the lusty hunger from earlier while he assessed me, and I fought the urge to hide behind Kairo again. Beside me, the air shifted, Kairo stepped further away, and my heart skipped a beat—and not in a good way.

It was clear Nolan thought I was a fool for coming here, and for a brief second, he seemed to consider the possibility that Kairo and I might be more than… whatever we were. And Kairo? One minute, he's protective; the next, he's acting like I have the plague. Why? Because of his cousin? Or because of the impact the idea of a relationship between the two of us might have on others like him?

"What kind of help do you need?"

"I need a blood oath," Kairo replied, his tone as casual as if he'd asked for a cup of sugar.

Nolan's head snapped back in surprise. "You," he pointed at Kairo, "need a blood oath?" he questioned, before swiveling his finger to me. "With her? With the Allorian?"

What's a blood oath? Whatever it was, it didn't sound good.

"Yes," Kairo stated flatly. "With the Allori—with Elle."

"With her?"

"Nolan," Kairo reprimanded.

My gaze bounced between the two of them before it landed on Nolan. Something about him pulled at me in a way I couldn't explain. That odd sense of familiarity returned, even if it made no sense given we'd just met. It was strange how easily I could read him, like turning the pages of a half-remembered book. I pushed away the unwelcome thought that maybe his earlier attention hadn't bothered me quite as much as it should have.

Nolan had this air about him, as if life was one big joke, and he was the only one who got the punchline. Kairo seemed like the type to dissect a joke until it lost all humor. I could imagine in a sticky situation, Kairo would be the one you'd hide behind. At the same time, Nolan seemed like the sort to leap headfirst into danger, consequences be damned. Danger like sharing a sanguinary vow with two people I barely knew.

"What's a blood oath?" I blurted.

They both blinked at me as if they'd forgotten I was there. That's great—either I'm being overlooked or looked all over.

"Think of it as a binding contract," Kairo explained, his voice softer now. "It would give us a link to communicate and solidify our agreement."

"It's also the dumbest idea I've ever heard come out of your mouth," Nolan retorted, rolling his eyes dramatically.

"Why?"

"Because he is Dothian, and you are… not Dothian," Nolan stated, raising a brow that conveyed 'obviously'.

"It doesn't matter," Kairo insisted, his jaw set stubbornly. "I have my reasons to protect her, and I will stand by my decision to do so." My shoulders relaxed at his words.

Nolan motioned wildly, his hands moving back and forth like he was conducting an orchestra of confusion. Struggling to find words, he sputtered. The idea of a blood oath settled like a heavy, cold weight in my stomach. I wasn't sure I was ready for such a binding, but I was desperate. And what other choice did I have? At this point, I was half tempted to go through with it just to see what would happen—and to shut Nolan up. Kairo's unwavering gaze finally made him deflate like a punctured balloon. Nolan took a long breath and shook his head as if realizing he was fighting a losing battle.

"Your funeral," Nolan finally muttered.

"What does he mean, your funeral?" I asked. I knew this was serious, but actual death? That wasn't a possibility… was it?

"He's just being cynical," Kairo replied, his tone reassuring, though his eyes never left Nolan.

Nolan pulled a row of vials out of a black pack sitting by the door.

"Are you sure you want to do this? I only have a few left," he said with an odd sort of weary indifference.

Kairo nodded firmly, his lips pressed into a thin line. His expression told me he hadn't come this far to bail on our deal now. My stomach knotted. He wasn't going to let me down; that much was certain. For a second, I replayed the moment he'd stepped away from me. It'd been like he was creating distance, so we didn't come off too close. But watching his determination… Had I read him wrong? His words still echoed in my mind, though: *It's not like that*—as if he didn't want it to be. I wasn't sure if I enjoyed being set aside so easily.

"Okay," Nolan replied, showing us a silvery black vial. "I'll do this under two conditions."

Kairo rolled his eyes. "What conditions?"

"You know the first," Nolan said pointedly. "The second is that I get to come with you."

Chapter Twenty-Two

We Were There

Kairo

I gave Nolan a critical look before motioning for them to follow me into the kitchen.

"Why would you want to come with us?"

My cousin lacked both an unwell Dragon and a plausible reason for targeting an Allorian or their Unicorns. No, Nolan's hidden agenda probably had more to do with the weird glint in his eyes that had appeared the second he laid them on Elle. I tried to quell the unexpected surge of jealousy heating my chest. Nolan was always a flirt, but this was different. He'd never been the type to turn eye contact into foreplay before. It set my teeth on edge.

Nolan smirked, clearly enjoying my discomfort. "I'm bored," he shrugged. "I know I said I like the quiet, but lately, it's been too quiet. I need some excitement in my life. Whatever you've got going on has to be more interesting than sitting around here."

Before I could respond, Elle asked, "What is the first thing?"

Catching Nolan's crooked smile, I couldn't help but roll my eyes. *Again.* Our situation was rapidly descending into complexity. We needed Nolan to complete the blood oath, and I'd come to the valley hoping he'd be here. Hoping that he wasn't off causing trouble somewhere else. Luck was on my side for once. Not that it surprised me much—Nolan was usually in the valley when there wasn't snow on the ground. The alternative would have been to ask someone from town or attempt the blood oath ourselves, which I'd never done before.

"He wants Tattu," I explained to Elle.

"No," Nolan replied, shaking his head with that infuriating grin still plastered on his face. "I just want to borrow Tattu."

Elle's inquisitive gaze settled on me. "Why would he want to borrow Tattu?"

I sighed, running a hand through my hair. "Nolan has a female Dragon named Caleda. The time window of your Sula-umbra will come to a close eventually, which means everyone with a female Dragon is most likely searching for a suitable male before the window closes."

"And those who aren't looking to mate their Dragons," Nolan cut in, "are looking for you."

I shot him a warning glance. The wheels were turning in Elle's head, and I braced myself for the inevitable barrage of questions. Instead, she clamped her lips together, fretting her fingers against her palm. She looked uncertain, perhaps as unsure as I felt.

When we got back, I would have to keep her safe from Koa and any other Dothian who deemed themselves a threat. The potentially more physical nature of my end of the bargain wasn't lost on me as I considered Nolan's demands. Another Dothian to assist in my task of keeping Elle safe wouldn't hurt. Reluctantly, I gave him a short nod of agreement, and his lips twisted in acknowledgment that he'd won an argument we'd never started.

"Why do we need another person to do the blood oath?" Elle asked.

"The third person is the binder. Think of it like a notary in your world."

Nolan laughed, shaking his head while he lined the vials on the counter. "Yeah, something along those lines."

I looked at my cousin with narrowed eyes and motioned for Elle to sit down on one of the dark wooden stools. "The ritual is pretty simple. We'll both make a small cut on our palms, hold them together while Nolan does what he needs. I state my intentions for the deal, you'll state yours."

"Dragon's blood," Elle interjected, staring at the black, silvery liquid.

"Yes, Dragon's blood," Nolan answered. "Bled from a Dragon during an eclipse and some mumbo jumbo like that. It has to come from a dominant male and a bunch of other important things. It's also used in a lot of potions, which is why I'm not too happy about giving it up. There are only seven vials left."

"I've told you, Nolan," I sighed, exasperated. "You cannot waste any more of Artok's blood on aphrodisiacs."

Nolan huffed and uncapped the vial. "You want to do this or not?"

Ignoring him, I took a knife from a drawer and went to Elle at the sizable wood-planked kitchen island. Holding up my palm, I made a cut from my thumb to my wrist, blood gathering quickly as the blade crossed my skin. It dripped down my arm and onto the floor. I held my hand out toward her.

Elle paled, her eyes following the trail of crimson liquid. "It'll sting a little," I told her, because I won't lie.

She turned to Nolan. "Will there be chanting?" she asked, deadpan.

Nolan chuckled and winked at her, his eyes bright with humor. Her ears colored and she leveled him with a blank expression.

"I like her." His eyes met mine before his attention returned to her. "I just have to end the ceremony with a drop of my blood as the person binding the agreement and say a few words. Once. No chanting, promise. Just repeat what Kairo says, but with the terms of your side of the agreement."

Elle's eyebrow quirked up one last time before she extended her hand, palm up. I cupped it in my own and made a small incision in the same spot I had made mine. Her skin was warm and softer than I'd expected. The blade kissed her palm, and she flinched, turning her head away as crimson welled up along the steel's edge.

I squeezed our hands together, aligning the cuts. She didn't wince, but her brow pinched tight. My thumb found hers, tracing small circles while our fingers interlaced. The tension in her shoulders eased, just slightly.

She sucked in a shaky breath, and an overwhelming impulse to shield from her pain dug its claws into me, coupled with a deep appreciation for her attempt at bravery. This wasn't easy, yet here she was, willing to bind herself to me—a Dothian—for her herd's protection.

Nolan eyed the vial sadly before tilting it over our hands. Nothing happened when the first drop of Dragon blood hit our joined palms. I'd expected as much, having done a couple of blood oaths in my youth. But as the second drop fell, the world tilted. The drops danced together into a single ruby bead, and my vision grew hazy. The blood trembled, catching the light before sliding down in an iridescent trail, seeping into our wounds like water into parched earth.

Numbness formed around our joined hands, spreading like ice over water until my entire body turned to stone. The cave walls bled into darkness, fracturing into endless nothing. I squeezed my eyes shut against the vertigo that slammed into me, but the sensations only intensified—my thoughts scattered like leaves in a storm, my breath no longer my own. Lungs filled with frost, my breath hitting the darkness in white wisps.

Elle's essence crashed into me, a wave meeting shore. Her fears, hopes, and memories flooded every corner of my mind until I was thrust into a void, stripped of all that made me… me. I floated, raw and unmade, as something ancient crackled between us, wild and untamed, weaving our souls together with threads of power older than time itself. My veins heated from ice to fire, the burning sensation far beyond any blood oath I'd known. Elle's terror mingled with my own—fear… confusion… anger swirling together in a tempest.

The air crackled with wrongness, sharp and acrid as lightning about to strike, while old stories whispered in my blood—tales of Dragons bound soul to soul, their hearts beating as one until death.

Slowly, I was whole again, my fingers tightening around Elle's, desperately seeking an anchor. Blood slicked our palms, making her hand slip from my grip. I clutched harder, but the void yanked us apart effortlessly. Her figure materialized opposite me, a ghostly beacon in the endless black. We spun—or perhaps the darkness spun around us—in a dizzying dance of shadow and starlight. Silver mist coiled up our arms like living smoke, bridging the space where our hands had been joined. I tracked its hypnotic path.

Elle thrashed against the dark, the fog swallowing her voice. Her fingers clawed at nothing; panic etched in every line of her face. I lunged toward her, but an invisible force snapped me back like a rubber band. Again, I surged forward, muscles straining, only to be wrenched away.

With each failed attempt, my chest grew tighter. Blood dripped from my palm, coiling downward like crimson snakes. It crept over my shoes, thick as tar, rooting me in place. My legs burned where the black substance wound around them, thorny tendrils climbing higher.

A deep, ancient voice circled us—one I'd never heard before. "Cursed Keepers," it whispered, sending chills down my spine, "you have found each other."

The guttural voice reverberated through the air, fading into an eerie silence.

Interesting, another voice said, lighter than the sound of a feather floating.

The swirling mist that enveloped us slowly retreated to wherever it came from. As it crept over her shoes, Elle's hoarse, desperate cries pierced the newfound stillness. My name tore from her throat in a ragged, frantic plea. Unconsciously, I held my breath, my lungs burning against my ribs until, with a gasp, I gulped the crisp, misty air. I lifted my foot slowly, anticipating resistance, but the fog parted like silky, black ink swirling away in ripples.

Elle's glittering eyes found mine, and for a heartbeat, she stood frozen. Then she broke—a dam bursting—and hurled herself across the abyss. She flew toward me, leaving wisps of silver in her wake, her feet barely touching the darkness. Opening my arms to her, I braced myself, and our bodies collided. The impact knocked the breath from my lungs once more, but I didn't care. I embraced her tightly, one hand cradling the back of her head, my fingers tangling in her hair. She trembled against me, her face pressed against my chest, her hot tears soaking through my shirt.

She smelled like lavender and vanilla, and it felt like home, so unlike the otherworldly encounter we'd just shared. The voice's words echoed in my mind: *Cursed Keepers… finally found each other.* What did it mean? And, more importantly, what had we just gotten ourselves into? Would this blood oath bind us together more profoundly than all others? Entwined in the slowly dissipating mist, I realized our lives would forever be changed.

Running my hand over her back, I grazed something warm and sticky. With a jolt of alarm, I realized it was blood—whether hers or mine, I couldn't tell. The crimson stain spread slowly, vivid against the pastel fabric as the illusion shattered. The mist evaporated, and we were back in my sunlit kitchen. The sudden shift was jarring, like plunging into icy water. Elle's eyes were wide, her face flushed when she searched my face. Her fingers trembled slightly against my arm, her expression stunned… disbelieving. With her eyes, she asked, *Did that just happen?*

"I… I think so," I whispered, my voice hoarse. I'd bitten my tongue and could taste the lingering tang of copper. That and the phantom sensation of mist on my skin were the only proof that something extraordinary had occurred.

"Are you going to say it?" Nolan prompted, seemingly oblivious to what had just happened. Elle shot him a look I couldn't fully decipher through the pounding in my head.

"Say wha…" I started, then stopped, realization dawning.

The blood oath.

Steadying myself on the counter, I forced myself to focus to avoid wasting the vial if I said the wrong thing. "I, Kairos Rimeair, Keeper of Dathon Valley and the Dragons Artok, Dalya, and Tattu, here and for the after, agree to protect you from enemies known and unknown until you find our oath fulfilled," I recited, the words heavy and significant.

Nolan touched Elle's arm and nodded to her. She was still staring at me, her eyes like saucers, her shirt covered in blood from the cut on my hand, but she cleared her throat and ran her bottom lip through her teeth.

"I, Ellise Portier…" she repeated. "Keeper of the Unicorns Flint, Nimue, Elska, Dolfan, Aire, Itha, and Ayda, here and for the after, agree to provide the blood of my Unicorns as necessary or until our oath is fulfilled."

I nodded to her encouragingly. A bead of sweat dripped down my back, and I wobbled.

"I, Nollaind Dracotta, Keeper of the Dragon Caleda, hereby bind this oath," Nolan stated, cutting into the thick part of his palm and dripping his blood over our hands.

He grabbed the vile and tipped it up, the last drop of Dragon blood hitting our joined hands. I let Elle go and rocked back on my heels. The finality of what we'd just done hit me like a kick in the ribs. Whatever had just happened, whatever this oath truly meant, we were in it together now. Destiny had found us.

Chapter Twenty-Three

At The Library

Elle

I could feel my heartbeat in every breath I took. *Thud, thud... thud, thud.* It was a battering ram bursting through my skull. My chest burned. I'd trusted Kairo to do what was right, given that he'd agreed to protect me. That trust was the only reason I followed him willingly, flew on his Dragon's back for hours, and let him lead me to this foreign place.

And then, once we'd landed, we were cutting our palms, and there was blood. Real blood—our blood and Dragon blood. Then there was nothing. Nothing but him and the thick mist. There was darkness swirling around us, and Kairo was standing across from me, standing so far away I had to squint to see him. Maybe it was the fact that I was an Allorian. Perhaps the blood oath took us to that place because I wasn't supposed to do it.

I screamed his name out of terror and then watched in horror as he tried to get to me, collapsing to my knees when I saw he couldn't. He was supposed to protect me. Yet, every step he took was sucked back by the mist creeping around us. My screams were swallowed by it; it clung to my limbs like tentacles of despair. I'd heard the gravelly voice and felt Kairo's confusion rip through me. What did it mean? *Cursed Keepers, you have found each other…* like it was some prophecy.

It was all gone in a flash, like some grand fallacy. One second, I was in his arms, and the next, I was standing in his home again, wildly searching Kairo's face. He looked like he was going to be physically ill, and I knew, at least, he'd undergone the same dreamlike trance I had. Kairo's pale, ghostlike expression revealed that he hadn't known any of this would happen, which frightened me. He was supposed to know the things I didn't, so he could warn me about them.

So ensnared by what had happened, I barely recognized that we still needed to complete the oath. Muttering the words I needed to, I waited with bated breath to see if we'd be sucked into the darkness once again. I begged whatever half-nightmare I'd stumbled out of not to drag me back.

After what seemed like seconds but also felt like a lifetime, pain crawled up my fingers, still sticky with blood from the wound on my palm. To my horror, the words we'd spoken curled up my arms in black, silvery Dragon blood. They twirled among themselves until I could barely understand them, before settling along both arms in intricate twists.

The ink burned itself into my flesh like a brand. I flinched, staring at it in fascination, holding my hands before me. It settled into a pattern of vines and flowers around the vow, overlapping and intertwining, ending in a Dragon's eye near the junction of my wrist. The small cut on my palm slowly healed, and the mixture of blood running down my arms was absorbed into my skin, where the tattoo now lay.

"What the…" I heard Nolan say, lifting his left arm to study the ink marking his skin.

His lips parted in confusion. Something had gone wrong—this wasn't part of the oath. Kairo raised a hand in front of his face and frowned at his own set of marks. The patterns were more reminiscent of the swirls of old scrolls, yet they landed at his wrists in the shape of a curved Unicorn horn.

The astonishment etched on his face while he examined the marks confirmed my suspicions. "This isn't supposed to happen?"

Nolan shook his head. "I've only ever had a small black spot until the oath is fulfilled, but nothing like this."

I let out a breath, closing my eyes and squeezing my shaking hands together.

"So, I take it that the darkness and the mist weren't supposed to happen either?"

It was Kairo's turn to shake his head. "It was all… different."

He was just as out of his element as I was. *Wonderful. We're all clueless together. At least we're not alone.* I rubbed at the etched ink on my arms, but it didn't budge. Out of the corner of my eye, I saw Nolan attempting the same. Wetting his thumb with his tongue, he scrubbed fruitlessly at the spirals of silver-black ink wrapped around his forearm. We looked like little kids scrubbing at temporary tattoos.

"What do you mean by darkness and mist?" Nolan asked, doing his best to ignore me, keeping his gaze on his arm while he scrubbed at it.

He was keeping secrets from Kairo, and I wasn't sure where my place was in saying anything, so I didn't. I kept my thoughts to myself and let Kairo briefly explain to his cousin what had happened. He didn't include the part where we'd ended up in each other's arms, but went into detail about the voice and how it felt to hear it. The way he explained it, it all sounded like someone else's nightmare.

"Did something go wrong?"

"I don't know… but I know exactly where we can find out," Nolan replied, shooting a meaningful glance at Kairo, his eyes lighting up with mischief.

Kairo mulled over Nolan's silent suggestion, his brow furrowing.

"We can't go there. It's not safe," he said, his voice edged with caution. He turned toward me, his eyes darting across my face. "Maybe there's something in your journals that could help?"

"Oh, come on!" Nolan exclaimed, throwing his hands up in exasperation. "We could be in and out before we're in any real danger. Where's your sense of adventure?"

A headache formed with each cryptic exchange. "What is he talking about?"

Kairo let out a long breath, running a hand through his hair. "There's a library," he explained, his voice low. "It contains the history of all Keepers. But…" He paused, his gaze holding mine.

"It's guarded by the librarian's Dragon. Nobody has taken a book out of it in a long time. I don't think the librarian has let anyone in since the curse was created. Their job is to protect the books from any and all who attempt to enter. I remember a book in there written about curses and blood oaths, but…" He paused again, shaking his head. "It's too dangerous."

"I can get us in," Nolan said. "There's a back entrance."

"It's not worth it," Kairo stated as if that was the end of the discussion. But I could see the conflict in his eyes—his desire for knowledge warring with his instinct for caution.

"Maybe we can tell the librarian why we want the books?" I offered, hoping to find a middle ground. "Surely whoever it is would understand if we explained our situation?"

Nolan looked at me as if I'd grown a horn smack dab in the middle of my forehead, then laughed like I'd said the funniest thing he'd ever heard. Kairo did his best to hold his composure until he could no longer. He, too, laughed—not as hard as Nolan, but enough that it made me stand up and cross my arms over my chest.

"I'm sorry. You guys are just full of great ideas," I stated, my voice dripping with sarcasm. "So far, I've been jetted to some empty dimension where a weird ghostly voice is telling me I might be part of some prophecy, and now I have these on me," I gestured to my arm, "like I'm a biker's girlfriend who drinks in a dive bar on Saturday nights. My face is covered in bruises from being kidnapped by your sister and thrown over her Dragon. My thighs are never going to recover from the umpteen hours I spent getting here, and to top it off, I have left my Unicorns completely defenseless while I've been gone."

Nolan's mouth dropped open when I mentioned Koa, but Kairo's mouth snapped shut. His eyebrows shot up, and he raised his hands in a sign of surrender. My breath hitched as I worked to calm myself. It was wrong of me to get so heated, but damned if it didn't feel good to let it out. Maybe Kairo didn't realize how much I'd been affected by what happened and needed to see it.

"Do you want to try the library?" he asked me, his voice cautious.

"As a matter of fact," I took a deep breath, "I do."

Chapter Twenty-Four

What Was Her Idea

Kairo

Nolan let out a grunt as he pushed a large log out of the way of the narrow entrance. The opening led to the center of the easternmost mountain, one of the peaks that made up the pass into the valley—the very mountain that housed the expansive library we were attempting to enter.

After we'd gotten some rest, we'd flown the short distance across the valley on Dalya and Caleda, with Elle tucked in front of me. She'd remained stiff and silent, her back straight against my chest. Tension had radiated off her. Her only words to me were ones of concern for her Unicorns. I'd done my best to reassure her. The wards over their location should prevent anyone from finding them.

I didn't mention that, despite my multiple attempts, I'd failed to breach those same wards. That particular detail wouldn't ease her worries since I'd managed to find where she lived despite the protections surrounding her home.

With that in mind, I sent Tattu to watch Elle's house without her prompting. However, speaking with my Dragon over such a long distance had nearly cost me all of my energy. Yet, the lazy Dragon, woken from his nap by the request, had reluctantly headed off to ensure no one went snooping. I was sure I'd get a full report if someone did—if only because I'd woken him.

Irritated I'd been talked into this, I let Nolan clear the entrance with Elle's help, only offering assistance when someone handed me a branch or stone. The truth was, I wanted answers just as much as Elle did. Still, I wanted to do it the smart way, not the reckless way that involved charging into a situation blindly, with severe injury as a possible side effect… which they'd chosen for me. My expertise in Dragons stemmed from generations of knowledge, with my ancestors having raised them for hundreds of years. Storming into the lair of a strange Dragon seemed like a great way to die. Nolan's boldness surprised me. I'd expected some level of caution from him, given that he, too, knew what Dragons were capable of.

"This is a ridiculous idea," I stated flatly when Nolan removed the last branch from the entrance.

"Do you have a better one?" Elle inquired.

"Don't ask him that," Nolan interrupted.

I glared at them both. Nolan shrugged with a crooked grin and squeezed through the entrance into the mountainside. Elle hesitated, holding onto the rocky ledge as she waited to see if Nolan made it through safely. She glanced back at me with a slight pout on her lips, her eyes searching my face. I could see it in her expressions. She wanted me to go in before her, ensuring I followed through with their plan by following them into the dank, narrow hole leading into the library.

"After you."

"Fine," Elle replied, tilting her head. "But if I get hurt, doesn't that mean your blood oath has been broken?"

I paused and considered her response. She was annoyingly correct. If Nolan's stupid idea got her injured, our blood oath would not be considered fulfilled, and this oath was unlike any I'd witnessed before. The uncertainty of its consequences should I fail made me hesitate. I had no desire to uncover the potential repercussions firsthand, so I had to go along with them.

"I promise, I'll be right behind you," I told her, motioning her forward.

Elle shot me a look before dipping her chin once with a clipped nod before she climbed into the cave. I ducked through the rocky opening after her. Rubbing my hands over my shirt to remove the moss and rock ash that coated them, I came through the other side of the tunnel. The air shifted as I straightened to take in what was around me. We were indeed in the very back of the library.

A powerful ancient magic protected the tall stacks of books no one could access anymore, keeping them neatly arranged and pristine in the countless alcoves carved directly into the living rock. The shelves were intricately woven into the mountainside, following the path of a massive spiral staircase that wound its way around the hollow heart of the mountain.

The steps disappeared into the shadows above, growing darker with each level where scholars once gathered to read and study. At intervals along the stone walls, narrow skylights had been carved—slender enough to deny entry to Dragons, yet wide enough to allow for a snout or claw. These openings allowed rays of light to filter into the cave, creating a mesmerizing play of light and shadow across the weathered stone steps and ancient tomes.

The faded recollections of the library from my childhood were nothing more than the fine dust swirling in the air around me. Only a hazy memory remained—an image of children and adults scattered across the various levels, reading and pursuing their studies in the naturally formed nooks and alcoves.

Elle looked up into the vastness where the spiral staircase disappeared, her mouth forming a perfect O. She turned to say something to me, and I held a finger to my lips. We were standing on one of the higher ledges that ringed the library's interior like the layers of a colossal cake. I pointed downward, past the intricate maze of staircases and stacks of books. A large golden Dragon lay below us, at the base of the cave, soundly sleeping as its scales glittered from the sun's rays that streamed down from the skylights. Even with his nose and tail tucked against himself, his immense size took up nearly the entire floor space.

Elle's eyes widened in understanding, and she nodded. I gave the Dragon a cursory glance over the balustrade before motioning them to follow me. Despite my reservations about this plan, I somehow knew exactly where to find the books we should look through as soon as we entered the library. As if I were drawn to it. Carefully, I led the way, weaving through the precarious stacks of books scattered across every flat surface.

Skimming over the spines of a group of books near a large bookcase, I took in their covers. I'd never heard of their titles before. Titles such as Ethereal Steeds of Horns and Wings, Starlight Steed, and The Compendium of the Ferrein featured tiny emblems of horned and winged beasts along the spines. Ferrein? Still puzzling over these unheard-of creatures, a warm breeze caught my hair when I rounded the corner. My arm itched, my body went rigid, and without thinking, I reached back and yanked Elle in front of me, my hand fisting in her shirt. Nolan looked up before I could and cursed under his breath. The Dragon was on the move, its massive head snaking through the labyrinth of books, searching for us.

"Did one of you touch a book?" Nolan whispered, his eyes wide with alarm.

I shook my head firmly. The rules of this place had been ingrained into my very bones. But when I glanced at Elle, I saw the dawning realization in her eyes.

"I turned one so that it wouldn't get knocked from its stack," she admitted, her voice small.

Nolan silently smacked his forehead, his eyes rolling with dramatic flair.

"In her defense," I whispered, surprising myself with the urge to shield Elle from blame, "we didn't tell her not to touch them."

Just as I finished speaking, it felt like flames blared through the blood oath marks on my arm. The Dragon had found us. I could sense its massive form looming behind me, hear its slow, deliberate inhale. A deep rumble resonated from its throat. Through the corner of my eye, I caught a glimpse of razor-sharp teeth lining its cavernous maw. My mind raced, assessing our options. About twenty feet and ten steps to our goal. Sixty feet back to the gap we'd come through. Neither distance was close enough.

What an absolutely ridiculous idea this was.

I didn't dare look back. I didn't need to. I could sense the Dragon's every movement as it rose on its hind legs, a living mountain of scales and muscle. The sound of its tail whipping through the air in agitation made my blood run cold. It snaked its golden head toward us, and I could feel its breath growing hotter against the back of my neck. Time slowed. My pulse roared like thunder, drowning out everything but the Dragon's rumbling growl.

Elle didn't know how to defend herself…

"Run!" I hissed, my voice filled with the panic that crawled up my throat.

As one, we burst into motion, the Dragon's roar of fury shaking the mountain around us. Its immense scales scraped against the ancient stone as it moved. We weaved through the library's maze-like structure, the shelves of ancient books towering over us. One misstep, one moment of hesitation, and we'd be nothing but ash and memory.

I grabbed Elle's hand, pulling her past Nolan. The Dragon struck, its spiked tail catching him and lifting him off the ground with a grunt. He sailed through the air, landing with a sickening thud on the next level, about five feet from the entrance to the nook I was aiming for. The impact echoed through the chamber, reverberating off the stone walls. Elle's fingers tightened around mine, and we both stared in horror at Nolan's motionless form. The Dragon's attention snapped to us, its eyes glowing with anger. Its nostrils flared as it scented the air. Behind it, Nolan slowly stirred, and I let out a breath of relief.

"Move!" I shouted at Nolan, motioning toward the alcove. He propped himself on one arm, his face flushed with shock.

The Dragon rumbled, shaking its head at the echo of my command. His home had been silent, and we'd interrupted it with noise and activity.

I took off again, pulling Elle with me. But the distraction of Nolan being thrown across the library had cost me, and her hand slipped from mine. Sliding to a stop, I spun around and watched in horror as the Dragon caught Elle's shirt in its teeth. Effortlessly, it sent her flying, her figure silhouetted against the sunrays like a bird thrown off course by a gust of wind. Her piercing scream drowned out the sound of ripping fabric. The noise caused the Dragon to whirl away, flames puffing from its mouth. Elle soared over me. Tracking her movement, I calculated her trajectory and sprinted backward, eyes locked on her falling form.

She struck me, her limbs splaying wildly. The impact knocked the wind from my lungs and sent us both rocketing to the ground. When we slammed into the mountain wall, pain exploded through me, but I clung to Elle, refusing to let go. We crumpled to the ground, my arms around her waist. The world spun, and for a moment all I could focus on was the weight of Elle in my arms and the thundering of our hearts. She was okay, sucking air into her lungs in great gulps.

"You're okay," I confirmed, setting her on her feet. "Run toward Nolan. I'll be right behind you."

We took off. The Dragon's wings stretched the entire length of the library. Its scorching breath licked at my neck, spurring us faster up the worn stone steps. The sound of the Dragon's thunderous roars vibrated off the ancient walls, shards of rock tumbling down around us. My desperation manifested in a flurry, shoving Elle forward through the arched entry with unintended force. She stumbled into the space, narrowly avoiding a collision with Nolan.

The Dragon's snout slammed against the nook's opening, a gust of sulfurous air blasting past us, causing us to scramble further into the alcove. We tumbled in an ungraceful heap of limbs and ragged breathing. I disentangled myself, catching sight of Nolan. He stood apart from us, observing our undignified sprawl with an infuriating smirk. Blood ran down his hairline, yet he seemed entirely unfazed.

"I could punch you right now," I told him, standing up and extending my hand to Elle.

The Dragon lunged toward us, but even its nostrils were too large for the arched doorway.

"Get the books," I demanded, pointing toward a row of them separated on a shelf. Nolan ran a finger over each spine, reading the titles aloud, their old leather-backed covers beautifully preserved.

The sound of Caleda's scattered chortles echoed through the space. The library's Dragon suddenly stopped trying to get in. It stretched onto its hind legs, and I could make out the darker golden scales of its belly. I poked my head through the opening to find it looking up, as if enthralled by something. Curiosity warred with caution as I risked a further glance outside.

What I saw made me pause for only a moment. The golden Dragon was fixated on something above it, its earlier aggression gone. Returning to the task at hand, I joined Nolan in his search through the book titles. The immediate threat had passed, allowing a small measure of relief.

"Dalya and Caleda are trying to get in," I said.

"Why would they do that?" Elle questioned.

"She doesn't know that Dragons can feel their Keepers' emotions?" Nolan asked, offering me a book.

I couldn't remember if I had told her about the emotional connection between Dragons and Keepers, so I shrugged. Our relationship was still so new, too new for the chaos we were creating.

Taking the book he held, I motioned us all toward the doorway. Caleda and Dalya's snouts and claws poked through the small skylight-like openings far above us. The library's Dragon stared up at them in rapt fascination. There was a palpable loneliness rippling off it, like it didn't want to be held prisoner anymore, and to it, that feeling was more important than our haphazard escape.

Placing my hand on Elle's lower back, we quietly retraced our steps. Miraculously, the Dragon had not tipped over a single book in its bid to rid the library of its intruders. Our progress was only halted by the stones and debris littering the narrow aisle, crowded by the tall stacks of books. We stepped carefully and quietly through the path, only glancing the Dragon's way if necessary.

Elle

Kairo's hand sprawled across my lower back, urging me through the stacks of books I dared not touch. Feeling guilty for causing such chaos by moving a single book, I tucked my arms in front of me, clasping my hands so I could carefully squeeze through. Despite the unsettling feeling that I should know this place, I was out of my element—all over one book.

Behind us, I could hear the library's gigantic Dragon calling hopefully to Caleda and Dalya. Its low rumble rattled the dust and pebbles lining our path. Kairo wrapped his arm around my waist. Silently, he signaled for me to take the lead when the path narrowed, his hand brushing through the air. When we neared our makeshift entrance, where the tunnel widened, I spotted a mysterious figure leaning against the moss-covered stone wall, barely illuminated by the dimming sunlight. I halted abruptly, causing Nolan and Kairo to stumble into me. At first, it looked like it was just a trick of the shadows, but then the figure shifted, moving its arm away from its body. A gasp escaped my lips, and the boys came to stand beside me, their expressions mirroring my apprehension. We all froze in place, an eerie silence enveloping us as we tried to make sense of the unexpected presence in the darkness.

"What do we have here?" the figure drawled, the voice neither feminine nor masculine. "Kairo, the Keeper of Dothan Valley, and Nolan, the rogue of Tobain, with a friend."

We stood stock-still, barely breathing. Something about this being felt off. As it approached, its hunched form slowly straightened, and the shadows shifted to reveal its attire. The cloak was dusty and tattered, the bottom covered in caked mud. It pulled back its hood, and my breath caught as the figure became a woman. Long silver hair draped over one shoulder in an intricate braid, and deep brown eyes fixed us with a hard, humorless stare. She looked so familiar.

Every step she took seemed deliberate, her boots leaving imprints on the dirt-covered earth. She was all angles and sharp edges, bony but far from frail. A strange glow danced around her silhouette, adding to her bizarre appearance.

"Who is your new friend?" she asked pointedly, her gaze boring into me.

When no one answered, her nose flared, and her upper lip curled in displeasure. She made me wish we were still facing the Dragon.

"Who is she?" the woman asked again, her bony finger jabbing toward Kairo.

"She is an Allorian," Kairo replied hastily, as if the choice for truth wasn't his. My heart skipped a beat.

The woman froze, her accusing finger still aimed at Kairo. Slowly, she processed his words. I could almost see the gears turning behind her piercing, red-rimmed eyes. Kairo pulled me behind him, his body tensing like a coiled spring. She approached us, her head tilting to one side, reminding me of a bird of prey searching for its next meal.

Her gaze suddenly locked onto the book in Nolan's hands, and I saw a flash of something dangerous in her expression. But it was her reaction to the ink sprawled on our arms that truly set my nerves on edge. Her eyebrows shot up in surprise, and the atmosphere around us became palpably tense, as if the air had suddenly grown heavy and oppressive. The woman's attention darted briefly to Nolan before settling back on me. Her gaze was so calculated it was like she could see right through me, past all my secrets and lies. When her lips parted, the sound that emerged gave me goosebumps—not quite a witch's cackle but so close I couldn't help but wince.

"An Allorian," the woman stated, her eyes still boring into me. "A Portier bound by a blood oath to the King of Dothan."

King?

"So, it is true. I felt the shift, and here you are." She dodged Kairo with predatory grace and placed a cold hand on my arm. Her gaze turned even more penetrating, stripping away my defenses and laying bare my core. I had no choice but to blink and look away, exposed and vulnerable from her touch. *I definitely know you... But how?*

"You'll bring the book back, won't you?" she questioned.

Kairo nodded. "I'll bring the book back."

The woman looked us over once more, shaking her head at Nolan before moving aside. "Next time, use the front entrance," she stated flatly, "and don't disrupt Volski's slumber."

I shot both of the boys a look. We could have come through the front door if they had just listened instead of laughing at me. Kairo gently gripped my elbow, guiding me through the narrow passageway we'd come in. We emerged from the library into a husky, fog-laced evening.

The Dragons spotted us and bound over, their eagerness at odds with my exhaustion. I sank onto a rocky ledge, every muscle protesting the movement. Reeling from the multitude of shocking truths and near-fatal moments, my grip on everything slipped further. Kairo and Nolan's quiet conversation, punctuated by the soft coos of their agitated Dragons, barely registered. Absently, I rubbed the tender spot on my leg where I'd collided with Kairo.

"King?" I muttered, the words slipping out.

The conversation between Kairo and Nolan paused.

"Semantics," Nolan stated, as if that explained everything.

Kairo elaborated, "My family is one of the oldest remaining Dragon Keepers. My mother traces back to the original Dothian."

"Dothian," I repeated, sitting up straight. "Like Dothan Valley?"

Kairo nodded in the way he does when he should verbally state his agreement but refuses to—all curt and short. I studied him momentarily, as he petted Dalya's nose. *Of course, he was a King. Why not add that to the growing list of impossibilities that had become my life? A couple of weeks ago, my biggest concern was a stack of papers. Now, I was sitting next to royalty.*

"Don't get too starstruck," Nolan smirked. "If I'm correct, Kairo might be a King, but you are a Queen in yours."

"What are you talking about?" I asked, my heart racing at the implication. I realized I'd missed most of their conversation, too caught up in my thoughts to pay them any mind.

Kairo's lips pursed, and he flipped the book open to the back cover, turning it toward me. On the last page was a lineage map. My eyes widened when I saw my name listed in black ink, right under my mother's, grandmother's, and so on, until it reached a notation at the top: *Alis Portier, The Original Keeper, The First Allorian.*

I stared at the page. *Queen? Me?* This was a mistake. I grabbed it, holding it closer and observing how the ink was fresher where the words *Ellise Portier* were scrawled. *Why was my name on this, and who wrote it?*

Chapter Twenty-Five

What Did It All Mean?

"I'm sorry, but this can't be right," I whispered, my voice shaking. "I'm just… me. Not a…not a Queen. This is insane."

Something strange stirred in my soul, as if awakening. I traced back to the original Allorian. Looking away from my lineage at Kairo and Nolan, I searched their faces for any sign this was all an elaborate joke. Their grave expressions told me otherwise, and it was a deeply unsettling yet oddly thrilling sensation to unravel the mystery of who I'm supposed to be.

"Wouldn't most Keepers trace back to the Originals?" I asked, likening it to Adam and Eve.

Kairo and Nolan shook their heads in unison.

"Centuries ago, Dragons and Unicorns were common. It was like owning a snake or a turtle," Nolan explained. "Some people kept them, and others didn't, but humans, Keepers, Dragons… we all lived together." He flicked something off his chest and straightened. "Some of our bloodlines are muddled, and some Keepers barely go back three or four generations. Other lines died out entirely. Today, Keepers, in general, are rare. Keepers that trace back to the Originals… honestly, at this point, it's probably Koa, Kairo, and you."

"Wouldn't my bloodline be muddled because my dad isn't a Keeper?"

"He doesn't have to be a Keeper if you are an Allorian," Kairo said. "Unicorn Keepers are all female. The males are," He paused, lips quirking. "Decorative. Have you ever heard of The Virgin and the Unicorn? There's some truth to that."

"No, I haven't heard of it," I admitted.

Nolan scoffed as if I most assuredly should know of the legend and held his hand up to Kairo, signaling him to continue. I held back the urge to give him a vulgar gesture because, for some reason, he was starting to grow on me.

"According to legend," Kairo explained, "the Unicorn was a powerful and elusive creature that could only be captured by a virgin maiden. The story goes that a Unicorn would be naturally drawn to a maiden and would become docile for her. This made the creature vulnerable to hunters who would use the virgin as bait to trap or kill the Unicorn." He leaned forward slightly. "The legends are loosely based on Allorians. Some parts differ in the retellings, but there is some truth to most of them."

His story, while interesting, only succeeded in bringing me back to our earlier conversation. "If you two are cousins, then why doesn't Nolan trace back to the same Dothians you do?"

"Nolan is my cousin through what you would consider marriage," Kairo explained. "His mother was pregnant with him when she met my uncle." He paused and looked away, the tips of his ears coloring before he spoke again. "Best guess is his real father is a Dothian, which explains how he can keep a Dragon. Humans without the right bloodlines cannot. Keepers have tried to pass their Dragons on to them, and it's failed every single time I'm aware of."

The flood of information made me realize I'd barely slept since we landed in Dothan Valley. Kairo had shown me to a spare room the night before and made sure I was comfortable, but I'd been restless all night trying to figure out how the blood oath worked while I picked futilely at the inky dark spirals on my arm. I'd woken before both of them, long before we left for the library in the mountains.

Too tired to piece the puzzle together, my eyelids grew heavy. Not the same tired as before, like when thoughts of my parents left me on the brink of despair—just… tired. Whatever Nolan and Kairo were discussing began to blur, and my knees began to buckle. Something hit my back, and I turned to find Dalya gently propping me up so I wouldn't fall. Snaking her head past me, she gave Kairo a look that clearly told him where she'd shove her horns if she could.

"I should get you home," Kairo said, interrupting what Nolan was saying. I could see the concern in his eyes, as well as the touch of fear at Dalya's threatening look.

"Your home?" I asked.

"No, yours," Kairo replied, walking to me.

Nolan stepped in to help, and despite his proximity, I didn't fuss as they lifted me onto the back of the Dragon. Kairo settled behind me, and I leaned back into him out of sheer necessity. He adjusted me so we were both comfortably sitting on the flat, broad scales between Dalya's shoulders before placing his arms on either side of me, caging me between them.

"Is Nolan coming?"

"He has some things to settle," Kairo replied, his breath warm against my ear. "He'll catch up with us. Caleda is faster than Dalya."

As I began to drift off, a nagging thought wormed its way through my fatigue. I was inviting not one, but two Dragon Keepers back to my territory despite the warnings in my journals. A part of me considered leaving them here and finding my own way back, but I realized I didn't know where here was. I'd have to trust that Kairo had sworn to protect me, and Nolan had sworn to uphold Kairo's oath. Besides, if the Dothians and Allorians were once close, perhaps some of that trust could be rebuilt. Having two Dragon Keepers and their four Dragons seemed like a good idea if other Dothians were around, searching for me—especially because Koa was probably still in the area.

My insides knotted at the thought of Koa. I hoped my Unicorns were safe in their meadow. Kairo assured me they would be, but being away from them for so long felt fundamentally wrong. I needed to check on them, to see with my own eyes that they were unharmed. What would it feel like if something happened to one of them? With a slow shake of my head, I dismissed the thought, unable to bear it.

Dalya swiftly took off into the sky, heading in the direction we'd come. The motion of her flight soothed me almost immediately, and my thoughts dulled as soon as she leveled out. The rhythmic beat of her wings and the warmth of Kairo's body behind me created a cocoon of safety I hadn't realized I needed. I tried to keep my eyes open for a bit longer… but…

"Goodnight, Ellise Portier," Kairo whispered, his voice barely audible over the wind.

Kairo

Nolan caught up with us a few hours into our travels, Caleda showing no signs of weariness as she kept pace with Dalya. Her amber-colored scales glistened in the bright moonlight. Dalya flattened her body, doing her best to keep pace with her, but she wasn't built for speed. With Elle nestled against me, I wasn't willing to race, but Dalya was too stubborn to realize she couldn't win. Pushing her urge to compete out of my head, I sent a firm mental nudge down the bond. Elle didn't need the jostling. The chase died down with a reluctant grumble from Dalya.

I adjusted Elle, tucking her head against my chest, her shirt slipping off her shoulder. Brushing her hair from her face, I marveled at its silken texture. Every instinct screamed at me to look away and forget what I'd been fighting tooth and nail for days. But the events swirling in our wake shattered any pretense of control over how I felt about her. We were in this together, deeper than either of us had imagined. The depth of my feelings for Elle, which I'd fought so desperately to deny, consumed me entirely.

I was hers…

Swallowing the lump in my throat, I held her tightly, my shoulders tensing as I ran my thumb over the yellowing bruises on her cheek. The softness was such a contrast to my rough skin. I brushed the back of my hand across her jawline, her warmth melting away my last shred of resistance. I wouldn't fight this anymore. She was too… Delicate. That was the word repeating in my mind as Elle slept against me. Delicate. Lost in her dreams, she remained blissfully unaware of the shift in our relationship, a change that both exhilarated and terrified me. Her weight in my arms was oddly comforting, a sense of belonging I hadn't realized I craved. But with that comfort came a fierce possessiveness, and I knew then I would shield her from the dangers that lay ahead, with or without the blood oath.

She was so perfect, molded against me. The soft rhythm of her breathing was peaceful, and I was mesmerized by the beauty of her vulnerability in slumber. Her collarbone peeked out from under the rumpled shirt. Damn it. My hand twitched, and before I could think better of it, my thumb grazed the exposed skin, sending a ripple of fine bumps erupting in its wake. She stirred, those gold-flecked eyes of hers fluttering open. Sleep-heavy, they locked onto mine, a flicker of something heated lingering beneath her hooded lids. Swallowing a curse, I leaned away from her.

Her hand, slow and deliberate, reached for mine, pulling it to her face in silent invitation. I glanced up—Caleda was a distant speck against the graying cotton-candy clouds. Nolan wouldn't see a damn thing even if he tried. Not that I cared if he could. I didn't care at all anymore; my earlier bluff at making it seem like there was nothing between us dissipated. When her eyes met mine, her lips parted, and I ran my thumb across her cheek again. I hesitated, but there was no hesitation on her end.

Brazenly, she hauled herself up, closing the distance between us. Her fingers gripped my shirt, pulling me closer, and the blush creeping up her neck mirrored the heat blooming in my chest. When it came, the kiss was slow and deliberate, a fire ignited under the surface. Her hand found purchase in my hair, twisting it around her finger. My thumb drifted to her chin, tilting it up, the pad tracing a line along her bottom lip. It parted under the pressure, and the kiss deepened.

A sharp buck from Dalya almost sent us sprawling. I tightened my grip around Elle, breaking the kiss with a groan that rumbled from somewhere deep. My chuckle was laced with a touch of annoyance. We'd gotten a little carried away, and Dalya wasn't having it. Being up this high, with the ground a dizzying blur of greens, meant respecting her boundaries.

Elle's cheeks flushed crimson, and she settled back down, a mumbled apology escaping her lips. I shrugged. What we'd done wasn't exactly unprecedented. Still, every Dragon had its limits. Maybe Dalya was just picking up on the raw energy crackling between us, or perhaps she knew what giving in to my poorly hidden intentions meant. Either way, she didn't need my emotions bursting through her while navigating the skies. Fair enough. It could wait… for now.

Elle sat quietly for a long while before drifting back to sleep. This time, I let her lean against my chest with one arm wrapped around her, the steady rhythm of her breathing syncing with my own. There were several moments when waking her was tempting. If she were awake, I could ignore the tiredness attempting to overtake my senses. The last few days have taken their toll, especially maintaining the long-distance connection with Tattu. The damn Dragon wouldn't shut up, bombarding me with useless updates: *House secure. Artok recovering. Bring fish.*

It was a good thing I was easily distracted from my exhaustion by the kiss and the way Elle felt in my arms. It was also a good thing I had time to reflect on what had happened back home. Though it all had an unreal quality, like a hazy dream I'd witnessed rather than participated in. She'd been so brave, strong, and effortlessly patient. I ran a hand through my hair, thinking about how she'd looked at me for answers, and I hadn't been able to give them.

Hell, I didn't deserve her. Her kindness, trust, and modern innocence—she wouldn't mesh with my life. Yet, the mere thought of her absence left me with an uncharacteristic hollowness, as if she was always meant to be with me, a missing piece finally slotted into place. She stirred something inside me, a forgotten part of my soul I couldn't grasp. This was falling, and it scared the hell out of me.

Lost in thought, the journey became hazy, and my energy reserves nearly depleted. Thankfully, we landed shortly after my limbs went numb. Unable to help her down, I told Nolan about my predicament. He eagerly assisted. Elle tumbled into his waiting arms, wrapping hers around his neck with a sleepy sigh. Stilling for a beat, he shot me a sly grin and adjusted his grip on her. The smug bastard. He was lucky. Carrying her was child's play for him, while every fiber of my being ached with lack of sleep.

We made it to her house quickly enough and climbed the stairs. I pulled open the unlocked door with a frown, reminding myself to tell her to be more careful. But for now, Nolan still gladly carried her, and she needed her rest. And I needed her out of his arms. I found her room and took her from him, gently placing her in bed.

A part of me wanted to stay to ensure she woke up all right. But my Dragons needed tending, and I knew she'd be desperate to see her Unicorns. With a final, lingering glance, I stepped away and returned to my Dragons.

Chapter Twenty-Six

Doubtful

Kairo...

I'd woken up disoriented, wobbly, and numb. Making my way to the bathroom, I stripped off my clothes and started the shower. It wasn't until I was under the stream of warm water that I remembered the marks lining my arms. Gazing down at them, I grew frustrated that Kairo hadn't left me with a way to reach him, despite his promise that returning to his home would provide a way. Was there a good reason for disappearing without telling me how to contact him, or was it just another one of his enigmatic quirks? He'd kissed me thousands of feet in the air, and I'd soaked him in the way the sun touches the earth. I'd wanted more. I'd never wanted more. There was something about how he'd made me feel that kept pulling me in. Not like a half-person just trying to survive, but like I was whole again.

Reluctantly, I went through the start of my day of dressing, eating, and putting the journals away so they weren't scattered across the living room. Afterward, I drove to the field, and the entire herd met me in the meadow as if they knew I was coming. I wasn't sure why I was surprised—they probably heard my loud, untethered thoughts the minute I pulled through the ward.

I doubted they'd stood at the edge of the meadow, near the dirt lane, the entire time I'd been gone, waiting for me. A pit formed in my stomach at the thought. I shouldn't have left without letting them know what was happening. But Kairo's plan had blindsided me, and I desperately wanted to protect them at any cost.

At least they were all still there, all in good shape. Their faces displayed a range of emotions that I understood all too well, from skepticism to hope to anger. My body protested as I climbed out of the car. The lines of sore muscles across my back, courtesy of the library's Dragon chucking me into Kairo's arms, ached, and it reminded me of how much I'd been through in such a short period.

"I have news," I breathed, my heart pounding anxiously.

Good or bad? Dolfan questioned.

For a second, I wasn't sure how to answer. Not that what I'd done was a bad thing—it was at least something, and there were few other options. Even if I was leaning toward it being good news, I was still unsure whether they would agree. I didn't like how weighty their expectations felt, even if I did understand them.

"I've found protection for us all."

How? Aire questioned, his doubt clear.

How could I explain the whirlwind of events that had led to this moment? The blood oath, the Dragon Keepers, the revelations about my identity? My only solution was to show them. I rolled up my sleeves, exposing the vine-like swirls etched on my skin. Taking a deep breath, I steeled myself for their reaction. By the confused looks on Aire and Dolfan's faces, I realized they'd never seen anything like it.

Aire was startled when his gaze fell on the Dragon's eye inked on my wrist, his ear tips pinning flat against his neck.

What have you done? he demanded.

Frustration sizzled in my veins. While I attempted to overcome Aire's reaction, I couldn't. I'd had enough of the doubt he continued to give me. I was exhausted and bruised, having risked my life to protect them, and all I got was suspicion?

Give me a chance to explain, I thought, struggling to keep my composure. *You have no idea what I've been through.*

One of them snorted, and I sucked in a quick breath. The Unicorns lived in their meadow, eating all day under the protection of the ward while I was out there finding ways to keep our lives from being totally upended. It was so exhausting expending my energy only to be met with mistrust. I tried so hard to rein in my temper to avoid exploding, but Aire stood there, his forelock dripping over his eyes, his nose in the air as if I should be ashamed of myself. Didn't they understand? My choices weren't even my own. Forces beyond my control had brought me and Kairo together.

They don't know, I reminded myself. *They couldn't possibly understand what happened. It's up to me to make them see.*

Make us see, Flint replied.

"Look," I said, my tone quieter now. "I know this looks strange, but please, let me explain. Everything I've done, I've done to protect us—all of us."

The way Aire's eyes narrowed made me snap—I could swear I heard him roll them.

"I went to Dothan Valley," I told them, my voice rising with each word as the frustration of the past few days spilled out. "I was kidnapped, pummeled by a massive Dragon, flew on another Dragon's back for hours, entered into a blood oath, and met a creepy old librarian to ensure you could continue living in this field without fear."

I took a deep breath, trying to steady myself before continuing. "I've secured protection for us. Not just one, but four Dragons and their two Keepers are now sworn to protect every single one of you. They've taken a blood oath to keep other Dothians away from this meadow, so you don't have to worry about being taken or harmed." My eyes swept over the herd, searching for understanding. "Everything I've done, every risk I've taken, was for your safety. Can't you see that?"

Flint approached my side while I spoke, leaning quietly into me as he ducked his head against my chest. The twisted point of his growing horn poked my skin. At least he could sense I needed one of them to trust me. At least he offered reassurance. Aire still looked at me as if I'd sold my soul to the devil, his ears pinned back mightily. The two younger mares cast squinty-eyed glances at me while Nimue and Elska stood quietly, waiting patiently for my mood to pass.

Please explain, Dolfan finally said.

"I took Flint's blood and gave it to Kairo, the Dothian, the Keeper of Dothan Valley, so he could give it to his Dragon."

Every single one of them froze, except Flint. He closed his eyes against the ripples of betrayal but kept his head gently tucked into my chest.

"And in exchange," I continued, ignoring their wind-swept emotions, "I asked him for protection. I asked him to stay and keep the other Dragon Keepers away, and he agreed. He was the one who wanted to make it official. We went to Dothan Valley and did a blood oath. When we performed it, Kairo's cousin also agreed to help."

You can't trust them, Aire cast out, his words twisting through me like flames.

She can, Dolfan replied. *They cannot break a blood oath.*

"They will not," I agreed. "Kairo has too much at stake, and Nolan is loyal to him. Kairo's sister, Koa, was going to find you guys. She kidnapped me and was close to finding out where the ward was. I didn't feel like there was a choice."

I let them see everything, closing my eyes and sharing the story of what Koa had done when she'd taken me. A different kind of stillness lapped around us as they absorbed the details. Suddenly, they were ashamed and frightened—not for themselves, but for me. The only one who still looked at me with cynicism was Aire, his neck arched and mouth tight.

Flint tossed his mane as he straightened and looked at the rest of the herd. *She did what no other Keeper has done.*

His words made me question how my mother and grandmother had managed when their Sula-umbras had to have been felt by the

Dothians as well. Maybe mine created a more significant shift because I was unaware? I'd need to read the journals to find out what my mother and grandmother had experienced.

I didn't want to leave the herd in this state, but I knew I couldn't stay. We all needed answers. "I'm not going to tell Kairo or Nolan exactly where the ward is," I assured them. "I'll give them a broad area to monitor for any danger, and I'll be coming by more frequently to ensure you're all okay."

Giving them one last once-over, I turned to leave. Dolfan, at the very least, seemed to regard me with a bit more respect. I hoped the change in his attitude would ripple throughout the herd. My desire to do right by them was a needy beast. Despite the doubt-filled gazes they'd held, I vowed to earn their trust. Somewhat defeated by my time with them, I headed back to my house to find answers. The collective stress of it all pressed down on me, but I was determined to see this through, for their sake and mine.

On my way home, I bought a new phone, and the store transferred my information from the old one. There were twenty-three missed texts and calls from Chase. I read over a few of his texts and sent him a quick reply explaining I'd lost my phone and just managed to get a new one. I wasn't interested in reading all his texts or listening to the voicemails, so I mass-deleted most of them. They likely all contained the same basic premise anyway.

Returning home to a quiet house, a part of me was sad that Kairo wasn't waiting for me. Another part of me relished the quiet, grateful for the solitude so I could pull out one of the journals in peace. My fingers traced the spine as I studied the cover. The material was familiar, and I remembered how Kairo had looked at them. His mask had been firmly in place, but for a brief second, sadness had passed over his face. Studying the covers, I realized… they were made from Dragon scales. Something inside my chest twisted at the thought of how many Dragons might have been used to make them, only for me to stash them in a box. Were the scales from the deceased? Had Allorians killed them?

I flipped open the journal labeled with a big number one to the first page and ran my finger over the inscription at the top.

Alis Portier

Bond of ruin, by the moon cast, A division born through the mountain's pass. Only through the union of two can I be undone. On the tenth turn of a cycle, their work begins. My onset drove some to shadow, others to chase. To save themselves, they ran a sacred race. For if they lose, they will not recall, Each day will pass, and end it all.

The Nine Valleys have fallen. None foresaw it, and the cause remains shrouded in mystery. Twelve years ago, the Dragons of the Valleys succumbed to an illness. One after another, they plummeted from the skies, unable to rise again. When Dothan fell, the Allorians scattered, fear gripping our hearts at what might come. The Dothians, in their desperation, cast baseless judgements upon Allorians, claiming their Dragons had been poisoned in an act of self-preservation. With the coronation coming, tensions have been high, yet I swear upon my life that the Allorians did no such thing. The Dragons of each Valley had long offered us protection from Keepers who did not share in the virtues of our cohabitation.

As the last of our kind fled, Albadine, the Keeper of All, cast her curse. She did so in the vain hope that one day, Allorians and Dothians might be reunited, that they would see the folly of their ways and return to the valleys once the curse was broken. The curse of bearing was cast so that neither Unicorns nor Dragons could bear young unless a new Keeper were awakened. The window for conception was three phases of the moon, in the misguided hope that Keepers would be compelled to seek each other out during these times. Alas, it did not come to pass.

The second part of the curse decreed that we Allorians must remain chaste to embrace immortality, while Dothians were forbidden to fall in love. Yet, all seemed to forget the specifics of who could be our lovers or the objects of their affections. This part of the curse became muddled and lost, for Keepers grew scarce.

The Nine Valleys shall not rise in my lifetime, for I have done exactly as I ought not to have done. I have taken a lover. I have borne a child, and I do not intend to relinquish the safety of my herd and my family for Albadine's ill-fated curse. May she rot in her mountain with her gold-flaked Dragon.

My lips parted in shock as I read the journal entry. Why had my mother only shared fragments of this story? Had she deliberately withheld these crucial details? The unification of an Allorian and a Dothian? A nagging suspicion crept into my mind, but it wouldn't voice itself. My head spun, and I pinched the bridge of my nose to stave off my building headache.

My gaze drifted to the Dragon's eye inked on my wrist, and I frowned. *Kairo,* I thought, half-hoping the blood oath might carry my thoughts to him. *If you can hear me… I could really use your advice right now.*

The silence that followed only emphasized how alone I was. I was adrift in a sea of centuries-old secrets and curses, with no idea how to navigate the waters. Part of me wanted to slam the journal shut and pretend I'd never read it. But I knew I couldn't. Whatever answers I needed, whatever path I was meant to follow, it started here, with these words written by Alis fricking Portier.

Chapter Twenty-Seven

He Wanted To Fly

Kairo

The world was a damn labyrinth of mysteries. For instance, how exactly did a giant female Dragon vanish so quickly after returning from a long trip? Dalya was blatantly ignoring my commands, cutting off our connection fully, leaving me to pace the flat ledge at the mouth of the cave. And Nolan? My cousin was grating on the last of my nerves. I must've answered enough questions about Elle and the months I'd been away to fill the library we'd almost died in. I was sure Nolan could pass an extensive exam on my comings and goings since I left the valley if I handed him a pencil and paper.

Picking up a rock, I hurled it down the mountainside, watching it disappear into the trees below. A curse slipped from my lips. While

Nolan's incessant questions and Dalya's disappearance were frustrating, they were just surface irritations. The real issue was how much I wanted to return to Elle. No, that wasn't right. I needed to go back to her.

Did she want me there? Our last interaction was complicated. The kiss we shared on Dalya's back kept circling to the forefront of my thoughts. But so did the burden of everything that had happened since. The blood oath, the revelations about her lineage, the danger we'd faced together. It was a lot to process. I ran a hand through my hair. What if I went to her and she wasn't ready for what I had to say? What if my presence only complicated things further? The uncertainty was wicked.

"She'll be back," Nolan drawled, lounging across my bed like a lizard on a sunbaked rock. "You'd know if something was seriously wrong."

It took me a minute to realize he meant Dalya and not Elle. "Not giving a response of some kind isn't like her," I stated.

Nolan sighed, scratching his chin. "Dalya is probably scouting out a nesting spot. You uprooted her from her lifelong home, remember? Now she's gotta find a new place to lay eggs."

Damn it, Nolan was right. Dalya was due to lay eggs in a few weeks. The thought of hatchlings was exciting. Still, I fought the urge to pace the cave like a caged wolf.

"Speaking of nests," Nolan replied. "Where is Tattu?"

"I'll call him," I said, grateful for the subject change.

Tattu...

Nothing.

Tattu...

Still nothing.

Tattu!

Damned Dragons.

Yessss, Tattu answered, landing on the mountain's ledge with a yawn. The lengthy Dragon settled all four limbs with a big stretch.

Were you sleeping again?

Tattu did sleep, he confirmed.

Lazy, I chided.

Our unspoken exchange was interrupted as Caleda emerged from the cave. As the sun touched her scales, they shifted to a deep, glowing scarlet. She was a lovely Dragon. Her scent must have hit Tattu hard when she moved into his space. He lifted his nose to the air, a guttural rumble erupting from his throat. It seemed inevitable. Caleda and Tattu, having grown up side by side, were fated for this union. They would make a formidable pairing, and their offspring promised to produce extraordinary Greeron-cross hatchlings.

"Bye, Tattu," I muttered as the two Dragons soared into the sky, Caleda initiating a playful chase.

Their graceful ripples glided through the cloudless expanse, and a flicker of envy twisted in my gut. For Dragons, relationships were black and white. Unbonded Dragons chose mates out of convenience, solely to reproduce and continue their lineage, while bonded pairs mated to produce the strongest possible offspring. The memory of Elle's kiss and unexpected willingness flashed into my thoughts again. That relationship was anything but black and white.

Nolan let out a sharp laugh. "Well, that went smoothly."

"We both knew it would," I said, spacing out as I stared into the back of the cave.

"What's wrong with you?"

I hesitated, unsure how much to reveal. "It's complicated."

"Aren't the little things always complicated with you?" Nolan teased, but his tone softened. " Is it Dalya?"

"It's not just Dalya. It's the blood oath, the library, Elle… It's like I can't catch a break."

Nolan's eyebrows rose at the mention of Elle. "Do you have feelings for her?"

I should have guessed that he'd focus on her and not my other concerns.

"I don't know. Maybe. When I'm with her, it's like…"

"Like what?"

I sank against the rough stone wall. "Like the world makes sense… but at the same time, it doesn't. I can't seem to focus around her."

A muscle in Nolan's jaw feathered almost imperceptibly. "What makes her so special?"

I hesitated, noting the subtle change in Nolan's demeanor. "It's hard to explain. There's this energy between us. It's like she understands parts of me… parts I don't even understand myself."

"Right," Nolan said, his tone carefully neutral. "And you've known her for how long exactly?"

"Not long, but time feels different. It's like I've known her far longer."

Nolan let out a short laugh. "That's quite a statement."

"What do you mean by that?"

"Nothing," Nolan said quickly, then sighed. "Just… be careful, okay? You've got a lot going on. Don't let some girl you barely know complicate what you came for."

I snorted. What an odd thing to say, considering we were both bound to her by the blood oath. "She's not just some girl, and I think we both know that."

Nolan held up his hands. "Okay, okay. I just don't want to see you get hurt. You know I've always got your back, right?"

"I know."

Right on cue, the inked symbol on my arm flared with sudden heat. A smile tugged at my lips. It could only mean one thing. Elle needed me. I rose, then froze. Tattu was gone, Dalya remained unresponsive to my inquiries about her location, and Artok was still recovering. I was stranded, effectively grounded. Elle needed me, and I, a Dragon Keeper, was useless without a Dragon.

"She is summoning me," I admitted when Nolan shot me a look.

"Take Artok," he answered, stretching himself out on the furs that made up my temporary bed.

"I can't do that to him."

"It'll do him some good to get out of here. I'm assuming it's not far."

The decision was a fissure, and rather than let it spread further, I chose to ask Artok. We were, after all, supposed to be partners. Approaching the cave's rear, I found the massive black Dragon stirring, his wings straining against the low ceiling. *Well, that answers that question,* I thought wryly.

I want to go, Artok rumbled, a low vibration resonating through the cavern, causing pebbles to skitter across the ground. Though undeniably improved, his voice lacked strength, and his movements were still tentative. Perhaps asking him wasn't the right decision. Yet, I knew Elle wouldn't hesitate to share more Unicorn blood if needed, not just because of the oath but because of who she was. And with Artok closer, I could get it to him faster. Besides, the resolute glint in his eyes told me arguing was a losing battle.

With a resigned sigh, I allowed Artok to carefully navigate the cave entrance, and, mounting his back, his steadiness eased my worry. It was like fragmented pieces of us became whole again. Artok basked in the sun momentarily, stretching his mighty wings before catching the breeze. The world fell away as we soared through the sky.

At first, I let Artok go where he wanted, allowing him to dip down near the trees, his wings barely brushing the top branches. We flew above the river, and I held in my laughter as we passed over a couple of fly fishermen who felt our presence but didn't see us. Their poles hit the water, floated away, and they looked around in confusion.

The exhilaration of flying with Artok was almost enough to erase the pressing urgency in my gut. Almost. Until Elle's beckoning echoed in my mind. With a gentle nudge, I steered Artok toward her home. The sun painted the sky with hues of pinkish oranges, creating an awe-inspiring view of the ice-capped mountain range.

When we landed, Artok was winded, his great hot breaths coming out in pants. Despite his exhaustion, he looked delighted as he lumbered to the tree line and stretched out against the mountain's edge. I gave him one last glance with a soft smile before heading to Elle's house. No matter how much the short trip had taken out of my beautiful black Dragon, it was good to see he was capable of making it.

Elle

I opened the door on the third knock, my heart skipping a beat when I saw Kairo standing there. Suddenly, I was acutely aware of my messy bun and the comfortable but decidedly unsexy outfit I'd thrown on—cotton pants so white they practically glowed and my favorite green T-shirt with a gigantic hole in the side from the washing machine. Why was it that every time Kairo knocked on my door, I was in a state of disarray?

I'd just finished eating waffles with tiny chocolate chips—the kind I had to make from scratch because my groceries were who knows where. Kairo stared at me with a crooked grin, his fingers twitching at his sides. The movement was so subtle I nearly missed it. I moved aside so he could come in, and my breath caught in my throat when his shoulder brushed mine. I hugged the door while he passed, trying to stop myself from leaning into him. What was wrong with me? I'd never felt this… needy for someone's attention.

"Hey," I managed, casually leaning against the doorframe while simultaneously attempting to cover the hole in my shirt with my arm. "What brings you here?"

He grabbed a napkin from the kitchen island, handed it to me, and pointed at the corner of my mouth. In the mirror by the door, I spotted the chocolate spot on the corner of my lip. Mortified, heat rushed to my cheeks, and I hastily wiped at it, silently cursing myself for not checking my face. When I was done, I realized I'd given him a clear view of the hole in my shirt, exposing myself from waist to bra. Tucking my arm to my side, I avoided his gaze.

"Thanks," I mumbled. "I swear I'm not always such a mess."

Kairo chuckled softly. "Don't worry about it. It's… endearing."

I met his eyes again. He must think I'm such a slob—disheveled, caught off-guard, and smeared with sugar. But something in his gaze made me think he might not mind at all.

"You called?"

"I did?" I questioned, my brow furrowing because that seemed impossible.

"Yes," Kairo nodded, his voice tinged with amusement. "Usually, the blood oath leaves behind a small dot, not something quite so large." He glanced out the window before looking back at me. "But regardless, if you say my name while under duress, it will alert me. Blood oaths bind Keepers. These marks sting if they're at risk of being broken." Holding out his wrist, he displayed the Unicorn horn tattoo as he sat on the couch.

"Wait," I replied, sitting across from him. "That's normal?"

"Yes, as far as I know, every blood oath links those who took it."

"Does that work both ways?"

"Yes. I'm sorry I didn't explain that before."

"Well… that's convenient."

Kairo nodded. "By the way, Tattu found your car. I can take you there if you want."

"That's amazing. Tell Tattu I said thank you."

"Sure," Kairo replied, leaning forward so his elbows rested on his knees.

"Before we go, can I show you why I wanted you to come?"

"Sure," he said again.

I pulled out the journal I'd been reading and showed Kairo the entry from Alis Portier. Handing it to him, our fingers lingered as they brushed. I pulled away and watched his face intently as he read, noticing how his eyebrows slowly drew together. He didn't know the information in the entry. I could see the struggle playing out in his features as he absorbed it. He continued reading. I held my breath, waiting for his reaction, knowing this information could challenge everything he thought he knew about his people's history.

Was he questioning why his parents had never explained this? Was their retelling different? Or was he realizing, as I had, that perhaps the Dothians kept these secrets to protect their reputation? That is… if the version in my journals was the real version. I chewed on my bottom lip anxiously, considering the possibility that our ancestors might have pitted us against each other by crafting their own iteration of events.

Kairo finished reading and looked up at me, his expression filled with various emotions—confusion, hurt, anger, and what looked like a desperate need for understanding.

"I… I don't understand," he finally said, quietly. "This can't be true."

"I know it's a lot to take in. I was shocked, too, when I first read it."

Kairo ran his fingers through his hair. "But why? Why would our people keep this from us?"

"I don't know. Maybe they thought they were protecting us. Or maybe… maybe they were ashamed."

"Ashamed? Of what? Making our lives impossible?"

I shook my head. "I don't have all the answers, Kairo. But I know we need to find out the truth."

He nodded slowly as his eyes met mine. "You're right. We need to know more. I'll bring the book we got from the library later, and we'll compare them."

Kairo

I did my best to process the information from Alis Portier's journal entry, but it all felt wrong. The idea that the Allorians weren't responsible for the curse that had befallen our Dragons shook me to my core. Part of me wanted to dismiss it outright, to cling to the version of history I'd always known.

If it were true, why would my parents and the entire Dothian community have lied to me all these years? The thought of such a massive deception made my stomach churn. I wanted to rationalize it, to find some noble reason for keeping this truth hidden. Perhaps they thought they were protecting us, shielding the younger generation from the burden of our ancestors' mistakes. Or maybe they feared that knowing the truth would weaken our position and identity as Dothians. But as much as I searched for justifications, I couldn't shake the feeling of betrayal slowly taking root in my chest. If we were wrong about this, what else might we have been mistaken about?

The thought of the curse festered, and I kept circling back to one line from the journal: the curse could only be broken by the unification of an Allorian and Dothian. *Uniting* could mean the union of hearts or bodies, aligning with the cruel irony of our curses. A Dothian couldn't fall in love, and an Allorian couldn't make love. For most of my life, either form of union would have been unthinkable.

Unification. I considered what breaking the curse implied, and its significance set my nerves on fire. I glanced up, catching Elle staring. The curse and its solution faded. All I could focus on was how she looked at me, as if I held the key to fixing everything. She rose, approached the couch, and settled beside me, her hand landing softly on my thigh. Every instinct roared to pull her close, to act on the undeniable spark simmering beneath my thin surface of control. Instead, I stayed rooted, hands clenched at my sides, waiting for her to make the first move. Whatever transpired next wouldn't just solidify our attraction. It would change everything, and I couldn't fight the pull between us anymore.

Lust crackled in the air, filling me with a mix of desire and uncertainty. Elle's lower lip caught between her teeth, and her eyes lingered on my mouth a beat too long. I leaned toward her, wanting to touch her so badly that my fingers twitched. I noticed the hint of chocolate still lingering at the corner of her mouth. It taunted me, begging me to lick it off and savor it. She pulled her bottom lip through her teeth again, this time painstakingly slow, her eyes nearly crossing. I leaned even closer, my fingers finding her sides, a warm sensation building in my abdomen.

Elle exhaled the moment my fingers grazed her arm. Her hands found my neck, tugging me closer, her breath warm against my cheek. Before I could register the power shift, her lips were on mine. Her kiss was wildfire, blowing the dust off urges that had lain dormant for far too long. Every fiber of my being ached to explore, to possess every inch of her. I surrendered to the building heat, letting her lead as my hands traced a desperate path up her side. My fingers brushed the soft cotton of her shirt, the fabric an agonizing barrier to her smooth skin. With a ragged breath, I pushed the fabric up. The gasp that escaped her lips as my fingers brushed her side was a melody. The kiss deepened, and her hands traced down to my shirt, gripping it.

Fueled by the heightened emotions of one of my bonded Dragons mating somewhere in the mountains, my control wavered. Usually, I was a master at compartmentalizing, keeping the storm brewing inside the Dragons separate from my desires. But tonight, the bond was causing the walls to crumble. The control slipped, turning to ash as her moan whispered onto my lips. And suddenly, I was a man on the precipice, teetering on the edge of hungry oblivion.

It took every ounce of self-control I possessed not to cave, not to let the beast within take over. I needed her like the earth needs gravity—to pull me back to the surface and breathe life into my existence. I gripped Elle's waist, a low growl escaping my throat as I pressed myself closer. Her eyes widened in startled surprise, a flicker of something unreadable crossing them before she melted into another kiss, her hands twisting into my hair, tugging at the roots. I traced a slow path further up her sides with my fingers, higher and higher. My thumbs brushed the edge of her bra, and I paused, breathing heavily.

Pulling back partially, I met her gaze. Her lips were parted, her chest rising and falling rapidly. This fire wasn't just mine. I could see it burning just as brightly in her eyes. But regret wasn't an option tonight, nor was recklessness. Taking a shaky breath, I squeezed my eyes shut, trying to dam the torrent of desire threatening to drown me.

When I opened them, Elle was studying my face, her expression relaxing into understanding as her hands skimmed down my chest, etching lines downward before coming to rest on my forearms. My body ached to erase the space between us, but a tiny voice of reason, buried deep within the storm, refused to be silenced. With a groan, I reluctantly forced myself further away, the distance agonizing. I stared at her, both of us grappling with the aftermath of what could have been. If there were a purgatory, I was sure this moment would be the one I'd have to live repeatedly.

I worked hard to put my mental shields back in place. If I didn't, I might have Artok crashing through the house's roof from the intensity of my emotions. The effort it took to control both my own raging desire and the overflow from my Dragon bond engulfed me. When I could finally muster some semblance of impassiveness, I sat forward, holding out my hand.

"That was intense," she said, adjusting her shirt as she took my hand and sat up.

"It was," I replied, my lips twisting.

Elle's eyes met mine, a mixture of desire and uncertainty swirling in their depths. "Kairo… about the unification. Do you think it might mean…"

I swallowed hard, and my throat went dry. "That we need to… make love?"

She nodded, a blush creeping up her cheeks. "It's just… the way the curse is worded. A Dothian can't fall in love, an Allorian can't make love. What if breaking it requires both?"

"The thought crossed my mind," I admitted, my heart racing. "It would be the ultimate union for two cursed Keepers."

Elle bit her lip, her gaze dropping to our intertwined hands. "I wouldn't have stopped you," she replied. "Except… what if we don't stop, and something happens that makes all this worse?"

"We need to know for sure," I agreed, with a slow nod.

"I don't even know half of what is going on," Elle breathed.

"Can I ask you a question?"

"Always," Elle replied without hesitation.

"Can you choose immortality?"

The question was reckless and intrusive, but somehow vital. The answer would determine if the fate hanging over our heads could be fulfilled. Yet, it was an intimate question tossed around by lovers, not people burdened with destiny. A selfish part of me yearned for her to say "no." It would mean there was a chance, a possibility to just be with her, consequences be damned. Knowing the curse couldn't be broken would be a twisted sense of liberation. It wouldn't change how I felt about her. Maybe that was the worst part—the weight of responsibility couldn't extinguish the spark between us. It just made the fire harder to control.

Chapter Twenty-Eight

They Know Each Other

Elle

The only reason I wouldn't be able to choose immortality was if I had already… oh. Was he really asking about my past, like some fumbling teenager behind the gym? A laugh bubbled up my throat but died there. Because underneath the absurdity of the moment, his assumption pricked at something deeper. A sharp retort formed—but I caught myself and forced a slow breath. No, that wasn't fair. He wasn't assuming anything; he had to ask. It wasn't the first time someone had asked me, and it probably wouldn't be the last. Yet, if someone had told me that my love life would become the linchpin of not one, but two entire species' survival, I would have told them they were certifiable.

"Yes," I stated. "I can."

Surprisingly, I admitted to Kairo I was still a virgin without even blushing. On the other hand, Kairo seemed embarrassed, clenching his jaw and averting his eyes. An awkward silence filled the room, and I tapped my fingers on the table. We were both assuming breaking this curse meant we'd have to go all the way—he'd have to fall in love with me, and I'd have to make love with him.

Could I love him enough to go through with it? Easily, I realized, feeling like I'd been hit by a ton of bricks. But could he love me? He was so hot and cold that it was hard to tell what was going on inside of him. But something changed after the blood oath. When he looked at me, I could tell he desired me. I'd dealt with eager guys before, but this was on an entirely different level.

"We should go," he said abruptly, changing the subject rather ungracefully.

Right, my car. Another Dragon ride. My body preemptively ached, but I got up anyway. After changing, I packed a bag with what I thought I might need and followed him out. I had to get my car back before someone found it and reported me missing. The last thing I needed was another issue right now. Especially knowing that everyday concerns wouldn't take precedence over Allorian issues. It would just become an outside problem for what was becoming an outside world.

We made our way to the field, and I nearly jumped out of my skin when Artok suddenly appeared.

"How does that work?" I asked, gesturing to Artok.

Kairo paused, considering how best to explain. "It's… complex. The Dragons' magic is ancient and not fully understood, even by us."

"But you can see them all the time, right?" I pressed, eager to understand.

"Once you get used to seeing the Dragons, the camouflage will lift for you from a little farther away," he said. "I can see them as long as I'm within about thirty feet, and if I'm on them, but they're nearly invisible once they fly away from me."

"Nearly?" I echoed, my brow furrowing.

"Yes. You learn to spot the outlines they create after looking for them for so long. It's like seeing a heat haze on a hot day, but more defined."

A thought struck me. "Wait. Are we invisible right now as well?"

"Yes," he admitted, a small smile playing on his lips. "When we're close enough, their cloaking includes us. I've always assumed it was so that Allorians or other Dothians can't easily find their enemies."

"That's incredible," I breathed, trying to take it in. "So, if someone were to walk by right now…"

"They'd see nothing but the empty field, and the air wouldn't sit right with them. It would feel like something dangerous was nearby."

"Even other Keepers?"

"Allorians would feel it, but not Dothians, since we're predisposed to it," he explained.

Odd. I wasn't sure I'd ever felt it.

"Does it ever wear off? The cloaking."

He shook his head. "Not that I've ever seen. They can turn it on and off, but it's part of their nature, as natural to them as breathing is to us."

I exhaled.

Kairo's expression softened. "I know it's a lot to take in. I grew up with this, and sometimes it still amazes me."

He took my hand and squeezed it reassuringly before helping me onto Artok's back. When I settled in, Kairo swung up to sit behind me, adjusting himself so that we were flush against each other. I couldn't stop the shiver that ran through me at his closeness. It was a little too late to hide my attraction for him.

Artok walked a few steps with a weary gait before spreading his magnificent wings and taking to the sky, carrying us into the open expanse above. He didn't move like Tattu or Dalya. His wingspan was far larger, and each great swoop moved the wind with a loud whoosh. Though his flight was capable, he didn't feel like a freight train underneath me, like Dalya, or a livewire, like Tattu. I wasn't sure if it was because he wasn't fully healed or if it was just his nature. The thought that he might still be suffering pulled at my heart. I made a mental note to remedy the possibility of his discomfort as soon as I could.

We climbed higher, the wind stinging my face, stealing whatever voice I might have used to ask Kairo how Artok was doing. It was obvious he was doing better than the last time I'd seen him. After all, he was carrying us across the trees, skimming his back legs over the top of them while thousands of leaves flew off. The way he tilted his wings to catch the breeze and the powerful strokes that propelled us through the sky made me realize how magnificent he was, unlike anything I'd ever encountered.

It fascinated me to no end that we could be so high up, and yet there were people completely unaware we were flying above them. The sky above was a brilliant shade of powder blue, with fluffy white clouds dotting the expanse like cotton candy. I wanted to savor every second, even though my body ached from being on the back of a frickin' Dragon. But it didn't take long before we were landing in a clearing by the road where my car was parked. Artok stayed near the trees, looking dreary-eyed and solemn. The way he leaned against an old oak concerned me.

"Is he going to be okay?" I asked.

Kairo looked at his Dragon with deep consideration before responding.

"He's stubborn," he replied. "I told him he didn't have to do this, but he wanted to, anyway."

"You can talk to him?"

Kairo nodded. "The same way you can talk to your Unicorns, I suppose."

I raised a brow, noting that Kairo knew I could communicate with my herd. The things he did and didn't know seemed so fragmented. Where did the information gap come from? Sometimes, his knowledge seemed endless; other times, we both seemed to be learning something new. Someone who has been alive for decades should definitely know more about his own history, and that bothered me.

I headed toward my car, leaving Kairo standing by the curb. When I turned to see if he would stay or come with me to say goodbye, the expression on his face stopped me in my tracks. His eyes were narrowed at the sky behind me, trying to spot something. A slight breeze whipped through the trees around us, stirring his hair and the dirt around him. A sudden, eerie feeling crept through the woods. His hands flexed as he made eye contact with me.

"Elle," he said, far too calmly. "Get whatever you need from your car, and let's go."

"I need my car, Kairo," I blurted. "The entire thing."

"You're not going to get away in your car," he hissed, still looking at the sky. "Hurry," Kairo reiterated, rubbing at the tattoo on his arm.

I didn't need to look up to know something was terribly wrong. Heart pounding, I rushed to the car and shoved some items into the bag I'd brought. Slinging it over my back, I sprinted toward Kairo. A roar filled the air, a chorus of rough, throaty booms that sent chills down my spine. My feet skidded on the gravel roadside as I reached Kairo and, without a word, he wrapped his arm around the small of my back to steady me.

Together, we crossed the cloaked barrier. On the other side, Artok stood as still as a statue, his giant snout pointing toward the sky. The sight of the massive Dragon frozen in suspense made my stomach drop. I wanted to ask Kairo what was happening or who exactly had roared, but I couldn't form words.

"He isn't strong enough to fight," Kairo told me, his voice tight. We both swung onto Artok's back, using his front leg as a mounting block. Artok trembled underneath us.

"Do you know who it is?" I asked, trying to keep the fear out of my voice. I wasn't sure I wanted the answer, but I needed to understand what we were up against.

"No. It's not my sister's Dragon, Chuff. It feels bigger."

Kairo tilted his head, a curse escaping his lips.

"Artok knows who it is?"

Kairo nodded, his lips forming a thin line as he searched the sky above us. I followed his gaze, squinting against the bright sun. As though it had been waiting for me to look, I saw it. It was just a small ripple against the clouds, but enough to make my stomach lurch. We were in trouble. I realized with a sinking feeling that no matter the Dragon's size, it was most likely not hindered by any lingering illness. Artok was obviously no match for the beast gliding through the air above us, easily kicking up wind in its wake.

"What do we do?"

"We won't have time to get back to the cave," Kairo explained.

Closing my eyes, I realized we only had one choice, but I also knew the Unicorns might never trust me again after I made it. Of course, if I ended up dead or kidnapped, they wouldn't have to worry about trusting me at all. If I were tortured, how much would I endure before I broke and told someone exactly where the Unicorns were? Decision made, I pointed my finger toward the highest peak and nudged Kairo so he'd look.

"Fly to the south. Follow the creek until it branches off, then make a sharp right at the clearing. There's a switchback in the mountain pass. If we're fast enough, we can probably ditch them there. It may take them a minute to notice they're no longer following us."

If we couldn't lose them and had to use the ward to our advantage, this route would put us close to the meadow. Kairo nodded, and Artok took off. In an attempt to dodge the other

Dragon, we headed in the opposite direction, flying low over the treetops. It only took a few seconds to realize our attempt had failed miserably when another roar sounded, so close that it rattled me like thunder. I sucked in a breath and ducked low on Artok's back, hugging my chest to the flat scales.

Artok flew hard over the creek bed. He glided over the trees, knocking off their branches. I felt the heat of the other Dragon behind us graze my back, and I could hear it breathing. We needed more speed. Part of me wanted to close my eyes and pretend this wasn't happening, but I forced myself to stay alert. I might be new to this world, but I wouldn't be useless.

"Come on, Artok," I urged. "We're almost there."

Right before we reached the branch of the creek, I caught sight of a bright red Dragon's nose at Artok's tail, and I squeaked. Kairo squeezed me around my midsection - whether for comfort or to keep me from falling, I wasn't sure. Suddenly, we ducked to the right, and I slid over Artok's back, my fingers scraping his scales for purchase. If not for Kairo's iron grip, I would've fallen into the trees below.

Scrambling to regain my seat, I gripped Artok so tightly I feared my fingers would snap. We banked left, straight over the cutback. The split in the mountain pass was nearly invisible, disguised by spring foliage that made everything look like one big green blur. Artok's altitude gave us an advantage among the tall aspens, and the ripples of the other Dragon faded completely when we dipped below a slight rise. Artok huffed in great, heavy pants, his wings bobbing. I knew he wouldn't make it much further, knew that we had to land.

"There is a meadow there," I pointed out, my breath catching on the wind.

"We might crash," Kairo warned. "Hang on to me."

We cleared the last stand of trees, the meadow opening before us. I turned and tucked myself against Kairo, and he braced his arm around me. The familiar willow tree rushed toward us, its branches whipping in the wind of our approach. Artok released a bone-rattling grunt. He was exhausted, and we were coming in too quickly.

He hit the ground hard, landing on one hind leg before collapsing heavily onto his shoulder. The impact sent shockwaves through his massive body and into mine. He tucked his wing tightly against his side with a sickening crunch. I prayed to the universe that it wasn't broken. Kairo tightened his hold around me, and the world spun as we tumbled across the grass and dirt. We hit the hard earth, Kairo's body cushioning my fall. Pain exploded across my side, the air whooshing out of my lungs, and for a moment, the world went white. My ears buzzed; everything went from a blinding light to the green wisps of grass surrounding us.

I rolled off Kairo in a haze of pain, checking him to see if he was alive, and dipped my sweat-soaked head in relief when I saw him suck in a stunned breath. We were both gasping for air like we were drowning. But every breath was agony, fire burning through my ribs. It felt like I'd been kicked by a horse. I pressed a hand to my side, biting back a cry as I probed for broken bones. My vision cleared slowly, but when it did, I made out the shape of two black hooves. My gaze traveled upward, meeting the wide-eyed stares of the Unicorns.

A Dragon, Flint's voice echoed in my mind, full of awe and accusation.

I had to… I started, forcing the words through our mental connection. It felt like pushing through a thick fog, but I was determined to explain.

Artok? Dolfan's voice cut through, sharp with recognition.

"You know him?"

Chapter Twenty-Nine

What We Knew Was A Lie

Kairo

A dull throb pulsed in my wrist, radiating agony every time I so much as twitched. Sitting up, I propped my hands on one knee, gritting my teeth against a wave of nausea. Every muscle screamed in protest, telling me to lie back down, but my duty to Artok bellowed louder. Even as I struggled, my eyes never left Elle. The Unicorns emerged from the foggy tree line, their forms mesmerizing. They were smaller than I remembered, their coats shimmering with a vivid radiance I didn't recall. Turning toward them, I kept Elle in my peripheral vision as she stood to face them.

Lowering myself onto my elbows, I ignored the fresh sting of pain flaring up my arm. The Unicorns glided across the meadow like phantoms, their manes and tails shimmering like shades of moonlight against the vibrant green surrounding them. Only three dared to approach Artok, the smallest and darkest standing before Elle. The rest maintained a watchful vigil beneath the willow tree, their heads held high.

Despite the vast difference in size, I felt uneasy as the Unicorns closed the distance. I braced myself against the tremor in my legs and attempted to rise. Stars danced behind my eyelids, and my breath grew ragged, and the world tilted precariously. My knees buckled, sending me crashing onto the unforgiving grass.

"Don't let them hurt him," I rasped.

Elle's raised brows laced her face with skepticism. I couldn't blame her, not when the Unicorns combined didn't come close to the size of my Dragon. Despite her expression, size mattered little when dealing with the unknown. Even with their serene appearance, these creatures might wield abilities I couldn't fathom. Abilities that Elle might not fully understand, like the ward that was so potent it had escaped my notice for countless flights above it.

The journal entry offered little comfort regarding their supposed docile nature. Not when my Dragon was so prone. Artok wasn't just something I was responsible for. No, he was the core foundation of who I was as a Keeper. Losing him now, on the cusp of unraveling the secrets that had bound our world for generations, was a monstrous prospect.

"They won't," she said. "Dolfan knows him."

Shocked by her confession, I turned to Artok.

Do you know The Unicorn? I asked him. He tried to lift himself onto his side with a heavy groan.

Yes, Artok admitted. *Yet, not in this form.*

I didn't know what he meant, but clarification would have to wait. Artok was injured, his wing hanging limply and his leg buckling under his weight. I attempted to rise once more, the world swaying sickeningly. Elle walked over to the other Unicorns, the black colt following behind her. She winced with every step, one hand clutching her side, but she was alive. The irony wasn't lost on me. Her sworn protector sprawled on the ground like a broken doll while she soldiers on.

"Dolfan wants to help him," Elle said. "He said he owes him that much."

"What does that mean?"

"I don't know," she shrugged. "Hand me my bag."

Searching the ground, I found it lying among a patch of bright white dandelions. I braced myself, got to my feet, and walked over to it. It took me a moment to hoist the canvas tote onto my good shoulder and make my way to her.

A few feet away, Artok stirred. He groaned, the sound raw and guttural. With great effort, he managed to rise onto all fours. His immense head drooped into the tall grass, half-lidded eyes glazed with pain. I couldn't stand the sight of him on the verge of collapse. I'd failed him.

"If we take enough from each of them who's willing to give it, will it help his injuries?"

"It's worth a try."

A tense silence followed as the Unicorns huddled, silently communicating amongst themselves. While they debated the future of my Dragon, Elle dragged out various tubes and containers, setting them at her feet. Then, the smallest of the herd moved forward with a quiet regality. Each hoof stepped delicately over the already bent blades of grass, stopping beside Elle with its head lowered in offering, the tip of its horn peeking through its forelock.

The sight of its horn was oddly foreign. Maybe the passage of time gave this encounter a surreal quality. Or it could've been Artok's cryptic words about the Unicorns and his apparent lack of recognition for these creatures in their current form. Whatever the reason, a disjointed memory flickered at the edge of my mind, just out of reach. A memory that had something to do with a white Unicorn.

Elle inserted the needle into the Unicorn's neck, filling a jug with shimmering blood. The scene unfolded in a slow, almost refined routine—the offering, the metallic liquid glinting under the afternoon sun, the desperate hope fueling our actions. The more I focused on unraveling the nagging suspicion that something was supposed to be different, the more distant the memory became, leaving me dazed.

She handed me the first jug, and I took it to Artok. He lapped at the silvery liquid, the thick fluid coating the rough texture of his tongue before he swallowed, his massive chest heaving with effort. A warm breath escaped his nostrils, kicking dozens of hand-sized dandelions into the air, silver tufted blowballs drifting on the breeze. The disjointed feeling eased as I handed the empty jug back to Elle.

The largest Unicorn and three others stepped forward to offer their blood. The remaining two lingered beneath the willow tree, their heads swiveling nervously. Elle made a final, open plea to them, hands extended in supplication. It was futile, and I understood why. We were trespassers, and their trust in this foreign Dragon and the person clinging to his side was understandably thin.

"Everyone but Aire is willing to help because Dolfan asked them to, but Aire refuses, and Nimue can't because she's…" Elle paused, considering her words. "She's pregnant. I won't force any of them."

I nodded curtly, the names blurring together. I had believed Unicorns were nearly extinct. Discovering so many of them, a ten-minute flight from the cave was overwhelming. Their ward must be exceptionally powerful, woven with magic so potent they had eluded me despite the numerous times I'd flown over this meadow. The thought sent a cold sweat prickling my forehead. Without that magic, their existence would have undoubtedly been discovered long ago. Elle would have been discovered also.

While the revelation of their numbers left me reeling, the urgency of Artok's condition yanked me back to the present. I pushed aside my thoughts of wards and hidden meadows. There would be time for those questions later. Elle approached with another jug, and I tilted it onto Artok's tongue, leaning against his giant maw as he swallowed. His breathing eased, his limbs steadied, and the tight knot in my chest finally loosened as the blood began to work. The Dragon's worried expression relaxed, and as his emotions eased, so did mine. For the first time in what seemed like months, my shoulders fell, and I let myself loosen the hold the stress of my Dragon's illness had put on me.

"Thank them for what they are doing," I told her, rubbing my hand across Artok's nostrils and nodding toward the Unicorns. These creatures, whom I'd long thought of as adversaries, were saving Artok of their own volition.

"They've been thanked. That's all they can give for now," Elle said, reaching back to pet the small black Unicorn beside her.

"How did you learn to do that?" I asked, motioning to the tubing in her hand.

"The internet," she shrugged. "My mom and I volunteered at a wildlife rehab facility once. The veterinarian used to draw blood, but I had to search for how to do it on a larger animal. Flint was the perfect patient." She patted the shoulder of the Unicorn that hadn't left her side.

My mouth snapped shut. I hadn't stopped to think about the simplicity of what she'd done. How had no Dothian ever thought of this? Giving the Dragons small amounts of blood would have preserved the Unicorns. It was possible that my parents had been so fueled by anger when the Allorians deserted them in their time of need that they lost sight of such a simple solution in their rage. Had we been so vengeful that we'd destroyed everything when there were other options beyond hunting them down? I tried to recall what had happened when everything had begun to fall apart, but dredging it up made my head ache. Unable to recall much, I swallowed my irritation.

"Hey, Elle?"

She turned to me, hand stilling against the animal's dark hide, her other tucked tightly against her chest. I'd wanted to ask her if she knew if the curse was worsening, but the words caught in my throat. Not when she stood there, so beautiful against her black Unicorn. It wasn't the time. I'd bring it up later, if I remembered.

"Introduce me so I can thank them myself?"

"I can," she replied.

Some of the Unicorns tolerated my presence, cautiously allowing me to approach. But any notion of nearing enough to touch them fled with the sting of their wary gazes. Instead, I offered a silent nod of thanks to each one, a gesture of respect for their willingness to help Artok. Only the young colt let me touch him, though he remained by Elle's side, seemingly captivated by her every move.

I couldn't help but feel a pang of kinship with the creature, a reflection of the admiration burgeoning within myself for Elle. There was an undeniable poise in the way she interacted with her herd, a quiet developing authority born of growing mutual respect. Respect that had undoubtedly been put into question when we'd crash-landed in their field. It seemed they'd come around enough to allow us to stay as long as needed, giving my Dragon the space he required.

Looking at the rows of brown dirt that lined the earth where Artok had skidded across the ground, I took a moment to revel in the fact that she had chosen to defend not only me but a Dragon. There was no self-serving motive in her actions, only a resolute sense of what was right. I grasped Elle's hand, and we walked away from the herd that was gathering under the willow's swaying branches.

"They're amazing," I admitted. Just like she was.

Elle was the catalyst for uncovering what decades of mistrust had caused, as the curse had buried the truth. The Allorians and Unicorns weren't out for our Dragons. They were protecting their own, as I'd once considered. Sometimes, the truth had to be right in front of you, no longer blurred in the stories whispered in the shadows or written in the words of our parents.

Chapter Thirty

We Can't Stay Here

Elle

The night air was crisp, and I rubbed my arms to warm them, settling against one of the headstones to rest my ribs. The rough stone pressed into my back, but I didn't move. I liked the way the catkins swayed in the breeze, gently brushing my side. From where I sat, I could see Artok still resting in the tall grass where he had landed. His camouflage flickered as he slowly regained strength, his wise eyes gradually brightening. It was fascinating to watch, like a mirage solidifying into reality.

Dolfan and the other Unicorns gathered around me, maintaining a respectful distance from the Dragon. I sensed their wariness, their bodies tense and alert. Some Unicorns seemed at ease, while a few, Aire in particular, still radiated distrust. I couldn't blame them; the sudden appearance of a Dragon and his mysterious rider would unsettle anyone. Judging by the way Kairo gave them space, he understood this as well.

"How do you know Artok?" I asked Dolfan aloud.

From the past, Dolfan said, his voice echoing in my mind. *Before the young Dothian was born.*

"What did you mean when you said you owed him?"

It is not something I can discuss, Dolfan admitted. *It is something you must discover for yourself.*

"Are you keeping secrets?" I raised a brow.

I cannot recall. It is indistinct. I know that we know each other, and I know that I owe him my life, but I don't remember the circumstances, Dolfan confessed.

"How do I break the curse?" I asked, hoping for guidance beyond what I had already learned.

Dolfan bent his long neck to peer at Kairo and the impossibly large, dark Dragon beside him.

The curse is indistinct as well. If I knew, I would tell you. I do think it has something to do with you and the Dothian.

I massaged my temples. Clearly, Dolfan didn't have any more information than the rest of us did. This curse wasn't intended to be easy to break. It reminded me of a jigsaw puzzle with pieces of the same size and shape, making it nearly impossible to solve. The only thing we could solve was the two pieces that were Kairo and me. What were the others? I scoffed at the question. What a wild position I was in… tasked with solving all of this. It was exhausting.

Pushing off the gravestone, I wiped my hands on my shirt to rid them of dirt and loose stone. If we were safer, I could focus. If Artok grew healthy enough, we might stand a real chance at some level of safety, and Kairo could live up to his end of the bargain. I was shoveling both sides of it. I glanced at the sky, wondering how far the ward extended, how long it had hidden the herd, and how long it could hold. There were so many unknowns, so many missing pieces to the damned puzzle. I ran my fingers over my side, probing at the puffy, hot spots, knowing I'd have to ignore the pain. Whatever the curse was, whatever role I played in it, I would solve it.

"Thank you for helping him," I said to Dolfan. "Our blood oath promised we would restore Artok's health in exchange for protection. I know you don't trust me, but I want you to know I'm doing my best."

I know you are, he replied. *You are doing your best. I'm sorry I didn't see that.*

"No need to apologize," I told him.

I'm apologizing anyway, Dolfan stated, watching me with a strange look in his eyes.

Mulling over Dolfan's words, my attention was drawn back to our immediate problem. Kairo approached, brow furrowed when he glanced at Artok.

"We need to move him," he told me, adjusting his ripped flight jacket.

"Can't he stay within the ward?"

"No. The Dragon that chased us might keep searching, which puts your Unicorns in danger. It's not fair to hide him here and risk their safety, and it wasn't part of our deal."

He was right, of course, even if I didn't want to admit it. There were only so many grassy flat areas that could house us around the pass where we'd lost the other Dragon. If Artok stayed, the Unicorn's location could be discovered.

"Will he make it back to the cave?" I asked. After everything we'd been through, I couldn't help but feel responsible for Artok's well-being now.

"As long as we're not found. I'll fly him out of the meadow and go back in the direction we came from. Once we are clear from here, I'll call for Tattu and Dalya to escort us back."

Considering Kairo's words, I realized he didn't include me in his plans to leave the meadow, probably assuming I'd want to stay. If I stayed, I'd have to walk back to my car or call someone to pick me up in the dead of night, scenarios I was less than keen on. I checked my pocket for my new phone, pulling it out to examine the screen with a grimace. Sure enough, a spiderweb of cracks from the crash spread across the display. Calling for a ride was out of the question. I pushed the phone back into my pocket and grabbed Kairo's hand.

"I'm coming with you," I told him.

He studied me momentarily, his gaze lingering a beat longer than necessary, until a hint of a smile played on his lips and he nodded, readily accepting my decision. We both watched the grazing unicorns. They seemed useless against the much larger Dragons, and I had yet to see the magical abilities Kairo believed they held. Were they holding back, or was I missing something?

"Don't give me that look," he told me. "We'll figure this out. They'll be safe."

I raised a brow, blinking at the Keeper before me. He assumed I was concerned about the herd, not realizing I wished they were somehow more helpful. But… Maybe they were. I'd been neglecting the journals. There had to be more to these creatures than just horses with flair. After all, Kairo wouldn't have warned me to keep them from hurting Artok if they were harmless. And Dothians had respected, or feared, them enough to let them co-exist with Dragons.

Kairo tucked a finger under my chin, gently turning my face toward him. The simple touch sent a jolt through me, a dizzying tangle of confusion, attraction, and a strange sense of purpose that created an almost painful need. I took a breath, facing my feelings head-on. The truth was, I craved Kairo. I craved his attention deep in my soul, his focus, his understanding, his… everything.

"Once we have Artok back to safety, I'll have Tattu take you back to your house if you want."

"I'd appreciate that," I replied.

There were journals to decipher, information to unearth, and a car stranded that would likely need a tow truck. I should be happy to have an issue as normal as my car, but explaining it, explaining everything to someone who knew me… the thought was exhausting. My life had taken a nosedive into something out of this world, and while a part of me missed the comfort of who I was before my parents had died, another part buzzed excitedly. This puzzle wasn't going to best me, and solving it, no matter how frustrating the journey, had become important to me. I would find the answers, piece by agonizing piece, even if it meant turning the world I knew upside down.

Chapter Thirty-One

She Needs To Stay

Kairo

Deciphering Elle's expressions was becoming easier. The stubborn jut of her jaw and her flickering gaze when I'd helped her onto Artok's back meant she was overthinking. I'd wanted to say something, needing to calm myself after what had happened, but I'd waited too long. With the wind whipping in her face, she might not be able to hear me, let alone answer, so my questions would have to wait. We soared from the meadow. Careful of her ribs, I tucked my arm around her and scanned the sky until Tattu swooped in.

Nice to see you, I greeted him.

Artok well?

Improved, I answered, surprised by his swift recovery.

Artok looked and felt more robust, not back to his usual self but rebounding spectacularly. The telltale ripples of two approaching Dragons disturbed the air around us. I froze, and Elle, sensing the shift, leaned back for stability, her eyes searching the sky. When Elle spotted them, she stilled against me as if preparing for conflict. I pointed toward the approaching ripples as Dalya's familiar rumble resonated in my head.

"Dalya, Caleda, and Nolan," I murmured in Elle's ear.

The tension seeped out of her, and she tilted her chin toward me in a brief nod. I adjusted my arm around her. It wasn't exactly the smoothest maneuver, and every jolt sent a multitude of aches shooting up my arm. When Elle turned her head, her stony expression told me her situation could have been better as well. Taking Artok felt more and more like a colossal mistake, even with the information we'd discovered from the Unicorns. It's a mistake that I wish I could take back, but it's a mistake nonetheless.

Momentarily distracted, I watched the Dragons that flanked us on either side. Their figures glided effortlessly against the clear blue sky. If another Dothian hadn't hounded us, it would've been a glorious day for Artok's recovery flight. The sun beat down like a furnace, a world apart from the cool darkness of the cave where he'd spent most of his time as of late. He stretched his dark, leathery wings wide, keeping with the others easily.

We made our way back to the cave without further incident. Elle and I dismounted, and Artok immediately retreated into the cave to make room for the others. The space that had initially felt manageable now felt suffocatingly small when the other Dragons landed. They fought for space in our cramped quarters with a flurry of jostling. Elle and I squeezed past them, settling onto my makeshift bed.

Dalya, perched on the edge of a giant boulder near the entrance, huffed a plume of annoyed steam and launched herself back into the sky with a powerful beat of her wings. The frustration followed her like a thick mist, and a pang of guilt settled in my gut. We'd dragged them all into this mess.

"We need a new plan," I muttered, primarily to myself. Elle's eyes met mine, a spark of agreement in their depths. She glanced at the ripple of Dalya fading over the horizon, forehead creasing.

"Where is she going?"

"I think she has a nest," I admitted.

"A nest?" Elle's eyes widened. "Like eggs?"

"Yes," I said, smiling. "She's going to have eggs."

"Oh…" She blinked. "Right."

Nolan strode into the cave, tugging off dark gray gloves and setting them on a ledge. He raked his curly blond hair back, deep lines creasing his brow. I recognized the look. He'd given me the same look whenever he wanted the leftovers I'd saved for myself. A fight was coming.

I tensed. Nolan's mood could be unpredictable, and given our situation, I couldn't blame him for being on edge. Still, I hoped we could avoid a confrontation. We had enough problems as it is. I glanced at Elle. She was still new to our group dynamics, and I was oddly concerned about how she'd perceive Nolan's mood. Judging by the way she drifted away and flipped open the book from the library, she wasn't interested in a fight either.

Puffing out a deep breath, I decided to head off the impending storm. "What's on your mind, Nolan?"

Elle returned to the bed, wincing as she sat and clutching her side. Watching her every move, Nolan marked her discomfort, and his expression softened. He reached into a small pouch at his belt, producing a vial filled with a shimmering, pale-blue liquid. Glaring at me as if he couldn't believe I let her get hurt, he handed Elle a vial.

"Here. This should help."

Elle eyed it cautiously. "What is it?"

"Something from the valley. It's safe, I promise. It'll ease the pain."

Without a fight, she nodded gratefully and downed the contents. Within moments, the tension left her face. I watched the exchange with interest, Nolan making no move to offer me any of the medicine. Instead, he returned to our previous conversation as if the interaction had never happened. I guess I'd have to ignore my swollen wrist and throbbing ankle.

"There will be more Dothians where that one came from," Nolan warned.

"I know," I responded quickly.

"Why?" Elle asked.

"The window of your Sula-umbra is coming to a close," he told her. "Faster than normal, I might add. We can all feel it. They'll be desperate to find you now."

"Who was chasing us?" Elle persisted.

"Oscur," I explained. "He commands the largest Dragon horde of any Keeper I know."

Nolan snorted. "That's an understatement. Even though he's lost a few, his numbers are still," he emphasized the word, "astronomical. But he won't bring the whole horde. The trip's too risky. He has bonded breeding pairs that he won't risk moving. He'll stick to his best, most likely Physk and Torcyur."

"Artok said the one on our tail was definitely Torcyur," I agreed.

"Either one is strong enough to take on Artok on a good day," Nolan said, leaning against the rocky cave wall.

"We've got four Dragons," I reminded him.

"Caleda isn't much of a fighter, and Tattu would be as useful in a battle against those two as one of Elle's beasts," Nolan shot back.

Is not useless, Tattu grumbled in my head.

"I know," I said to Tattu and Nolan. "Dalya will defend the valley with her last breath now that she has a nest."

"You want to risk the nest?" Nolan's nostrils flared.

"What do you suggest?" I pushed.

"We need to move the Dragons and the Unicorns," Nolan said.

"If we move the Unicorns, someone will see them. Right now, the ward is protecting them," Elle put in, glancing up from her book. "It's obviously strong enough. They haven't been found yet."

"Yet," Nolan threw in, the single word hitting hard because Artok had crashed through it, may have given Oscur an area to search.

"How are we going to move the Unicorns safely?" I asked.

"I don't know. Maybe the answer is in that damned book?" Nolan said, eyeing the volume in Elle's hands.

"Or in the journals I have," Elle offered. "If you take me back, I can start on them while you guys read the book."

"I don't think that's a good idea," Nolan said. "You should stay here where we can keep an eye on you."

"Stay here?" Elle shook her head. "Why would I do that? My house is warded."

"Kairo found you," Nolan insisted. "When–not if–someone tries hard enough, they'll find you sitting alone in that house while we're a twenty-minute flight away. I don't want to test the repercussions of failing this blood oath."

"He's got a point," I admitted.

Nolan was right, and it irritated me because I hadn't thought about what leaving Elle at her house meant. Doing so could be a recipe for disaster. But bringing her into this den of Dragons–and two Dothians– seemed almost as risky. Elle's mouth opened, ready to argue, but her defiance fizzled out, replaced by a heavy sigh.

"Alright," she conceded, her cheeks coloring. "Doesn't seem like I have much choice."

I wasn't sure how to feel. Part of me hoped she'd agreed because she trusted us—trusted me. Yet the red tint on her cheeks made me wonder, and I wanted to question it. If I push too hard, she might change her mind, and having her close was the safest option. I couldn't shake the desire for her to want to be here, not just see it as the lesser of two evils. I pushed that thought aside, reminding myself that her safety mattered most, not my wishes for… what? I wasn't sure myself.

"I'll take you to get your things," I offered.

Her gaze drifted to the back of the cave where Artok stretched, then she nodded somberly. The quiet acceptance didn't fade, and it was a resignation that ate at me. Artok caught my eye and lifted his head, his eyes flickering between Elle and me. Intrigued, I tilted my head in question. Artok's expression was… ambivalent. His usually unwavering golden eyes were hooded with a concern I rarely saw, even when he was in the throes of his illness.

She needs to read the journals, Artok stated.

Is there a specific reason?

The answers are in them, he stated.

Unsure of why he was being cryptic, I frowned but nodded. *I'll push her to read them.*

Tattu lumbered toward the cave entrance. His exhaustion was evident in the low droop of his wings and the uncharacteristic slump in his usually playfully proud posture. Elle flinched at the sound of his approach, her shoulders hunching forward and her gaze drifting into the distance.

We go, Tattu said, in a hurry to get back to Caleda.

Ignoring him, I turned to Elle. "You'll be safer here," I reassured her.

"I know," she replied, her voice lacking conviction. "But the Unicorns…" She trailed off.

"The ward is holding for now," I told her. "We'll figure out how to move them once we have to, but not until then. Leave them in the meadow. I'll have Tattu scout the area, and if we need to, we will lure others away."

Elle offered a faint smile, but it didn't reach her eyes. "I just hope they'll be okay."

Pulling her into my arms, I held her until we both relaxed and she stepped away so I could help her onto Tattu's back. We launched into the sky, a familiar rush trickling through me, but this time, it was laced with a strange discomfort. Damn, I hadn't considered the emotional fallout of Tattu's activities with Caleda. Activities that left me shifting uncomfortably with Elle tucked in front of me, giving her space as we dove through moisture-filled clouds, with tiny raindrops clinging to our faces like a damp veil.

The situation was snowballing. Elle needed to read the journals so that we could get answers. Everything else – the tension, the uncertainties, the residue of Tattu's lust, and the inexplicable pull toward Elle—could wait. Right now, I have to be the leader, the protector. Personal feelings were a luxury we couldn't afford right now.

Chapter Thirty-Two

They Can't Remember

Elle

Crossing my legs, I fixed the corner of the blanket I'd brought from home and spread across the cave floor. Despite the tight bandages and the pain reliever Nolan had given me, my ribs still ached so much that it was hard to find a comfortable position amid the journals scattered around me. Each time I moved, I sensed Nolan's eyes on me as he assessed my condition with concern and something I couldn't, or didn't want to, identify.

We'd been at this for two days—reading, questioning, taking notes, then flipping through more pages. Some information was repetitive, some useless, like the lists of deceased Unicorns or long-gone Allorians. Some information was relevant, and when we stumbled upon it, we took turns discussing it.

Kairo was thumbing through the library book, lines forming between his brows. He couldn't understand the archaic text, and he didn't like being confused. He'd given up on notetaking despite my prompting. I shot him a look, and the corner of his lip twisted, acknowledging his deliberate disobedience. Puffing a strand of hair from my face, I turned to Nolan. He leaned against the opposite wall, one of my newer journals on his lap. I'd hesitated to share them since my ancestors meant for them to be protected from Dothians at all costs. But I'd quickly realized I'd never get through them alone in enough time to offer us insight. There was an unexplainable sense of urgency surrounding our task.

I'd given Nolan one of the newest volumes, hoping it held the least controversial material. What choice did I have? The stakes were too high to let old prejudices stand in our way. I turned back to my reading, but I couldn't focus.

"Break time?" I asked, stretching my arms up and cracking my aching shoulder blades.

"What are you thinking?" Nolan asked, suppressing a bored yawn.

I held up the book. "On page one-hundred-forty-seven, it mentions the Keepers' confusion after the curse. But here's the thing - that confusion wasn't listed as an original component of the curse. What were the original components again?" I glanced at both of them to gauge their reactions, and when neither answered, I continued. "The Dragons and Unicorns mating, and the immortality aspect, right?" This time, I didn't wait for them to respond. "What if the person who created the curse wanted to motivate those attempting to break it? What if forgetting key historical facts was built in as a fail-safe?"

As I spoke, I wove my hair into a braid. "Think about it. If you can't remember why the curse was created, wouldn't that drive you to seek answers? It's like having a puzzle with missing pieces–you want to fill in the gaps. So, my theory is that the confusion is intentional. It pushes the Keepers to uncover the truth rather than accept the curse as it is. Does that make sense?"

Kairo and Nolan frowned, looked at each other, and then back at me. Their expressions told me that they didn't fully understand.

"I guess," Kairo replied, an apparent attempt at pacification.

"Let me try something," I said, opting for a question that should be fairly simple to answer. "Can you tell me what year the curse was cast?"

Kairo blinked and tilted his head, his expression growing contemplative. He set the book down and looked at Nolan. "I can't remember," he confessed. "Nolan?"

"I know it was several decades ago," Nolan said, "but the exact year? I have no clue."

I winced at the 'several decades ago' comment. These men before me were several decades old. By the looks of it, they hadn't aged past their early to mid-twenties. I shook my head and returned to the conversation.

"That's what I mean," I said, smiling because I knew I was on to something. "I noticed that both your memories are fractured. You can recall some things in great detail, but not others, and most of the confusion surrounds details of the curse specifically."

That is why Kairo could tell me some things but acted confused when I asked him about information he should have known, given how long he'd been around.

"Some of my memories are hazy," Kairo admitted.

"Not just hazy," I replied, "not there at all. Think about it. You were old enough that you should remember more, or at the very least old enough to have heard it from others - unless they didn't know it. On top of that, the Unicorns and Dragons are missing major parts of their past, and we all know they have been around long enough that Dolfan should know why he owes Artok his life. Parts of the curse shouldn't be indistinct. Let me read this to you."

I ran my finger over the words in one of the journals as I repeated them: "*The curse spiraled through the lands in a thick, ugly green fog, eating away at the normalcy of every Dragon, Unicorn, and Keeper in its path. It was like our past was replaced with a suggested history. Even the lesson the curse was meant to teach was nearly lost in the confusion.*"

When I looked up from the journal, my mind raced. The passage confirmed my suspicions, adding a new layer to the curse's effects. The vivid description of the green fog played out in my mind, flowing over grass and trees, and covering the forms of the Unicorns. The curse was more insidious than we'd initially believed. It was less of a magical barrier to be broken than a veil over reality itself. It distorted perception, sowed discord, and obscured truth, leaving us to grapple with the unsettling fact that any understanding of the past was compromised.

"Do you see?" I asked. "This isn't just forgetting a date or two. The curse has altered your perception of history itself."

Kairo leaned forward, brow furrowed. "So, what we think we know might not be accurate?"

"Exactly," I said, nodding. "And it's not just facts that are muddled; even the purpose of the curse is forgotten. If the lesson it was meant to teach was lost, how can anyone break it?" I paused, rethinking what it might mean. "Or maybe that's the point: to motivate Dothians and Allorians to act before their entire history—everything they are—slips away."

Nolan's eyes narrowed in thought. "So, we can't trust our memories or the stories passed down to us?"

"But it also gives us a new angle to explore," I countered, a surge of determination rising. "If we can spot the gaps in memory, those inconsistencies in the histories, we might piece together what really happened and maybe even why."

"Where do we even start?" Kairo asked, sounding overwhelmed.

I took a deep breath. "We start by questioning everything. We look for patterns in what's missing and what doesn't make sense. Most importantly, we keep digging into the book and the journals—anything that might have escaped the curse's influence."

Nolan parted his lips as if he was going to argue, then closed them again when I held up a finger.

"What if each Sula-umbra deepens this amnesia?" I asked, puzzling them both. "We need to figure out if there is a deadline because it's possible that we either break the curse or your memories will vanish for good." I filled my lungs and continued. "We also skipped over the part where Alis Portier says the librarian who gave us that book is the Albadine."

"What are you talking about?" Nolan asked, squinting at me.

Flipping to the front of Alis's journal, the one Kairo and I had already read, I pointed to the last sentence. The boys leaned closer. Nolan's eyes widened, and he looked at Kairo for an answer. But Kairo appeared shocked that he'd missed that part, his eyes narrowing as he reread the page.

"Damn," Kairo muttered.

My brow furrowed. Were they unable to retain some of what they were reading due to the curse?

"That might be why you can't read the book," I said. "Hand it to me."

Kairo looked at the volume blankly before passing it over, the tops of his ears reddening. Everything probably made him feel lost, possibly even angering him, because I felt the same way. Our predecessors intentionally ruined so many lives, especially Albadine. For what? To push someone to break it? To begin something? Or end it?

Muttering under my breath, I flipped to a random page and ran my finger along the first paragraph. The slanted script was in a different font than I was used to, and the words were old English, but it was nearly the same as reading Shakespeare.

"I'll paraphrase," I said. "This section covers blood oaths. Blood oaths between Dothians are sealed with Dragon blood. Allorians with… Alicorn blood?"

"Alicorn?" Kairo echoed.

"Unicorns with wings," Nolan supplied.

I looked at him in surprise. "What?" he said, shrugging. "I do read. Sometimes."

I stuck my tongue out at him and went back to the book. "Why would it say Alicorn and not Unicorn?"

"I'm not sure," Kairo admitted.

We fell silent, each of us was processing. Each stared off into the distance, waiting for the silence to break. We were answering questions while creating more, like a dog chasing its tail. I ran my fingers through my hair at the top of my forehead and squeezed, frustrated by how my brain refused to connect the dots.

"I think you guys should switch," Nolan finally said.

"Switch what?" Kairo asked.

"She should read the book, and you should read the journals."

"I agree," Kairo said at once.

I sighed. "We've got a lot of work to do."

Kairo

Hours later, I scratched the back of my neck and yawned. It was growing dark, and we were still reading by candlelight or by the cracked light of Elle's cell phone, plugged into a square device that kept it charged. Elle hadn't asked for a break since Nolan returned with fish for dinner. He'd cleaned the fish, seasoned the filets with salt, and cooked them over a small fire. We'd eaten in silence, Elle refusing to put the book down.

Her emotions shifted so rapidly that Nolan and I were afraid to interrupt her. Though her intensity unnerved me, her tenacity fascinated me. Instead of reading the journal she'd given me, I caught myself watching her: the way her brow was drawn as she scribbled notes, the black lead from her pencils caking the sides of her fingers. Without a doubt, solving this mystery had become inevitable for her.

Part of me felt a spark of excitement at the thought of change. My life before I'd met her had grown stagnant. Despite needing a reprieve from that monotony, the rest of me was weary, a foreboding feeling creeping through. What if something went wrong? I tried to focus back on the journal in my hands, but my thoughts kept drifting to Elle's determination. It was both inspiring and unsettling. She was diving headfirst into a world she barely understood, yet she seemed more driven than Nolan and me. I'd nearly given up after learning the odds we had stacked against us.

"Break?" Nolan finally questioned, eyeing us hopefully.

"What do you have?" I asked, squinting up at him in the darkness.

"These new journals don't say much that we, amazingly, don't already know," he admitted. "Beyond your mom going on and on about breaking the immortality part of the curse because she loved your dad, and a few pages about your birth."

"I'll have to read those," Elle said sleepily.

Nolan glanced at her before continuing. "She didn't elaborate on much, Elle. In one paragraph, she talks about how she isn't going to drag out the information from the other journals because she has to rewrite them all. So, she condensed them and was afraid that some of the information might have gotten lost in the process."

"I found out they attempted to break the curse once before," I offered. "Your great-great-grandmother thought the curse would be lifted if she found and fell in love with a male born from an Allorian. Maybe she translated the original journals wrong?"

"How did my mom translate them?" Elle asked.

I held up journal number eleven. "She created her own decoding system. The original journals were written in a language that no longer exists."

"What language would that be?" Nolan asked.

"It's going to sound cliche at this point…"

"You don't remember?" Elle asked, smiling softly at me.

"It doesn't say," I replied, stretching out my legs in front of me. "Did you find anything useful?"

"This book's chapters are not in the right order," Elle told us. "I hunted through it to find what the Dothians believe happened when the curse was cast. There isn't much difference between what it says in the first journal, except for where the blame is placed. The illness didn't come from the Allorians or the Dothians. I think it came from Dragons themselves." She held the book out to show us what she meant. "One Dragon killed and ate its bonded mate to save its Keeper," Elle explained. "I'm not sure why, but it fell ill soon after, and the illness spread."

"I had no idea," I said, attempting to read the words myself. My forehead creased as I tried to decipher what she could easily read.

"How could you?" Elle asked. "According to this book, the library was closed as soon as the illness hit the valleys. Whoever wrote this wanted the information locked away so no one else would read it. Someone wanted everyone in the dark."

"How could that be included in the book?" I asked. "That book has been around since before the library was closed. I distinctly remember my father reading it."

"I don't know," Elle answered.

Could the Dragon's illness be a direct symptom of the curse itself? A disease woven into the very fabric of their existence by the ancient magic? If so, breaking the curse might be the true cure, negating the need for Unicorn blood entirely. No. That would be too simple, too easy an answer to a problem that had plagued us for centuries.

My gaze drifted between Elle and Nolan, searching for answers that weren't there. Bathed in the flickering candlelight, Elle fought a losing battle against fatigue. Her phone, dimming by the minute, lay forgotten on the table. The book, held precariously close to her face, cast shadows that danced across the wall. Tapping the blanket as a signal for her to lie down, I took the book from her and gently placed it on a stack.

"I'll take the first watch," I announced, my voice low and firm.

Nolan's features relaxed, and he readily surrendered the journal he'd been studying intensely. Within minutes, both were lost in sleep, Nolan's snores providing a temperate counterpoint to the silence. Elle had barely paused in the whirlwind of activity over the past few days. Her ethic was immeasurable, from trips to her house and then the meadow to ensure the Unicorns' safety to devouring every scrap of knowledge she could glean from the books. It was no surprise that sleep claimed her so quickly, her arm draped over the side of the bed.

Gazing out into the moonlit distance, I watched as a ripple shimmered across the night sky. A brief mental message – a simple *hello* – flickered through the bond before Tattu vanished. Our Dragons hunted under the cloak of darkness, avoiding unwanted attention from Dothians and their Dragons.

For a fleeting moment, a yearning for normalcy tugged at me—returning to the serenity of the valley, living without fear of Dothians hunting Elle or harm befalling those in our care. A future where we could live together. A future painted with the simple joy of existing. It was a dream, I knew, shrouded in uncertainty, but a dream I held onto nonetheless.

Chapter Thirty-Three

What We Truly Were

Elle

I took my turn keeping watch in the early-morning hours. During each shift, I'd studied the long, silvery clouds, teaching myself to spot the faint ripples of cloaked Dragons. I knew Caleda had flown off to find food. Artok had already eaten and was tucked into his familiar spot along the back of the cave. The large Dragon was finally strong enough to hunt, and for that, we were all grateful. The Unicorn blood had worked. Behind me, Tattu slept soundly, belly-up and limbs sprawled like an oversized puppy.

Dalya had yet to return. Kairo had told me that she would only come back if necessary. Her priority would be her nest. He knew it was close, but he also realized it was safer not to know exactly where it was. The Dragon would defend the nest with her life because poachers would eagerly snatch Dragon eggs to sell or keep if they were unguarded.

Nolan and Kairo were soundly sleeping. From my vantage point, I could only make out Nolan's curly blond hair and one of his legs that stuck out from his blankets. I didn't want to admit how much he'd grown on me in the short time that I'd known him. Even though he still looked at me oddly from time to time, he was goofy, cooperative, and almost supportive.

Pulling the ancient book open, I crossed my legs underneath me and set the book splayed across my lap. Stuck on the fact that the book kept referring to Alicorns, I stared at the old font. There wasn't mention of Unicorns yet; they were all Alicorns and Allorians. The names were so similar. When I'd asked Kairo and Nolan about it, both seemed completely clueless about the connection. They'd never seen an Alicorn. I'd pushed to see if I could break through their muddled memories, but both had stared at me with near-blank expressions - the same expression that threatened their features whenever I asked about anything they couldn't quite remember.

I heard someone stirring, and my attention was drawn to the inside of the cave. Nolan was sitting upright in the makeshift fur bed he'd made that was too small for him. He rubbed a hand through his hair and looked over at me. The sleepy look was cute, and I couldn't help the smile that crossed my face as I darted my eyes back to my book.

"Back at it already?" he asked, voice rough with sleep.

I rolled my eyes dramatically. "Someone has to do the reading around here," I teased. "I'm starting to think you two just like the sound of my voice."

The corners of his full lips twisted into an easy smile. Nolan always looked nonchalant about nearly everything that happened around him. It was as if he were privy to some inside joke or hidden truth. It was intriguing and slightly maddening, like he was constantly on the verge of revealing something important but always held back at the last second.

Nolan pulled his shirt off, tossing it to the ground by his feet before pulling a clean one out of his pack. He pulled the new shirt down over his defined abs, pulling it away from his body so that it settled more naturally against his broad shoulders. I tried not to stare, but it was hard to look away. Nolan certainly wasn't an ugly man. In fact, he was pretty easy to look at. But there was no way I would be caught staring at Kairo's cousin… I cast one last glance in his direction before sighing and attempting to clear my head of him by returning to my reading.

Reading the next paragraph, my hands stilled on the edges of the worn leather binding. My mouth gaped open, and I read the section again. The words on the page sharpened as the truth smacked me upside my head. My heart rate quickened at the implications of what I'd just read and glanced back at Nolan, wondering if I should wake Kairo to share this epiphany immediately or take a moment to process it myself first.

It is justly held in surmise that the Allorians shall suffer a great loss when the Alicorns return to their truest and most base form. Survival's very instinct doth demand that they be hidden with greater ease and tended as Unicorns, for their Alicorn guise shall surely draw unwarranted attention. Once this shift is wrought, their horns shall possess a wondrous, elemental magic that keeps them concealed; an ability which they do not retain in the Alicorn form. Yet, the Allorians must never know that they may revert to their former selves with but a simple plea: *Alsaforus.* But, should this reversion be commanded, the sacred magic of their Unicorn state is forthwith lost.

Nolan walked over to me and stared down at the book, creases forming on his forehead. "What is it?"

"The Unicorns," I breathed, eyes wide. "They're the Alicorns."

Kairo

Nolan and Elle's voices bouncing off the cave walls woke me. Resisting the urge to burrow back under the covers, I let out a groan that rivaled Nolan's snoring and reluctantly sat up. Elle held the book to her face, peering over it, while she teased Nolan. He scowled at her with a sour expression, his pride visibly wounded. It seemed I'd missed the good part…whatever sparks had ignited this squabble. Swinging my legs off the bed, I stretched my arms and stood up. I could really use some coffee.

"What'd I miss?" I mumbled, shuffling toward the commotion.

"It all makes sense now," she told me. "The Unicorns are Alicorns."

"What?" I asked, yawning.

Her eyes lingered on me briefly, and heat reflected in her enlarged, excited pupils before she returned to the book.

"The curse didn't change them. They changed themselves to make it easier for the Keepers to keep them safe. Having a horn is one thing, but having a horn and wings is more noticeable. We can cut off their horns, but I don't think they'd appreciate us hacking off wings."

The realization hit me like an erring wave. This changed everything we thought we knew about Unicorns. "Artok said that he knew Dolfan," I stated, "but not in his current form."

Elle's smile grew.

"See," she said, turning to Nolan. "I told you I was right."

"I didn't say you were wrong," he said with a playful glare.

"You said there was… and I quote, 'no way that the Unicorns were Alicorns,'" she replied, rolling her eyes.

"Okay, okay," Nolan responded, throwing up his hands. "You were right."

While Elle and Nolan bantered, I found myself lost in thought. If the Unicorns could change their form at will, what other abilities might they have been hiding? And more importantly, how would this affect our plans to protect them? Could they protect themselves if they were in their other form?

"How do you change them back?" I asked, interrupting them.

Elle's response was surprisingly simple. "I just walk up to them and request it," she told me.

"When do we do it?" I pressed, eager to see this transformation for myself.

"We don't," she replied, shaking her head twice. "Not until we know more. According to the last sentence in this section, I'm pretty sure the ward breaks if they change back, and we don't know what makes them more adept at protecting themselves with wings versus without them."

I frowned, considering her words. Moments like these reminded me why having her perspective was so valuable. She always thought of things I didn't and was usually right. Seeing the Alicorns in their true form could provide valuable insights, but we couldn't risk compromising their safety.

"That certainly makes one option easier," Nolan said. "If we need to move them, we can."

"What's the plan now that we know this?"

"Unfortunately…" Elle started to say.

"No, don't say it," Nolan replied, earning him a glare.

"We are going to have to…"

Nolan groaned.

"Keep reading…" she finished.

"She said it," Nolan sighed, falling back into the cave wall.

Elle's response, though predictable, still elicited my own internal groan. More reading. As much as I shared Nolan's sentiment, I knew Elle was right. We needed more information before we could make a move.

"So, we read," I shrugged, hiding my own reluctance behind a mask of practicality.

"I'd rather fight Oscur," Nolan muttered, picking up a journal anyway.

"If we don't find out how to keep Elle and the herd safe, you may do just that."

Silence settled back over us while we burrowed into our respective texts. I stole a glance at Elle. She devoured the pages, tracing each line as she went, her lower lip caught between her teeth. While she rarely slumped, when she did, it was a controlled slouch, her back maintaining a hint of straightness, only the curve of her shoulders betraying lousy posture. Now and then, she'd tilt her head inquisitively, her jaw set with a distinct cant. Occasionally, the tip of her tongue would peek out, caught between her teeth. The gesture was so oddly endearing that I found myself chuckling softly, shaking my head.

The self-deprecating chuckle died in my throat when I realized I'd been caught up in observing her again, her eyes finding mine. Returning my attention to the journal, I reread the same page for the fourth time. I flipped the page as a blast of hot air tickled my cheek. Touching the hot skin, I glanced up to see Artok stalking toward us, his head lowered menacingly. He paused in the cavern's center; his fiery gaze fixed on its berm. A sense of dread coiled in my gut. It had been a long time since I'd seen Artok radiate such raw, unbridled fury. His eyes narrowed, and his head tilted back slowly.

"Damn it," I cursed under my breath, tossing down the journal, and instinctively pressed against the wall. A shift of power, followed by the signature of another Dragon, pulsed across the bond. It was there, just beyond the edge of the cave's entrance, invisible to my eyes but clear as day to Artok. My entire body tensed. We were close enough to see the cliff face, yet the Dragon remained hidden, no more than a ripple in the air. Sheer terror crossed Nolan's face as he scrambled out of the Dragon's path, shoving Elle to safety behind him.

Chapter Thirty-Four

Why Did He Do That?

Elle

Before all hell broke loose, my last clear thought was that Nolan was scratching his arm right where the oath was. I found my gaze drawn to the small, intricate symbol that circled the back of his hand, wondering what the details created. Then, the air around us suddenly grew thick, and I clutched the book we'd gotten from the library tightly to my chest as if it could shield me from whatever was about to happen.

My heart leaped into my throat when Artok stalked forward, his massive form radiating an aura of barely contained aggression. My pulse thundered in my ears as he stopped in front of us, his front talons digging into the dirt by our feet and his giant head rearing back with a snarl. The air went fuzzy, and for one terrifying second, it looked as if he'd gone mad and was coming straight for me.

In a blur, I was yanked behind Nolan, pressed so hard into the rough cave wall that I could barely breathe, the pressure aggravating my already sore ribs. Artok worked his jaws, his long, forked tongue flicking out as he lowered his head. With a rumble reverberating through the cave, he opened his mouth, exposing rows of gleaming, razor-sharp teeth. Saliva stretched across the expanse of his maw, flicking across the ground and sticking to the dirt.

"Ohhhh, shit," Nolan muttered. "Stay behind me."

When the last word left his mouth, fire erupted from Artok's mouth. The flicks of heat from the wave of flames hit me, and the stench of singed hair made my stomach lurch. Even with some distance, the intense blaze was unbearable, and sweat instantly beaded on my skin. The roar of the flames was deafening, drowning out everything else. I held the book as tightly as possible and covered my face with my other hand, feeling the rough leather binding against my chest. Nolan turned his head away from the heat, a tear forming in his eye as he took most of the blast.

As slowly as it started, it stopped suddenly. Artok lifted his head and stomped one powerful leg so near us that the impact reverberated on the ground under our feet, sending large rocks tumbling down the mountainside. The cave walls rattled, pushing me further into Nolan.

"The journals!" I cried, spotting smoldering pages scattered across the cave.

Our valuable sources of information started to go up in flames, and my heart sank. As if he knew I was going to try to save the journals, Nolan reached for me, but I twisted under his arm, darting under the angry Dragon. I landed on my knees next to the one closest to me and hastily patted it with my free hand, ignoring the pain as the hot paper seared my palm. Artok froze, glancing under his front legs with a surprised look as Nolan and Kairo rushed toward me, with the intent of getting me away from the Dragon.

Nolan got to me first, pulling me to my feet by my arm, but once Kairo's hands touched me, Nolan threw his hands up. He let Kairo take me toward his side of the cave, and when Kairo hauled me into his arms, I couldn't stop the tears from falling. The adrenaline that propelled me to save the journals suddenly drained away, leaving me shaking and overwhelmed. I buried my face into Kairo's chest, the scent of smoke and burnt paper filling my nostrils. My hand stung from patting out the flames, but I still clutched the library book desperately. Kairo's heart beat rapidly against my cheek.

"The journals," I choked out between sobs. "We needed them…"

His arms tightened around me. "Shh, it's okay," he murmured. "We'll figure it out."

I pulled back, looking up at his face and then at Nolan and Artok. We'd nearly been roasted alive, and for what? What did Artok see that caused such a violent reaction?

"Why did he do that?" I managed to ask, my voice trembling.

Kairo whispered in my ear, "Artok saw another Dragon. We have to find it."

My heart skipped a beat. I should've known. I should have realized. Kairo's arms dropped, and he walked to Artok, swinging onto him effortlessly. Pulling himself to his full height, the black dragon stalked out of the cave and launched himself into the sky. I watched their forms turn into a ripple through blurry eyes.

"Artok is feeling better," Nolan noted. I could see the burn marks across the side of his face and the burnt clothing draped across his chest. A wave of guilt washed over me when I realized he'd taken the brunt of the blast to protect me. I stood so that I could help him with his burns, but Caleda appeared.

Nolan turned toward me, his lazy grin faltering. "Stay here," he told me. I chuckled under my breath because how would I go anywhere?

Tilting my chin up with a finger, Nolan's eyes searched my face. "It'll be okay," he whispered. Then they were gone as well.

Standing in the middle of the cave, I took in the damaged journals around me as tears spilled. *What a mess*, I sobbed internally, *all of our hard work*. The sight of the charred pages scattered across the cave floor made my chest tighten. Each burnt page represented hours of research that was now lost to us. Tattu appeared suddenly, his nose to the sky. He positioned himself diagonally across the entrance and glared at the clouds while he guarded me.

I sighed and knelt to gather the damaged books. The ones burnt beyond recognition were tossed into a pile; each one felt like I was discarding pieces of hope. I gathered the ones we might still get information from, placing them carefully on the makeshift bed. My fingers shook as I handled each journal, afraid they might crumble at my touch. I pulled one open and wiped my face, trying to compose myself. At least the book from the library was safe, I thought, feeling a small measure of relief. I delved into journal number five, determined to salvage what information I could.

As I read, questions raced through my mind. Who was the other Dragon? Why had they come? And, most importantly, what did this mean for our safety now that the Dothians knew where I was? My gaze drifted over the heaps of ash and shredded paper, and I forced myself not to crumble along with them.

Nolan

Returning before Kairo, my boots crunched on the scorched cave floor as I dismounted Caleda. Tattu scrambled out of her way, snapping at her playfully before settling near the entrance. Elle was sitting on Kairo's bed, and the sight of her made me falter. Murder was written on the tight brows and thinned lips she wore. She set down the journal she'd been reading and sat up straighter, her chin set stubbornly.

Coming to a stop in front of her, I raised a brow, my hands held out at my sides, palms up. Even though she was looking at me like she was going to shove me straight off the side of the mountain, she was so fucking hot. I swallowed, and my heart thudded in my chest; I wasn't supposed to think of my cousin's girl that way. Yet, those thoughts were constantly on my mind, eating at me like a welcomed parasite.

"What's wrong?" I asked, keeping my voice casual. "Did you find something particularly horrifying in there? Or are you just practicing your 'death glare' for when Kairo gets back?"

"You were reading this one?" She held up one of the few journals that survived the blast. Her tone was sharp enough to cut glass.

I looked at the cover briefly and nodded. Then it hit me. I knew what this was about. Every ounce of saliva left my mouth. I attempted to remedy the grating feeling it left behind by running my tongue across the ridges of my palate, but it didn't do any good. I carefully schooled my expression. Elle and I argued playfully before, but we might be about to have an actual argument. I suddenly wished I could be anywhere else…anywhere but here.

"Yeah, I was. Why? What'd I do this time?"

She flipped open the book and found a page marked with the crispy remains of another journal's cover.

"It states here," she turned the book to face me, "that journal six was never rewritten because my mom never found it. Why didn't you tell me that there was no hope of finding it?"

My brows stitched together, and my shoulders relaxed. She hadn't gotten to the part I'd been avoiding yet. Relief flushed through me, but it was short-lived. Her face melted, and tears began to spring into her eyes. My thumb twitched as I resisted the urge to go to her. She was basically with my cousin in every stupidly destined way, but I couldn't deny the pull she had on me. Puffing out a breath, I went and sat beside her on the bed, pulling her close and letting her lean her head on my shoulder.

"Don't play dumb, Nolan. It's right here in black and white," she muttered.

"Well, slightly singed white," I responded.

She hiccupped a laugh.

"I didn't tell you," I admitted, "because I didn't think it mattered yet. We need to finish the journals we have. Worrying about a missing one wouldn't have helped. It would have taken us off task."

Elle tensed. "That… actually makes a terrifying amount of sense."

She relaxed against me. The scent of her hair—smoke from Artok's breath mingled with something sugary and uniquely Elle—quickened my pulse. I desperately wanted to pull the journal away from her, wishing it'd been among those in the pile of non-recoverable. There was no stopping her now. She was going to read it and discover the secret I hadn't shared with a single soul.

I took a slow, deep breath and nearly kissed the top of her head, but stopped, instead resting my chin on her hair. *Silly girl*, I thought, *didn't know how special she was.* She was too damned clever, too brave, too everything. If I weren't entirely enthralled by her, I probably would hate her for making me feel this way – caught between loyalty and desire, duty and what my heart wanted.

"We need to find it," she told me, sitting up to wipe her eyes.

I didn't respond; my heart was still pounding in an odd, erratic rhythm. Letting out a sigh, I wrapped my arm around her shoulder and tugged her closer, letting the warmth of her skin heat me. My thumb traced the edge of the sleeve of her T-shirt, and when I turned to look to see if she'd stopped crying, I saw her studying me. Elle's lips parted in confusion.

Just as I formed the words to tell her how I felt, though what exactly I would've said, I had no idea, Kairo flew in on Artok. Without hesitating, his beautiful black Dragon skulked toward the back of the cave, looking angsty. Standing up, I put space between myself and Elle, concealing the slight twisting in my chest. I walked over to the pile of burnt journals and picked one up in an attempt to look unaffected by how close we'd been, though I wasn't entirely sure whose benefit it was for.

While Kairo questioned Elle about which journals were lost, I found myself only half listening. The tension in the cave was palpable, and I knew Kairo noticed our closeness. But how could I explain to him that it wasn't just physical attraction? That somehow, amid all this chaos, I'd found a connection with Elle that felt both new and ancient, like rediscovering a part of myself I never knew was missing.

I'd never try to take her from Kairo, but I wouldn't stop her from leaving him. However, I had no clue what that would mean for my relationship with one of the last members of my family. Standing there pretending to examine the burnt journal in my hands, I thought to myself, W*ell, you outdid yourself this time.*

The thought almost made me laugh out loud, but the reality of our situation kept me silent. Whatever came next, I knew one thing for certain: my feelings for Elle weren't going away anytime soon.

"We didn't find the Dragon," Kairo stated, looking between us.

"I was on its tail for a while," I admitted. "The Dragon didn't have a rider. It wasn't one I recognized, either. It was long-scaled and medium-built, with twisted horns like Caleda's. It was super quick. It lost Caleda around the mountain's north side, heading away from town. Do you know any like that?"

Kairo shook his head before pausing and giving me a once-over, one eyebrow raised. "Your shirt is missing."

I looked down and frowned, noticing my shirt was indeed gone. I'd been a bit distracted. Lifting the shreds that remained, I grimaced and pulled them off. Angry red marks traced across my skin where the Dragon's flames had licked at me. I ran a finger over them, and the nerves awoke; the sharp sting of pain burned through me from the singed flesh. Amazing how that works.

"Artok burned most of it. The rest must have blown off. Dang it. That was a new shirt. I was hoping to make it a whole week without ruining my clothes."

"We'll have to treat your burns," Elle said quietly.

Nodding, I moved away from them and pulled out one of my packs to fetch the vial of burn medicine. I could sense Kairo's eyes on me when I handed the meds to Elle. The muscle in Kairo's jaw rippled, but he didn't say anything. The dim light in the cave cast long shadows while he moved to stack the rest of the journals.

Wincing as Elle brushed the salve over each raised mark, I let out a breath. The cave felt more cramped by the minute. Kairo gave me one final look before collapsing onto his bed. I glanced up at Elle. She was intently applying the medication, her fingers brushing my skin as she worked. The tip of her tongue caught between her teeth, and the sight made my heart pound in my chest all over again. I grabbed her wrist.

She paused, the vial frozen over my skin, and our eyes locked. I felt a jolt of something. Attraction? Guilt? Both? I wasn't sure anymore. This whole situation was confusing as hell. I pried the vial from her fingers and pointed toward Kairo, jutting my chin in his direction. Elle blinked, swallowed, and stepped back. I was dismissing her, even though a part of me wanted her to stay.

She walked away, and my shoulders sagged. I capped the vial and set it down with my belongings, then lowered myself against one of the boulders at the cave entrance so I could take my turn on watch. Looking out at the dark clouds forming in the sky, I pinched my eyes closed, letting the breeze cool my heated skin.

Maybe I should have stayed in Dothan Valley and enjoyed the quiet. Nah, this was far more fun. Elle was more fun. I chuckled to myself, though there wasn't much humor in it. *What was happening to me? Since when did I get all tangled up in feelings? Why was I pining after a girl and feeling guilty about it?* I shook my head, clearing my thoughts. *Focus on the task at hand, Nolan. Keep watch. Worry about your messed-up love life later. Or never. Never sounded good, too.*

Chapter Thirty-Five

When We Were Alone

Elle

"We should move," Nolan said that evening as a storm rumbled in the distance.

"Move where?" I asked, looking up from the book.

"I don't know," Nolan replied, adjusting his position as he leaned against the cave's opening. "Another mountain? To the valley? We can't stay here. Once that Dragon returns to its Keeper, they'll most likely be back."

"Just because they found us doesn't mean they know we have an Allorian," Kairo responded.

"Right," Nolan said, raising a brow sarcastically. "It's just Kairo and Nolan sitting in a cave with a random pretty blonde female that your sister kidnapped, and that Oscur has most likely seen flying on the back of your Dragon. Nothing. To. See. Here." He tapped his finger on his thigh as he emphasized each word.

Kairo sighed, setting down his book and running a hand through his hair as if the situation was giving him a headache. "Look, I get it. We're in a tight spot here," Kairo said, trying to keep his voice level. "But we can't just move without some sort of plan."

I caught Nolan's eye from where I sat next to Kairo, and a flush crept up my neck. Did he honestly think I was pretty? And why did that suddenly matter so much? The whole thing was scandalous. *Get it together, Elle.* He'd been a shameless flirt since I met him, but he'd laid off the last few days, as if something had changed or he was respecting boundaries. I chastised myself for not focusing on the rest of what he'd said. Now was not the time to gawk at the cousin of my boyfrie… I blinked; what exactly was Kairo to me? Was he my boyfriend?

"Then we move," Kairo was saying. I'd missed a part of the conversation.

"We can't go back to the valley," I stated. "If we fly out of the mountains with a herd of Alicorns, we'll be too easy to spot."

"I'll scout for a new location tomorrow," Nolan said, glancing toward the lightning that ran through the clouds.

"I need to check on the herd."

"Tattu circled the meadow between breaks in the storm earlier. Nothing to report," Kairo replied.

I smiled softly at him. That'd been nice. He'd either known I was worried or was being cautious on my behalf. The corner of Kairo's lip twitched as he moved the half-burnt journal from his lap.

"I'd still like to see them," I told him. "I have questions for Aire."

"The one that doesn't like you?" Kairo asked.

Nolan glanced over as if the conversation suddenly interested him.

"Yes. One journal mentions that he wasn't originally part of the herd."

"He wouldn't be," Nolan stated. "Normally, the herds consist of one male and several females."

"Just like a horse herd," I nodded. "But Aire was thrown into the herd, and I want to know if he knows why. I'd like to know who he used to belong to."

"To see if there are more Allorians?" Kairo asked.

"No," I shook my head. "Something Alis said about Aire being beholden to the Ninth?"

Nolan perked up at that, his earlier sarcasm forgotten. "The Ninth? What does the Ninth mean?"

"I'm not sure. I want to ask him. Plus, I just… I need to see the herd. Make sure they're okay with my own eyes, you know?"

Stretching his arms, Kairo yawned impressively, and as he recovered, his expression softened. "I understand. We'll figure out a way to get you there safely."

A loud crack of thunder made me jump. "Preferably when it's not about to storm, though. I'd rather not get barbecued by lightning."

Nolan snorted. "Yeah, that'd be a hell of a way to go."

I rolled my eyes but was grateful for the moment of levity. Another rumble of thunder shook the cave, and I huddled closer to Kairo. Nolan turned away to face the horizon, his broad shoulders tense as he studied the raging storm outside. The thunder was so loud it felt like the mountain itself was shaking, and I couldn't help but flinch at each boom. The rain came down in torrents, a sheet of water obscuring everything beyond the cave's mouth. I breathed a sigh of relief, realizing what this meant for us.

"At least we're safe from any Dragon riders tonight," I murmured, more to myself than the others.

I glanced back at the Dragons, huddled together at the cave's rear. Poor things looked restless, their eyes fixed on the downpour outside. I could sympathize, being cooped up here wasn't my idea of fun either. A gust of wind sent a spray of mist into the cave, and I shivered, wrapping my arms around myself. We were lucky the storm was blowing away from us. If the wind changed direction, I didn't fancy the idea of everything we owned getting soaked through. I'd dealt with enough damage to the journals to last a lifetime.

Another flash of lightning illuminated the cave. I caught Nolan's eyes briefly before he quickly looked away again. There was something in his gaze I couldn't read, and my cheeks warmed a little. *Stop it, Elle*, I chided myself.

"Is Dalya okay?" I raised my voice so that I could be heard over the thunder. Kairo blinked, coming out of his near sleep.

"What's the Ninth?" he asked, out of nowhere. He hadn't really been listening.

I shook my head. "I don't know. The journal didn't say much, and this book," I tapped the one on my lap, "hasn't mentioned it yet. It could be related to the Nine Valleys?"

Kairo nodded thoughtfully, then let out another massive yawn. I couldn't help but smile a little. Even Dragon riders needed their beauty sleep, I supposed. Nolan's voice cut through the patter of rain.

"I'll take the first watch," he said, moving to sit on a curved rock near the entrance. He leaned his back against the cave wall, seemingly unbothered by the rain spattering his arm. His silhouette was stark against the stormy night, and for a moment, I was concerned about him. He looked so alone there. I almost offered him a blanket, but stopped myself. If he gets too comfortable, he might fall asleep too. Instead, I leaned over and blew out the candle. Carefully, I went to the back of the makeshift bed, curling up on the other side of it without disturbing Kairo. The storm quickly lulled me to sleep.

Kairo

I blinked awake, immediately aware of Elle's arm draped across my chest. For a moment, I allowed myself to savor the warmth of her touch, the soft curves of her body pressed against mine. But reality quickly set in, and with it a twinge of decency. My eyes flashed over to where Nolan should be, sitting out on the rocky ledge. He was gone. He must have left knowing that I would wake soon to resume watch.

I couldn't continue to ignore how he looked at Elle. This situation was complicated enough without him developing feelings for her. Carefully, I extricated myself from her embrace, and she spread herself across the furs, still deep in slumber. The morning light that filtered in caught her hair, making it shine like spun gold against the deep russet of the bear pelts. Even in sleep, she was breathtakingly beautiful. Noble. Delicate. The gentle rise and fall of her chest and the soft parting of her lips nearly drew me back to the bed. Her long lashes fluttered, dreaming perhaps, and I found myself captivated by the curve of her cheek and the arch of her brows.

My mouth went dry, and I made my way to the water flasks. Artok's rumbling voice filled my mind. *You need to teach her the ways of the Dragon.*

I took a long drink, buying myself time before responding. *I know,* I admitted.

She almost got herself killed, Artok pressed.

I'll warn her, I promised, glancing back at Elle's sleeping form.

She needs to tell them what they truly are.

I'm glad you feel well enough to complain. I was worried about you.

His recovery was remarkable; how he held himself proud and strong almost masked the slight labored breathing that betrayed his recent fall. Seeing him so much like his old self was a relief.

Artok's response was typically gruff, but there was an underlying contentment. *I'm feeling well enough to fly us out of this cramped cave if everyone can stay awake long enough.*

I chuckled softly, careful not to disturb Elle while she slept. He shifted restlessly in the back of the cave. We'd been through so much together, Artok and I. The bond between Dragon and Keeper was something I struggled to put into words, even in my own mind. It was more than friendship, more than family. It was a joining of souls, a shared destiny. And now my destiny had become inexorably linked with Elle's, with the Allorians, with whatever this "Ninth" business was about, and with the threat of losing my immortality.

Soon, I promised Artok silently. *We'll be in the air again before long. Until then... telling the Unicorns what they are is Elle's decision to make.*

I'd advise her to tell them, Artok responded. *Strongly advise.*

"I'll take that into consideration," I replied, the words slipping past my lips.

Elle's eyes bounced open, and she looked from Artok to me as if, for a second, she could hear our conversation. Her face was slightly pale and puffy. She pulled herself up to sit, looking as if she might be sick. I grabbed one of the flasks and brought it to her.

"Are you okay?" I asked, handing her the flask.

"Yes," she said, taking it from me. "It's just… that…" She looked around the cave as if searching for something or someone. "It was just a dream," she breathed. "I'm fine."

"Did you have a nightmare?"

She frowned and then nodded. "You could call it that."

"What was it about?"

"About the night of the blood oath. It was all the same—the darkness, how I felt—but something was different."

"What was different about it?"

"I…I don't remember," she told me, her forehead creasing.

"It's okay. It was just a dream."

She looked at me sadly, searching my face before nodding slowly.

"Can you take me to the herd now?"

"Yes." I reached down for her bag and handed it to her so she could change.

"I'll need to swing by the house," she said as she stood. "I've got to get some things, and I need a shower."

Elle disappeared behind the rocks and then emerged in jeans and a black blouse moments later. Slipping on her shoes, she pulled her hair back. She looked so… normal. She looked like she was heading off to class or meeting friends for coffee, not preparing to fly on a Dragon to check on a herd of Unicorns. For a brief moment, I regretted her being with me. What if she could have that normal life? What if she'd never been thrust into this world of Dragons, danger, and destiny?

She wouldn't. Wouldn't be her if she hadn't, Artok's voice rumbled in my mind, sensing my thoughts.

He was right, of course. The Elle I'd come to know, brave, curious, and determined, was shaped by these extraordinary circumstances. Still, I couldn't shake the feeling that we were robbing her of something precious.

"Ready?" I asked, forcing a lightness into my tone that I didn't feel.

Elle nodded. "As I'll ever be."
Pausing, I turned to her, grabbing her upper arms and running my thumbs across her skin as I looked down at her. I needed to know. "Would you change any of this?"

"Any of what?"

"If you knew what you know now, would you want to be an Allorian?"

She paused, placing her hands on my chest, seeming to contemplate my words. Her eyes traced over my face.

"I wouldn't change anything unless it meant my parents were still alive."

"I wish it could be different for you," I said candidly.

"Why?" She smirked. "This has all given me a reason to live."

I raised a brow.

"I don't think you understand how depressed I was," she admitted. "I was perfectly okay with sleeping every day and night in my bed. When I had to talk to people, their words went straight through me. I answered every question, but the words were automatic. I went through every motion, but it felt like someone else was in control of my body. This new life has given me purpose. I don't fear how fast or slow the days are going because I'm not simply existing anymore."

Every word Elle spoke resonated deep within me, stirring emotions I hadn't even realized existed. Without thinking, I closed the little space between us. My arms encircled her, drawing her close. I guided her arms around my neck, feeling a thrill rush up my back when she complied without hesitation. Leaning in, I pressed my forehead against hers. My hands found the small of her back, and I couldn't resist caressing the gentle curve of her spine.

"You are so beautiful," I murmured, my voice low.

Elle wasn't just physically beautiful, though that was undeniable. Her spirit, courage, and compassion genuinely took my breath away.

In that moment, with her in my arms and her familiar sweet scent enveloping me, there was a connection that went beyond our physical touch. It was as if our souls were having a conversation our bodies couldn't fully articulate. How could I have ever dismissed the idea of love?

I breathed her in, feeling the warmth of her body against mine. My heart raced, and I knew she could probably feel it. I wanted to kiss her, to show her exactly how much she meant to me. But I held back, savoring the moment, not wanting to rush or pressure her.

She smiled at me and leaned forward until our lips were close, stealing the hesitation I was offering. Kissing me, she moved closer, our bodies aligning tightly. Bringing one hand up to the small of her neck, I threaded three fingers into the base of her gathered hair. I deepened the kiss with a low groan and moved her backward, a silent invitation she readily accepted. She stumbled, her knees giving way as she met the edge of the furs. I followed the movement smoothly, the heat of her body a welcome counterpoint to the cool morning air. Her hands braced on my chest, momentarily pushing back before surrendering to my weight.

"Ellise," I muttered into her lips.

She hesitated, and as I looked down, I caught a glimpse of something in her expression. Before I could decipher it, she pulled me to her, her hands reaching for the back of my neck. We nearly fell off the bed, and suddenly, I found myself on top of her, her body soft beneath mine. I tucked one hand under the curve of her back, propping myself on my elbow, and she sighed into our next kiss.

Nipping her bottom lip gently, I lost myself in the moment until a low rumbling sound from the back of the cave caught my attention. Looking up, I found myself staring into Artok's narrowed golden eyes. The Dragon's disapproving gaze was unmistakable. Very aware of our compromising position, I sucked in a breath and pulled away. Elle looked surprised for a moment, then followed my gaze to Artok. She sat up, frowning at our scaly chaperone.

"I'm never going to get used to that," she mumbled.

I snorted and adjusted my shirt. "I don't think he will either," I admitted, glancing at Elle and noting the flush in her cheeks and the slight pout of her lips. It took all my willpower not to pull her back into my arms.

"We should probably…" I started, gesturing vaguely toward our gear.

"Yeah," Elle agreed, standing up and smoothing her clothes.

Chapter Thirty-Six

Stop Me

Elle

Enjoying the simple luxury of a comfortable couch after a nice hot shower, I scrolled through my phone until movement caught my eye. Kairo was coming down the stairs, and my heart stuttered. He was shirtless, water droplets still clinging to his skin. He was drying his hair with a towel, and a crooked grin played on his lips. When he glanced at me, my fingers faltered on the phone screen. I slowly sat up, unable to tear my eyes away from him.

"Kairo," I breathed, his name escaping my lips almost involuntarily.

I traced the contours of his muscles with my eyes, the defined lines of his chest and abs. I'd known he was fit, but seeing him half-naked caused a reaction I wasn't prepared for. My cheeks flushed, and I grew warm. Part of me wanted to look away, to pretend I wasn't so obviously staring. But a larger part couldn't bear to break this moment. Looking away seemed like a sin.
I swallowed hard. "I, um… how was your shower?" I managed to ask, wincing internally at how breathless I sounded.

Kairo's grin widened, and my gaze hooked onto his distracting dimples.

"Much better than using a stream," he replied, his voice low and rich.

As Kairo moved further into the room, I became acutely aware of the distance between us. He was only ten steps away, nine steps. Eight. My mind flashed back to our interrupted moment in the cave, and I crossed my legs.

We had a mission. We had responsibilities. We…

"We should probably get going," I said reluctantly, looking away briefly.

"Right," Kairo voiced, but he made no move to put on his shirt.

Using the towel to dry his hair one last time, his pants dipped low enough to reveal the V-shaped muscles of his torso. *Damn…* He set the towel and his shirt on the back of a chair and stood in front of me. When he offered me his hand, I took it, my fingers shaking. He was insanely gorgeous. His muscles spiraled down his long arms, over the dips of his clavicles, to his well-defined pectorals and the fine, nearly invisible black hairs that trailed down his abs. I placed a hand on his chest, the tips of my fingers tingling as I barely brushed his skin.

He curled his fingers under my chin, his thumb resting on my bottom lip. His lashes covered his heated, unfathomably blue eyes. I traced my fingers downward, and he tilted my face so that our noses were almost touching. I heard his breath catch as he leaned forward, our lips lingering. Inclining his head toward me, he brought his mouth to my ear.

"If we go too far," he whispered, "stop me."

I swallowed hard, my heart thudding rapidly in my chest. He waited, nearly frozen, until I finally agreed to his condition with a nod. *Yes...yes, I'll do anything.* Though I wasn't sure I could stop myself. With a deep growl, he lifted me by my thighs and wrapped my legs around him. Placing one hand on my back to steady me, he walked me backward until my back thudded lightly against the wall. He held me there gently, careful of my bandaged ribs. But the ache was easy to ignore when I was clinging to him. Instead of pain, my body hummed. Dipping his head, his lips met mine. I wrapped my arms around his neck, pulling myself up as he pressed tight against me.

His hand slid under my shirt, maneuvering beneath the soft, silky fabric. I pulled away with a shaky exhale, his fingers tracing the bottom of my bra. His lips found my forehead, and he pressed his hips into mine. I splayed my fingers across his back for purchase, his skin blazing under them. My eyes flashed to his when he pulled my bra up, his fingers exploring. *Oh, my G...*

"Don't let me interrupt you."

Looking around Kairo's shoulder, I went as still as a statue. Nolan was leaning casually against the doorframe, looking as if he'd just stumbled upon a mildly exciting art exhibit. Kairo set me down, my feet hitting the ground with a soft thump. I winced as pain shot through my side. Kairo scowled at his cousin with a look that suggested he was seriously considering fratricide. He stepped back, snatching his shirt from the chair and yanking it on. I couldn't help but mourn the loss of that gloriously distracting view, even as embarrassment coursed through me.

"Nolan, how… um, how long have you been standing there?"

"Oh, long enough," Nolan drawled, his eyes dancing with amusement. "I particularly enjoyed the part where you two were doing an impression of a pretzel. You guys looked very cozy."

"Seriously," I muttered, running a hand down my face. *The ground was free to swallow me whole at any second… time is ticking… No? Fine.*

Having regained some of his composure, Kairo folded his arms across his chest and glared at Nolan. "Your timing, as always, is impeccable," he growled.

"What can I say?" Nolan shrugged, grinning. "It's a gift. Though I have to say, cousin, I never pegged you for the type to get handsy in someone's living room with the door unlocked. I'm almost proud."

Kairo lifted an eyebrow, his silent rebuke for the unlocked door sending a jolt of heat to my cheeks. My eyes flicked to the handle, and I recalled that I was the one who'd forgotten to lock it. *I think…*

"What are you doing here?" Kairo said tightly.

"I found out who the other Dragon belonged to," Nolan said, moving to the side so that a tall, auburn-haired, brown-eyed girl could pass.

"Aiska," Kairo said, surprise crossing his features.

The girl smiled and pulled Kairo into a hug. With tears in her eyes, she looked past him and shot me a knowing grin, one that was utterly devoid of jealousy or resentment. I shot Nolan a curious look. He shrugged boredly and closed the door behind him.

Kairo

Aiska stood before me, in the flesh. As I stepped back to get a better look at her, I tried to recall how long it had been since I'd last seen her. She looked great physically, but there were bags under her eyes, and the spark that had once been in them seemed duller. Her hair was dyed a muddy reddish-brown and cut in a short bob, which was unusual. I remembered her hair always being long, tied in a ponytail for flight, and a darker red.

"I thought you were gone," I said, still processing her sudden appearance.

"No, I've been pretty busy," Aiska replied.

"The Dragon at the cave," I breathed. "That's the little hatchling of yours?"

"Yes, Fynch."

My shoulders relaxed. We wouldn't have to worry about who the visitor had been. Aiska wasn't an enemy. She'd been one of the only Dothians who still held a healthy regard toward Allorians. Eager to make introductions, I turned to Elle. "Elle, this is Aiska. We've known each other for years."

"Hello," Elle said, giving Aiska a soft smile.

"You're an Allorian?" Aiska asked, pulling Elle into a short, enthusiastic hug.

"Yes," Elle replied, her cheeks flushed as if she were still reeling from the high of intimacy and the shock of being interrupted.

When the topic of Elle's Allorian heritage surfaced, my blood oath caused a possessive instinct to flare. Even though I trusted Aiska, I perked up protectively when she embraced her. Elle's face went blank, her arms stiff at her sides, and her shoulders tensed. Aiska's smile didn't falter; she just pushed on, ignoring the lack of reciprocation.

"It's been years since I've seen a Unicorn," Aiska said. "Beautiful creatures."

"What are you doing here, Aiska?" I interrupted, keeping my tone light.

"I don't have a sick Dragon, if that's what you're thinking. I heard a rumor that you were nearby and had your males with you." She shrugged.

"You came all this way to mate your Dragon?" I questioned.

"Boy," Aiska laughed. "You and your cousin… he already ran me through the same gamut of questions."

Aiska's laughter made me feel a bit sheepish. "I'm sorry."

"It's okay. I heard about the blood oath. I'm not here to harm anyone or take anything. I thought I'd try my hand at raising some hatchlings. Then Fynch found your cave, and I knew the rumors that you guys were in the area were true. After Nolan gave me the rundown, I figured I might stick around to help."
"Rumors?" I asked at the same time Elle questioned, "Another Dothian helping?"

"Another one," Aiska replied, still grinning. "I heard you guys need a hideout."

"We do," I responded, though not as urgently now that we knew who the Dragon from the cave was.

Aiska took in the house briefly before settling herself onto the couch with one leg propped across the arm, making herself at home. Elle's gaze followed her, her brow lifting comically. She was deciding whether to like or dislike the woman who'd blown into her house from nowhere.

"I also heard you have a few things to take care of," Aiska said. "Mind if we hang out until you get back?" She motioned toward Nolan.

I caught Elle's gaze and grabbed her hand, squeezing it lightly. "Aiska is one of my closest friends."

"I get that, but…" Elle hesitated.

Nolan cleared his throat and walked over to us. "I trust Aiska with Caleda's life."

"Every cell in my body is telling me that one more Dothian is a bad idea," Elle admitted, her gaze flickering between Nolan and me before settling on Aiska, who was casually picking her teeth with her nail. The sight was quintessentially Aiska. "But if you guys trust her, then I do."

I took a breath. Elle's leap of faith was a testament to how far we'd come since that day at the diner. Perhaps she trusted us because we were bound to her, or maybe because she was outnumbered in the decision. Either way, I was grateful. Having Aiska with us made me feel safer and more at ease.

"We'll be back," I told Nolan and Aiska, leading Elle out of her house and down the road to where Artok waited. He'd insisted on flying us for the day, too restless to remain behind.

"She seems nice," Elle said, her steps slowing.

I nodded. "I've known Aiska for a very long time."

"How long?"

"Her family has been friends with mine for generations."

"Where has she been all this time?" Elle asked, pausing on the edge of a crosswalk.

"I'm not sure," I told her. "The last time I saw Aiska, her Dragon was a hatchling, barely bigger than that cat." I pointed at a black cat up the road.

Elle's lips pressed together.

"I know it's hard to trust someone you just met. But Aiska is one of the only Dothians I know who wasn't after Allorians for one reason or another."

"I get that you trust her," Elle responded. "I really do. But you haven't seen her in years, and who knows what has happened during that time." She reached out and touched my arm. "It might take me a while to allow her to get close."

Wrapping my hands around her upper arms, I pulled her closer, dipping my forehead to meet hers. "I understand," I whispered. "I can assure you she won't do anything that will put you in danger. If anything happens, I'll protect you."

"I hope so," she whispered back. "At least that's what I'm counting on."

Chapter Thirty-Seven

I Do Not Recall

Elle

In the field where we'd left Artok, we found Aiska's curious Dragon. She was larger than Tattu but smaller than Dalya, with a tiny head, silvery wings, and dainty features that gave her a distinctly feminine air. Shamelessly, she flirted with Artok, her playful chittering stopping only when he nipped at her in mock annoyance.

Kairo's light laughter rang out at their antics, his dimples popping at the edges of his cheeks. With my semi-broken phone, I snuck a quick picture of him, standing in front of his Dragon, before he could help me onto Artok's back. It was mildly fascinating that I could take a photo of them, as if it were proof that he truly existed and wasn't a figment of my imagination.

When I grabbed onto Artok, his scales felt cool and solid beneath my hands. Kairo seated himself behind me, and we took off, heading toward the herd. We hovered around the area until we were confident we weren't being followed, and then I nodded to Kairo. He guided Artok down to land in the meadow. As soon as we touched down, Artok shook, the clinking of his realigning scales loud in the quiet field. I found the sound oddly satisfying.

Most of the Unicorns kept their distance, their wary eyes following our every move. It pained me to see their hesitance, but I understood it. Kairo, seemingly unfazed, approached Flint. He scratched the colt's chest, causing his big eyes to close in contentment. It was a small gesture, but it gave me hope that a relationship could be built between my herd and my… I blinked, still unsure of what to call him.

I found Dolfan and checked him for any signs of harm. He sensed my scrutiny, eyeing me wearily. I tried to figure out how to say what needed to be said. *Just get on with it, Elle…*

Yes, Dolfan responded. *Please get on with whatever this is.*

"Did you know that you guys are actually Alicorns?"

He startled but then froze, his eyes going blank.

"You don't remember?" I pressed.

Vaguely, Dolfan responded. *Where did you acquire this knowledge?*

"From this book," I told him, pulling it out of my bag.

He eyed the book, and his ears folded backward. *The curse?*

"It's part of the curse," I nodded. "It altered everyone's memories. Even the Keepers remember only fragments from before it. That's why your stories are considered folklore."

Are you close to breaking it?

"I'm close," I responded. "I could turn you back into an Alicorn right now."

He tensed.

"But I won't, because I don't know enough to know whether you'll be safe if I do," I reassured him. "Unless you can tell me that you will be?"

His eyes narrowed, and he shook his mane lightly.

I do not recall. He responded with a heavy breath.

Of course, you don't… Why would anyone recall anything useful?

He didn't respond, his attention turning to Nimue, who grazed a few feet away. Despite my agitation, I gave him one more look and returned the book to the bag. I knew he wouldn't have the answer I was looking for, so I didn't ask whether I could restore the Unicorns to their original state without breaking the wards. I wanted to try it, but not at the cost of their safety, and only if they were willing. The way emotions rippled through the herd made me fear that if I requested something of one, it would be for all.

It was impossible to tell what was real and what wasn't. What the books and journals stated… What if it was all a trick? What if the proposed solution made the curse worse?

Walking over to Kairo, I searched the ground as if it would give me answers. He dropped his hand from Flint's chest and met me halfway. Tucking an arm around me, he tugged me to his chest, and butterflies filled my stomach.

"What did he have to say?" Kairo asked.

"He doesn't remember much," I sighed. "And he agrees that we shouldn't try just yet."

"Flint would let you."

"He would," I replied, looking over at the maturing Unicorn toying with the Dragon's tail. "But I'm afraid that if I ask him, it'll trigger the change for all of them."

"Maybe Aiska can help research?"

I leaned away from him and eyed him carefully. Aiska… At first, I had no idea what to make of her or her sudden appearance, and her closeness to Kairo and Nolan caught me off guard. But when she hugged me, something unexpected happened. I felt safe. It was as if I knew her, which was impossible, yet the feeling was undeniable.

The more I thought about our brief interaction, the more I realized that Aiska could be a potential friend and ally in this strange situation. The warmth and sincerity seemed trustworthy, and her eagerness to help felt genuine. I hadn't fought her staying because I didn't feel like I needed to, even though I pretended to question it.

"It's impossible that I know her, right?" I asked Kairo. It seemed my beliefs were constantly being tested.

"I don't know how you would."

"Right." I sighed. "I've got one last thing to take care of."
I walked over to Aire, pulling out the journal I'd brought. Mom's handwritten translation of a Keeper's words long ago was still clear and crisp on the charred and water-damaged page. Running my finger down the text, I searched carefully until I landed on the paragraph I sought.

"And it was with Aire that the Valleys have truly fallen," I read, my words slow and steady. "With him, the final part of the curse swept the last Valley. Blanketed behind him as he flew through the sky. Leaving behind the blood and pain of his past. Aire was beholden to the Ninth."

Aire's body stilled, his nostrils flaring as I read. He closed his eyes and held his breath until I spoke the last word.
I asked, "What is this Aire? What does it mean?"

It means you will break the curse, he said. *It means that I was wrong about you.*

Aire turned to face me. With one elegant movement, he dropped his front knee, his half-grown horn nearly touching the ground, and bowed before me. I couldn't move, save for the widening of my eyes, as I watched the magnificent beast lower himself. It felt surreal and overwhelming. Around me, I could sense the other Unicorns watching with rapt attention. Then, one by one, they bowed their heads as well. Their obeisance felt profoundly right, as if this level of respect was exactly as it should be.

Aire stood slowly, letting out a heavy breath. When his gaze fell on me, it was as if he saw every piece of me. I waited for him to speak, my chest rising slowly.

Do not break the curse before our horns are fully grown, he warned. *We will never return to our full forms if they have not completed their growth.*

"What do you know?" I asked.

I'm afraid that if I tell you too much, it may alter your choices. I will only say that when you returned to Dothan Valley, you set things into play. Even your mother could not correctly translate what you just read.

"It's in her handwriting," I whispered, my eyes drawn back to the page.

Aire tipped his horn at the journal, and I gasped as the letters before me shifted, transforming into an indecipherable blur. *She attempted to translate those pages for years,* he said, his voice soft with respect. *When she couldn't, she wrote them in her journal as they were.*

The words shifted back to the text, allowing me to read clearly. The contrast between what I saw now and the scratch from a moment before left me reeling. Two realities existed on the same page, separated only by my ability to understand them.

"How is this possible?"

Chapter Thirty-Eight

They Bowed

Kairo

The scene unfolding before me felt wrong, especially when the Unicorns bowed before Elle. *No, no… they aren't supposed to bow to her,* my insides screamed. The feelings were so sudden and unexpected that I had to check myself. There was no reason for me to think their respect for Elle was unwarranted. Yet, even as we prepared to leave, I couldn't shake the odd sensation that their groveling was a mistake. Artok's subtle inclination of his head in her direction only deepened the enigma.

Mounting behind Elle, I gazed down at the herd and noticed an inexplicable change had washed over them. Their forms seemed to shimmer, their eyes locked on Elle, a silent reverence emanating from their collective being.

"What happened?" I inquired.

Elle's gaze was fixed on her herd, her expression a blend of amazement and poise. "They know," she whispered. "They know I'm going to break the curse."

"Why did they bow to you?"

A soft smile curved her lips. "I don't know… but it's a start, right?"

I couldn't meet her gaze. Something inside me was unraveling, a sense of disorientation creeping into my consciousness. Artok launched us into the sky, and I clung to Elle, seeking a semblance of balance in her nearness because the world felt off kilter. I was standing on shifting tides. Every one of my senses seemed imbued with a new, unsettling energy. I grasped that changes were truly upon us, and I was unsure what they meant for our future.

Returning to the meadow near Elle's house, I found Fynch and Caleda nestled in the trees. Their peaceful slumber was the opposite of the madness within me. We dismounted swiftly, steadying my unstable limbs. After a moment of scrutinizing me, Artok joined them, his heavy body settling with a rumble. He had been quiet the entire trip, and his silence was uncharacteristic, given the depth of emotions I'd felt.

"What's wrong?" Elle asked as we walked toward her house.

"What do you mean?"

"You were quiet the entire way here. Usually, when we land, you help me down."

"I'm sorry," I sighed. I wasn't even sure why I didn't want to open up to her. "I just have this feeling that a lot is going to change soon, and I don't know if I want it to."

"You don't want me to break the curse?" she questioned, tilting her head.

"No," I shook my head. "That's not what I meant. It's just…" I let out a breath. "I keep getting the feeling that something is off."

"Something is off. Your memories. Your Dragon's safety. My entire herd. It's all off because of the curse."

"I know," I agreed, running a hand through my hair as I glanced away from her. "I just can't shake this feeling that something will drive a wedge between us when the curse is lifted."

Elle paused, pulling on my arm until I faced her. "Between us?"

"Yes."

Leaning toward her, I tucked a stray strand of hair behind her ear. If she was trying to distract me from the onslaught of tumultuous emotions, she was doing a great job with her doe-eyed, innocent look.

"Kairo," she breathed. "The only people who can let a wedge come between us is us. So, unless you are hiding some dark secret I don't know about, you shouldn't worry."

Running a finger down her neckline, I lightly grabbed her upper arm, tucking my fingers under the soft fabric of her blouse. I smiled down at her, loving the silky feel of her skin. If she wanted to be the voice of reason, she could have at it; my mind couldn't handle everything going through it right now. The anger that had developed from seeing them bow to her was something I didn't understand and refused to hold onto. She was too important to me.

"Good," I told her. "Because I wouldn't know what I would do if something happened to us."

Her lashes lowered. "Don't let something happen."

"I won't," I promised.

She smiled softly in response. "We'd better get going," she said. "It'll be dark soon."

Elle

Opening the door to my house, the heavenly scent of pizza hit me like a freight train. Gospel music played in my head, and my stomach let out a loud growl. I had to bite the tip of my tongue to keep myself from drooling. *So much for dignity.* Setting my bag on the floor, I entered the living room where Aiska and Nolan lounged on my furniture, eating pizza, and watching a reality show. My couch never looked so inviting or so occupied.

"He's cheating on her," Aiska declared.

"No, he's not," Nolan argued, adjusting his long legs that nearly hung over the edge of the couch as he took a bite of pizza.

"Told you," Aiska laughed, as a dramatic scene played out on the television, punctuated by a change in the music.

"Know-it-all," Nolan said, shaking his head at her.

I narrowed my eyes in his direction. He was good at being wrong, like it was on purpose, or it was intended to make the person he was arguing with feel better about themselves.

"Oh, hey, guys," Aiska smiled, waving us in. "We saved you some pizza."

"Thank everything that is holy," I replied, practically levitating to the pizza box. "I was about to start gnawing on the furniture."

I grabbed a slimy, greasy slice of meat-lovers' pizza and scarfed it down in the most unladylike fashion, wiping at the corners of my mouth with the back of my arm.

"Guess you must be holy," Nolan teased, winking at Aiska.

"Thank you," she replied, sticking a finger up at him. "I've been told I'm downright saintly."

Kairo slowly made his way over to the pizza. Lifting the lid with two fingers, he looked inside the box, hesitated, then grabbed a slice. He sat on the edge of the recliner and took a bite, his expression changing to one of mild appreciation.

"Have you never had pizza before?" I asked, my gaze filled with amusement.

"Not like this," he admitted.

I raised a brow at him. "Welcome to civilization. We have pizza."

There was a knock on the door, and everyone froze. Being closest to the front window, Aiska pulled the curtain back, glanced out, then let it fall back into place. Her expression gave nothing away. For all I could tell, it could be the mailman.

"There is a short human boy outside," she said flatly.

"Chase?" I asked, grabbing a second piece of pizza before heading to the door. I wasn't facing his wrath on a semi-empty stomach.

"Elle," Chase exclaimed, his voice urgent. "I didn't think you would answer, but I saw someone through the curtains and thought I'd at least knock. Who is here?"

"Oh…Uhh… come in?" *Eloquent, real eloquent.*

Chase walked in, took one look at Nolan lying across the couch, Kairo sitting on the edge of the recliner, and Aiska on the loveseat, and stopped in his tracks. His eyes went so wide I thought they might pop out of his head.

"You have guests," he stated, captain of the obvious. "Multiple guests?"

"I do," I nodded and ate another bite of pizza, wiping at my grease-covered lips again.

Chase took in each visitor again, and his face paled, especially when his gaze landed on Kairo. He looked from the pizza to the television and back to the front door so rapidly, I half expected his neck to snap. Gripping my arm, his face tightened, pulling his lips into a scowl. He spun me through the doorway, and with a sharp click, the door shut behind us. I huffed, resisting the urge to tell him I wasn't a toy for him to fight over.

"Who are they?"

"My friends," I responded, because it was the truth, even if it felt strange to say it out loud.

Chase's mouth flew open, and his eyebrows formed a canyon between them. He shook his head as if I'd just told him something he couldn't fathom.

"Like from college?"

I faltered, biting my lip. It wasn't easy to lie to someone who didn't deserve it. But the truth might send him running for the hills.

"Yes."

His face reddened.

"I think you are getting involved with the wrong people," he chastised, as if he were my parent.

"Chase," I replied, ready to tell him exactly where he could stick his unsolicited advice.

Before I could respond further, the door snapped open. Kairo's steady gaze met mine. He leaned in the doorframe, his forearm braced above his head, and his other hand still on the doorknob. Nolan stood behind him, his face tense as he glared over Kairo's shoulder. *Great, Chase, you've alerted the bodyguards.* I stifled a snort.

"Is there a problem?" Kairo asked, his tone bored.

"No," I told him. "Chase was just leaving." Hoping my expression conveyed that everything was under control. Kairo gave me a look, silently indicating that there was no way he was leaving me alone.

"You have to go now, Chase," I told him. "I'll text you later."

Chase narrowed his eyes at Kairo. "You better not hurt her."

"Or what?" Kairo growled, his expression heating.

Chase looked from Kairo, who nearly filled the entire door frame, to Nolan, who was holding himself back on the other side of it. His mouth dropped open, and his hands fisted. Standing there, caught between my past and present, I looked down at the pizza grease still on my fingers. I considered, not for the first time, if it was too late to pretend I ever saw a herd of horses standing in the field my mother had left me. But I knew I couldn't go back, I didn't want to.

"I really think you should go now," I told Chase, my voice steady.

Chase blinked and then looked at me, his cheeks flushing. "I'll call you."

"You do that," Kairo responded for me. I shot him a look that said, *Not helping.*

Chase eyed Kairo one last time before turning away. I watched him go, relief and guilt swirling in my stomach.

"That wasn't very nice," I whispered, watching Chase disappear down the porch before returning to the living room.

Though Chase was being an abnormally judgy asshole and I didn't want to deal with him fathering me, I still felt bad that he was obviously disappointed in me. Life had been simpler, if far more boring, when one of my biggest concerns was Chase and his approval.

"I thought Kairo and Nolan were going to kill him," Aiska commented, wiping her hands on a napkin. Her casual tone made it sound like she was discussing the weather, not potential murder.

"He is harmless," I responded, though the words felt hollow. He knew where the Unicorns were… even if he thought they were horses. My stomach knotted. I had to believe he wouldn't tell anyone.

"He is a liability," Nolan stated.

"A liability?" I asked, setting my pizza on the box.

"He's a tie to your past life. Anything beyond discovering your true roots can be used against you."

"He's right," Kairo cut in, grabbing my slice of pizza. I briefly considered fighting him for it, but decided against it. It'd been so long since I'd had real food. "Koa is tricky enough that she could have figured out where you live by now. If she sees him walking away from this house, he's at risk. Someone might snatch him, thinking you'll come to save him."

My lips pressed together as the reality of his words sank in. If I planned to stay with Kairo, I would have to make sacrifices. It was good that I wasn't overly attached to my previous life, but letting it go still stung. I'd have to sever Chase's attachment to me if I wanted to live the rest of my life knowing I'd kept him from being dragged into my mess. Letting Chase live his life in ignorance of this world was a relatively easy choice. It was for the best, even if it felt like closing a chapter for good. I would let him go. No, I needed to let him go. He and everything else that came before my life had changed.

"Are you guys ready?" Aiska asked, tossing the pizza boxes away. Her question snapped me out of my introspection.

Yes, I am.

"I hope it has cable," Nolan responded, standing and stretching his arms. "I need to know if that guy really was cheating."

"No electricity," Aiska told him as she walked back into the living room, crushing his reality-TV dreams, "but it does have actual beds."

"Where is this place?" I asked.

"Up on the mountainside," Aiska answered, a wicked tilt to her grin.

I took one last look around my house as we prepared to leave. It was strange how easily I was walking away from everything I'd known. But when I glanced from Nolan to Aiska, and finally to Kairo, I realized that maybe I wasn't walking away from everything. Maybe I was walking toward something.

"Well," I said, grabbing my bag, "here's hoping whatever else is out there doesn't involve any more near-death experiences."

Kairo snorted, Nolan grinned, and Aiska laughed outright. Something told me my hopes for a quiet mountain retreat were wildly optimistic.

Chapter Thirty-Nine

We Went Looking

Nolan

Guiding Caleda down to land on the long, wide old drive that led up to the expansive resort, I took in my surroundings. The stone structure climbed into the trees like a castle straight out of folklore–if those lores included dilapidated, abandoned buildings, that is. It was so well hidden that I'd almost flown Caleda straight over it. The weathered roof blended seamlessly into its surroundings. The oldest part of the resort had been reclaimed by Mother Nature herself, vines covering the crumbling walls from the ground to the old ceramic rooftop. It looked…charming.

The weathered building was near a steep switchback that had crumbled into the mountainside, so the only way to get there was from the air. The trees were so dense that the Dragons had to tuck in their wings when we dove through them, causing Caleda to grumble about scratching her scales as she bristled underneath me. I had to give Aiska points for the seclusion. Finding us here would not be easy unless you knew where to look. Jumping down from Caleda, I nodded in appreciation.

"You like?" Aiska asked, Fynch nosing her from behind.

"I've been sleeping in a cave for what feels like forever. Rooms and a roof are just what we needed," Kairo replied. I resisted the urge to roll my eyes. The cave had been pretty decent. Forced proximity had been fun, especially when it only included Elle and me.

"I forgot this place was here," Elle admitted. "It used to be a private school and then a members-only hotel. It closed down several years ago. The road collapsed, and they didn't want to pay to fix it."

"What conditions are the beds in?" I asked, trying not to sound too eager.

"Everything on the south side should make you feel right at home," Aiska replied with a smirk. "But don't expect breakfast in bed."

"Now, Aiska," I sighed, putting on my best wounded expression. "That's not very hospitable."

"You can sleep in the tool shed," Aiska said with a laugh.

I scoffed, watching Elle smile out of the corner of my eye. Her amusement at our banter warmed something inside me, a feeling I quickly pushed aside. I let everyone go in before me, doing my best to play the gentleman while my paranoid side checked that we hadn't been followed. As I shut the door behind us, I took in the expansive entryway, the massive stone fireplace at its center, and the furniture covered in white sheets. It was impressive, but also like walking into a dusty, old, forgotten time capsule.

An image flashed through my mind, causing me to swallow hard. In it, Elle was stretched across the couch with a baby in her arms, reading a book. Its domesticity hit me like a punch to the gut. Blinking away the homey, unbidden image, unsettled by the longing it stirred in me, I made my way over to an old wine cabinet. Pulling open the door, I retrieved the only remaining bottle and turned to the group, plastering on a grin.

"Drinks are on me," I announced, waving the bottle like a trophy.

"Why didn't I check in there?" Aiska replied glumly, eyeing the bottle with desire.

Laughing, I searched for cups and found a few hidden in the cabinets surrounding a lone bar. I poured the wine, stealing a glance at Elle as she explored our new hideout. Lifting a white sheet off a couch, she sent dust flying into the air and promptly dropped the sheet in favor of covering her nose. There was a familiar tug in my chest, a slow, gathering warmth that started deep in my lungs and spread outward with every breath. It was a feeling I'd pushed down so many times, but watching her smile, it bubbled up like an irrepressible spring, rising into my throat and catching my breath.

I knew I was treading dangerous waters. Elle was… well, Elle. Strong, beautiful, destined for great things. And she was totally not mine to be ogling. And me? I was just along for the ride, nothing more than a supportive friend. I wasn't blind to the way she looked at Kairo or the way they sucked faces like it would take a pry bar to get them apart. It stung, but I couldn't blame her. Kairo was the hero type, all brooding good looks and noble intentions. Next to him, I was just the jokester. But still, a part of me hoped… hoped that maybe, just maybe, Elle would see me as more than just a friend. It was a foolish hope, probably, but I clung to it anyway.

I lifted the coffee mug that held the red wine I'd found toward the center of the room and turned to Aiska with a wide smile.

"Here's to dusty sheets and free wine," I cheered, my stomach twisting when I caught the glint of delight in Elle's eyes.

Aiska

"What exactly are we looking for?" I asked, adjusting my legs to sit cross-legged against a cracked leather sofa that had seen better days. The rough edges running from the armrest to the cushions dug into my back.

"Anything to do with breaking the curse," Elle told me, "or anything to do with the location of the original journals."

Great, vague, and impossibly broad. Just how I like my research tasks.

I looked down at the crisp journal unceremoniously dumped in my lap and frowned. This was going to take years, perhaps decades. I'd never admit to the others that I had trouble reading. Often, the words seemed to desperately twist themselves into complete and utter nonsense, like attempting to read the alphabet after it had been blended into a smoothie. At least a smoothie would be tasty. This was just frustrating. I pinched the bridge of my nose, trying to ward off the headache I could feel brewing. Across from me, Kairo leaned against the fireplace, which crackled to life thanks to Nolan's ability to produce fire with matches and fallen branches. Show-off.

Reading his own journal, Nolan lounged on a wide, flat ottoman. He stifled a yawn and made odd doe-eyes at Elle, who kept shooting him glares as if scolding him for being tired. The anticipation rolling off him was so palpable you could bottle it and sell it as an aphrodisiac. He shot Elle a flirty smile that she blatantly ignored, returning her attention to the extra-large, daunting book she held in both hands. Their barely hidden teasing was odd. I'd seen her making out with Kairo. She was obviously his girl. Or was she?

I shook my head at them and flipped the page I hadn't even read. But something pricked up my spine when Elle glanced up at the tall, dark-haired, crystal-blue-eyed boy I'd known since I was young. Something about it felt off, but I couldn't place it. Maybe it was merely that it'd been far too long since I'd had a lover to sit amid the sexual energy the two shared. Note to self, get laid or get out more, preferably both.

My eyes flicked back to Elle. She reminded me of someone I couldn't quite place, like a word on the tip of my tongue or a half-remembered dream. She sat against the armchair of the long sectional that took up most of the front of the fireplace. Her book rested in her hand as if it were second nature. I crinkled my nose. I didn't understand the fascination with reading, yet Elle definitely made it look alluring. Her chin dipped, and her bright hazel eyes ran the lines on the pages, studying and restudying each paragraph. Show-off number two.

Sighing, I returned to reading, the words swimming before my eyes like drunken fish. This was going to be a long night. At least the company wasn't terrible, even if the sexual tension was thick enough to cut with a knife, a very dull and very frustrating knife.

"I'm already bored," I complained, my voice low.

"Tut tut," Nolan replied out of the corner of his mouth. "Nobody called break yet."

Break? My forehead creased, but I returned to studying the page, doing my best to make sense of it because the group felt this task was necessary, or so they kept telling me. Seemed repetitive and mundane to me. Staring at incomprehensible squiggles was about as helpful as reading tea leaves in an empty cup, but who was I to argue?

What would be more interesting would be to see the Unicorns… Alicorns. It'd been centuries since I'd laid eyes on them, actual centuries, not the exaggerated ten years people use when telling stories. Knowing an entire herd was nearby piqued my curiosity to such an extent that it was almost hard to sit still. My legs were practically itching to run off to find them, journal be damned.

I'd never hurt them, of course. I just wanted to see them. But no, here I was, stuck inside. I knew Elle didn't trust me yet because our relationship was still new and still in an awkward phase. Unicorns would have to wait. For now, I had to be patient and hope that someday Elle might trust me enough to let me near her herd.

"Focus," Elle said, giving me a soft smile.

I tried again. One line took me nearly three minutes to read. At this rate, finishing felt impossible. Frustrated, I flipped through the pages, hoping for divine inspiration or a conveniently placed informational insert. The pages gaped open in the middle, splitting naturally where there was a folded-up paper. Interesting. Lying it on my lap, I pulled the old sheet from the seam of the journal and carefully tugged it open, half expecting it to disintegrate in my hands. It was a map so crudely drawn that I almost didn't recognize it. I turned it upside down.

Well, what do you know? It was Dothan Valley, recognizable by the peaks of the mountains and the way the river ran through it. There were words on the bottom that I didn't recognize because the handwriting was so poor that it looked like a child's scribble.

"What's that?" Kairo asked, walking over. Looking at him, I held out the paper.

"It's a map of Dothan," I told him, relieved that his curiosity spared me from deciphering the words scrawled across the bottom. Sometimes it's nice when others do the heavy lifting. Or, in this case, the heavy reading.

Kairo turned the map so the words were at the top of the paper. I let out a breath, feeling like an absolute idiot. Of course I'd been reading it upside down. Elle noticed we'd found something and set her book down to join us. Her curiosity dulled when she read the words, a frown pulling at her mouth. I was concerned. If Elle was frowning, it probably wasn't good news.

"What does it say?"

"It's a map to the library," Elle told me. "We already know where that is."

I blinked. "That's what the words say?"

It seemed like there were more words than just 'Map to the Library' on the page.

"No," Elle shook her head. "It says 'Alis Portier's Guide To A Secret Society can be found at the library in Dothan Valley'."

Wait. Why did that name sound familiar? Narrowing my eyes in concentration, I tried to dredge up the memory it provoked.

"Why would we need a guide to a secret society?" Nolan asked from the large ottoman. He didn't even look up from the journal he was reading. His attention seemed to be rapt on the page he was thumbing.

"Maybe it's not important?" Kairo offered.

"At this point, we have no clue what is important and what isn't," Elle replied, walking back to her seat with the map in hand. "But I am definitely not ready to go back to the library, especially since we know that the librarian is the Keeper of All."

"She's what?" I blurted.

"According to Alis Portier, the librarian is the Albadine," Kairo stated.

Oh, perfect. Because dealing with the Albadine was on my radar, right beside getting worms. My stomach twisted at both ideas.

Kairo continued, "She seemed to recall me in great detail, but I only very vaguely remember her, and she was oddly young but old at the same time, like she'd been desiccating under the mountain for far longer than any of us have been alive."

Suppressing a shudder, I tried not to imagine the librarian slowly mummifying under a mountain while surrounded by dusty tomes. It wasn't an image I needed in my head when my stomach was cramping the way it was.

"If she is the Albadine, why doesn't she break the curse?" I asked.

"My guess is that she can't," Nolan replied, finally looking up from his journal. "She put it in place with stipulations that have to be fulfilled by others and made it impossible for herself to break it because of that. Now she's just been waiting for someone to undo her stupid mistake."

I let out a long, exasperated sigh. "So, let me get this straight. We're dealing with an ancient librarian who set up an unbreakable curse, hid the solution in a bunch of books, and is now waiting for a group of bumbling idiots to clean up her mess?"

The silence that followed was all the confirmation that I needed.

"Fantastic," I muttered.

Elle

Half-listening to the conversation between the others, I studied the map. Something caught my eye; there were faint lines beneath the visible markings. Squinting, I could decipher the willow tree and the markers of the meadow. Someone had drawn another map underneath, and if I was correct, there was something written at the top that said *originals*. My heart quickened.

"See if any of the other journals have a map," I stated, interrupting their conversation. They all turned to look at me, but Kairo was the only one who showed genuine interest. The others looked tired and bored.

"Whoever drew this one drew another on the page before it. It might be the location of the original journals."

We divided up the remaining journals, with each of us taking a couple to flip through. Out of the corner of my eye, I caught Nolan tucking the one he'd been reading close to him. My teeth clenched involuntarily. He was keeping secrets again, just like the night of the blood oath. But now wasn't the time. We searched for the other map page by page and journal by journal, over and over, until Nolan tossed down a mostly burnt journal and stood stretching. We weren't going to find it tonight. I pushed the book aside and pushed my hair out of my face.

"Damn it," I muttered, earning a surprised look from Nolan. "Nothing can be easy." I rarely cursed, but the situation warranted it.

Placing the map on the couch, I shone my cell phone light on it, grateful I'd had the foresight to recharge it at the house. The lines weren't clear enough to make out where they went, but they ended closer to the lane than the willow tree where I'd found the others. Another piece of the puzzle… just out of reach.

"Why are Allorians always hiding things?" Aiska pondered rhetorically.

"Because of Dothians," I replied, my tone dripping with sarcasm. Sometimes, I wondered if we'd ever get everyone else to move past the rivalry. Maybe that was exhaustion talking.

Nolan laughed, picked up the journal he'd hidden, and walked toward the rooms. We were going to have a conversation later, and I would get that journal. They seemed to have forgotten that the journals belonged to me, which meant the information inside them also did.

"I'll search the meadow tomorrow," I announced.

"Can I come?" Aiska asked, a little too eagerly. I eyed her, and she blushed. "I'm sorry," she added quickly. "That seemed a little pushy. I just… haven't seen Unicorns in so long."

I glanced at Kairo, who pointedly avoided the conversation by burying his nose between crisped pages. Her question had caught me off guard. I didn't know whether to trust the newest member of our group with the location of my herd. Aiska seemed sincere enough, but our connection wasn't quite there. It was too new.

"Maybe some other time," I finally said, trying to soften the rejection with a small smile. Aiska's expression fell flat, but she responded with a short nod of understanding.

For a moment, I stopped to consider whether her intentions were harmless, but I dismissed the thought when she immediately returned to helping us by offering to retrieve food.

Chapter Forty

His Secrets To Tell

Nolan

Sitting on a rocky ledge at the far side of the resort, I watched Caleda fret about in an attempt to get comfortable. She pushed herself against a boulder, rubbing her scaly side against the rocks as she maneuvered under the ledge. Caleda was a big fan of coverage. She liked every bit of her body hidden. For that, among other things, I respected her.

I ran a small knife under my nails, cleaning the accumulated dirt and grime under the edges. *What I wouldn't give for a real bath.* Even my hair was greasy, sitting in knotted curls on my head. I pulled at one for good measure and winced at the straw-like feeling.

"Bad hair day?" Elle's voice startled me, and I jumped. She climbed the rest of the path to get onto the large rocky ledge.

"I might have to use your bathtub," I admitted, keeping my tone light. "The creek leaves a lot to be desired."

"That's fine."

"Done reading?" I asked, though I already knew the answer. She was never done reading.

"I wanted to look something up, but you have the journal I need."

I tried not to wince, but my eyes squeezed shut anyway. The moment I'd been dreading had arrived. I'd been tempting fate for far too long to continue to get away with being bold about reading the journal in her vicinity. She sat down next to me and brushed her hand over my arm.

"What are you hiding?"

My heart thrummed against my tightening chest. I swallowed and looked away from her. She was going to read it all anyway. When she did, she would discover the truth; if I kept it from her, she'd be livid with me. I sucked in a nice, long breath and pulled my canvas sack onto my lap. Digging through its contents, my fingers closed around the scale-bound journal, and I held it out to her.

Elle took the journal reluctantly and flipped it over. She squinted at the cover in the bright moonlight. I could see the moment she slowly deciphered what was inscribed in the varnished scales. *Journal VI*

"It's an original," she whispered.

"It is."

"How did you get this?" she asked, running her finger down the aged binding.

"It belonged to my mom. I found it in her things."

"Why would your mom have it?"

"Because my mother was an Allorian," I answered, looking at her grimly. I took a deep breath.

Elle's reaction was exactly as I'd expected. Her gaze darted between the lines of text in her palm and my face; her lower lip caught between her teeth. She opened her mouth to speak, paused, then slowly closed it, a flicker of suspicion clouding her eyes before she forced herself to face what I'd confessed.

"An Allorian… Why did you keep this from me?" she questioned, tears forming on her lower lashes. She'd been alone, surrounded by Dothians, and I'd confessed that I knew an Allorian. Had known one well, in fact.

The hurt in her voice cut me deep. I didn't know how to handle her tears. Huffing, I ran my hand across the back of my neck. Aiska wouldn't cry over something like this. She'd be so angry at me that I was sure she'd smack me over the head with the journal rather than clutch it to her chest and shed tears on it. But Elle wasn't Aiska. She was far softer and empathetic.

"Because nobody else knows. My mom chose to keep it a secret, so I did the same."

"Why?" Elle replied, wiping at her eyes.

"I don't know."

"You can't remember?"

"No, it's not that. She never told me," I clarified. "I only found out after she… after she was gone."

Elle's brow furrowed. "But how? How did you find out if she never told you?"

I gestured to the journal in her hands. "That book. It was hidden in a false bottom of a trunk. I found it when I was going through her things."

"And you're sure it's hers?" Elle pressed, her fingers tracing the worn edges of the cover.

I nodded solemnly. "She made notes in the margins. Her handwriting is unmistakable."

Elle took a shaky breath. "Kairo doesn't know?"

I shook my head. "No. And I don't know how to tell him. How do you tell a Dothian you're half Allorian with how they feel about each other?"

Elle reached out and touched my arm.

Throat bobbing, I fought back my emotions. "I just… I don't understand why she hid it, why she never told me. Was she ashamed? Afraid? I have so many questions and no way to get all of the answers, and now, because of the curse, the answers might not even be the truth."

I looked out into the darkening night, the fog of my partial amnesia, and the confusion caused by the curse twisting in my gut. The gaps in my memory were like wounds that refused to heal, constantly reminding me of what little of my history I was left with. I'd tried to find answers in Elle's journals, but there'd been little mention of who my mother had been. Pressing my teeth together, I leaned back on my elbows.

The cool night air washed over me, and I considered the relief and apprehension I held over the fact that the secret was out now. I no longer had to hide it, and I couldn't imagine confiding in anyone else but Elle.

We sat in the moonlight for almost an hour, quietly talking about my mother. Both of us were perplexed by how little I knew. The basics of my past seemed unaltered, such as the type of parent my mother was or some traditions she upheld. I could almost see the gears turning in Elle's head as she tried to understand it all. With her, the weight of a lifetime of solitude felt lighter, as if her presence alone was a sanctuary.

"Your father was a Dothian?" Elle asked, leaning back on her elbows.

"He has to be," I admitted, suppressing a bitter laugh. "You can only keep a Dragon if you have Dothian blood running through your veins." And I do have a Dragon. Caleda was the only uncomplicated relationship in my life right now.

"I thought it wasn't common for an Allorian and a Dothian to have relations?"

"No, it wasn't."

"Is your mother related to my mother?"

"No," I told her, shaking my head. "According to my mother's notes, the journal was a gift from a friend, given to her before she died. She passed away nearly seventy years after the curse. I don't know who gave it to her, but there was a note in it that said, 'for you' with a heart." Which, if you ask me, is about as clear as mud.

Elle returned to the earlier conversation by asking, "Why didn't you tell Kairo?"

I frowned, unsure of why I didn't tell anyone else. It didn't feel fitting to share it, as if the words would be stamped across my forehead and others would consider me a traitor or unworthy.

"It wasn't my secret to tell," I repeated, knowing how weak that sounded.

Elle sat up, wiping her hands together to remove the dirt that had dug into her skin. "So, we are on the same page. It doesn't change anything with me."

"Thank you," I said with a soft, sad smile. It meant more than I could express that she didn't devalue me based on my parentage. My face grew solemn as I studied her. She nearly reached out and took my hand to comfort me, but stopped herself. I pretended not to notice, even as my heart somersaulted.

"Is there anything else I should know?"

I shook my head. "Everything I know is in that journal. Thanks to reading through what you have found, I've learned more about my past in the last week than I have in many years. I just wish we could break the curse and remember everything."

"I'm working on it."

"You are doing it."

"Not fast enough…"

"Faster than anyone else has," I countered.

She looked up at me, pulling the edge of her bottom lip between her teeth. The muscle in my jaw twitched. In the last bit of moonlight, she looked like a damned goddess. Her gold hair fell in soft waves around her, and the shimmering silver shirt she wore cast a faint reflective glow from the light onto her face. I nearly sat on my hands in my desperation to touch her—just one touch. But I knew better. I wasn't a complete idiot... most of the time.

"I better get inside," she told me, looking down at the candlelight flickering in the window of the room Kairo had chosen for himself in the resort.

"Yes," I agreed because she wasn't mine, and the sooner she walked away, the sooner I could try to get a grip on my feelings. Or at least pretend to.

I wasn't fast enough to offer her my hand, so she stood alone, looking back at me once before she climbed down the path. As soon as she made her way to the resort's back door, I crumbled onto the rocky earth, flinging my arms to the side. She was going to be the absolute death of me, and I did not care one bit because I would lay down my life to protect her without her ever returning a single one of my feelings.

Maybe it was the damned blood oath or pure male competition that made me feel like I would take on the world if it meant keeping her safe. Perhaps the way she made me feel was something I should fight for. Yet I saw the way she looked at Kairo. I'd been there when the universe claimed they were fated mates. It ripped me apart knowing I couldn't stop them, but I also couldn't make myself walk away because I'm a glutton for punishment, apparently.

Their destiny was written in the stars. As sure as the morning sun would show, Kairo and Elle were meant for each other. My job was to ensure I didn't stand in their way. Yet I couldn't help feeling like dying every time I saw Kairo touch her. It was a feeling that poured from the very foundation of who I was, as if it had been sitting there for an eternity, waiting to bubble over.

My upper lip curled at the thought of it. I should hate Elle because she was unknowingly driving a wedge between us. Even though Kairo didn't say anything, I knew he saw my unintentional glances. He was paying attention when I unwittingly slipped into the role of the person falling in love with his girl.

No, not falling. Already fell. Head over heels, crash and burn, no hope of recovery fell.

Chapter Forty-One

The Heat In Yours

Elle

"Where did you go?" Kairo asked as I entered the room. His voice was casual, but I could sense an underlying tension in the way his shoulders stiffened.

"I needed to talk to Nolan for a second."

The cold glint in Kairo's eyes looked like jealousy, but he quickly masked it. I couldn't blame him. Lately, I'd been feeling… confused about Nolan. It wasn't that I preferred his company over Kairo's; it was that I didn't mind it. The thought itself felt like a betrayal. Kairo was my constant, the person I was supposed to want. But lately, when I was with Nolan, I wasn't just tolerating his presence. I was finding it easy to exist without the weight of expectations that came with Kairo. It was a terrifying, quiet comfort.

"What did you guys talk about?"

"He found the missing journal."

I wasn't sure why I wasn't elaborating beyond what Nolan had said—it wasn't my secret to tell.

"How did he find it?" Kairo inquired, straightening the furs on the bed to cover the musty mattress underneath. His movements were deliberate as if he was distracting himself.

"You'll have to ask him," I responded delicately.

I wouldn't lie to Kairo about his cousin's secrets, but I wouldn't tell him them either. That decision was up to Nolan. It was up to him to confess to it. But why did keeping Nolan's secret feel so… intimate? Thumbing the cover of the dark, scale-bound journal, the strings that tied it shut started to give under my finger. I couldn't wait to read it, but my body was tired. My eyes were tired. More than that, my mind was a whirlwind of warring thoughts. I eyed the bed and yawned, hoping sleep might bring clearness.

"Want to sleep here tonight?" Kairo offered, his voice invitingly soft.

I faltered, surprised by my own hesitation. We'd unintentionally fallen asleep next to each other before, but this felt different. Sleeping in the same bed on purpose was a proposition, and I wasn't sure we could keep our hands off one another. A shiver ran through me, yet my shoulders relaxed. My gravitation toward him was strong, even with my recent confusion about Nolan. In the dim candlelight, his blue eyes were shadowed, but the desire in them was unmistakable. Heat bloomed. Our attraction was a steady current beneath the surface; Nolan was just ripples.

"We don't have to do anything."

He can always read me so well. It was one of the things I lov… liked most about him. He was willing to give me space to figure out what I wanted.

"Honestly," I sighed, the long day settling into my bones, "I'm too tired to do anything anyway. It's past midnight." As I said it, I realized just how exhausted I truly was. Taking my words as 'yes', he held up the comforter I'd brought from my house. I folded myself onto the bed, grateful for the soft surface after the hard, rocky ledge I'd been sitting on earlier.

Kairo climbed in after me, giving me enough space to get comfortable. He was always so considerate and patient with me. Within a few minutes, I drifted off, my mind spinning into a vivid dream. In it, I saw a great golden Dragon, its scales glittering like sunlight on water. It was trapped, desperately trying to free itself from a prison inside a mountain. I could feel its frustration, its yearning for freedom. As I watched, unable to help him, I couldn't shake the feeling that this Dragon was supposed to be important to me. But the dream faded before I could decipher the reason, leaving me floating in a sea of questions. Even in sleep, our quest for answers continued.

Kairo

When I opened my eyes the following day, Elle was curled against me. The morning was unseasonably chilly, a chill that filled the room even with the furs. She'd managed to wiggle out of half of the blanket and shivered lightly in her sleep. I pulled the blanket around her, my arm instinctively seeking the curve of her back.

Recalling Elle's private conversation with Nolan, the jealous, green-eyed brute inside me rumbled. They'd been alone together again… for quite a while. I wasn't oblivious that Nolan's interest in her had evolved from casual flirtation to something far more intense. The possessive glint in his eyes reflected my own. He was getting too close to her.

I thought I could handle it because Nolan's interest in Elle arguably kept her safer. But every part of me wanted to confront Nolan and demand that he stay away from her. What frightened me was that it wasn't just him. I'd seen the subtle shifts in their interactions, the guarded glances, the unspoken crossed boundaries. Moving the hair off her neck, I tugged her closer, letting my body warm her so that she would stop shivering.

Nolan was treading carefully, somewhat respecting the growing bond between Elle and me. But it wasn't enough. Not even when Nolan did everything he could to give her space if she came too close, or when he averted his gaze when I caught him watching her, I could recount several instances of Nolan holding his hands up in apparent surrender when I approached. The three of us were dancing precariously on the edge of a conflict none of us were particularly interested in confronting.

Elle stirred next to me, her gold and sea-green-flecked eyes slowly opening. A lazy smile curved her lips when she met my gaze, her fingers curling against my skin. Even with sleep in her eyes, her hair tangled around her, and her clothes rumpled, she was breathtaking. I ran my hand under her shirt, gently skimming the bandage that was still wrapped around her ribs with my fingers. Her body responded with a symphony of goosebumps and trembling skin.

"Morning," she murmured, her voice husky with sleep.

"Good morning," I replied, pulling her closer, my lips brushing against her temple. Her scent was intoxicating, a blend of cinnamon and something sugary.

"How long have you been up?"

"I just woke up," I admitted, cupping her jaw and leaning down to kiss her.

She returned the kiss lazily and leaned her cheek against mine, her lashes brushing my skin. Inhaling deeply, I used the arm under her to flip us both so that I was lying on top of her, resting my weight on my knees and one elbow. Brushing a strand of hair from her forehead, I kissed the spot it covered. Elle looked up at me, her cheeks coloring prettily in the sunlight streaming through the grimy windows.

"I can see the sun rising in your eyes," I murmured, tracing the delicate lines of her brow.

"I can see the heat in yours," she countered, a playful glint in her eyes.

I chuckled, lowering my head until our foreheads touched. The slow, lazy intimacy of the moment caused me to roll my hips into hers and intertwine our fingers. Suddenly, the morning chill was forgotten, replaced by the growing heat between us.

"I wish I could touch more of you," I whispered.

Elle's eyes darkened, a silent promise in her gaze. "I know," she replied, her lips brushing against mine.

Tracing the skin under Elle's bra with the back of my hand, I tugged at it lightly. Her lips parted, and her breath stuttered. She squirmed under me, untangling our fingers, and softly wrapped hers around the beating pulse inside my elbow. The touch was so gentle and tentative that it made the hair on my arms lift. It emboldened me. My hand found the back of her neck, and I squeezed lightly as I pulled her in for a kiss. The taste of her lips was the sun, and it warmed me to my core.

I hooked her bra under a finger, my breath becoming hers. Her nipple grazed my palm. Her back arched off the bed, stomach pressing against mine. I wanted to devour her, to lose myself in the intensity we were creating. Yet, a part of me held back, waiting for her to stop me if she wished. She twisted her thighs, and my throat rumbled.

Giving her one last chance to stop me, I waited for her to pull away or tell me that she was too tired. But when I opened my eyes, hers were glued to my face. The intensity of her look mesmerized me. She worried her bottom lip, filling the space between us with heart-pounding desire and wanton arousal. Savoring the moment, I waited for her next move, acutely aware of every point where our bodies touched. Elle hesitated, a subtle resistance like a taut bowstring. I understood it because I felt it, too. We shouldn't be doing this, not now. There were too many loose ends and too many unknowns. One wrong move and our world could unravel.

Would taking this step before we knew how to break the curse result in our failure? The lust swirling around us created a fog of uncertainty that threatened to cloud our judgment. But we both knew we couldn't risk it, not if something might happen to my Dragons or her herd. It would be selfish of us to risk them because we couldn't control ourselves.

However, despite these fears, I couldn't stop myself. My body seemed to move of its own accord as I ran my hand down her body, my fingers tracing the band of her loose-fitting pajama bottoms. Her eyes widened, but she didn't stop me. Desire, fear, and a raw vulnerability drew me in like a moth to flame. I wanted to consume her, claim her, and make her forget everything else. A deep red bloomed across her cheeks and the tops of her ears.

I leaned down to kiss her, hoping to ease away her hesitation— and maybe my own. Drawing her lower lip between my teeth, I savored the soft gasp that escaped her. But even as I lost myself in the kiss, a nagging voice in the back of my mind whispered doubts again and again. Were we being reckless? What if this moment of passion jeopardized everything we'd been working toward? I pulled back, searching Elle's eyes and saw my own conflicted emotions reflected there—desire warring with caution, need battling with responsibility.

"Kairo," she breathed, her thighs tightening.

A micro-shift, a mere whisper of motion, ignited a fire in my groin. The fire was consuming, a savage hunger that tormented me. I ground my teeth, a low growl trembling in my chest. Silently cursing the day pants were invented, I realized there was far too much clothing between my bare skin and hers.

"I'm going to stop," I told her. "I promise."

Elle nodded, her eyes holding onto that raw vulnerability that excited and terrified me. She was surrendering, offering herself on a silver platter, but a part of her was still holding back. I could feel the precipice, the edge. One more move, and we'd tumble over it together. I could feel just how badly she wanted me when my hand made its way between her thighs. Her name was a prayer, a curse, a desperate plea as I dipped my head forward and moaned it against her neck, the sound escaping me before I could stop it. My lips found hers as I reluctantly pulled back, my hands trembling with restraint. Gently, I pulled her bra back down, tugged her shirt to cover her torso, and lay next to her.

"Are we any closer to answers?"

"Closer than we were," she replied. "We'd be closer if I found the original journals."

The journals were a smokescreen, a desperate gambit to quell the inferno raging within me. I didn't need to spell it out. The hunger etched on her face was just like mine. She adjusted her clothing and sat up. Wrapping her arms around her bent legs, I admired the graceful curve of her back as my finger traced down it.

To her, my eyes must have seemed blank, lost in thought. In reality, I was internally tamping down the part of me that wanted her naked on top of me, locking up the lust-filled beast that nearly lost control. Yet, metaphorically, I set the keys to that lock next to the door, just in case. The possibility, the potential, was too tempting to dismiss entirely. She was too irresistible.

"I'm hungry," Elle whispered.

Released from my stupor, I stood up easily and took her hand to help her from the bed. She squeezed my fingers, followed me through the door, and down the hall. We found Aiska already up, with muffins and coffee on the table. She had a journal open before her; her face scrunched in deep concentration.

"For us?" Elle asked, pointing to the food and hot cups.

Aiska looked up from the journal and grinned, her eyes bouncing from my face to Elle's as if she could sense what we'd been doing.

"Don't get used to it," Aiska paused, tapping her lip with her finger. "I have somewhere I think we should go."

Chapter Forty-Two

Explain Yourself

Kairo

The Bad Saint. That was the name of the club Aiska dragged us to. She'd only convinced us by saying she knew someone who might give us more information. I sat with my arms crossed over my chest, sulking because Aiska and Nolan had fake IDs and I had never bothered to get one. Which meant they didn't have to wear a bright white stamp on their hand that glowed in the garish black lights surrounding the bar. Not that I wanted to drink. It's the principle. I was, after all, far older than the twenty-one years required if you counted the years and not the fact that I stopped aging at 23.

I wasn't thrilled to come in the first place, especially when my demands to know who we were meeting were met with Aiska skirting names and information. The only slight comfort was that we'd chosen a neutral location away from Elle's little hometown. Across the table, Elle seemed unperturbed, sipping a virgin daiquiri. Nolan, sitting opposite her, was cradling a Bahama Mama the size of his own damned head. The music was a sonic assault, a relentless beat that pounded in my skull.

Out of place in my scuffed tall boots, black pants, and a T-shirt that Elle had found in her dad's closet, I felt exposed. I'd reluctantly taken a solid black T-shirt with a small, stitched hippopotamus on the pocket, leaving me entirely underdressed compared to Aiska and Elle. Tugging at the T-shirt's sleeves, I glanced at the girls. Aiska had borrowed one of Elle's fancier dresses - a tight-fitting, silky, dark green number with a small slit on the side. At the same time, Elle wore a silver-on-black shimmering low-cut top and a flowing, flared, short black skirt.

She'd dug both out of one of the suitcases she'd never unpacked when she returned home from college. The shirt still had the price tag on it. It had dangled from the bunched fabric under her arm, and I pulled it off for her before we left her house. Both girls looked stunning, but Elle, in particular, exuded a dangerous allure in her outfit, which made me edgy in the heady atmosphere. There were more than a couple of pairs of eyes on her.

Despite my reservations, Elle looked comfortable, almost happy. The relentless pursuit of the original journals cast a long shadow over us all. Days bled into nights, each minute a painstaking crawl while we'd searched the meadow blade by blade. We still couldn't find them. With every fruitless hour, our resolve eroded, replaced by creeping despair. When Aiska suggested a reprieve, Nolan readily agreed. Elle had hesitated until Aiska insisted, explaining that the research was going to give her wrinkles. This information would be easier to obtain if given by whoever Aiska had found.

"I'll be right back," Aiska yelled over the booming bass of the music.

Only Elle nodded. I eyed the crowd warily, curious who Aiska was retrieving. Spotting a flash of bright red hair over the sea of dancing figures, my eyes narrowed. I looked at Nolan, who was obliviously drinking his fruity alcoholic slushy as if he didn't have a care in the world. The skin surrounding the oath pricked. If that red hair belonged to who I thought it did, this night was about to go from a break to a catastrophe. I snapped my fingers at Nolan.

"Zayn," I mouthed, feeling a knot form in my stomach. He turned slowly, lips still on his straw, but I saw the moment recognition hit him.

"Shit," Nolan muttered, echoing my thoughts.

"What's wrong?" Elle asked.

"It's okay," I said, a brittle reassurance coating my words.

Elle's golden hair snapped into my vision, screaming that she wasn't a Dothian and serving as an open invitation for trouble with others nearby. A deep ache settled in my gut, a yearning to shield her, to somehow erase that telltale blonde from existence. And it wasn't just her hair. If anyone here started asking questions, they'd realize in a heartbeat that she wasn't one of us, wasn't a Dragon Keeper. Every word she uttered, every unfamiliar mannerism, would expose her. Nolan must have felt it, too, because he slid his chair closer to hers.

"Whatever you do, don't let him know you're an Allorian."

Elle's eyes widened in fear before she schooled her expression. Smart girl. She focused intently on her drink. I tensed as Zayn approached, his red hair brighter than flames. Like a snake, he was a coiled spring, tense and unpredictable. Aiska's voice cut through a lull in the music.

"Kairo," she said, her tone cautious. "Nolan… I know that you guys know Zayn and that you have history…"

I couldn't help but raise an eyebrow at her understatement. Everyone had history with Zayn. He was a trader, after all.

"But," she pressed on, her voice steady, "he might have something to offer." The word 'might' hung in the air, a compelling uncertainty.

Another song played, somehow even louder than before. I studied Zayn's face, searching for any hint of his intentions.

"Why don't we go somewhere more… private?" Zayn suggested, gesturing toward the back of the club.

Hesitating, I weighed our options. On one hand, Zayn's presence spelled trouble. On the other hand, he got around a lot. He might have information that could help us… I glanced at Nolan, seeing the same conflict warring across his features. Whatever we decided, Aiska had a lot of explaining to do.

Nolan

I'd drunk enough to openly admit to everyone at the table that I despised Zayn. Despised was putting it mildly. My memories before the curse may have been fuzzy, but it didn't take long to develop a burning hatred for the guy after he screwed me over. Repeatedly. Zayn was a trader, which was a polite way of saying he was a glorified con artist with delusions of grandeur. He had sold everything from stolen Dragon eggs to priceless artifacts. His idea of a fair trade was whatever shiny object caught his eye that day.

The idiot's gambling habit meant he lost as much as he gained, but hey, at least he was consistent in his stupidity. Zayn was smart in the way a calculator was smart - all facts, no wisdom. It was Elle who motioned us to get up from the booth. Reluctantly, we followed the walking disaster toward the club's backroom. I tugged on Kairo's arm, trying to motion that he should take her literally anywhere else. Hell, I would have settled for the dumpster out back… Anywhere but here. I'd get the information. She didn't need to stay for it.

Kairo frowned at me. *She won't go*, he mouthed, *you know that.*

"Elle," I hissed, trying to catch her attention. "You sure you want to do this?"

"We're here for answers," she hissed back.

I didn't give a rat's ass if she wanted to go or not. I was half-tempted to throw her over my shoulder and make a run for it. But I knew if Elle suddenly vanished, it would raise more red flags than I did… sometimes… unintentionally, of course. I cursed under my breath, silently damning Aiska for putting us in this mess. What game was she playing?

Zayn led us through thick black curtains that were covered in stains of various sizes and colors. They probably hadn't been washed since the club opened. I positioned myself behind Elle, close enough that her shampoo wafted up my nostrils. My blood oath tattoo itched like crazy as Zayn ushered us through a door.

Grimacing, my nostrils flared, and my head swam from too much slushy booze. The room we'd entered looked like it had been decorated by someone with a crush on a Vampire—circular black couch, glass table, shag carpet that had seen better days. The walls were a charming shade of "murder scene red," and two sad-looking iron lanterns were pretending to be fancy in the corners. My nose wrinkled involuntarily at the sweet bouquet of vomit, industrial-strength cleaner, and stale cigars.

"Charming place, Zayn," I drawled, sarcasm dripping from every word. "Matches your personality."

Zayn's smile didn't reach his eyes. "Always the comedian, aren't you, Nolan?"

The door clicked shut behind us, muffling the club's music. Zayn motioned for us to sit. Elle moved toward the center of the couch like it was just another night out, and Kairo practically teleported to her side, wedging himself in before she even settled. It was a smooth way of showing that she was, in fact, the most important thing in the room.

I didn't sit. Something didn't feel right, and it wasn't just the questionable crunchy texture of the carpet under my boots. Instead, I stood watch as the others sank into the cushions. Someone had to keep their wits about them, and I wasn't placing any bets on anyone but myself. Everyone else had clearly lost their minds.

"Why are we here?" I grumbled.

Zayn's lips curled into an infuriating smirk. "I have something that you guys might want to see," he offered as if he were doing us a favor.

Before I could retort, Kairo cut in, his voice sharp. "I have a better question. Why does Aiska know you're here?"

Zayn rolled his eyes. "Aiska owes me a debt."

We all turned to look at Aiska, who splayed her hands out in a gesture of mock innocence. A hollow feeling spread through my chest.

"Explain," I demanded.

Aiska's face fell. "I lost Fynch in a bet," she admitted. "That's why I left Dothan Valley. I couldn't hand her over."

Her admission was another blow to the gut. Beside me, Kairo's voice was incredulous. "You bet Fynch?"

"I didn't have a choice," Aiska replied, crossing her arms defensively. "You wouldn't understand…"

"Try us," Elle interjected, her reaction unnervingly calm. "We're all ears, Aiska."

Kairo's jaw clenched, the muscles jumping beneath his skin. He was furious, and so was I. Zayn and Aiska were working together. He must have given her an ultimatum to get Elle here. I could not have been more livid at her.

"Later," Aiska muttered, avoiding our eyes. "We'll discuss this later."

Kairo turned back to Zayn. "What do you have and what do you want?"

Zayn's smile widened, and the look made me want to vomit. "First," he purred, "tell me who she is."

Kairo stiffened, instinctively tucking Elle closer to his side. It was a protective gesture that didn't go unnoticed by Zayn. His gaze sharpened, focusing on them like a predator spotting prey. Elle didn't so much as flinch under Zayn's stare, but her fingers tightened around Kairo's arm, leaving indents in his skin.

"She's nobody," Kairo stated, but the lie in his voice was made obvious by his deep tone. Damn it, Kairo. You're playing right into his hands.

Zayn raised both eyebrows, leaning forward on the table. His attention bounced between Elle and Kairo as if he were jumping from one wrong conclusion to another. I decided to step in before anything got worse.

"She's from Ashen Valley," I stated, letting the lie roll off my tongue as smoothly as possible. It was a gamble, but it was better than allowing Zayn to think Elle was Allorian.

Zayn didn't buy it. "Nobody has left Ashen Valley in centuries," he replied, his eyes glittering with suspicion.

I caught Kairo's appreciative glance. I might make a decent liar out of me, yet. Ashen Valley was a charming little slice of paradise - if your idea of paradise was a desolate, rocky wasteland populated by a few dozen paranoid Dothians. They were so scared of "corruption" from the outside world that they'd practically become hermits. Of course, Elle's golden locks were about as Ashen Valley as white feathers on a raven.

"She came on her own Dragon," Kairo shrugged, cool as a cucumber.

"Why?" Zayn asked.

Elle opened her mouth to say something, but snapped it shut when I shot her a look.

"For the same reason, we all are here," Kairo replied, and I nearly snorted at the irony.

Zayn raised one brow and reached under the couch - *please don't be a weapon, please don't be a weapon* - and pulled out a briefcase. Well, that was… anticlimactic. He snapped it open with both thumbs. Inside was a scroll that looked older than dirt itself, wrapped around a wooden dowel with golden Dragon ornaments on the ends.

"What is it?" I asked.

"I have no idea," Zayn admitted. Shocker. "I don't understand what language it's written in… but I was told it contains the instructions to cure the curse."

My heart danced into my throat, and I reached out to grab the scroll. But Zayn yanked it away. He turned to Elle, pushing the case toward her. Oh, this can't be good.

"I'm going to gather by the ink on your arms that you three have a vested interest in seeing this," Zayn stated, his eyes gleaming with an infuriating know-it-all look. "Aiska didn't tell me much, but I'm assuming your newness to this group brought about the search for information on the curse."

Kairo moved to block him, but Elle moved his arm out of her way.

"I believe you are the one with the answers," Zayn continued, focusing on Elle. "I'll let you see it… If you tell me what it says."

"And if she can't read it?" I challenged. "What then, Zayn? You'll have shown your hand for nothing."

Zayn didn't bother responding to me, a sly grin crossing his face. Well, shit. We'd walked right into the fox's den, hadn't we? And now the fox wanted a story. I glanced at Kairo, then Elle, my mind fuzzy but sobering. How the hell were we going to get out of this one? Maybe if I created a distraction? I'd heard setting things on fire worked. Or I could try my hand at ventriloquism. *Oh no, Zayn! The scroll is talking! It says you should give it to Nolan immediately and jump into a lake!* Maybe I was a tad more buzzed than I thought I was.

The tension in the room ratcheted up another notch when Elle reached for the scroll. Maybe Zayn was on a search for information just like we were? He watched Elle like he could only hope she had all the answers. If he wasn't searching for information, we might be trading one curse for another. Elle's cheeks flushed when she pulled the scroll out of the briefcase. I wanted to yank it away from her, like some paranoid lunatic. But after slogging through endless journals, I'd probably read the back of a cereal box if it promised answers.

Elle cautiously unfurled the parchment as if it would bite her. Her eyes narrowed, her head tilted, and the tips of her ears grew pink. After what felt like an eternity of silently looking over the thing, long enough that I finally had to sit, Elle rolled up the scroll, placed it back in the briefcase, and pushed it back to Zayn.

"What does it say?" Zayn demanded, practically salivating.

"I'm not sure who you got that from, but it's not instructions on anything related to curing the curse," Elle stated.

Zayn's face fell. "Then what is it?"

"It's a detailed rendering of how the curse was created," Elle explained. "It's not complete, though. At the end of the last part, a notation states that this scroll is part one of three."

"Three parts?" Kairo interjected, leaning forward. "Where are the others?"

Zayn cursed under his breath, running a hand through his red hair. "How the hell should I know? I was told this was the whole thing."

I shot him a look, which he promptly ignored. Again.

Apparently, this was less valuable than he'd hoped. Shoving the briefcase away like he was angry with it, he turned to Elle and searched her as if looking for a way to decipher if she was being honest.

"That was helpful," I sighed in an attempt to draw his attention away from her.

Zayn snapped, "I didn't drag you all here for nothing. There's got to be something useful in that scroll."

Elle shook her head. "It's mostly historical context. Nothing about breaking the curse."

Zayn studied Elle again before his expression turned flat. He motioned for us to go as if he couldn't bear the sight of us any longer. We all stood to leave. Before she could make it to the door, Zayn grabbed Aiska's arm, whispering something that made her go pale. Whatever the terms of the debt she owed, I was starting to think running had been the best option. I was also still considering whether to trust her after this. Kairo whisked Elle away before Zayn could ask any more questions. Zayn's eyes lingered on Elle long enough to make me consider the merits of a good old-fashioned brawl.

"Mind what you are looking at, Zayn," I warned, stepping into his line of sight. "Those eyes might wander somewhere they shouldn't."

Zayn's smirk widened. "Protective, aren't we? Interesting."

Shit.

"Hey Zayn," I said, "If you're looking for the Allorian, the last time she was spotted was in a town north of here called Sherman."

"Seems like a lie. But I'll take your word for it."

Knowing I hadn't convinced him of much, I turned to leave, hiding my agitation behind a mask of indifference.

"Must be hard," Zayn's voice stopped me cold.

I paused in the doorway, looking back. "What do you mean?"

"To be in love with his girl," Zayn replied, smirking like a cocky bastard.

I arched an eyebrow, giving him a once-over. Well, well. Maybe there was a brain cell or two rattling around in that thick skull after all.

"And what makes you think that?"

Zayn chuckled. "Please. The way you look at her, how you position yourself to guard her… It's written all over you."

I forced a laugh. "You're seeing things that aren't there. Must be an occupational hazard of being a professional liar."

"Am I?" He pressed, his grin widening. "So, you're saying you feel nothing for her?" He gave me a skeptical look.

I met his gaze steadily. "Impossibly hard," I relented because sometimes the best lie was wrapped in truth. "To feel nothing for someone so important to our cause. But love? You're barking up the wrong tree, pal."

Zayn narrowed his eyes, studying me for a long moment, then shrugged. "If you say so. But remember, Nolan, in our world, unspoken feelings have a way of becoming very loud at the worst possible moments."

I turned away, my hand on the door. "Save the fortune cookie wisdom. It doesn't suit you."

Chapter Forty-Three

Trust Me

Aiska

"Why would you let us take Elle there?" Kairo demanded when we all piled into the Jeep.

His voice was sharp and accusatory, and I couldn't blame him. I'd walked them into a trap. But they never would have come if I'd told them. Zayn had practically demanded an introduction in trade for more time with my Dragon before he planned to take her. How could I have refused?

"I didn't have a choice," I muttered, knowing how weak it sounds.

"There's always a choice, Aiska," Nolan growled from the back seat. "You just made the wrong one."

I took a deep breath, steeling myself. "She's going to have to face the others eventually. Zayn is mild in comparison to many," I replied, catching Elle's eye in the rearview mirror and mouthing an apology. It wasn't enough, but it was all I could offer.

Elle's gaze was steady, but there was hurt in her eyes. "A little warning would have been nice," she said softly.

"Eventually," Kairo cut in. "Did you think for one second that Zayn won't look into who she actually is?"

"He won't bother," I said, trying to sound more confident than I felt.

Nolan's voice cut through the vehicle. "What makes you believe that?"

I swallowed hard. "Because Zayn didn't originally come for her," I responded. "He's here for me."

The inside of the Jeep grew quiet, the silence broken only by the engine's rumble as Elle started to drive off. I could feel their confusion and betrayal in the silence that surrounded me.

Elle was the first to break it. "Could you elaborate?"

Closing my eyes for a moment, I gathered my courage. "I lost Fynch to him in a bet years ago," I confessed, the words tasting bitter. "I've been on the run since I left Dothan Valley. He was searching for me and came here. He told me that if I found you guys and made you talk to him, he would give me more time with Fynch. I didn't know… I hadn't met Elle when I agreed to do it."

"Why would you bet your Dragon?" Kairo asked, the disappointment in his voice cut me to the core.

With a stuttering inhale, I looked at Elle in the mirror. "Because Zayn had my mother's necklace, the one she was supposed to give me before she died. He got it from my drunk ass father." The memories of that moment flooded back, and they were still sharp enough to be painful. "I bet Fynch, thinking I could win it back, and I lost. She was the only thing I could offer more valuable than the necklace."

"Oh, Aiska," Elle sighed.

"That doesn't excuse putting us all at risk," Nolan countered.

Kairo shook his head. "I can't believe you'd gamble with Fynch like that. She's not just a possession, Aiska. She's your Dragon."

"Don't you think I know that?" I snapped, tears pricking my eyes. "I've regretted it every day since."

I'd been carrying this secret for so long, running from it, and now it was all crashing down around me. The apologies and explanations became lodged in my throat. All I could do was hope that they'd understand and forgive me for dragging them into this mess. But their shocked faces meant that forgiveness might be too much to ask for. My imperfections stood out, especially next to someone like Elle. I wanted to hate her, but I couldn't. Elle seemed like someone who would never do what I'd done, and I suddenly found myself holding to the moral compass she embodied.

The silence in the Jeep was deafening as if sound itself was banished. Even the passing cars seemed muted, afraid to intrude through the tension. I watched the lines on the road pass. My reflection stared back in the window, the recollection of all my mistakes shadowed across my features.

The curse. That damned curse that didn't even have the decency to grandfather in existing relationships. Every Dothian and Allorian had been forced to choose between solitude and companionship, most not even realizing they had a choice. Only those close to the Albadine knew the details. Those like my mother, she'd known. She had chosen to stay with my father anyway, lasting thirty years after that wretched curse swept across our valleys. Her decision haunted me still. He'd been a drunken bastard who treated me like an inconvenience instead of his only child.

"I understand," Elle's voice broke through my reverie. I caught her eyes in the rearview mirror, a fleeting moment of connection.

"To clarify… I understand a little," Nolan echoed. "I just don't know if I can trust you now."

His words stung, but again, it was hard to place blame. "I've been helping," I protested weakly, knowing it wasn't enough.

Kairo twisted in his seat, his eyes boring into me. "How do we know you won't go to someone else? How do we know you won't return to Zayn and offer Elle in exchange for Fynch?"

"Because I won't," I insisted.

The very thought of betraying them and Elle had made me nauseous. As soon as Zayn had laid eyes on her, I'd realized the danger I'd placed her in. Elle was our only chance to break the curse. Had he… had he taken her. I wouldn't have been able to forgive myself.

"How can we trust that?" Kairo pressed.

"She can do a blood oath," Elle suggested, and a surge of gratitude for Elle's attempt at a solution toyed with my emotions.

Nolan groaned, his head thumping against the window. "Not another blood oath."

"We have bigger things to worry about," Elle declared, trying to shift the conversation. Part of me was relieved, while another wanted to finish this, to prove myself. To do something.

"What do you mean?" Kairo asked.

"When I was reading the scroll, it all clicked. I know how and in what order to break the first two parts of the curse," she stated. The energy in the car jolted.

This was the moment we'd all been waiting for, the reason we'd been searching and struggling. As the others reacted, I found myself torn between hope for our future and fear of my past catching up with us. Whether they trusted me or not, whether I had to take a blood oath or prove myself in some other way, I knew one thing for certain: I was done running. It was time to face the consequences of my actions and do whatever it took to help break this curse, for all our sake. Even if it meant losing my Dragon…

Elle

Flipping open the map of Dothan Valley, I compared it to the vague, riddle-like entries in journal number six. We'd gone over this journal so many times, my dreams had become convoluted analogies focused on its entries. Some pages were like cryptic poetry. But one entry kept drawing me back to it, and the scroll had confirmed my suspicion.

"The curse was first cast in Dothan Valley?" I asked, looking up at the faces hovering around me like anxious vultures at a picnic.

"Likely," Kairo replied. His features grew serious.

"We have to break the curse in Dothan Valley," I explained, pointing to a pass between two mountains on the map. One mountain housed the expansive library with its golden Dragon. The other was full of shadowy rock faces and steep inclines.

"What do we do?" Kairo asked.

I took a deep breath. "The first part of the curse is to change the Unicorns back to their former selves and take them to the valley. We have to return to where it started, following the path it took during the seventh phase of the moon. They must pass through these two mountains where the curse was first cast. Once I request that my herd return to their original form, the scroll states that I change them all. Just like I thought, all of the Unicorns that exist right now will transform into Alicorns, and their wards will be broken."

The words tumbled out of me, and they felt like coming home. It was almost as if I'd known them all along, buried deep in my subconscious like forgotten song lyrics. An eerie sense of déjà vu crawled up my spine as my fingers traced the passage I'd read a dozen times before. It was like the scroll had flipped a switch in my brain, turning the riddle into crystal-clear instructions. The uncertain fate of the other Allorians loomed over me. How many were out there, blissfully unaware of the time bomb ticking away? The time bomb that I was holding the detonator for was ticking. I swallowed hard.

"I don't understand…" I muttered, suddenly feeling very small.

"What?" Aiska asked absently, scratching at the small ink spot from her brand-new blood oath.

"I don't understand why you all trust that I'm doing everything right."

Kairo frowned, his expression softening. "Elle, you've been ten steps ahead of us. Whenever we come to you with new information, you're already connecting the dots. I think it has become pretty obvious that you are meant to bring us back to how things used to be."

His words warmed me, but Nolan cut in with a dose of doubt before I could bask in the glow. "I don't understand why you would want to break the curse. We could hang around and protect you until your Sula-umbra wears off, and then you could return to your normal life. You don't have to help us."

Normal? That ship had sailed, waved goodbye, and was probably halfway across the ocean. "My life is never going to be normal again," I said, the truth settling in my chest. "Things will never go back to how they were for me, but things can go back for all of you. Since my parents died, I don't have anything tying me here. I can do and go where I please as long as my herd can follow. If this is what it takes to keep them safe for as long as they can live, then it's what I'll do." I paused and swallowed. "Besides, I'm almost positive that this is the last chance to do this. I think I am the last of my lineage that can break the curse, and I don't know what happens if I don't break it."

"Then let's do this," Kairo murmured.

There was a flicker of hesitation in his eyes, his throat bobbing. I understood. I wasn't feeling one hundred percent about any of this, but I nodded, returning to the map. There was more to tell him – the second part of the curse affected both of us. But that was more of a private conversation. I couldn't dive into our love life with Nolan and Aiska as an audience. It was too awkward.

I was lost in thought, my mind racing with plans and possibilities, when Nolan snapped me back.

"So," he said, "breaking the first part of the curse is returning the Unicorns to their former form... What about the Dragons?"

There was still so much we didn't know, so many pieces of this puzzle that didn't quite fit. Frowning, I reached for the paper I'd scribbled on as soon as we'd arrived at the resort.

"The journals were all written by Allorians. The only thing I have found about the changes in the Dragons is something about it being internal," I explained, my eyes running over the words I'd written in a frenzy. "I think it means the ones who are sick will fully heal. Maybe they won't need Unicorn blood anymore?"

It wasn't much, but it was something. I thought of all the Dragons suffering from an ailment they didn't understand. The thought of being able to help them, to restore them to their full glory, was one of the reasons why I couldn't back down.

"What's the second part?" Aiska asked.

Heat rose to my cheeks, a blush I couldn't control. Turning toward them, I placed the paper down with a deliberateness that felt almost ceremonial. My eyes found Kairo's, and for a moment, it was like we were the only two people in the room.

"It's personal," I stated, my voice barely above a whisper.

The burden of what I knew, of what we needed to do, was merely confirmation. The second part was something we both already knew had to happen. Yet, it seemed so profound... so intimate... I took a deep breath and held it, my chest rising. The others were looking at me expectantly, but this wasn't something I could just blurt out in front of everyone. Nolan and Aiska had no idea that to break the curse, a Dothian must fall in love, and an Allorian must give herself to him.

In its cruel design, the curse hadn't just affected our creatures. It had twisted the very nature of love and the connection between Dothians and Allorians. And now, to undo it, Kairo and I… Nolan and Aiska had followed me down this rabbit hole of ancient magic and generational curses. But this next step… was something Kairo and I needed to face together.

"I'll explain more later," I said. "For now, we need to focus on what comes next."

Chapter Forty-Four

They Are Up North

Aiska

Sprawled across the couch, I fiddled with Elle's phone as if I'd never seen one before. To be honest, the last time I'd touched one, they'd folded in half. Having been on the run for so long, I found technology so foreign. Though I quickly realized why humans walked around like zombies. Even without reception, these games were more addictive than fresh cannoli. Sure, I'd done plenty of modern things like watching television and playing arcade games a time or two, but this tiny screen was far more euphoric. The world was at my fingertips. Since I was finally up to date on what my companions had been through, I had nothing better to do than embrace my inner zombie.

Elle had only lent me this miraculous distraction as a bribe for fetching her chocolate ice cream from town. She was sitting across the living area, spooning the ice cream straight from the carton as if it were paramount to her. Maybe it was. It seemed to be helping her with something. We had hit another lull in our grand adventure when Elle mentioned the timing wasn't right. We needed to wait at least another week, maybe two, before attempting to break the first part of the curse. I suspected she was buying time to figure out how to warn the other Allorians that their Unicorns were about to sprout wings, because she was incredibly fucking responsible.

The delay didn't bother me. It gave me more time to lose myself in this ridiculous game where a worm swallowed smaller worms, growing longer and faster with each meal. It was oddly satisfying in a morbid way, and it kept me from dwelling on the Zayn situation. My eyes flickered at the thought of him. He was the bane of my existence, and his new deadline for handing over Fynch was approaching fast. I should prepare my heart for when I have to hand her over. It was breaking at the mere thought.

I'd been hoping against hope that Fynch would nest soon, that there would be eggs to snatch before she was hauled off to be auctioned to some creep like Oscur. Gag. Or, better yet, she'd have been too busy guarding her nest for Zayn to touch her. But no, my stubborn girl showed no signs of settling down despite her obvious dalliances with one of her two male admirers. Instead, she stuck to me like glue, appearing as if by magic every time I stepped outside the resort. It was as if she knew what was happening despite intentionally not being told. *The clever beast.* Zayn would probably need a crane and an army to haul her away.

The reality was, I wasn't going to be able to go with the others when they left here. It was time for me to face the music. Going with them meant Zayn would follow, and I couldn't allow that, especially not after betraying them the way that I did. Swallowing hard, I realized I'd lost another round of the worm game. Fitting, really. I set the phone down and looked over at Elle. There was something about her, a hope that lingered around her like a subtle perfume. Seeing that glow and quiet determination made me want to help. It led me to take the blood oath, itchy aftermath and all.

Elle might save us. It was a lot to put on such young shoulders, but if anyone could do it, it was her. And maybe, just maybe, when all this curse-breaking business was done, Zayn would have bigger things to worry about than collecting on old debts. Maybe Fynch and I would get our happily-ever-after after all, and we could stop running. It was a long shot, I knew, but anything is possible. If needed, I would keep playing this silly worm game, fetching ice cream, and hoping. Because what else could I do?

Picking the phone back up, I restarted the game and was still fiddling with it sometime later when Elle finally piped up.

"I figured out the first few pages of this riddle." She was talking more to herself than to me, but I couldn't help but be intrigued.

"What does it say?"

Elle looked up at me, eyes narrowed. She was wondering how much she could trust me, and I couldn't blame her. I'd already created a problem. While I understood it, her hesitation stung a bit. I'm trying to make up for my mistakes by helping, damn it.

"It's a list of possible Allorian locations," she finally said, "but it's decades old. Who knows if they are still there?"

"Where's the closest one?" I asked, scratching my blood oath.

Elle furrowed her brow, looking adorably earnest as she sat cross-legged on the ottoman. "Somewhere where the cold lasts but eight months of the year," she stated, "near an iced mountain and a valley of cliffs and evergreens."

"North?"

Elle tilted her head, continuing, "Possibly. The journal states it can only be accessed by air or sea. It lies along the coast and has a never-ending bay, and it mentions something about where the whales play and sweet strawberries?"

Before I could respond, Nolan materialized behind us like the riddle had summoned him. He'd been asleep while Kairo was on watch.
"Sounds like Gustava," he said, casual as ever.

We both turned to look at him, and I stifled a laugh. He was decked out in human clothes—a thin T-shirt that I was sure belonged to Elle's dad and black sweatpants that were a tad too small.

"What," Nolan shrugged, noticing our stares. "I like geography, and I like to travel."

"Where is Gustava?" Elle asked.

"Alaska," Nolan and I said in unison. *Great minds, I suppose.*

Elle's face lit up like she'd just won the lottery. "We should go there," she declared, snapping the book shut with finality.

Nolan cut in, "And leave the Unicorns unattended with Zayn and Oscur nearby?"

I saw an opportunity and jumped in. "There are enough of us that two can stay behind, and two can make the trip," I offered, mentally packing my bags.

"My Dragon is nesting," Nolan stated. "Yours should be. Kairo is the only one with male Dragons, and if one is gone, that only leaves one to protect the resort and the meadow."

"About that," Elle said with a grimace, "we should move the nests into the meadow."

"What?" Kairo said, coming through the double set of doors that were left open to let in the cool breeze.

"You guys said the Dragons protect their eggs with their lives, but that they could be found and the eggs could be snatched," she said. "If the nests are in the meadow, the ward will hide them, but if they are found, the Dragons will protect the meadow and their nests."

"Double security," I replied with a grin.

"Triple," Elle corrected me. "You and Nolan could also stay in the meadow. Kairo and I can make the trip."

"What trip?" Kairo asked.

Nolan's lips puckered, and his nose scrunched. "Why?" he whined, and I realized he'd gotten too comfortable with resort living. Or maybe his displeasure had to do with the hint of jealousy creeping across his gaze as he eyed Kairo and Elle. Elle's reasoning was sound, though. She would get to play savior to the Allorians, the Unicorns stayed protected, and if the ward protected Fynch, maybe I'd get those eggs after all. Out of sight, out of mind for Zayn.

Elle pointed to Kairo. "After the Dragons have settled in the meadow, you are going with me to Alaska to find the Allorians and warn them," she pointed to Nolan, "you are going to the meadow to protect everything while we're gone."

Nolan grumbled. "You're the boss," he sighed. "Camping. Can't wait."

I bit back a smile. Poor Nolan, forced to rough it. Such hardship. I'd slept in worse places than a Dragon-guarded, warded meadow with Unicorns. Unicorns I'd actually get to lay eyes on.

Elle

Standing in the middle of the meadow, I ran my fingers down the defined arches that made up Flint's massive jowl. He was larger in size and presence, and his horn had grown to a fine point. The image he presented was breathtaking, a living embodiment of a fairytale. His silky hide gleamed in the sunlight, his long flowing mane floated in the breeze, and his arched neck curved with a grace that seemed impossible for a creature of his size.

Flint lipped at my palm, his hot breath skirting my skin as he quietly traced his whiskers against my wrist and up my arm. The gesture had become a habit. It was like I'd known the herd a lot longer than just a few months, but Flint…his soul was mine and mine his. Perhaps it was because he'd been born from my mother's Sula-umbra. Maybe that is what made him special, just as it was for my mother with Elska.

I'd told the herd what was happening, bracing myself for resistance, but instead, I was met with a surprising amount of understanding. Not one of them, not even the usually peevish Aire, argued when I said that the Dragons would be sharing the meadow.

They seemed resigned that I wouldn't let anything stand in the way of breaking this curse, not even them.

Once again, the magnitude of my role settled into my bones. The path that had been chosen for me, and the one I chose for myself, was one I couldn't stray from. It was like it'd been etched into my DNA as the blood dried from the oath carving into the marrow running through my bones. Each step forward felt both inevitable and terrifying.

"Am I doing the right thing?" I asked Flint, the question echoing through the herd like ripples in a still pond.

Two heads popped up and glanced my way, a set of silvery-tipped ears flickering in my direction. They awaited Flint's answer as if his response would determine whether his wisdom grew to match his impressive stature. He regarded Dolfan before twisting his long neck so his nose rested on my chest. He was careful to keep his horn from poking me, a gentleness that belied his enormous strength.

I believe in you, he replied, his voice warm and reassuring.

It was an answer, but also not an answer. More of a vote of confidence, but not a guarantee. I ran my fingers through his silky mane, taking comfort in the texture as I puffed out a long, slow breath. Dolfan and Nimue returned to grazing, seemingly satisfied with Flint's response.

"I had a dream," I confided, my voice low. "We were in a field of wheat that ran along the bed of a river. All of us. The Dragons, the Dothians… You… Me. I was lying on your back, enjoying the sunset as a flock of birds flew overhead. It was so peaceful."

The memory of the dream was vivid, a teasing glimpse of a future that seemed both possible and impossibly distant. Flint's eyes softened, empathy radiating from his gaze. I let his mane drop down before running a finger over the spiraling black and silver horn that split his forelock. The horn hummed, its power coursing through me.

"I want that," I told him, my voice thick with longing. "That peace, that harmony."

Break the curse, he responded, his mental voice firm and unwavering.

Doubts flooded my mind, a torrent of fears I couldn't silence. *What if I'm not supposed to? What if it's a trap? What if I break it, and something terrible happens to all of us? I can't bear the thought that it was my fault everyone trusted me, and I made things worse.* They were mere thoughts, but I could tell that the herd had taken in every doubt-filled question. Flint stepped back and rested his nose on my shoulder. His whiskers tickled the small space of skin exposed on my neck.

Break the curse because it's supposed to be broken, he told me, his mental voice filled with a certainty I envied. *Break it because we aren't supposed to be here like this. If something goes wrong, we will not think less of you. You are fulfilling the destiny that has been handed to you. There is no fault in that.*

"That's so wise," I smiled, tears slipping from the corners of my eyes. "So very wise."

Even though it was what I'd sought, the depth of Flint's understanding and the unwavering support of the herd were almost too much to bear. The sound of beating wings drew my attention, and I felt more than heard Tattu land in the field behind me. For once, Kairo was not with him. The Dragon stretched his wings impressively, scales glittering in the sunlight as he waited by the meadow's edge to give me a ride back to the dilapidated resort. One by one, my gaze fell on each herd member. They continued grazing, despite the Dragon's appearance. The scene was so peaceful that I could imagine everyone living in harmony, and it felt so right. Like that was how it was always meant to be.

Passing my hand over Flint's flank one last time, I murmured a goodbye and made my way over to Tattu, using the hard scales along his foreleg to climb onto his back. The Dragon's powerful muscles bunched beneath me, preparing for takeoff, and my stomach twisted with a different kind of anxiety. Thoughts of Kairo, of the label 'boyfriend' and all it implied, mingled with my worries and anxiousness about the curse. I'd have to talk to him about what we were and what we'd need to do soon.

Nolan

The cold, hard rocks bit into my palms as I climbed up the boulders that lined the surface where grass met stone. Finding Caleda's nest was relatively easy, thanks to our bond and the relentless, restless growling she'd emitted once I'd gotten close enough. Unlike Dalya, she'd chosen to stay in the area, nesting under an overhang with just days-old eggs. I'd stumbled upon them, seeing her scales glint through the dense woods.

It didn't matter how easy locating them was, though, because moving the nest was venturing into uncharted territory, and I was woefully unprepared. I'd never relocated a Dragon's nest before, and it's not something our parents covered because it wasn't something that was done. As a rule, you left Dragon's nests alone… unless you had a death wish.

The closer I drew to the nest, the more the air seemed to constrict. Caleda's deadly glare made me pause as the raw power within her was barely veiled behind her fiery gaze. I reached for the two obsidian-spiked eggs nestled among twigs and stones. Her massive head whipped around as she bared her sharp, curved teeth. I almost stopped breathing, almost died. This wasn't just Caleda anymore. No, this was raw motherhood at its most fierce.

"Shit," I breathed, my voice barely audible over the sound of my pounding heart. "Easy, girl."

Leave, she hissed.

"I'm taking you somewhere safer."

The words felt hollow, inadequate in the face of her maternal instinct.

Safe? The spikes along her beautiful, angular head settled ever so slightly.

"You're not safe here." I motioned to the resort. "Others can find you. We've got to move further down the mountainside."

I held up my hands to show her that I mean no harm, managing to crouch beside her. Despite her obvious distress, she let me close enough that I could reach the eggs with the tips of my fingers. She watched me warily as I gingerly placed them in my pack, each movement feeling like disarming a bomb.

Caleda's low grumbles reverberated through me, tugging at my heart. Mounting her, I was acutely aware that these were the future of her lineage. She had every right to be angry with me.

I'll keep hold of them.

Better, she huffed.

She thrust herself off the boulder, soaring down the mountainside to where Elle and Kairo waited at the clearing by the resort. Tattu was there, too, looking like he'd rather be on the other side of the moon than anywhere near a female's eggs. I couldn't blame the poor Dragon because when Caleda saw Tattu, she snaked her head at him. A low rumbling growl came from deep inside her, filling every gap of air around us. Her intense irritation made me taste ash, my nose tingling against the overwhelming anger that she cast into me.

"You guys go on ahead of us," I warned them.

Kairo didn't pause. He tugged Elle close and climbed onto Tattu so that he could take flight. As Caleda prepared to follow, a new wave of anxiety washed over me. It didn't feel right to move them, as if it was instinctual on my part to leave them where Caleda had laid them. The sudden lurch when she leaped into the air nearly sent the pack flying. My desperate grab for it was fueled by more than just reflex. I'd rather not die at the teeth and claws of my own Dragon once she figured out that I lost grip of the pack that held what might be her only chance of becoming a mother.

"Don't make me drop them," I pleaded, voice strained.

The words were as much for me as for her. I clung to the pack for the rest of the flight. Feeling the weight of the eggs pressed against my chest made me want to protect them with my life.

After an eternity, we finally approached our destination, and my shoulders relaxed. Landing in the meadow, I was struck by the surreal nature of what was going on around us. The Unicorns' nonchalance was almost comical. They were utterly indifferent to the female Dragon huffing as I set up her nest. Looking them over, I walked back through the meadow without the pack. They were weird, lanky creatures that moved as if they were floating across the ground. Beautiful, yet ethereal.

Caleda settled onto her nest, her anger evident in every puff of steam and glare. I was proud of her. She'd do anything to keep her eggs safe. Despite the ward and her motherly instincts, I still held a touch of fear for the potential consequences of our actions.

When I was sure that she was settled, I made my way toward Elle and Kairo.

"They won't mess with the nest," Elle reassured me.

"I know they won't. I've never seen Caleda this angry or difficult. She wouldn't let one of them within ten yards." I scrubbed my hand through my hair. What if this plan backfired spectacularly? Caught between Caleda's fury and the aloof presence of the Unicorns, I couldn't shake the feeling that we were balanced on a knife's edge.

I asked myself, once again, why exactly were we all so hell-bent on ending this curse?

Chapter Forty-Five

Stay Away

Kairo

Already on edge from watching Nolan handle Caleda, a cold sweat prickled my skin as I inched closer to my Dragon's nest. Dalya was an inferno of scales and fury. She let out a throaty roar. Yet, I persisted, driven by determination. I wouldn't admit it to anyone, but I was recalling less and less with each passing day. The memories of my parents, the time before the curse, and the way it had all once been, were like wisps of smoke. The same smoke that poured out of Dalya's nostrils, curling around my shaking arms. One single misstep away from her biting my head off, I peered over the boulder's edge. Dalya's ivory-colored scales reflected the moonlight when she spun angrily around the mound of rocks and bramble that made up her nest. The air grew turbulent as I crept closer.

It'd taken us the rest of the day to find her, making pass after pass over each mountainside. If it wasn't for the low, threatening noise she'd made when Tattu came too close, we might never have noticed her in the stone gorge where she lay. Her head and tail were tucked around the nest so entirely that she was camouflaged into the mountain.

Dalya, I tried.

The Dragon hissed and lowered her head in a clear warning.

Stay away...

I swallowed but stood tall.

We need to move the nest, I told her.

No... You will not.

For a brief second, I marveled at her voice in my head. It'd been so long since I'd heard her rustic and eloquent cadence. As if to remind me she was there, Dalya's talons dug into stone with a shrill cry. Maybe this wasn't the greatest idea. I couldn't imagine what she would do to the Unicorns if she were this angry with me so close. I crossed my arms over my chest. She snaked her neck in my direction and wound herself around the nest so I couldn't see a single inch of it.

I'm not trying to take them from you, I said through our shaky bond.

Stay away...

You aren't safe here.

Go!

Dalya... please.

If you do not go, I will do harm.

Closing my eyes, I sucked my teeth with a tsk. Nature demanded that female Dragons be overprotective of their nests when they were halfway to hatching. Yet, if we had a better connection, I should have been able to get closer than where I crouched. She might understand, and it wouldn't be so difficult. Our bond was too fragile. I couldn't comprehend why she wouldn't allow me the connection that secured a Keeper to their Dragon. There was something there, a faint something that precariously hung between us, but it wasn't the same as it was with my other two Dragons.

Her refusal to yield irked me. If it wasn't for my pride, I would've given up and let her stay where she was, unprotected by the ward while I was gone. But reason whispered caution. Moving her eggs was necessary. I needed to put my anger aside to make it happen.

I command you...

Do not.

As your Keeper, I growled. *I command you to let me move your nest.*

The ground rumbled under my feet when Dalya stood up and stalked over the rocks. She reeled back her head, and another steady stream of hot steam coiled around me. Her eyes were narrow slits as she studied me. My hands fisted at my sides. She seemed to be daring me. Take one step, and you die, her low, lidded eyes read. My back teeth clacked together, and I squeezed my jaw shut.

We need to move your nest. There are too many Dothians. They will find you.

Let them.

Oscur is nearby.

Dalya froze. Her entire body became a statue. Only the slight flap of her wings, catching the wind that spiraled around the gash in the earth she'd chosen, dared move. My suspicions were confirmed, and I cursed under my breath. Oscur was the one who tortured Dalya as a yearling. I'd wondered how Oscur kept his Dragons in line. They were more like soldiers than willing partners, following his demands mindlessly.

We need to move your nest.

Dalya snapped her gray eyes to me and sucked in a giant breath before moving slowly out of my way. The revelation of Oscur's shadow over her attitude shift was gut-wrenching. Her fear, her pain, was palpable through our connection. I faced a choice. I could break her spirit or save her soul. The decision was a heavy burden to bear. She watched my every move as I collected the three spiked eggs: one red and two dark silver. Once they were in the sack, I climbed a rock and mounted her. She eyed the empty nest with grief-filled eyes and took to the sky.

Thank you... I breathed in relief.

When we landed in the meadow, Dalya showed no interest in the Unicorns or the other Dragons. She followed me and the pack with her eggs, away from Caleda, and watched as I set the eggs on the nest the others had made for her. She balefully eyed her surroundings before curling herself on top of them.

Thanks, she whispered.

I will always protect you, I replied, *and therefore them.*

Dalya blinked at me, taking in my words, before tucking her nose under her wing.

Elle

I'd been up most of the night, gnawing worry eating at my stomach until I could no longer lie still. Moving the Dragons had been incredibly hard on all of us. Though it had ended well enough, seeing the Dragons so upset over the transfer had been stressful. The day after we'd moved them, the four of us spent most of our time roaming around the resort like ghosts—quiet, sullen, and exhausted. Nobody complained when the sky darkened with a storm, sending us to bed early.

Kairo stood in the window, watching the rain come down. His expression was blank, lightning framing his handsome features. Sitting down with the book from the library, I forced my tired eyes to focus as the words swam on the page. The chapters on the blood oath were the hardest to get through because they were filled with contingencies and punishments. Half a dozen pages detailed consequences ranging from lifelong scars to death, all dependent on the severity of the oath or how it was broken.

My heart stuttered when I found a small paragraph about blood oaths between Allorians and Dothians. The text read that, although ill-advised, oaths between the two weren't forbidden, and they still carried the same consequences. It wasn't much, but it was something. Setting the book aside, I dove back into journal six. The first half was riddled with cryptic passages, potentially meant to confuse anyone who acquired it through disreputable means. Since I lacked knowledge about Allorian history, I couldn't decipher all of the hidden messages on every page, even after reading the scroll.

When I could no longer bear the confusion, I climbed off the bed and paced across the dirt-covered floor. Breaking the first two parts of the curse would be relatively simple, but the timing was a challenge. The parts of the curse I was aware of needed to be broken around the same time, with other parts following soon after. The scarcity and muddled nature of the details made me want to hurl the remaining journals into the crackling fire.

"You okay?" Kairo's voice startled me. He walked over to stand behind me, wrapping his arms around my shoulders, his breath against my neck.

"Not really," I admitted, my hands coming to a rest on his.

Leaning my head against his chest, I looked out at the flashes of lightning covering the night sky. There was comfort in the way he held me, firmly but with a tenderness that made the tightness in my chest lighten.

"What are we?" I asked quietly.

His fingers stilled. "What do you mean?"

"Do you love me?"

"Elle…" He turned me around, his hands cupping my elbows.

"It's just the curse…"

"It is what we'd assumed, correct? Do we need to break it together?"

"You need to fall in lov—"

"Elle," Kairo sighed, tugging my chin upward so that I would look at his face.

I met his gaze steadily. "The texts say you have to truly be in love. It can't be forced or faked."

Kairo looked away, his jaw clenching. I could see the internal struggle playing out on his face. When he finally spoke, his voice was rough with emotion. "Elle, I… I think I already am. In love with you, I mean. I just… I haven't said it because I was afraid. Afraid of what it might mean, afraid of losing you… Afraid of losing…"

"Your Dragons?" I breathed.

He nodded, his chest rising as he sucked in a breath. He'd admitted that he was in love with me, and I was so tired that it didn't truly sink in… until it did. Kairo loved me. My heart fluttered, and heat washed over my middle at his admission. Kairo was in love with me. The most beautiful man I'd ever met was in love with me.

"What about the second part?"

"The second part," I barely whispered, "we need to… make love. But it has to be on the exact night we plan to break the curse. Not before, not after. It has to be in Dothan Valley, as the half-moon passes between the peaks."

"The half-moon? When is that?"

"It's coming soon," I told him.

His eyes narrowed, his lips pressing together. "Are you still willing to break the curse?"

I nodded. "I don't think I have a choice now."

Kairo's breath hitched. "I see," he said, his voice low. "But… are you willing to be with me to break the curse?"

I nodded again, still processing his confession. "Yes, I am."

We grew quiet under the flickering flames of the fire before us, both considering what the other had said. I put a hand over my mouth and yawned. He pulled me against his chest.

"Come to bed," he urged gently.

"I can't sleep," I confessed, even as my body betrayed me with another yawn.

"We've got a long day ahead of us," he reminded me, his voice a mix of concern and gentle insistence.

"I'll try to sleep then."

Without warning, Kairo lifted me off the ground, his strong arms cradling me as if I weighed nothing. I relaxed against his broad chest, breathing him in. He laid me gently onto the furs, and I sighed when he pulled the blanket over us. He made a noise in his throat as he moved to climb in next to me. I felt the pull of sleep, more potent than any worry or fear. Before he could settle, I was already drifting off.

Chapter Forty-Six

Looking For Me

Kairo

If I had learned one thing from my years of flying on the back of a Dragon, cloud-high, it was not to look down unless necessary, or the world would shrink to an abstract canvas, a dizzying quilt of blues, browns, and greens. When I made that mistake, I realized the ground was both desperately far away and far too close. Trees became dots, lakes shrank to ponds, rivers thinned to streams, and sometimes even mountains were reduced to mere boulders.

But Elle? She was different. Fascinated, she watched the ground whiz by underneath, lying forward on Tattu's back while we glided along the coastline. Her curiosity and wonder amazed me. And

Tattu, for all the flack I'd given him, was managing the trip quite well. I'd been worried about him carrying us and our gear, but he'd been stoic, taking on the journey without complaint, even as the air shifted from lukewarm to muted cold.

Neither of us had been to Alaska before. However, it seemed logical that we would eventually find Gustava if we followed the western coast. The wind whipped around us in brisk, unforgiving tendrils as we flew further north. Elle shivered, and I pulled out a thick wool jacket for her, wrapping it around her shoulders. The gesture felt inadequate against the vastness of our journey, but it was all I could offer. Despite it being early summer, the evenings were still bitter.

Our plan was to stop at the edge of Gustava. Elle used her phone to search for photos of the area so we could spot it from the air. The small town attracted various tourists during the season, so we would blend in easily enough. Elle had the wherewithal to bring clothing that would make us inconspicuous. To most, we would, hopefully, appear as nothing more than visitors enjoying the beautiful little town.

When we spotted the icy peaks, both of us relaxed. Elle leaned back into my arms, and I was struck by how natural she felt against me. It was nice to have her alone, without Nolan or Aiska disrupting our privacy or stealing her concentration with the journals. Selfishly, I wanted to be the center of her attention. I splayed my palm across her abdomen, and she covered my hand with hers, interlacing her fingers with mine.

Despite my need to have her to myself, I was determined to hold to the time we'd set to return to Belview. The longer we were gone, the more chance Nolan or Aiska could mess something up in our absence, and we had no idea if the Allorians were still in Gustava.

Elle had explained that a lot of Allorians may move after every Sula-umbra to keep their herd from being found. They were harder to find if they kept moving. She wasn't sure if the Allorians knew that the horns provided protection, as her predecessors had discovered this. So, despite what the journals and book said, things may have changed with how Allorians behaved. We also couldn't find an accurate count of how many still existed. I'd thought Elle to be one of the last, yet the riddles listed at least twenty locations.

Twenty vague locations, with no way to pinpoint them exactly. How were we going to find them?

Elle turned her head so I could hear her over the wind. "Too bad we can't lure them with treasure like the Dragons," she said as if reading my thoughts.

I smiled, even as the gravity of our mission settled over me. We were searching for others that might not even want to be found.

"We could scare them out," I replied.

"How?"

"Drop Tattu's cloaking near the flat meadows where they'll be grazing," I offered with a shrug.

"They wouldn't know I was with you. We could scare them away by doing that," she sighed. "Besides, if they know more than I do, that might put Tattu and you at risk."

"What's your idea?"

She didn't answer as my little, green Dragon set all four feet on the ground, yawning and stretching his wings languidly. I slid down his side and landed on my feet. Elle's face was flushed, and she put a hand to her chest.

"We should ask around," she replied, dismounting into my arms.

"Ask around?"

"Yes," she breathed, "When was the last time you felt a Sula-umbra in this area?"

"I've never…" I snapped my mouth shut. She was a genius.

"All we have to do is find the right person with the right information."

"Small towns?"

"I'm hoping that's the case," she replied. "But it's late, and I'm tired. I booked a room for us at an inn."

Shouldering our packs, I told Tattu to stay in the area, and we headed into Gustava. The town was a picturesque blend of snow and sunlight, painted with the hues of winter's end. The snow-capped horizon lined the sky to the bay, with the town lights glittering against the fading sunlight. There was a large white ship at the docks. It seemed she'd aligned our arrival with the group of tourists on the vast cruise ship.

There was a closed sign on the hotel door, but Elle didn't pause. She passed the log-style main part of the inn, huddled amongst sparse pine trees, and found the cabins in the back. Looking down at her phone, she walked past the ones out in the open and found one among the denser woods. When we got to the door, she entered a code and twisted the handle. I was too tired to ask how she'd found the place or how the lock worked.

The interior was cozy and efficient: a bed, a kitchenette, and a window that framed the natural beauty outside. Two overstuffed sage green chairs sat under a floor-to-ceiling window with a small table between them. Setting the bags down, I went over to the kitchen sink and grabbed a cup. I downed three glasses of water before leaning against the counter. Elle disappeared into the bathroom. When she came out, she was wearing a long T-shirt and a pair of flannel pants. Pulling her hair onto the top of her head, she smiled at me.

"What do you think is going to happen after this?"

Her hands stilled. "I don't know."

I wasn't sure where the question had come from, a raw thought ripped from some desperate corner of my mind, but it was too late to take it back. "Do you think we can be together?"

"I think so," she answered, twisting a band into her hair. "I hope so."

A muscle in my jaw twitched. Elle's face fell as she walked over. Wanting to rid her of her warring emotions, I lifted her onto the counter, caging her between my arms.

"What's wrong?"

My forehead found hers, and I exhaled, long and slow. "This is nice," I whispered. "Being alone with you. Letting all the distractions wait."

Elle's chest lifted. "It is," she agreed, wrapping her arms around my neck and tilting her head for a kiss.

I lost myself in it, imagining a world where we didn't have to worry about so much. A world where I could love her endlessly and without regret.

It didn't take us long to ask around the small town. Only two stores sold the clothing and supplies someone would need to survive on the outskirts in this bone-chilling cold. Most tourists weren't in the area long enough to require fleece undergarments and insulated socks. As Kairo and I went from shop to shop, my stomach started to churn. We'd crafted our story carefully. We were looking for my cousin, visiting from the lower states. "We have something for her," we'd say, trying to sound casual. "Do you know her? Blonde hair hasn't changed much over the years." I cringed internally at the description, wondering if it was too specific or telling.

The vendors' lips were sealed tighter than a drum. Both shook their heads at us, their eyes darting away before they hurried to send us down the road. But there was something about the first one – call it intuition or maybe just desperation. The way he looked at me, tight lines formed at the corners of his mouth as we turned to leave. Kairo wasn't oblivious to the signs either. I caught his subtle nod as we exited the store, confirming he'd seen the once-over the man gave him. We relented quickly, showing we weren't a threat. Just tourists, nothing more.

That evening, we played our parts to perfection. We ate at the local diner, bought postcards we'd never send, and snapped photos of the quaint town center. But beneath our carefree facade, my nerves were frayed. We walked back to our cabin, strolling down the unpaved sidewalk. I couldn't shake the feeling we were being watched. The town center faded behind us, streetlights growing sparse. I instinctively moved closer to Kairo, brushing my hand against his. He tucked me into his side, an arm around my waist so we could soak in each other's warmth.

We turned a corner, and my heart nearly stopped. A figure stepped out from the shadows, their face obscured. For a second, I thought it was the Albadine.

"I've heard you've been looking for me."

Chapter Forty-Seven

Guard Dogs

Elle

The figure stepped out of the shadows of the white cedar building. Kairo moved to stand before me, his arm forming a barrier. He widened his stance, causing me to peek around him. The stranger stepped into the moonlight, slowly lowering the hood of her thick, black fur-lined coat.

Long, straight blonde hair cascaded over her shoulders, catching the silvery streetlight. Her pewter-colored eyes locked onto mine. I cataloged her features. She had an upturned button nose, full lips, and an almond-shaped face. The pale hair that would have framed her face was neatly tucked back, emphasizing her hooded, slanted eyes and the short length of her forehead. Our features were so similar that we could have been sisters. It was like looking into a mirror, yet not entirely. Like we were related…somehow. Though she was a complete stranger.

"I didn't know Allorians had guard dogs now," she muttered, her gaze flicking to Kairo before returning to me. "Or that we were allowed to have them now. Interesting."

She searched my face, eyes darting from chin to brow. She was deciphering something, working through her thoughts. Like she was attempting to conclude how she would place me. Whatever she decided, her chin tilted, and the corners of her lips twisted into a friendly smile. She reached her hand out, and I stepped from behind Kairo and took it. I was surprised when she pulled me into a hug, her arms tightening around me.

She smacked my back lightly, her breath warm against my ear as she whispered, "A Portier. How exciting."

"Who are you?" Kairo's voice was tense and protective. His hand hovered near the small of my back, ready to pull me away if needed.

The girl's attention shifted to him, her demeanor changing like quicksilver. Ignoring his question, she scrutinized him, her welcoming persona shifting. A hint of her grin remained when she sighed and shook her head in something akin to acceptance. Her easygoing attitude reminded me so much of my mother. Yet, unlike my mother, there was a sternness about her, as if she didn't know how to back down from a challenge.

"This is Kairo, and I'm Elle," I said, shooting him a look that I hoped conveyed, 'Play nice'. This was why we were here, after all. To find her. Another Allorian.

"A Dothian?" Her tone was laced with amusement. "I could spot the arrogant attitude rolling off you from miles away." She turned back to me, her lips flattening in clear disapproval. "Why would you bring a Dothian here?" She had a heavy accent that I couldn't place, each upturned vowel emphasizing her displeasure.

Kairo tensed beside me, and I turned to him. A look of confusion crossed his features. *What*? I questioned, with a raise of one brow. He shrugged and motioned for me to respond.

I kept my voice steady and replied, "To break the curse."

The girl tilted her head. "What do you know about breaking the curse? You are so new. I can smell it on you like an unfledged falcon."

Her words hurt, but I didn't let it show. "I know everything I need to know about the curse," I stated flatly. "Enough to know that the Unicorns are not actually Unicorns."

She blinked, her brow furrowing and fingers curling. I shocked her. Something I'd said confirmed something she suspected, or she'd just confirmed that I was on the right track. My shoulders relaxed for the first time in a very long time. If she was verifying what the journals said, she knew things. We weren't being led astray by the conflicting information in the old journals and the old book we'd stolen from the library.

"Tell me what you know," she demanded, motioning for us to follow her.

As we walked, I told her of everything from the time my parents died to when we landed in Gustava. We passed the inn, the dock with its quietly swaying boats, the last of the roads, and walked into a field that ran the length of tall glacial cliffs. Despite my down coat,

I shivered in the biting cold, my words forming small clouds in the frigid air. Neither Kairo nor the girl said a word as I spoke.

Kairo kept close, his arm brushing mine while we moved across the ground. Oddly quiet, his eyes were glued to the ground. The woman smiled politely, signaling me to continue when I hit a lull or paused to consider my words. Her youthful face gave very little away, other than a soft kind of friendliness.

"What do you know?" I asked her.

"It sounds like I know less than you do," she admitted. "Like your mother, I've kept journals to remind myself. As the years pass, I have to do more of that. Remind myself, that is."

"That's the curse. I believe this is our last chance to break it," I told her. "I'm not sure what the repercussions are if we don't. From my mother and grandmother's journals, the curse worsens with every Sula-umbra."

She was quiet for a moment before she finally asked. "You are here to warn the Allorians?"

"Yes," I confirmed. "During the day before the next half-moon, I will request the Unicorns to shift, and the wards will fall."

Her face grew somber. She looked at the greening field to our right, slowly nodding. When she turned back to Kairo, her eyes cooled slightly. Her upturned chin made her appear regal and wise.

"It is about time," she stated. "I will warn them."

"You know how to reach them?" I asked, hope blooming in my chest.

"I do. I will take care of it."

"How many—" I began, but she cut me off.

"I cannot say," she interrupted firmly. "Even though I trust your Dothian is not here to harm me, I will not give away their positions or numbers."

I grimaced. "We understand."

"It sounds like there isn't much time. We all have work to do… no?"

"Yes," I agreed, taking Kairo's hand. As I turned, I hesitated. "I didn't catch your name?"

"Alex," she smiled. "My name is Alex."

I nodded to her as she waved goodbye. Turning to Kairo, he looked perplexed, his brows drawn together. "What is it?"

His reply sent a chill through me that had nothing to do with the Alaskan cold. "I didn't understand a word that either of you said."

Chapter Forty-Eight

You Are A Liar

Nolan

I plopped down next to Aiska, who was sprawled on her belly, engrossed in some puzzle game on her new tablet. She'd bought it at a resale store - probably charmed the poor cashier into downloading games for her, too.

Everything around me was so peaceful while Elle and Kairo were away. Well, as peaceful as my tumultuous mind would allow. The second they'd flown off, it felt like they'd taken a piece of me with them. Then it'd grown quiet because they were gone, and I didn't have my cousin to pick on or Elle to bicker with.

Her absence was a persistent itch I couldn't scratch. I wasn't supposed to fall in love. It was practically rule number one. Admitting I was in love meant potentially losing the many years I'd planned on sticking around. Unless it was marrying someone who shortened our lives? Maybe having feelings wouldn't condemn me unless I acted on them? I nodded to myself. Surely other Dothians had fallen in love but not allowed themselves to act on it. This was a good thing because I was sure this was what falling in love felt like. And boy, did it suck. I missed her, even if she wasn't mine, even if she was Kairo's. Even if... Oh, for crying out loud, I was becoming a lovesick fool.

"You're thinking about her again," Aiska noted, not looking up from her game.

"No, I'm not," I denied with a snort that probably didn't fool her.

Aiska set the tablet down, apparently having lost her game. Join the club, sister.

"Liar."

I ducked my head and tousled my hair. "I don't know why I feel the way I do," I admitted, my voice pathetically whiny even to my ears.

"Elle is special," Aiska replied, and I could almost hear the unspoken 'duh' in her tone.

"She is," I agreed, lying back on the grass with my hands under my head. If I stared at the clouds long enough, perhaps they'd form into a sign telling me what to do. 'GET OVER IT, DUMMY' would be nice.

"Want to blow off some steam?"

My brows drew together. "What do you have in mind?"

"Well… we can't fly… but we are alone."

I looked toward where the Unicorns had been. They'd wandered over the slight crest in the field, disappearing. I briefly recalled Aiska's fascination with the beasts when we'd first landed in the meadow. She'd been starstruck until they'd finally shown their annoyance at her attention with pinned ears and swishing tails. None of them had been mean to either of us, but they'd made their feelings clear. Stay a few yards away, or we'll show you what hoof-sized bruises in the middle of your chest felt like.

Part of me was still adjusting to being near them. The blood oath prevented me from acting on my initial impulses of protecting my Dragons. Time had shown me that they were far more peaceful than the lies I'd been led to believe. Mostly, they just wanted to be left alone. They were incredibly docile.

Blinking, I looked over at Aiska. Wait a minute. Did she just proposition me? And there I lay thinking about horned beasts. Talk about missing social cues. I closed my eyes, rolled them dramatically, and flattened my bent legs onto the grass.

"You want to have sex, Aiska?"

"So, what if I do?" she replied. "It's not like either of us is committed."

"Like we could be?"

"It's a possibility if Elle breaks the curse. Not that you would want to be."

"I am not your type." I snorted.

"Evidently, I am not yours," she shot back.

"Don't take it personally," I told her, wondering how to reject an offer like hers without making things awkward for eternity.

"I'll try not to," she sighed.

"It would complicate things."

"For you," she replied.

Yes… for me, I thought. I didn't want anyone else until I was sure I didn't have a chance with Elle. I just wanted her. My heart twisted, and my gut tingled, actually tingled like there were butterflies in it. I needed to get a grip.

We both fell quiet and she picked up the tablet, returning to her game. I tried not to dwell on turning her down. Instead, I took a deep breath through my nose and let it out through my mouth, noticing from the corner of my eye that Artok was watching the sky. The Dragon looked like his old self, steady on his trunk-like legs, without the wobble the sickness had given him. Looking up to where he was searching the horizon, I saw a ripple and stood suddenly. Either they were back early, or we were in for trouble. I breathed a sigh of relief when I spotted a flare of green and could make out that it was indeed Tattu coasting through the ward, dropping his cloaking as he neared the ground. Aiska jumped to her feet and nearly ran to them.

Seeing that Elle was okay sent a wave of relief through me, and the fact that they both looked content meant that the trip hadn't been for nothing. I paused. That meant that the curse was going to be broken. My stomach twisted. I'd thought long and hard about what the second part of the curse could be and had drawn only one conclusion. If we were going to break it, that meant that soon Kairo and Elle would… I shook my head and walked toward them, ignoring the voice that sounded suspiciously like jealousy. Wonderful. Not only was I in love, but I was turning into a douche with the emotional maturity of a virgin human. Just perfect.

Kairo

I let Elle explain everything while I muttered something about going to check on Dalya. It was a flimsy excuse. I just needed a moment, a solitary breath, before diving back into the energy of Elle's enthusiasm to process everything from our time in Gustava. To come to terms with the unknown of everything that might come.

Dalya was soundly sleeping over her eggs, her wing hiding them from view. She peeked at me through heavy eyelids when I approached, but didn't bother to rise. I checked the perimeter of her nest without getting too close. Seeing that all was well, I let out a breath and leaned against a tree. But the relief was short-lived. There was an aching feeling that I couldn't control, creeping up my spine like poison ivy.

Elle was hell-bent on ending the curse, and I knew I wouldn't stop her. How could I? But I couldn't shake the feeling that maybe I should. On the trip back, I'd wrapped my arms around her, pulling her close. She'd looked at me with such enthusiasm that I couldn't discuss my doubts. I helped her tuck her flowing hair into her jacket, and she turned to kiss me. That kiss was a validation. We were going to do this. We were going to break the curse.

The entire ride back, I felt like I was going to be sick. I couldn't help but ask myself repeatedly, what if something went wrong? I'd lost the chance to voice it to her. My role in setting everything in motion made it seem like I would sacrifice anything to return to the days before the curse. Yet, I couldn't remember how things used to be or what would change. What if I changed? What if I didn't feel the same? What if we didn't do it? Was Elle right? Would we forget everything?

I swallowed against the knot in my throat and bowed my head. A more horrifying thought struck me. What if she didn't feel the same way about me once the curse was broken? I knew I should be excited about breaking the curse. I should want the possibility of a future without it hanging over us. To have the Dragons and her. But all I could think about was what we might lose in the process, what I might lose—Elle's love, her trust, maybe even Elle herself.

A cloud cast a shadow, dimming the sunlight that filtered through the tree leaves. Sitting down amongst the roots, I rested my cheek on my knees. It felt fitting, somehow, like the world was echoing my mood. That's when I spotted something shining between two aspens. Narrowing my eyes, I saw the glint of a silvery string dangle from a branch far above my head. Reluctantly, I stood and walked over to it. The string was about four feet too high for me to reach. I tried once anyway, stretching as far as possible, but my fingers came nowhere close to it.

Giving up, I turned and returned to the meadow.

Elle

"Careful," Aiska cautioned as she helped me onto the back of Flint.

I couldn't help but smile at the concern in her voice. "Believe it or not," I replied, trying to sound more confident than I felt, "I've done this before."

Standing tall on the Unicorn's back, I reached for the cord dangling tantalizingly above me. We had all come a bit too close to Dalya for comfort, and I could practically feel the Dragon's angry gaze boring into us. Kairo spoke softly to her, attempting to keep her calm, but we all knew it wasn't working. Beneath me, Flint's skin trembled, and his muscles tensed as if ready to leap away at any sign of danger. His instinct was to protect not just himself but me.

Stretching my arm as far as it would go, I brushed my fingertips against the cord. So close, yet not quite there. Rising onto my tiptoes, head down and shoulders high, I finally managed to grasp it and pull hard, but it held firm. Determined, I went up as far as I could on the balls of my feet and gave it a good yank. Suddenly, something gave way. When I looked up, a large duffel bag plummeted toward me.

Shit.

"Heads up!"

Flint moved beneath me, his sudden shift throwing me off balance. My arms wobbled and I tumbled onto his back, my fingers clutching at his mane to keep from falling off. Nearby, I heard Dalya rise to her feet, an angry rumble in her throat. Flint snorted while he skirted away, bumping into the tree. The large sack landed with a heavy thud, partially in Aiska's arms. The weight of it knocked her backward, and I winced when she landed on her backside with an audible "oof." An old leather-bound book fell out of the sack, sliding onto the ground quietly.

"What is it?" Nolan asked, from where he stood several trees away, avoiding Dalya.

"The original journals. We must have looked at the map backward. They were on the opposite side of the meadow all along."

Jumping from Flint's back, I gave him a grateful pat. He puffed out indulgent breaths of air and tail rising over his back, and he trotted back to the safety of the meadow. Extending a hand to help Aiska up, I laughed. We'd done it. We'd actually found them.

I tucked the cord attached to the duffel bag into my back pocket and grabbed the handle. The bag was beyond heavy, nearly bursting at the seams with various-sized, oddly dry diaries. How were these diaries so perfectly dry when the ones we found earlier, despite being in clear sacks, had been damaged by the elements?

"Great," Nolan's dry voice cut through my thoughts as he strode toward us, "more reading."

I shot him a look, half exasperated, half amused.

"There are probably more answers inside these than anything else we've been reading," I reminded him, unable to keep the excitement from my voice.

I glanced at Kairo, but when our eyes met, he looked away, his lips pursed. We'd come too far to turn back now. Whatever these journals held, whatever challenges lay ahead, we had to face them no matter how uncertain he was.

Chapter Forty-Nine

Hear Me Out

Elle

The following days passed as if I were caught in a time warp. I sat in the room I shared with Kairo, surrounded by journals, taking notes, and reading pages before collapsing into bed from exhaustion each evening. Occasionally, I would go home to shower, change, and check on the Unicorns, but the journals consumed most of my attention. Since I was the only one who could read them, they became my sole responsibility.

What I learned from the old pages was the heart-wrenching history of the Allorians after the curse displaced them from their homelands. I discovered how groups fractured, families split, and herds divided. My heart ached as I read about relationship after relationship where each Allorian in my lineage fell in love, each union resulting in a mortal life span. Many Allorians managed to avoid the fate of my ancestors, choosing to stay with their herds. It seemed that the curse of falling in love was mostly Portier-specific, leading me to confirm that a Portier had to break it. As I suspected, with each generation and every Sula-umbra, the confusion and memory loss among Unicorns, Dragons, and Keepers worsened.

I reread the riddle written in the translated version of Alis Portier's journal: *Bond of ruin, by the moon cast, A division born through the mountain's pass. Only through the union of two can I be undone. On the tenth turn of a cycle, their work begins. My onset drove some to shadow, others to chase. To save themselves, they ran a sacred race. For if they lose, they will not recall, Each day will pass, and end it all.*

The order was written not only in the riddle but in the margins of one of the old journals, and the clarification was a blessed relief. I'd had it mostly right. First, restore the Unicorns to their true form; then fly through the pass on the half-moon; and defy the curse by the unification of a Dothian and an Allorian. If we succeeded, the lost memories would be restored. If I didn't break this curse, it would mean the rapid decline and eventual extinction of Keepers and the species we cared for. The truth of it all made my head spin. I rubbed my forehead with two fingers and set the journal aside. If I never saw another again, I would be elated.

"You need a break?" Nolan's voice startled me. I looked up to see him leaning his shoulder against the door frame.

"Yes," I said, resting against the headboard.

"Good," he told me, "I need to talk to you."

I eyed him warily. Nolan had intentionally distanced himself from me for the past week and a half, appearing only at meals and occasionally helping with what he could read. He'd claimed boredom, but I could tell something was wrong. I didn't want to hurt him, but there was nothing I could do about it. Determined to break the curse, I knew admitting something was there would not help my cause. Despite my attraction to him, he wasn't Kairo.

"Nolan."

"Hear me out."

Crossing my legs, I rested my elbows on my thighs, readying myself for whatever was coming. He eyed me softly, swallowing his hesitation. His expression made my skin prickle.

"Go ahead then."

"I wanted to tell you…" he breathed, glancing over his shoulder, checking that the hall was empty.

"Do you think this is a good idea?" I stopped him, my heart thudding.

"No," he admitted. He shook his head and ran his fingers through his hair, mussing the curly blond strands until they haloed his brows. "Elle, I…"

"Nolan," I said, raising my hand to pause him, "think about what you are going to say."

"I have thought about it," he blurted out. "I think about it every single moment of every single day."

His chest heaved, and he trembled slightly. Swallowing, I looked out the window, my chest tightening with emotions I couldn't place.

"But I'm not here about that. Not really."

"Then what are you here for?"

"I'm here because you need to know something about the day of the blood oath."

I froze, unblinking. A chill ran down my spine.

"I already know," I told him, my voice barely above a whisper.

His breathing quickened, nostrils flaring.

"What do you know?"

"You were there. You were standing in the darkness behind Kairo. I saw you."

Nolan paled. "You knew and you didn't say anything?"

"I did not," I agreed. "Because of Kairo."

Lips parting, he balled his fists and crossed his arms. The pain in his eyes was almost unbearable.

"Don't you see? I was there. Breaking the curse could involve me, not Kairo. If you had done the blood oath with me instead of him," he paused, fists clenched. "You might be making a mistake," he said, voice so low I almost didn't hear him.

"I might be making a lot of them," I admitted. "I'm doing the best I can."

Nolan looked like he might beg me to reconsider. Stepping toward me, he extended his hand in my direction. If he came near me, I wasn't sure I could hold back because feelings for him did linger in the depths, waiting for me to acknowledge them. Memories played out in my mind. The day Nolan saw me for the first time, I noticed the hungry gaze in his eyes. He laughed over how little I knew about the blood oath. He pinned me against the wall when Artok stormed into the cave. The way he looked at me when I cared for his burns and the worry that crossed his features when he saw I'd been hurt after Artok crashed into the meadow.

Damn it.

Holding up my hand to stop him, my eyes moistened as I shook my head. If he came closer, we would both feel the impact of what I would say next, because I would choose Kairo no matter what, despite our time together, despite the laughter, despite the fact that I cared for him. I wasn't sure what my feelings were for Nolan, but they didn't matter. I would choose Kairo. Every. Time. The realization was both painful and liberating.

"Nolan… I like you. I don't want to break your heart."

"You already have," he replied, turning and walking away.

Kairo

Standing in the doorway of the empty room next to mine, my heart pounded. I'd heard every word they'd exchanged and could just make out the desperation lacing Nolan's voice. He wanted Elle to admit she had feelings for him. Fighting the urge to burst in and interrupt on Elle's behalf, I leaned my head against the doorframe, fingers clenching so tightly my knuckles turned white. Then she said something that made my blood run cold.

Nolan was there the night of the blood oath, in the mist.

He had the same markings wrapped around his arm as I did. I figured it was because Nolan was the binder. But he'd been there, standing behind me in that strange place, which meant so much more than simply being the binder. Nolan's footsteps sounded down the short hall, and I tucked myself on the other side of the wall, cursing under my breath. The curse was about choices. A Dothian's chance to fall in love. An Allorian's choice to take a lover. If Nolan had been there and he had the marks… He was an option. A choice.

I inhaled a thrumming breath and slowly lowered myself to the floor, my back sliding down the wall. What if I was the wrong one? What if I'd just been in the right place first? What if it was meant to be him?

The thought of Nolan being an option for Elle to break the curse filled me with a toxic mixture of fear, jealousy, and self-doubt. Nolan was more a friend than a cousin. But knowing he could potentially be the one to break the curse with Elle, it was like I was looking at a rival. Someone I would pummel without thinking to ensure that Elle never took a shaky, sobbing breath again.

My throat bobbed, swallowing the doubt that threatened to dominate me. I met her first. Elle was a descendant of the first Allorian, and I… I shook my head, cutting off that train of thought. No, I couldn't let myself spiral into these what-ifs and maybes. Elle chose me. She'd said it herself. But still, the nagging persisted. Was I truly the right choice for her?

Leaning back against the wall, I realized it was time to confront Nolan. I needed clarity, and so did he, not just for our peace of mind but for Elle's. Pushing to my feet, I let determination replace doubt. Despite my reservations, it was time. For Elle, for our future, and for the chance to finally break this curse once and for all.

Nolan

Sitting on the cliff's edge, I threw pebbles at the resort's rooftop. My chest was so tight that it was hard to breathe. I didn't expect anything different from Elle. She was too stubborn. Even if she could admit to herself that she held feelings for me, Kairo had gotten to her first, and she would stand by her choice. Her choice burned like acid in my chest.

Angrily, I heaved a handful of stones toward a window, frowning when the small rocks merely bounced off it. When I heard footsteps, my heart skipped a beat. It was filled with the foolish hope that Elle had come to find me. Glancing over at the small trail, I saw Kairo's boot before I saw him and ducked my head. *Great. Just what I needed.*

"I don't blame you," Kairo spoke as he approached.

"What do you mean?"

"I don't blame you for loving her."

I looked up at my cousin, my stomach somersaulting. I'd admitted to myself that I loved her a while ago, but admitting it to Kairo felt different. It felt wrong.

"How? Did Elle tell you?"

Kairo shook his head and sat down beside me. "I heard you just now in the room. But we both know this has been going on for a while."

Great, I'd made a mess of things and couldn't take any of it back. I rubbed a hand through my hair. Perhaps I wouldn't even if I could.

Telling her everything had been a long time coming, and it was my fault I'd told her how much I cared for her too late. She should have known she had options the day we figured out how to break the curse.

"I'm sorry," I said, the words tasting bitter. "I didn't mean for this to happen."

"When did you know?" Kairo asked.

"Know what?"

"That you were in love with her?"

"I don't want to have this conversation," I admitted, shaking my head ruefully.

"I knew the moment she lured my Dragons to a meadow by burning a bag full of coins from an old seaside carnival," he said, smiling as if the memory was bittersweet. "I had feelings for her before then, but seeing her waltz out of the trees with that look she gets when she's on to something. Then, when she saw Artok for the first time, she didn't cower. She walked right up to him and asked how she could help."

Leaning forward, I rested my arms on my legs, fingers intertwined, and head low.

"I knew there was something about her when she demanded to go to the library," I confessed. "The way she stood up against both of us. It all clicked when she risked her life to save the journals by diving under Artok."

Kairo smiled, blinked, and then grew serious. The shift in his demeanor made my stomach clench. "She's mine, you know?"

"I know," I replied, swallowing roughly. The words felt like sandpaper in my throat.

"I know you'll protect her with your life," Kairo said. "That's why I haven't said anything, but I can't let her go."

"You would be stupid if you did," I replied, looking at Kairo. The admission cost me, but it was true.

"I need you to give her more space."

I dipped my head but nodded anyway. What else could I do?

"In exchange, I'm going to tell you something I think you need to hear," Kairo said, leaning away from me slightly.

"What?"

"Years ago, I found something that belonged to my dad after he died. It was the small silver dagger with our family crest on the hilt, the one he carried around everywhere. For whatever reason, he loved that blade, and it hurt to look at it. So, I stashed it in their house and forgot about it. You came back from being gone for almost a year, and you were throwing a dagger into the dead tree that Caleda had accidentally burned nearly to the ground."

When he finished talking, I stilled, my expression growing perplexed. A growing sense of unease crept up my limbs as I lifted my shirt and pulled a small silver dagger from a sheath at my waist. I held it out to Kairo.

"This one?"

"Yes," Kairo admitted. "I thought to myself when I saw it…how can you have a twin to the one that belonged to my dad? I even asked you how you'd gotten it. You told me it was a gift from your mother, and she told you?"

"It was a gift from my dad," I replied, blanching.

The world tilted on its axis when his words sank in.

"Nolan," Kairo breathed. "We share the same father."

"It's just a coincidence," I stated, refusing to believe it. This couldn't be happening. Not now. Not like this.

But images flashed through my head. There'd always been a gift for me on my birthdays, wrapped in the same silver paper as Kairo's. One time, his father smiled down at me and called me "son," then cleared his throat and walked away. The memories ran deeper, to the time his father had gifted me my Dragon and then shown me how to fly. Things only a father would do. It wasn't true. I pressed a hand to my chest above my splintering heart.

"I thought it might be as well," Kairo admitted. "The memories were muddled from the curse, but back then, your mother was still alive, so I confronted her. I demanded to know, and she confessed."

"It's not true," I declared, standing.

Why would he tell me this as if he were doing me some kind of favor?

"You are my half-brother."

I balled my fists. "Stop lying!"

"It's true," Kairo pushed.

"Why would you keep it from me all this time?" I questioned, my voice trembling. "Why would you tell me this now?"

"Because your mom made me promise," Kairo told me. "She told me the last thing she wanted was to cause you pain. And then the curse confused me. I didn't remember until… until we looked at the stupid genealogy tree in the back of the wretched book we got from the library."

Kairo's explanation only fueled my anger. I narrowed my eyes at him, suspicion flaring.

"What are you doing? Is this payback for telling Elle how I feel?"

"No," Kairo answered, shaking his head.

"It feels like it," I spat, my emotions boiling. "It feels like you will do whatever it takes to drive a wedge between us. All so I will leave her alone? I've got news for you. I was going to leave her alone. She made her choice, and I was going to respect it. You could have taken that information to the grave. The King of Dothan has a brother. Competition. A challenge to succession."

"It's not like that," Kairo asserted, "you need to know. I couldn't hide it from you any longer."

Tears stung my eyes. I wiped at them angrily, hating the vulnerability.

"Nolan…"

I raised my hand in dismissal. "I don't want to talk to you right now."

"Don't do this."

"I need you to go," I told him, my chest heaving as I held in the anguish burning below the surface. "I don't want to see you right now. I'm bound by the blood oath to protect Elle, and I'll stand by that. But right now, I don't want to see your face."

Kairo turned to leave, and bitterness rose in me. "I hope she changes her mind. I hope she sees you for who you truly are and changes her mind."

Even though my words vibrated off the mountains, Kairo never looked back.

Chapter Fifty

Signs Of Trouble

Elle

"What did you say to Nolan?" I asked Kairo while we packed the last of our belongings.

Today was the day. After relentless preparations, we had a plan. Soon, we would head to the meadow and find out if the Unicorns were really Alicorns. If it was true, and they were, we'd fly straight to Dothan Valley, passing through the mountain peaks as the moon hit its apex, just like the book from the library had detailed. After that… I wasn't sure what would happen. Which is why I regretted that whatever we couldn't carry would have to stay behind. We couldn't bring all of the journals, just the ones that might offer some relevance.

Would I return home? Would I stay in the valley? If I never came back, what would happen to my house and the things I'd leave? What would people think?

"You'll have to ask him," Kairo replied.

My eyes flicked to his face, recognizing my words thrown back at me. Yet, his tone wasn't harsh. I doubted he even remembered me saying it.

"He's been avoiding us both." A knot formed in my throat.

The first day Nolan avoided me, I'd expected it. But he looked at Kairo as if disgust didn't even begin to define how he felt. It made me uneasy and, if I was honest, a little hurt.

"I'll tell you later," Kairo stated, lugging the heavy pack onto his back.

"I'm going to hold you to that."

Nolan's attitude worried me, and I missed his easy smile and playful banter. I cared for him that much was certain, but in what way? The line between friendship and something more was blurred, and I felt guilty for even considering him as more than a friend with Kairo so close.

I held Kairo's riding jacket out to him, and he took it gently, pulling me to him by the waistband of my black leggings. He wrapped his arms around me, the warmth of his touch calming. A small part of me couldn't help but wonder if being in Nolan's arms would have the same effect. My face heated as I pushed the thought away, ashamed of my wavering heart.

"If there are any signs of trouble," Kairo muttered into my ear, "I want you to head in the other direction."

"Sure," I lied, hating myself for the deception. I wasn't going to duck tail and run.

"I mean it," he kissed my cheek, "Fly to Gustava. Just don't look back."

"Kairo, we'll be fine."

"Famous last words," Aiska said from the doorway. Kairo and I broke apart reluctantly.

We walked outside with our packs, and I placed mine on the ground. My eyes drifted to where Nolan sat atop Artok, his expression stony and distant. He looked to the horizon, the familiar, playful glint in his eyes gone. Seeing him so standoffish, my heart ached, and I found myself stuck between wanting to comfort him and knowing I shouldn't. Nolan would have to be a problem for another time. Besides, I wasn't sure what I could do or say to make anything better for him. Or for myself, for that matter. I'd made my choice. I just wish my thoughts would follow suit.

Biting my tongue, Kairo helped me onto Tattu and tucked his arm around me. I melted into him, my back relaxing into his chest. He squeezed me gently as we took off, leaving Aiska behind to deal with her bargain with Zayn. I couldn't shake the trepidation coursing through me. I was dizzy with the anticipation of breaking the curse and realizing that my feelings for Kairo and Nolan were far more complicated than I'd allowed myself to believe. Even with Kairo's breath on my ear, I was lost and alone in my worries. It was too late to say anything now. We were too close to the peak to stop climbing the mountain.

Nolan

Something is going to go wrong. I tried to breathe past the feeling, but it clung to me like a second skin. A sense of impending doom sat like a boulder on my shoulders. I dismounted Artok, using his hind leg to slide to the ground.

Hands trembling, I moved to collect Caleda's eggs. Looking through the tall aspens, I spotted Elle and Kairo waiting together. I'd done my best to ignore them after their admissions. I was duty-bound to go along with whatever crazy ideas they came up with, but my heart wasn't in it anymore, not after everything that happened.

They should wait. The thought nagged at me incessantly. *I should make them wait.* Who was I to make demands? Just the discarded third wheel, the unwanted half-brother, the unrealized love interest. The semi-carefree existence I once complained about now seemed like a fantasy.

After securing the eggs in the leather rucksack between Caleda's front talons, I stepped back to study my work. The sack wasn't going anywhere, especially with Caleda clutching it in her talons and intentionally favoring her leg in the air. My beautiful Dragon looked at the sky excitedly, and I felt a pang of envy at her simple joy. While I dreaded every moment that brought us closer to Dothan Valley, the Dragons were craving the familiar air and earth their grounds offered.

Home, Caleda sighed.

I know.

The sprawling canyons and ranges that surrounded Dothan Valley were perfect for nesting. No Dothian would dream of attempting to locate or retrieve eggs from the steep declines and ravines that made prime hatching spots.

Once the bag was truly secure, I gently rubbed Caleda's nose, drawing solace from her stability. There was a time I'd looked forward to returning to the valley. Now, it felt like a prison sentence. One where I would be alone, while Kairo and Elle create a life together. It wasn't home anymore, not with Kairo's revelations haunting me. I swallowed hard to push back the misery and pain of his confession. The taste of his betrayal and Elle's confession was bitterly acidic. Why hadn't he told me that we were half-brothers? Why hadn't I told Elle about my feelings sooner? I couldn't shake the feeling that this journey held a sense of finality. For me, it felt like a death sentence—the death of my old life, my relationships, and my place in this world.

Shaking my head, I glanced at Elle and Kairo. He was holding her, his hands tucked around her waist, her head on his chest. Their closeness opened a gaping wound that festered inside me. My teeth clacked together as I forced myself to look away. My duties might have been fulfilled once Elle safely touched the ground in Dothan Valley. If so, I would stay in my mother's old house until Caleda hatched her eggs and the fledglings were ready to travel. Then I would retreat to whatever life I could to avoid Kairo and Elle.

The thought of a solitary destiny stretched before me, bleak and empty, but it was better than this constant pain, this reminder of what I could never have. This trip marked the end of everything I had come to know and love in such a short time, and I wondered if I would ever truly recover from it.

Elle

The meadow was quiet. I took in every detail as if for the last time. The tall grass danced with the breeze, and the willow tree branches twirled within themselves, seeming to bid their own farewell. I was going to miss this place desperately. Even if I planned to return one day, its familiarity would leave an ache in my chest. Slowly stepping through the marked graves under the tree's boughs, I committed the names on the stones to memory. The women who'd written the original journals. My grandmother, her mother, and her mother before her. Seven generations are buried beneath the tall willow.

Only Kairo and Nolan waited, sitting atop their Dragons expectantly. One was solemn, while the other was anxious. Kairo sat tall and proud on Tattu, with Dalya at the meadow's edge, ready to take flight when commanded. Nolan avoided my gaze, leaning forward and running a flat palm down Artok's scales. The females were splitting off once we reached the valley, the packs with their eggs in them secured to their feet so that they could pull them off themselves. Aiska wasn't coming; she'd decided to stay back to face the music, and watching us leave was too difficult. We'd said our farewells the night before with the promise to meet again once she'd settled her affairs. Leaving her felt wrong, but I wouldn't make her go.

The Unicorns watched me expectantly, Dolfan and Aire standing at the head of the herd with their ears pricked and necks arched. I walked right past them, drawn instead to Flint, the Unicorn who'd been by my side whenever I was within the ward. He was the one who had calmed me on so many occasions, and now he looked at me as if I were the giver of the greatest gifts. I chose him to initiate their shift, a decision that came easily.

Standing before Flint, he nudged me softly, and I ran my hand over his neck. Curling my fingers into his satin mane, I tried to memorize the feeling in case this was the last time.

"Are you ready, Flint?" I asked in a whisper.

He tipped his nose patiently, his kind eyes watching me. I rubbed my hand up his handsome face, and up the fully formed horn that split his forelock. It was time, and my heart raced with anticipation and a touch of fear. Taking a deep breath, I moved to stand directly in front of him, my hand resting on his nose. I bowed my forehead to his and grabbed his horn. It tingled against my skin.

"I have a request for you," I murmured, my voice trembling, "Fl...Flint... Aslaforus."

The moment the words left my lips, the grass stilled blade by blade. Chirping birds ceased their calls, and the grasshopper's two-beat song grew quiet. The tall grass stood straight, the breeze sucking upward out of the ward. My ears rang as I stepped back from Flint. A flash of bright light from the top of the ward blinded me. I hid my eyes under my arm, shadowing them while I looked up. The ward was gone. I could feel it, a sudden vulnerability stinging my senses, making my skin prick.

A nose pressed into my shoulder. Gasping, I took in the black beast before me. Flint had transformed into something truly glorious. Where a solid coat had once been, long black webbed wings stretched outward, tipping into a claw at the joint. His once-soft coat now gleamed like leather. His beautiful face had transformed, with flat, armor-like scales surrounding his enormous, glistening black horn, which swept upward sharply like a curved sword. His mane lay thick and glorious around his neck.

I had expected feathered wings to appear, not this. The others had changed as well and looked like aged beasts who had survived tremendous wars. Running a hand down Flint's neck, his skin felt like firm velvet, as if the worst weapons would have difficulty penetrating it. A sharp intake of breath rattled through my ears. The same unwavering eyes looked back at me, and for a moment, all else was lost save for me and my Alicorns. Flint bowed gracefully before me.

"The ward is down," Kairo called from Tattu's back, breaking me from my trance. "We have to go."

The Dragons didn't wait, heading off into the horizon. I jumped onto Flint's back and grabbed his mane, my fingers tangling in the thick strands. We took to the sky, the others behind us. They moved as one, forming a V formation with Flint at the front. Riding on his back, far above the ground, was nothing like flying on the Dragons. His strength rippled beneath me with every flap of his endless, leathery, gossamer-like wings. His legs were tucked beneath him as if flying was as natural as breathing.

We climbed higher, staying above the clouds as planned. The dew clung to my arms, and I laughed, flinging my arms out to the side. Despite the potential danger of others seeing us, I couldn't help but revel in the beauty of it all. This felt so right, so perfect. Nolan looked over his shoulder, and I shot him a smile, unable to contain my joy despite our last shared words. And for a moment, I saw the slant of his lips as he turned back, a glimpse of the old Nolan shining through.

Chapter Fifty-One

We Flew Forever

Elle

We flew for what felt like an eternity. My body ached in ways I never knew possible. I quickly learned to tuck my legs under the mantle of Flint's wings to maintain a secure seat while he split the air effortlessly. It allowed me to stretch and crack my aching muscles without holding on to his mane.

When we left the familiar terrain of my homeland, my kidneys screamed at me, making my entire pelvis burn. Eventually, I had to give in to my body's demands, and I guided Flint up to the Dragons to signal that I needed a break. Kairo chose a large, tilled field lined with trees to land in. We all took the opportunity to relieve ourselves, eat, and awaken our dead legs before taking to the sky again.

This time, I didn't have the luxury of leaning back into Kairo to nap. Since I couldn't secure myself to Flint's back, staying awake was necessary. To distract myself from how tired I was, I focused on the landscape passing below. We were in such a rural area that we would likely go unnoticed in the sky– nothing but green hills, tiny dots of trees, and seaside cliffs under us. It was like a beautiful painting made by the curves and passages of time.

In the distance, Dothan Valley formed, the shapes of the peaks appearing through the clouds. I revisited our plan in my head. Kairo assured me that most of those who remained in Dothan Valley were content not to cause trouble. Despite his encouragement, my primary concern was still flying a herd of Alicorns into the valley and essentially serving the Dragons that resided there dinner. Kairo promised to take care of that part, and I trusted him. But, as we drew closer, dread caused his sketch from the cafe to keep flashing through my mind. In grave detail, I recalled the image of the Dragon he'd drawn with a deceased Unicorn in its clutches.

The group banked to the right, and Caleda and Dalya chuffed behind us in farewell, flying to the left to find places for their nests. While the boys watched them disappear into the distance, a movement caught my eye. Squinting, I tried to make out what was coming: Birds? No. A large airplane? Definitely not. Dragons? My throat tightened. Oscur… No. The shapes were too distinct, bodies too short, legs too long. It wasn't Dragons. There were dozens of Alicorns approaching. The wind shifted when they flew nearer, and I felt Flint's muscles stiffen beneath me when he caught their scent.

Are we in danger? His thoughts echoed in my mind. The herd shifted restlessly behind him, awaiting my answer.

I'm not sure.

The Dragons in front of me whipped their mighty heads in the direction of the approaching Alicorns' flapping wings. Tattu dipped when he caught sight of the number of winged, leathery beasts coming toward him. I couldn't see Kairo's face, but I saw him tip his head, signaling Nolan to switch positions. They did, as quickly as kites dancing in the wind, putting Artok between me and the newcomers. Surprisingly, the rider in front wasn't headed for the Dragons. Instead, they flew directly toward me. When it neared, I recognized Alex atop a great Palomino-colored beast, its eyes a wild amber red. It glided to my side.

"There are Dragons," Alex huffed, her voice urgent. "We came to meet you at the pass and found them. It looked like they were waiting for you."

Dragons at the pass. The words thundered through me, filling me with fear before trickling slowly to determination. We were flying into a far more complex situation than anticipated. Depending on who the Dragons belonged to, our plans might already be unraveling.

Suddenly, Tattu was beside me, causing Flint to dart into the startled Palomino. His wings drew inward to give both fliers space. I glanced at Alex to make sure she wasn't frightened, but she barely flinched at the sight of the Dragon so close.

"How many Dragons?" I shouted, my voice barely audible over the howling wind. Kairo's eyes narrowed as he processed the information he'd missed, his expression growing grave.

Alex's voice came out in ragged huffs, her face ashen. "At least twenty, maybe more."

Kairo cupped his hands around his mouth, struggling to be heard over the deafening sound of massive wings beating the air around us. "Can you describe them?" he yelled at Alex.

Alex nodded. Brow furrowed in concentration; she recounted what she'd seen at the pass. Twenty Dragons of various colors, sizes, and types. Kairo's face grew tighter with each detail she shared, and my fear deepened.

"We need to land," Kairo yelled over the wind, and pointed to a wide ravine at the base of a cliff that stretched along the wild ocean tides.

I nodded, my lips pressed into a thin line, but inside I was torn. Every fiber of my being yearned to press forward. We were so close now that I could feel the pass calling to me, pulling at my very soul. The urge to answer that call was almost overwhelming.

When we descended, I took in the sight of the numerous Alicorns gathered around us. There were at least fifty of them, their coats gleaming and hooves dancing on the sandy ground as they landed. Among them, I counted no fewer than a dozen riders. The moment my feet touched the ground, I walked to Alex, my mind racing over what to do.

"Why did you come?" I asked, taking in her appearance.

She looked eerily ageless with her long pale hair cascading down her back in a tight braid, dressed in leather pants, boots, a loose white shirt, and a brown vest.

"If you are going to break the curse, I want to be there."

"Why?" I frowned.

She shrugged a gesture too casual for the uncertainty of our situation. "Because we've all waited too long, and it's time."

Either Alex knew far more than she should, or she had pieced together what I hadn't shared. I wasn't sure which possibility unsettled me more. The ground trembled beneath my feet as the Dragons landed on the flat rock behind me. Their sudden appearance startled the Alicorns, who were unaccustomed to such a presence, sending a ripple of nervous energy through the herds. Within moments, Nolan and Kairo were at my side, providing an odd sense of balance at my back. One was ready to protect me no matter the cost, the other was prepared to stand behind me for support.

"Oscur," Kairo said, grumbling the name.

"How do you know?" I asked, turning to face him.

His eyes held mine, the icy hues shadowed under his lashes. "He is the only one I know with a pale moon-blue Dragon," he explained, echoing Alex's earlier description. "And one of the only ones who doesn't want the curse broken."

"Why?" I asked.

"I'm not sure. He acquired a lot of dragons through unethical means. Maybe they'll abandon him?"

Alex stepped forward. "How do we get around them?"

"We don't," Nolan interjected firmly. "Call it off. It's not safe."

"We have to do this," I insisted.

Nolan's face contorted, lips thinning and forehead bunching in anguish. "And risk something happening to you?" he pleaded, reaching out as if to shake sense into me before he thought better of it. His hands dropped to his sides, but his shoulders remained tense.

Kairo grabbed Nolan's arm, pulling him back a step. "What do you want to do?" he asked me.

"We need to go through the pass," I declared, my resolve strengthening through the underlying fear.

"No," Nolan said softly, his face so full of worry that it threatened to drown me in guilt.

Ignoring him, Kairo gestured to the herd of snorting Alicorns behind us. "We might stand a chance with them."

"Two Dragons and a herd of ponies against a horde?" Nolan scoffed.

We're not ponies, Flint snorted.

Shhh, someone replied, and Aire pinned his ears at the younger colt.

"We could distract them," Alex offered.

"No," Kairo's voice was quiet but firm. "I'll distract them."

"With Artok?" Nolan shook his head, disbelief evident in his tone.

Kairo's lips twisted, clearly offended by the implication. "With Tattu."

"They'll follow us," Alex cut in, "out of mere curiosity. Once you fly through the pass, the curse will be broken, and as you said," she nodded to Kairo, "some of those Dragons may abandon his horde."

"I can't ask that of you," I told Alex. "I barely know you."

"We know you," she replied, her voice steady and sure. "We've been waiting for you for years." She motioned behind her, and I felt the weight of dozens of expectant gazes. "All of us have been waiting for this very moment, and it's too close not to see you do what must be done."

My shoulders slumped, the enormity of it all pressing them down. Yet, beneath the pressure, I felt it again—that undeniable call vibrating through every fiber of my being. *Come... come to me.* I studied the two distant peaks. The wind whipped around me, tousling my hair and carrying with it the strong feeling of fate. We needed to go. There was no other choice.

I shifted my gaze to Kairo, finding his eyes on me, expectant and ready. He was willing to do whatever I asked, his loyalty unwavering. Then I looked at Nolan, my heart constricting at the frustration written on the tightness of his body. He'd already read the answer in my eyes, and I could see the pain of knowing he couldn't fully protect me once we took to the air again. Taking a deep breath, I made my decision.

"We will walk til we get closer to the pass. Aire knows the way," I announced, pointing toward him. His ears shot up as if surprised, but I pressed on, the plan forming in my mind while I spoke.

"You will fly in from the opposite direction," I told Kairo and Nolan, my voice growing stronger with each word. "They are searching the skies for us. They won't expect us to be on the ground, and the cliffs should provide cover. We will get as close to the pass as possible and wait until we see you fly over. Then we'll take to the sky and scatter. Maybe they won't know which of us riders needs to cross the pass. Keep his Dragons on your tail so that we can get through."

I was asking so much of these people, most of whom I didn't know, yet they were willing to risk everything for me and this cause. The wind picked up again, and with it came that haunting call, stronger than ever. *Come...come to me.* It sang in my blood, urging me forward, singing me forward. *You are not alone, as you once were. They will help you. Come to me.*

"Are we ready?" I asked.

The nods I received in return were all the affirmation I needed. With one last look at the looming peaks of the pass, I inhaled deeply, my shoulders rising against the weight that had been placed on them. It was time to face our future, whatever it might be.

Nolan

I dipped my head in surrender when she spoke. Elle would *have* to be at the center of it all. She was the only one who had to cross the pass, and it wouldn't take long for Oscur to notice her. Not with that brilliant glow that seemed to brighten the closer we got to the valley. She was impossible to look at, yet impossible to look away from. Elle jumped onto the back of her black Alicorn, his mane bobbing as he tossed his head. The Allorian riders mounted, the larger steeds bowing so the riders could swing onto their backs. The air swirled around us when they took to the sky, Elle in the lead. They planned to fly a bit further, land, and walk toward the pass until we gave them a signal. It was foolish.

I shot Kairo an apprehensive look. I wanted to scream at him and demand that we protect her, but the way Kairo turned his back on me told me it would do no good. We would do as Elle instructed. I followed after him, grabbing him by his shoulder.

"I don't understand. Why are we following her orders so blindly?"

"This is her mission," Kairo replied, maddeningly calm. "We are blood-oathed to support her, and that is what we will do."

"We are blood-oathed to protect her," I argued, my grip tightening.

"Then let us protect her, brother," Kairo replied, meeting my gaze with a challenge.

My mouth snapped shut, and I let him go.

"Grow up, Nolan. Undoing the curse has been the goal from the very beginning. Have you seen Artok? He is cured. We need this, not for us," he nodded to the Dragons, "for them. I've accepted it. Why can't you?"

I opened my mouth to argue, but hesitated when something crossed Kairo's face as he walked away. There was uncertainty in the way he shrugged me off. Tilting my head, I grabbed Kairo's arm again and turned him back to face me.

"You don't want her to break it," I accused.

"It doesn't matter what I wanted then or what I want now. She will do it with or without my blessing. My job is to pick up the pieces once it is done."

"Bullshit," I spat. "Let's stop her. We can find another way."

"You don't think I've considered that?" Kairo asked, pain etching lines around his eyes. "I read every one of her notes, I studied every journal, and I even tried to decipher that damned book. This is the only way."

His words sucked the breath from me. I let him go, my arms dangling uselessly at my sides. The fight drained out of me, replaced by a hollow ache inside me. There was no other way. I followed

Kairo to the Dragons and mounted Artok, my movements mechanical.

The Dragons shifted their weight onto their hind legs, preparing to take flight. I silently vowed to myself: I would do whatever I must and be there to pick up those pieces that Kairo couldn't. And then I would leave. I couldn't bear to stay and watch Elle sacrifice herself for a curse we didn't fully understand.

But for now, I had to protect Elle, even if it meant it was from herself.

Chapter Fifty-Two

I Will Not Run

Kairo

The mountain pass grew closer as we entered the valley from the opposite side. The tall wheat below danced in tan ripples under the draft from the Dragons' wings. I caught sight of Chuff near the top of the peak and hesitated, Tattu bulking beneath me. Tattu was outmatched. He would be of very little use against even one of the Dragons watching restlessly from the mountainside, let alone the entire horde. A cold dread settled over me when I realized the extent of the trap I was flying him into.

"It's okay," I said aloud, trying to sound more confident than I felt. "We can run."

I'm not running, Tattu replied in my mind, his voice resolute.

Since the curse of the Alicorns was broken, the Dragons had found their true voices. They no longer spoke in clipped phrases. During the flight here, they conversed with each other freely for the first time in decades. Their excitement at being freed from the language barrier was clear as they talked endlessly about what would come once the curse was broken.

Artok had looked youthful while he considered the possibilities. Remembering his enthusiasm brought a bittersweet smile to my face. Even if I were reluctant to see what changes breaking the curse would cause, what Nolan refused to understand was that this wasn't only for Elle. I was pushing forward for the Dragons as well. They deserved a chance to have a full, healthy life.

It was all bigger than me, bigger than any of us individually. To see this through, I needed to be selfless. If I had considered my own wants and needs, I would never have allowed Elle to fly away from me into the ravine. Watching her go, knowing the danger she was flying into, had wrenched me apart. The last thing I wanted was for her to be harmed. I glanced down at the blood oath tattoo, which itched and burned as if she were calling me, before returning my gaze to the mountain peaks.

Swallowing hard, I took in the number of heads popping out of the crevices. Was I leading my Dragons to their doom in the name of the greater good? It didn't matter. There was no turning back. We'd come too far and risked too much. Elle was coming, and I needed to be there for her, to protect her if I could or to support her if I couldn't. I took a deep breath, barring myself against the trepidation I shared through the bond with Tattu and Artok.

"We can do this," I murmured to Tattu, feeling his agreement rumble through his body. "We're in this together, old friend. No matter what happens."

"Shit," I heard Nolan curse, and I couldn't help but agree as we both looked to the top of the mountain that held the library.

The sight of a massive red Dragon, nearly twice Artok's size, snapping at its companion was horrifying. The air filled with a sense of impending doom, settling over us like heavy fog. Contemplating our slim chances, I heard the sound of wing beats behind us and turned to see Fynch flying in our direction. I faltered. Aiska smiled when she neared, waving her hand.

"What the hell are you doing here?" Nolan asked.

"Thought you guys could use some help," Aiska replied with a crooked grin. "Fynch was restless. She couldn't find a place to nest."

She surveyed the mountain. "This isn't going to end well," she said, shaking her head. "I saw Elle and a lot of Alicorns heading this way. What's the plan?"

"Elle and the others are walking to the pass. One of her Alicorns knows the way. When they get close enough," I started to explain as Tattu's wings swept the air so we could hover closer.

"We are bait," Nolan interrupted.

"Bait?" Aiska rolled her eyes, clearly unimpressed.

"Do you have a better plan?" I asked.

Aiska's face scrunched in thought before she replied, "Let's be good bait then."

I pointed to the less populated peak. "Let's come up behind the Dragons on the south side and lure them into the valley. I'll head around the other side of the library as soon as it's safe for Elle to fly through to see if I can scatter the Dragons there."

Using the wind to our advantage, I guided Tattu low, knowing we needed to be seen at the last possible second for this to work. We passed a cluster of weathered log homes, and a silver beast of a Dragon spotted us. It chortled at us and spread its wings, the spikes along its back rising as it took flight. Tattu responded instantly, spiraling away so quickly I nearly lost my grip on the large flat scales meant to keep me seated. We narrowly avoided colliding with Artok, the great black Dragon, clambering out of our way.

Tattu dived, flying low, weaving through buildings and trees. I glanced behind us, spotting Nolan and Aiska as they evaded their pursuers. But my momentary pride turned to dread when I realized how many Dragons were giving chase. Almost half the horde was after us, and the sheer number of massive, angry Dragons bearing down on us kicked dirt and debris into our faces. The plan lost its luster.

Oscur screamed from atop his massive blood-red Dragon, but his words were lost in the chaos when Tattu dipped under the branches of two large oak trees. The Dragon that was pursuing us, not nearly as agile, smacked into them with a resounding thud. I winced as its wings hit every branch on the way down, sending it tumbling to the ground in a daze.

Nice move.

Patting Tattu's side, I sucked air into my lungs. Two more Dragons filled the gap left by their fallen comrade. My momentary elation faded when we flew over the Dragons that were still perched on the mountainside, not yet involved in our aerial chase. We'd never get around the mountain to give Elle the signal with this many against us. Tattu's dark green wings grazed past Chuff, who watched

Artok with bristling intensity when another Dragon dove off the mountainside to join the chase. I knew their history. They'd been raised together, and Chuff did not look happy about being on Oscur's side.

"Artok!" I called out, hoping to catch his attention, but Artok didn't acknowledge me, gamely evading the sleek, smaller black Dragon on his tail.

Chuff spread his wings, intent on joining the fray. Turning as far as I could, I saw the moment Koa realized she no longer had control of her mount. Her shouts were lost to the roar of her Dragon. They were partners now, not possessions, and some clearly weren't keen on blindly obeying their Keepers anymore. If only Oscur's Dragons felt the same. Though if they had suffered under his hand, it might take more than newfound coherence for them to break his control.

Chuff lifted off with Koa clinging to his back. He grabbed one of the smaller Dragons by its tail, spinning it into the mountainside with a sickening crunch. Still twisted on the back of Tattu, I didn't notice when he started to turn away from the pass. Suddenly sideways, my legs dangled toward Tattu's back.

If I didn't know any better, I would think you were trying to lose me, I complained to Tattu as he flew diagonally between two houses at the river's edge.

If you would pay attention and hold on, Tattu demanded, his sides heaving, but I could hear the pleasure in his tone.

The tip of Tattu's wing skimmed the river, splashing cool water onto my face. My hair plastered itself to my skin, and I raised a hand to push it back, acutely aware of my precarious position. Tattu used the riverbank to launch us straight into the sky. I tightened my grip, my heart lurching into my throat.

Despite the danger, a rush of exhilaration filled my veins. This was what it meant to truly fly with a Dragon, not as master and beast, but as partners working in perfect harmony. We were meant for battles, for wars. We climbed higher, evading our pursuers still. I allowed myself a moment to appreciate the beauty of how Dragons worked. The way they moved was almost effortless. But reality quickly set in. We were still outnumbered, still in danger, and Elle was out there somewhere, counting on us to clear the way.

We need to find a way to draw more of them away from the mountain. Any ideas?

Tattu's muscles bunched beneath me, and I prepared for whatever crazy maneuver he'd planned next. We banked hard, cutting across the flight paths of several pursuing Dragons. I looked back and cursed when one of the Dragons recovered quickly, too quickly. It was on us in seconds.

We've got to make it around the mountain.

There are too many Dragons at the pass, Tattu replied.

I scrutinized the mountain, searching its craggy face for any potential advantage. My gaze swept over jutting rocks, hidden crevices, and sparse vegetation. An idea crystallized. It was risky, possibly suicidal, but it might be our only chance. Glancing back, I saw Artok holding his own, thanks to Chuff, who brazenly disobeyed my sister while he chased off the smaller Dragons. Fynch had three on her tail, but she was moving like a fox, quick and deft, leaving several in her dust.

Are we going to do something dangerous? Tattu asked.

Yes, I responded, tightening my grip on his scales.

Tattu trembled beneath me. *About time,* he replied, a thrill of anticipation running through our bond.

Taking a deep breath, I leaned close. "We're going to use the mountain itself against them. See that narrow ravine cutting through the rock face? We're going to thread that needle."

Tensing, he processed my words. *That's insane,* he responded, but I heard the eagerness in his voice. *I love it.*

We only have one shot at this, so wait for my mark. The Dragon behind us was closing in, massive jaws snapping at Tattu's tail. Just as it lunged forward, I shouted, "Now!"

Tattu banked hard, and we shot into the ravine. The sudden change in direction caught our pursuer off guard, and I heard its roar of frustration when it struggled to follow. We plunged into the narrow gap between the rocks, stone walls blurring on either side. Tattu's wings folded against his body to keep us from smashing into the unforgiving rock. Sideways, he ran, claws scraping stone. Behind us, I heard the sickening crunch of scales against rock as our pursuer, too large to navigate the tight space, collided with the mountain. A pang of guilt hit me, but I pushed it aside. This was about survival. When we emerged on the other side of the ravine, I let out a whoop of triumph.

"Tattu, you magnificent beast!" I shouted, patting his neck. "That was incredible!"

We're not done yet, Tattu reminded me, but I could feel his pride.

He was right. We still needed to clear the pass for Elle and face down an army of Dragons. But for the first time since this mad chase began, I felt a glimmer of hope. We might just pull this off after all.

Nolan

I've heard plenty of curse words in my long life, but none as colorful as the ones spewed from Koa's mouth as she berated her Dragon. For his part, Chuff looked about as interested in her tirade as I was in learning proper teatime, which was to say, not at all. Despite Fynch and Chuff's unexpected help, we were still four against dozens. Dragons poured off the peak to join the aerial scramble, while a few lingered on the mountainside, watching us wearily.

Artok grappled with a Dragon near his own size, causing me to duck out of its way when he flung the beast over our heads. When the Dragon fell into a large ravine, I caught sight of ivory scales and did a double-take. Dalya rammed two Dragons off their perches, sending them cascading down the rocks in a grey blur. To my horror, Caleda was right on her tail. We must have gotten close to where their nests were. The lingering Dragons skittered out of their way, pleading silently for reprieve with their maternal instincts.

A rock struck my arm and snapped my attention back to Kairo climbing skyward. He was headed straight for Oscur and his monstrous red Dragon. I lost my breath, and not in a good way. He either had a brilliantly heroic plan or a spectacularly stupid one.

Kairo was going to give Elle the signal, the only way he could, when Oscur was so intent on staying in the pass by flying Tattu right under the red Dragon's nose. Artok realized his intention at the exact moment I did, launching himself upward with enough force to trigger an avalanche. Fynch, proving quicker on the uptake, darted in front of Artok, her spiked tail nearly skewering him. When we neared the peak, I spotted what Kairo was aiming for. A small V-shaped split in the rocks under Oscur's Dragon, his legs splayed like a scaly mountain goat. With Kairo climbing one side of the peak, and us racing up the other, we were going to head toward the path he needed to escape. Artok bounded off boulders, his claws scraping and smaller rocks tumbling in his wake.

"We're going to be in the way!" I yelled to Aiska, pointing at the narrow passage. She nodded, and Fynch dove left to lure more Dragons into flight as Artok skidded to a stop.

Kairo guided Tattu straight under Oscur's massive Dragon. The red beast roared in rage, but Kairo cleared the other side. I cursed his timing: throwing Elle and the Alicorns into this chaos didn't seem wise. Oscur bellowed a command that was lost in the sounds of the roaring Dragons nearest to him. Their agitation distracted me from my thoughts. His effect on them was immediate and chilling. The Dragons' eyes grew angrier, and I recognized the scars from shackles when they took flight.

Artok was suddenly pinned against the mountainside, two Dragons grappling at his neck and stomach. He grabbed the smaller Dragon in his teeth and slammed it against the mountainside. My leg scraped stone, rock shrapnel peppering my face, my eyes burning from the dirt. Chuff took hold of a dark grey beast, talons wrapping around its middle, and he yanked it away from us. Thrashing it into the air, it tumbled toward the ground, its limbs drooping. My heart sank. Dragons peppered the cliffs below us, all covered in blood or broken in some way. I scanned for anyone familiar, and when I didn't see anyone, I let out a breath. This was getting uglier by the second. Would I end up dead, sprawled amongst the injured?

Another Dragon plummeted to the ground, brushing its wing against my side as it fell. *Such a shame.* Artok sprang skyward with Chuff hot on his heels, and Koa was missing from his back. Without her, Chuff was free to defend his own. Like a monster freed, he spun from us, latching onto a light-green Dragon and tossing it like a discarded toy. Artok launched himself to follow, a low growl vibrating the scales under me.

Behind us, at least six Dragons were still chasing us. Too many. A blast of heat flicked over me, and sweat dripped down my forehead. We neared the mountain pass, Artok's wings flung as wide as they could go. A snarling copper colored beast halted midair so close to us that I braced for impact. Nostrils flared, it eyed the pass with curiosity, and my focus shifted.

The setting sun's rays bounced through the mountain pass, nearly blinding me. I squinted through spots dancing across the horizon and onto the half-moon peeking through. There were so many dots. I blinked again, wondering if I'd been blinded. But no, the Alicorns had arrived. Flint released a proud war cry as he neared the other side of the pass. Behind them flew at least four Dragons with Zayn at their helm, red hair standing out against the slate-grey scales of his mount.

Zayn didn't hesitate to enter the fray. He charged Oscur like a man with a centuries-old grudge. From the valley below, half a dozen Dothians rode their Dragons into the chaos as if they'd been waiting their entire lives for this moment. Which, given the oppressions from the curse, they probably had. Even if they didn't know our intent, they knew us and would stand behind us.

I wiped the dirt from my brow. This was no longer a skirmish but a full-blown war for the future of Dragons and their riders. I leaned forward, patting Artok's neck.

"Ready to make history?" I asked, voice barely audible over the battle's din.

Artok's answering roar vibrated through my bones. I grinned despite the danger. We might be out of our minds, but we weren't out of the fight. Not by a long shot.

Elle

The pass rose above us, and the air became suffocating with the sounds of battle. Dragons were fighting their own kind, teeth gnashing and claws digging into flesh. I tried not to look down, where the broken bodies were scattered across rock and dirt. Instead, I kept my eyes fixed ahead on the shimmering barrier that marked our destination. The last rays of the setting sun painted the other side of the pass in hues of orange and pink while the rising moon cast an eerie glow.

Flint was giving it his all, his body nearly parallel to the ground, dodging one Dragon after another. His muscles strained with each wing beat. We were so close, just a few hundred feet, and we'd cross that golden line between the mountains. A cry rose in the air, but I didn't dare look back. I couldn't afford any distractions with our goal so near.

But then the voice became clear, and I recognized it.

"Come back!" Koa screamed.

Against my better judgment, I turned my head. Koa was astride a light blue Dragon with impossibly long wings, anger reddening her face. She gained on us. Her Dragon bit at Flint's wing, forcing him to dodge hard to the right. The sudden movement nearly unseated me. I let out a surprised yelp and desperately clung to Flint's mane, wrapping the strands around my hand.

"What is your problem?" I yelled back at Koa.

Koa screamed again, but her words were lost in the wind whipping past. Flint's nose crossed the barrier.

Time seemed to slow as we passed through—first Flint's nose, then his neck and wings, and then me. When I crossed that invisible line, a surge of energy coursed through my body. The clouds parted, revealing the half-moon cresting the sky, and suddenly it felt as if I was being torn apart and put back together all at once. The Alicorns had returned home.

My body exploded with sensation, pain, and pleasure, hot and cold, light and dark. Every nerve ending was on fire, every cell in my body singing with an ancient power I couldn't comprehend. In that moment, suspended between two worlds, I became the catalyst I was meant to be. This wasn't just about breaking a curse. It was about reshaping the very essence of our world, restoring balance to a realm long fractured.

Praying that we were doing the right thing, I let Flint's mane go. There was no going back now. For better or worse, we'd set events in motion that would change everything. The world around me blurred and shifted, and stars danced in my vision. I could see Dothians and Alorians united in a way they hadn't been for centuries, the way things were meant to be.

I'd done the right thing.

Chapter Fifty-Three

I Got You

Elle

Something twisted over us, its body spiraling, blue-tipped claw grazing Flint before knocking into me. Everything vanished in an instant: sound, light, and feeling were all gone. Then, I felt Flint panic beneath me as my body lifted off his back. The air seemed to suspend me, spinning me slowly. As I whirled, my hair came loose, spilling around me. Gravity suddenly reasserted itself, and I fell. A black Dragon, so dark he was almost a shadow, flew toward me as I tumbled toward the unforgiving ground below. Then there was Aire, blocking the shadow with light.

I've got you, I heard him say.

He flew under me, and I attempted to right myself before landing on his back, but the impact sent us hurtling forward too fast. The ground loomed closer. Aire pushed his front legs outward in a desperate attempt to save us. His skin flickered, ears pinned, and the feeling of resignation washed over me. He knew what was coming before I did.

"No!" I screamed, but it was too late.

Aire hit the ground hard, both front legs snapping upon impact. He twisted to keep me from flying over him, but in doing so, his head slammed into the ground. His horn caught at an odd angle, wedging into the unyielding surface of the dirt. I felt the sickening crunch of his neck before I heard it.

"NO!"

I was thrown from his shoulder, my body scraping against the hard earth. My anguished cry echoed through the valley, followed by a tremendous rumble from the library. The ground shook beneath me. I scrambled to Aire, draping myself over him. Tears poured from my eyes onto his dirt-flecked coat. He was gone, his eyes empty, his sides still. Flint landed beside me, sweaty foam flying from his coat. Sadness filled all the cracks inside of me. Cracks that had been designated for the joy of giving others their freedom from the damned curse.

The ground shook again. Everyone looked to the mountain in time to see the Golden Dragon burst through one of the library's skylights, its wings stretching across the span of the mountain peaks. It snaked its neck until it spotted me, lying over my dead Alicorn. The Dragon reared its head and bellowed, flames shooting from its mouth and nostrils. Creatures and Keepers froze.

On the peak of the mountain, a red Dragon bristled, its rider a dark figure on its back. The red Dragon's head reared back, smoke billowing from his nostrils. It crouched onto its hind legs, ready to take flight. Oscur's commands to stay echoed off the stone, but his Dragon didn't listen and didn't falter when it left most of his horde behind. Only half followed, subdued by the mating bonds of far-away nesting females.

Alicorns landed in a circle, and one by one, they lowered their heads in respect to Aire. Each sky-bound creature landed, but none of them had the impact of the library's guardian. The ground rattled beneath me, and the Golden Dragon stalked toward us until he was so close I could feel the heat of his breath. He smelled of ash and fire when he nudged Aire gently.

He did what he must, the great beast told me.

My grief turned into an ache that settled into my bones. But as I gazed into the Golden Dragon's ancient eyes, I felt the promise of something else—hope, perhaps, or the first stirrings of purpose. I ran my hand down Aire's leathery white pelt. He didn't get a chance to tell me the secrets he'd promised.

"What happens now?" I whispered.

The Dragon's response reverberated through my mind. *We create a new world from the ashes of the old.*

I sobbed. What did he know? He'd been sequestered in a mountain for years, while I'd been tasked with protecting my Alicorns. And I'd failed. Aire was gone, his body cooling beside me. Yet the Dragon didn't leave. I didn't understand why. Where was the librarian? Why didn't someone come to fetch him? Through my tears, I saw Kairo approaching, hands fisted and steps careful.

Standing, I stumbled toward him. He caught me in his arms, and I sagged against his chest, my grief threatening to pull me under. Over his shoulder, I glimpsed Nolan dismounting Artok, blood flowing from a wound on his face.

"Do you remember? Have your memories returned?" I asked Kairo quietly.

He shook his head, his face buried in my neck. It was stupid to assume flying through the pass would work. I knew that for them to recall their lives before the curse, I needed to take the next step. But I couldn't fathom that thought in the fog of my sorrow. Pulling away from Kairo, I realized the fighting had ceased and all eyes were on us. Shame washed over me, and I ducked my head into Kairo's chest again.

"I don't remember," Kairo said softly, "but nobody is fighting anymore."

He gently tilted my chin up, forcing me to meet his eyes. "You have brought us together."

His words pierced my grief. I turned my head, truly seeing the scene for the first time. Dragons and Alicorns stood side by side, their enmity forgotten in the existence we'd created. Yes, Aire was gone, and the pain of his loss would stay with me always. But his sacrifice wasn't in vain. We'd broken the curse, ended the fighting, and now stood on the precipice of what we'd wanted. The one I'd worked so hard for. I turned back to Kairo, then to Nolan, who'd joined us, and finally to the Golden Dragon, who watched over us with ancient, knowing eyes.

"What do we do now?" I repeated.

The Golden Dragon's voice resonated in my mind. *We heal. We learn. We build.*

My heart fluttered as I waited for the golden Dragon's snores to rumble behind me, for Flint's protective gaze to finally drift, for Nolan to stalk off with Kairo in pursuit. When I was sure most eyes were turned away, I stood, stretching my aching muscles, and made an excuse for a moment of privacy. Instead of staying close, I slipped off toward the library. The ornate wooden door clicked open easily under my touch, and I stepped inside, half expecting to find the Albadine waiting. But the library was empty, silent save for the whisper of my footsteps and the soft rustle of my clothes.

Silver streams of light poured through gaps in the mountain's side, illuminating dust motes that danced in the air. I moved quietly through, letting the expanse of the space humble me. I didn't have to wonder where to go because I was drawn upward by the pull of vague memories, level after level, until I reached the top. A small terrace greeted me: two modest shelves bearing a plaque that read *Alis' Trove*. My fingers shook as they skimmed over dry, cracked spines until they found what I sought—Alis' *Guide to the Secret Society*.

Slowly, reverently, I pulled the leather-bound journal from its resting place. The significance of it in my hands somehow felt substantial. With a deep breath, I flipped it open to the first page and ran my finger down the elaborately sprawled words.

Alis' Secret Society

Alisyn Portier–The Rightful Heir

Nollaind Draccota–The Heir Majesty's Hand ♡

Nikoa Rimeair–Captain of the Guard

Ailiaska Denira–The Heir Majesty's Royal Advisor

Alexxa Ruthar–The Heir Majesty's Royal Treasure

Zayin Threshin–The Heir Majesty's Captain of the Leggio

Artim Kreol–General of Horns and Wings

Onalee Kadril–The Royal Messenger

Larklin Barvello–Keeper of Royal Records

My heart sank deeper with each name. The realization dawned on me that these were extended versions of the names I knew. Alisyn was Alis, Nollaind must be Nolan, Nikoa was Koa, Alexxa likely Alex, Ailiaska was Aiska, and Zayin probably Zayn. But Kairo's name was nowhere to be found. The absence of it left a hollow feeling in the pit of my stomach. Who were these other names? What did it all mean? And the heart drawn beside Nolan's name, what hidden significance did it hold?

As I was about to turn the page, I felt warm hands slip around me. Kairo's heated breath found my neck, and he kissed my collarbone. Taking the book and setting it down, he pulled me against his chest. His lips brushed my ear, sending heat blooming despite my troubled thoughts.

"What are you doing here?" he asked, his voice low and intimate.

For a moment, I hesitated. The truth hovered on the tip of my tongue, but something held me back. Instead, I heard myself say, "I was trying to find the other scrolls." The lie tasted bitter, and I wasn't even sure why I'd said it.

Guilt became a sliver of doubt. Kairo deserved the truth, especially after everything we'd been through together. But how could I explain what I'd found, or rather, what I didn't find? How could I tell him his name was missing from the list Alis Portier had made? I leaned back into his embrace, conflicted. Part of me wanted to show it to him, to share my discovery. Another part of me, the part that lied, wanted to protect him from it until I understood more. It could mean nothing, but I knew it didn't. There was a great big reason why his name wasn't on that list. I could feel it in my soul.

"Elle?" Kairo's voice grew concerned, probably sensing my conflict. "Is everything okay?"

"Yes," I told him. "Everything is fine."

Chapter Fifty-four

He Pulled Her Close

Kairo

Caught up in my need for her, I ignored the want to think things through, the warmth of her body against mine too inviting. I knew she wouldn't initiate this. It would be too awkward for her to find the right moment. But after everything we'd been through, I couldn't wait any longer. We'd almost lost our chance to be together, and watching her sob over her broken Alicorn made it all seem more urgent. His death would be for nothing if we didn't take the next step. My soul had threatened to shatter when I saw her flying through the air. I'd known Tattu wasn't fast enough to catch her, and for one heart-stopping moment, I thought she was going to plummet to the earth. If she had died, I would have willingly followed.

But she'd lived, and I hadn't given a damn about Aire. Elle standing there, in one piece, was all that mattered. The world could have collapsed around us both, and I wouldn't have blinked twice as long as she was still standing in the middle of the ashes. I wanted her then. I needed her so badly that I almost couldn't let her go. But there were too many eyes on us. Now, though, we were alone in the library. Not a soul knew where we were.

I'd given up the conversation I knew I needed to have with my brother to find her. Standing in the shadows, I couldn't keep myself from reaching out any longer. Letting her think she was walking away on her own, I'd waited. When the moon started to disappear over the pass, I followed her slowly, giving her time to find what she was seeking. Then I found her, glowing in the streams of moonlight as she held something I was sure would interrupt our plans if I didn't act.

I put my finger under her chin, turning her face to me. Her cheeks were smudged with dirt, but that wasn't going to stop me. When I kissed the tip of her nose, her lips parted. She pulled her bottom lip through her teeth, leaning her forehead against mine. Wrapping my arm around her waist, I pulled her closer. She hesitated, and I couldn't help but sigh. Was I misreading this? Did she not want this as much as I did?

"Elle," I murmured. "If you don't want this, tell me now. But know that I've never wanted anything more in my life."

"It's okay," she told me, her voice carrying through the library's layers. "It has to be tonight. It has to be here. I want this."

Despite her words, I studied her face intently, searching for any sign of hesitation. When I saw the reluctance fade from her eyes, replaced by a heated gaze, a surge of adrenaline filled my chest. Her fingers found the edge of my shirt, and as they grazed my skin, my breath caught in my throat. She lifted my shirt over my head, her fingers tracing the contours of my muscles. I swallowed heavily, brushing errant strands of hair from her face. When she leaned forward and kissed me right over my heart, I tugged her to me, my lips finding hers.

She searched with her mouth for an answer I wasn't sure I had, but I let her attempt to find it anyway, our kiss deepening. The black shirt she wore came off with a swift yank, discarded over the edge of the banister, and floated through the air like a glittering, inky spiral. I pushed her backward until her body molded to the flat rock behind her. My hands fumbled with the binding, wrapping her ribs. I wasn't moving fast enough. When she reached down to help, I pulled her hands away, using one hand to hold her wrists above her head as I found the edge of the cloth and pulled it loose.

Her eyes searched my face, her chest rising in pants. Undressing her quickly, I leaned back to take her in. She stood breathless and trembling, but willing. In that moment, everything else faded away. The challenges we'd faced, the mysteries still unsolved, and the uncertain future ahead are daunting. But all that matters is Elle, here with me. I reached out, tracing the curve of her cheek with my fingertips.

"You're beautiful."

I ran my fingers down her back, tiny bumps coating her skin. Tugging her down onto the stone ground, my mouth traced the shape of her neck, down her collarbone, until I found the soft flesh of her breast. She shuddered under my lips as I tugged softly at her nipple, her back arching upward. Her gasp echoed off the open spaces below us, sending a thrill through my body. My fingers found her wet. Ready. Huffing, I pressed my forehead to her chest. I pushed a finger inside her, and her thighs squeezed around my hand.

"Kairo," she breathed, her fingers curling tightly into my hair.

My name on her lips was fuel. I let it linger, circling my thumb until her breath caught. Eyes widening, her hands clutched my back. Kissing the soft skin between her breasts, I guided her toward release, reveling in her response. She pushed her hips into my hand, her nails raking my back, leaving sharp, stinging trails of pleasure behind. Her moans filled the mountain, reverberating off the walls, and the sound was intoxicating.

I could feel the Dragons growing restless, their primordial need echoing down the bonds that tied us. The intensity of their emotions mirrored my own. They scuttled against the sides of the library, their restlessness loud. Elle's eyes shot to the square dormer that illuminated us. Golden scales shifted near the opening. I touched her side reassuringly, my finger filling her again, determined to keep her focus.

"He is keeping Artok and Tattu away," I told her as an angry roar filled the air. My voice was husky with desire as I added, "Don't worry about them. Pay attention to me." I wanted nothing more than to lose myself in this moment with her, to shut out everything but the heat between us. If only she'd do the same.

She bit her lip and nodded, her eyes returning to mine. I brought her back to that high we were chasing, curling my fingers and pulling her toward me. Tossing my pants somewhere against the wall, I was above her, my knee prying her legs apart. Control was an illusion. A haughty, kept secret. One wrong move, and it was lost. Her fingers traced the muscles on my back as I guided myself deeper. I wanted this to be perfect for her, but the need, the aching desire, demanded its own pace.

"Fuck," I panted, slowly finding my way.

For one fraction of a second, I felt her tense, and then her legs wrapped around me, her desire matching my own. I moved within her as she surrendered. The world around us halted. Our breaths and soft moans were the only noise. We clung to each other until her body relaxed around me. Only then did I dare to move, letting her adjust as I made love to her.

We became one, our souls merging. The curse whimpered at our connection. She met my rhythm with unyielding ease, and we both climbed the summit. Kissing me, she spoke my name, and it vibrated against my lips. We fell together. When she shattered, I splintered into a million pieces. Over and over, until we were both spent, panting as we held each other. Still trembling, I lowered myself to lie beside her, pulling her close so her back rested against my chest. Guilt, rage, fear, and confusion fiercely coursed through me. I sucked in a ragged breath and brushed damp hair from her face.

I remembered.

Chapter Fifty-Five

Wish I Could

Elle

"I love you," I whispered, lacing my finger with his.

Kairo stilled behind me. He leaned forward and breathed me in. I could feel the tickle of air caress my cheek when he exhaled. He kissed the back of my neck and let out a low sob, heart thundering against my back. My own faltered, waiting for him to say it back.

There was something dreadful in his silence. Something had changed. I could feel it. It was heavy in the air. Memories flooded me, fragments of doubts and fears I'd pushed aside. Turning to face him, my nerves frayed completely. For a painful second, he looked the same. Sweet, loyal, supportive Kairo. The man I'd fallen for, the one I trusted with my heart. And then Kairo was gone.

Hardened eyes met mine, unfamiliar and cold. The corner of his lips twisted maliciously. He cupped my face, pinching my chin. My chest constricted, and I couldn't breathe.

"I wish I could say the same," he replied, his deep voice like velvet night.

Somewhere, an agonizing roar rent the air, and behind Kairo, heavy white fog poured through the skylights, filling the library.

The End

Bonus Chapter

He Was Too Late

Nolan

Lunging up the stairs two at a time, my heart hammered in my chest. Minutes ago, I'd realized why Kairo's Dragons had lifted their heads, rumbling deeply before taking off toward the library. The Golden Dragon flew after them, attempting to cut them off. The wind from his wings blew the flames from the bonfires across the long dirt road, Keepers scattering in his wake.

My lungs burned as I fought to reach them, desperately attempting to prevent what I knew was going to happen. This was my last stand, one final attempt to throw myself at Elle's mercy. It was a fruitless effort to get to her. But I needed to try. She would see that she was making the wrong choice if I could tell her the truth. Kairo was my brother, and I was an option.

Nearly tripping, I scrambled up the next flight of stairs. The journey seemed endless, yet I could hear their voices. I was so close that the realization that I was still too far away crushed me. Swallowing hard, I panted against the strain in my legs. I was already so tired from the flight and the battle. It wasn't enough. Their voices grew closer, and I heard Elle's serene tone at the edges of my senses.

"It's okay," she said.

The words threatened to demolish me entirely. I quickened my pace. It was not okay. None of this was okay. I needed to get to her.

Nearing the center of the towering staircase, I caught sight of the shimmering gold and black fabric of her shirt twirling in slow motion toward the ground like a dark flame. I shattered, tears springing to my eyes. The moans and the muted pants of passion vibrated off the walls, each sound a dagger to my heart.

Her shirt drifted toward me, and I caught it with an outstretched finger. Pulling it to my chest, I closed my eyes and squeezed the tears from my lashes. The pain was too much. I couldn't handle it. Sinking to my knees, I hit the stairs with a thud, the noise drowned out by the Dragons clamoring above the library.

Sobs wracked my body as I leaned against the hard stone wall. I was too late. Defeated, I pressed my face into the fabric, letting it soak up the tears. My eyes filled with its blackness and, suddenly, memories of so long ago consumed me. The curse had begun to break. With those long-forgotten memories, the agony swallowed who I was.

A room high in the tower of a castle. Needy breaths and hushed moans. My hands on her, wandering over the smooth, soft skin of her sides while she leaned into my touch. She was glorious under me, the sun leaving golden rings on her chestnut-colored torso. She tugged at her slip and ran a hand down my naked chest. A smile played on her lips—bright hazel eyes through dark lashes.

"Alis," I whispered into the vastness, opening my eyes to find myself without her.

"Ellise," I cried, the name tearing from my throat.

The Dragons settled beyond the thick rock walls, leaving the library silent enough that I heard Elle tell Kairo, "I love you." My heart fragmented into shards at her words. Ears straining, I heard Kairo's reply, and I knew I would do what I'd said. I would be there to pick up the pieces my brother left behind, even as my own soul lay in tatters.

Koa

I'd failed… in a way.

The moon dripped down on me, mocking my failure with its half-covered face. Chuff grumbled and stretched his large frame against the rocky ground below the ledge where I sat. At least he'd come back. At least he'd been loyal enough after all these years to know what was at stake. His steadfastness inspired me to keep trying even though my responsibility kept attempting to get herself killed, thanks to my brothers.

I rolled my eyes and itched at the ink on my arm again, glancing up at the Golden Dragon circling the library. His presence meant my duties were somewhat fulfilled. The second part of the curse was breaking. I could feel the pressure releasing as the moon settled behind the library. Even though the curse never tampered with my memories, its release still erased the tension from my body. I rolled my shoulders backward and let a small smile form.

Finally.

My smile faltered as the irony of her choices trickled through my illogical happiness. My twin hadn't been who I'd intended for her. I'd arranged everything to bring Nolan and Elle together, gave him a reason to come, and planted seeds amongst the people to drive him toward her. But he hadn't shown. He'd ignored my attempts and remained behind in Dothan Valley while Kairo had come instead. It was my fault. I hadn't realized how ill Artok had become because I was too consumed by my oath-bound duty.

Seeing Kairo had been a shock. His anger had been an even greater one. The curse had warped his memories so deeply that I'd become his unintended enemy. The target of his disappointment, and I'd inadvertently used that rift to get them here. I'd driven them together with the rumors I'd placed to keep people off my trail and unaware of my actions. I'd been the reason he'd come to save her from me—the absolute irony of it. I'd been trying to save her. I'd intended to take Elle to Dothan Valley myself and present her to Nolan. To say, "Here you go, she's meant to be yours, you absolute idiot." They would have loved each other. I was certain of it.

The wrong one. I huffed. *She'd chosen the wrong one.*

The repercussions of her choice would smoke themselves out in time, and they'd be dealt with accordingly. I'd do what I must to keep her on the path laid out before her, but now I could get closer to her. I could right the wrongs I'd been unable to. The silvery ink of the Unicorn horn adorning my wrist winked up at me, and I rubbed it lightly. Alis would be furious at what I'd allowed to happen, but then she would see that it was necessary.

It wasn't like I could stop them anyway. I tried. It was like they'd been driven together by something beyond my ability to prevent. Still, my best friend's cocky voice filled my head as the last remnants of the second part of the curse shimmered down the other side of the valley.

The tenth descendant. She must end it. It must be her. Guide her to him. Bring me back, Koa. Don't let me linger here in the after any longer than necessary.

One night, not long ago, in the haze of a nightmare, I'd awoken covered in sweat. Time was ticking. The clock in my dreams was counting down. *Tick, tick.* The panic filling me had sent Chuff soaring to the sky, and through his eyes, I saw him land on the road near the tiny town I'd spent years monitoring. I saw the headlights glint against the surrounding trees. His camouflage lifted as the car came into view, and I saw the fright in their eyes as the man driving twisted the wheel. The sound of Chuff's snoring startled me back to reality. Swallowing back the tears, I looked over the valley, taking in the peaceful view of Alicorns and Dragons resting around the meadow together after their battle.

Her parents' sacrifice hadn't been for nothing. It'd been a means to an end. Though I hadn't given him the command, I couldn't fault Chuff for his actions. He'd felt the rush of time passing each day after the tenth descendant had been born. He'd felt me pass those days with anticipation that bordered on mania. Chuff had only done what I couldn't.

And for that, I hoped Alis would be proud.

To be continued

9 798218 867478